KU-216-422

Reaper

STEVEN DUNNE

Reaper

Copyright © 2007 Steven Dunne

The moral right of the author has been asserted.

Apart from any fair dealing for the purposes of research or private study,
or criticism or review, as permitted under the Copyright, Designs and Patents
Act 1988, this publication may only be reproduced, stored or transmitted, in
any form or by any means, with the prior permission in writing of the
publishers, or in the case of reprographic reproduction in accordance with
the terms of licences issued by the Copyright Licensing Agency. Enquiries
concerning reproduction outside those terms should be sent to the publishers.

Matador
9 De Montfort Mews
Leicester LE1 7FW, UK
Tel: (+44) 116 255 9311 / 9312
Email: books@troubador.co.uk
Web: www.troubador.co.uk/matador

ISBN 10: 1 905886 50 0
ISBN 13: 978-1-905886-50-0

Typeset in 11pt Stempel Garamond by Troubador Publishing Ltd, Leicester, UK
Printed in the UK by The Cromwell Press Ltd, Trowbridge, Wilts, UK

Matador is an imprint of Troubador Publishing Ltd

Dedicated to my beautiful wife Carmel,
whose wholehearted and constructive support
made this book possible

Acknowledgements

Special thanks go to Jeff Fountain and Patrick Raggett for their invaluable advice and help during the writing and marketing of this book. As fellow writers, their consistent encouragement and cajoling has ensured the project bore fruit.

I'd also like to thank my loyal friends who have helped me to get copies of the book into people's hands. Thanks to Martin Bowen, Chris Fisher and all my friends from Camberwell and the Weekenders.

www.the-reaper.com

Prologue

The cat froze, suppressing its instinct to run, and peered into the swirling gloom towards the noise. To break cover, even in this fog, could be its undoing. That's what its own prey did. That's when it had them. The animal stared, unblinking, head locked in the direction of the approaching footfall.

From the gasps of fog a figure emerged as though exhaled from the bowels of the earth. The boy was tall and though his clothes were baggy, he was identifiably lean as the cold breeze folded his roomy, low-slung trousers around his legs. He scuffed his Nikes along the rutted pavement, as though wiping something from them, before stopping to sniff the air. The peak of his grimy baseball cap came up as he looked around, sensing the animal nearby.

For a second he stopped hunching himself against the cold and looked toward the cat. He saw its eyes and stood perfectly still.

Softly the rumble in the boy's throat grew until his armoury was fully loaded and he let fly. An arc of spittle landed near the cat's front paws, splashing its legs. The cat tensed then leapt to the side, wide-eyed.

To banish any chance of feline forgiveness, the boy darted towards the animal and aimed a kick at its retreating rear.

"Here puss puss," coaxed the boy bending down to click his fingers, scouring the dark ground for missiles. Surprisingly there were none. The boy had alighted upon the only spot on Derby's Drayfin Estate that wasn't crumbling.

"Shit." The boy continued to grope but with dwindling enthusiasm. He cursed the absence of street lighting, forgetting it had been he and his crew who'd spent a diligent evening the month before breaking as many as they could find still working. The only illumination now shone from limp Christmas lights winking out from the odd door and window. No-one on the estate put on much of a show at this time of

1

year. It didn't do to advertise.

The boy stood up without ammunition and shrugged his shoulders. The cat had already taken the hint. No point trying to catch the little sod anyway – he'd run out of lighter fuel. Plus it was no fun torching the little bastards without your crew there to see it.

He peered down at his pale hand clutching an old tab end from the ground. Too big to throw, so he buried it deep in the pocket of his Stone Island jacket for future consumption.

After a noisy piss into a puddle – pissing quietly didn't unsettle nervous residents – he adjusted his baseball cap and hunched himself into the position offering greatest protection against the biting wind. By happy coincidence, it was also the posture designed to radiate maximum menace, the posture of choice for that invisible brotherhood of disaffected youth around the world. Wicked.

Jason Donovan Wallis wiped his moistening pink nose on his sleeve and stared up at the gun-metal sky through the billows of fog. Nothing but grey. Shame. He liked a clear sky. Enjoyed seeing all those stars and planets and meteors and stuff. Not that he was so gay that he wanted to learn anything about the universe. Fuck that. But one day he hoped to meet an alien and be abducted, taken somewhere with a spaceship full of supermodels to colonise a new world. Then he would return in triumph, a split-second after being taken in earth time. He'd be a hero, the most famous man on the planet. Gash would be queuing round the block to screw him then. Safe.

※

The man placed the boxes onto a blanket then covered them over to keep the food warm. He closed the back doors of the van and returned to the driver's seat, darting a glance from side to side. The fog rolling down from the Peaks was perfect. No-one was braving the cold on such a filthy night. The streets were already empty. He had them to himself.

He looked at his watch and smiled. The time was near.

He pushed the cassette into the stereo and closed his eyes to let the soft music flow over him for a moment, then pulled the leather gloves from his hands and placed them on the dashboard. He had on a pair of surgical rubbers already and his hands were clammy so he extracted a container from a hold-all, tapped a little powder on each wrist and shook it down under the surface onto his palms.

Having returned the powder to the hold-all, he placed the bag into the back of the van and picked up the small leather case from the floor

2

and gently drummed his fingers on it, nodding. He looked at his watch again. The time was right. His final contribution was about to begin.

He picked up the brand new mobile the second it began to ring. He thumbed the answer button, lifted the phone to his ear and listened for a second. Then he ended the call, removed the battery and SIM card and placed the pieces in the leather bag for future disposal. He reached for the ignition, turned on the engine and lights and drove away. The time was now.

*

Jason examined the murky sky. No aliens tonight. Still, no moon meant a good night for teafin' though there weren't nothing worth stealing on the Drayfin no more.

He resumed his trudge to The Centre, a moribund sixties complex of boarded shop windows and grim food stores, housed in a cold grey slab of a building, surrounded by dark and windy walkways: the brainchild of an architect who doubtless lived in an ivy-covered cottage in the Peaks.

He peered into the gloom as he walked. What the fuck to do tonight? There were only so many things he could break to sustain his interest and the council had given up replacing the glass in the bus shelters.

Drugs were great but once the free samples from Banger had been toked, it was hard finding the cash to buy. Booze was easy to get but with no money, he'd been forced to apply for a Saturday job, washing cars at the Jap garage. Already the taste of a life turning sour.

There was always sex to take his mind off things, but that was nothing special. Sure he'd bust his cherry last year, at the age of fourteen, but somehow the way it was offered by the slappers at school put him off. He wanted more than to plant it up the downy fuzz box of those slappers followed by all that crap about him being their *boyfriend*. Even before he'd washed his dick. Fuck that!

Plus they enjoyed it too much for Jason's liking. Slags! He liked it better when they didn't want to, even though they really did. They all did. Like in those videos his dad let him watch. They were the best. So was his dad. All his mates said. *Their* dads got narked about them being out all hours. Not his dad. Jason was dead lucky. He'd hate a dad who did his head in.

Mum could be a drag though. That was women for you. "Only good for one thing," his dad would say.

"That's one more than you then," his mum would shout back.

3

There'd be a slanging match after that. Weird. Sometimes his mum seemed tougher than his dad, though Jason knew that couldn't be right.

*

The man drove the unfamiliar van slowly along the unfamiliar roads. It didn't matter. There were no other road users to complain. The only sign of life he'd seen was a foraging cat.

He glanced at the A-Z and peered at the nearest street sign through the waves of fog. He nodded, took a deep breath and turned left. He could sense he was near.

*

Jason pulled his mobile from his pocket on the first ring. He stared at the display and pulled a face. "What?"

"It's me. Your mother."

"I told you to text me if you need me, woman. I could have been wi' my mates."

"Piss off yer little shit or you won't have a phone."

"Er, likely? What do you want?"

"We've ordered those pizzas we won."

"Tonight?"

"Yeah, yer coming back?"

Jason hesitated. It was cold plus he was hungry. "Save me some," he ordered, before ending the call without waiting for a response.

He walked on, pulling his jacket tighter. He thought again about the film his dad had shown him last week and felt the stirring of a stiffy to warm him. The slag in that film hadn't seemed keen at first. She'd soon warmed up, mind, after the first two or three geezers had popped her.

Fuckin' aaay! The best sex he'd ever had was the blow from that girl at the posh school. Fatboy and Grets had picked her up and led her off the footpath by the lane. It was wicked. She hadn't wanted to either, not at first, but it was clear by the end she was into it. There were a few tears but you expect that.

"It's all part of the act," his dad said. "Bit of attention. Makes 'em feel loved." That's why Jason's teacher said what she did. Frustrated cow, she was. His dad supported him all the way. He knew about women. Got married at seventeen – though Jason was too young to remember the wedding. Rape Mrs Ottoman? A teacher! Er, likely? Sayin' it was one thing. Doin' it was another. All he'd done was feel her

4

up a bit when he grabbed her, but she couldn't prove nothin'.

Got him suspended from school just the same. A month. Some kind of record Mr Wrexham, the head teacher, said. Not that Jason cared. He loved all the fuss. School was for gays. As soon as he was old enough he'd get himself on the Social and win the lottery. That'd show those fucking teachers, telling him what to do. Jason Wallis looked after Number One. Nobody else mattered. It was the law of the jungle.

"It's a hard world out there," his dad had said. Not that he'd seen much of it. Bobby Wallis had lived in Derby all his life.

"Have some fun; play around as long as you can. Don't let some bitch trap you, son," he'd said.

"Thanks a bundle," his mum had replied. "Stop filling that boy's head with crap. It'll have more in than yours at this rate."

Funny. His dad had turned to him with *that* look. See what I mean, son. Keep clear. Sow a few wild oats. Not that I couldn't walk away any time...

"Jace!" shouted Grets from the doorway of the chip shop. The only intact window in the Centre glowed warmly at Jason. Like a moth to flame he headed for the only bright light for miles since the pub had closed its doors and boarded its windows for the last time.

"Yo!" shouted Jason back at his friend who also wore the de rigueur baseball cap and Stone Island top, over low slung baggy jeans. These guys knew how to big themselves up.

"How's it hanging, man?" said Jason, with a faint Brooklyn twang – Manchester was out – offering a clenched fist which Grets punched in greeting.

"Safe, man." Grets held out his chips and Jason helped himself.

"Thanks man. Starving, innit?"

"Eh! It's the superstar. How's it hanging, bro?" cried another of his crew, Stinger, emerging from the chip shop's cocoon of light and steam. "You're a Celebrity; get me out of 'ere."

Jason would've tried to look modest if he'd ever had anything to be modest about. Instead he savoured the inner heat stoked by acclamation and basked in his notoriety. It was the only reason to venture out on a bitter December night. He was famous, on the Drayfin at least, and he had to milk the attention before the whole thing blew over.

There'd been something about his suspension in the local rag, but that was two weeks ago. It cracked on about what the world was coming to and why schools had stopped using the cane. Like any kid would stand for that. They got rights, you know.

There was also a snippet on *East Midlands Today* though Jason's name hadn't been mentioned. His dad was hoping they'd let it slip so he could sue the arse off 'em. His dad was dead proud of the family honour.

Then the clincher – his passport to a thousand backslaps – a brief clip of him strutting out of school with his dad. Everyone local would know who he was.

"How you coping man? Bitches still lining up to daisy chain yo ass?"

"Chill guys. It's chilling a bit now," he said, making more of an effort to be self-effacing.

"Dread. Wish I'd been there man," grinned Stinger shaking his head. "Tell us what Grottyman did again?"

Jason grinned, feigning a reluctance that lasted no more than a second. "She freaked man..."

"Safe."

"...started crying. She's fucked up, man. Like I'd risk my dick in that dirt track."

"Fucking aaay to that man," laughed Grets and they tapped fists.

"Got any smokes?" asked Jason, fingering the tab end in his pocket.

"Nope, we're busted man, but I know how we can get some. Banger promised me some gear and some folding in exchange for help with this gig."

"Safe," drawled Jason. "Lead the way homey."

*

The van drew to a halt outside the house and the man got out and stepped to the rear of the van. He wore black overalls and a black peaked cap.

A crack of light from the house fell on the van as a curtain was pulled aside and was gone. The man closed the back doors more carefully than seemed necessary then moved towards the house, well camouflaged against the blackness except for the white boxes in his hands. The door of the house opened.

"Pizza Parlour?"

Chapter 1

Detective Inspector Damen Brook woke with a shudder and gathered himself for a moment, eyes clamped shut, damp fists clenched, poised between realities, each one disagreeable. With a mind divided he could escape both, have a foot in neither, bliss, for that second, before he opened his eyes to take in the blankness of his conscious world.

He raised his head from his desk and looked around his spartan office. He scanned the floor and listened. Nothing. No scratching, no telltale scurrying.

He pulled himself upright and massaged his aching neck, then stood to do the same for his back. He checked his watch. Gone midnight. His shift had finished four hours ago. He could have been at home now. Home. He could never resist a smile at the word. What would he do there?

He picked up the phone and yawned, tapped a pencil on his notepad and began to doodle. He moved his head from side to side in a silent *Eeny meeny miney mo* then punched the keys.

"*Taj Mahal.*"

"I'd like to order a takeaway please."

"*Hello Mr Brook. How are you tonight?*

"Never better. I'd like Chicken Jalfrezi…"

"*…and pillau rice. Would you like any bread with that?*"

"Do I ever have bread?"

"*Never.*"

"Well then. How long?"

"*Ten minutes.*"

"I'll be right there." Brook replaced the receiver and left, closing the door of his office softly. He walked quickly and quietly towards the main entrance.

He was in luck. Sergeant Hendrickson had his back to the counter and Brook was able to slide across the door to Reception without being noticed. He was in the clear and about to stride away when Hendrickson's voice held him.

"Bastard! He wants stringing up."

"Too right," replied a voice. Brook recognised PC Robinson – Hendrickson's straight man.

"Well if we get whatever bastard's done this, you'll see me at the front of the queue when the knuckle sandwiches are being served up."

"Me too."

Another voice, too indistinct to hear, said something by way of disagreement, judging by Hendrickson's response.

"No good at all. But it'll make me feel a fuck of a lot better."

Brook stood poised, grimacing, urging himself to make his escape. But he couldn't let it go. He was a DI. He had rank. He took a deep breath and stepped back in front of the counter. "Sergeant." All heads turned. "I could easily be a member of the public standing here listening to that language," he said, with an effort to sound forceful. "Or worse the Chief Super…" He stopped in mid-sentence when he saw WPC Wendy Jones was the third person in the conversation. Their eyes locked briefly before each looked away.

Brook pursed his lips and let the sentence hang, hoping it would appear a natural break. He should have said nothing. He knew it. He could have been away. His resolve was melting so he pretended to examine the desultory Christmas streamers darted around the ceiling before returning his eyes to Hendrickson.

"Still here? Sir." Sergeant Harry Hendrickson wore the mocking smile he reserved for his dealings with Brook. The pause he took before acknowledging Brook's seniority was a new technique for him though Brook knew it well enough. It was one he'd used himself when dealing with any Joe or Josephine Public who stimulated his contempt. That was in the days when he could still be stimulated.

"And people wonder why you didn't make detective," smiled Brook, with a bravado he didn't feel. Hendrickson's grin vanished and Brook heard sharp breaths being sucked in. He took one himself and decided he had to play on for all it was worth. "Well?"

"Well what? Sir?" replied Hendrickson.

"Foul language and threats of violence. Explain yourself." Brook knew he sounded lame. Hendrickson sensed it. He found his mocking smile again and stared back at Brook with unconcealed hatred.

PC Robinson decided to step in. "There's been a murder, sir. Some old dear. Strangled and beaten to death."

"I see…" began Brook.

"And some of us with mothers get very hot under the collar," spat Hendrickson, "when we see what some scumbags will do for a few quid. Sir!"

There was a crackling silence that prompted even WPC Jones to look up for Brook's reaction. When it came, it surprised even Hendrickson. Brook smiled a sad little smile and nodded. "Who took the call?"

"DI Greatorix was on duty, sir," said Robinson.

"Right." Brook turned from Hendrickson's triumphant grin and his eyes sought the floor. A second later he spun back to face Hendrickson, trying to get control of his voice. "Some of us who had mothers also got hot under the collar, sergeant, until we realised those feelings made us worse policemen who couldn't do their job properly. I may not find your language offensive in itself but it's a symptom of a mind that's not under control." Brook paused before adding softly. "And control is what they pay us for."

Hendrickson's grin remained but it had lost some of its wattage. Now it was Robinson's turn to look at the floor as Jones looked up at Brook. He, in turn, permitted himself a brief dart towards her eyes and fancied he detected a scintilla of approval in her expression. He couldn't hold the look for long and turned away, throwing a "Good night" over his shoulder as he left.

Brook walked away more calmly than he felt, listening for the telltale mutter and laugh that signalled some further insult. It arrived, as usual, as Brook rounded the corner and descended the stairs to the car park. He shook his head.

"Why didn't I just slip away? Why?"

∗

"Who does that twat think he is?" spat Hendrickson. "Fucking London ponce."

"He's from Yorkshire originally," offered Jones, not looking at either of her colleagues. This was a subject best avoided.

"Yeah. So what the fuck was he doing in the Met then?"

Jones took a breath and looked straight back at Hendrickson to signal her final say on the matter. "He was some kind of rising star, they say. The best criminal profiler on the Force. Until he got sick."

The portly figure of PC Aktar walked in. "Come on my duck. Let's get out there," he said to Jones. "We've got a city to look after."

"Coming."

"Sick my arse. I've seen his file. He had a fucking breakdown. So what's he doing here then?" asked Hendrickson. "I'll tell you what he's doing here, my girl…"

"I'm not your girl…"

"…he couldn't hack it in the Met, see. A college boy who thought he could do a better job than us ordinary coppers but he couldn't handle it, could he? So what happens?" He glanced at Robinson as though he wouldn't continue unless people insisted then carried on a split-second later. "We have to take him off their hands, don't we? Why? Because Derbyshire's a second class county and we can make do with middle-aged burn-outs who are treading water until they retire. That's why. We're shit and he's better than us so we should all bow down and kiss his arse."

"Sounds like fun, sarge," laughed Robinson.

Hendrickson smiled back at him. "Ai. It's true though, innit? And there's not a copper in this nick who doesn't agree with me."

"He does his job," chipped in Jones, on her way out.

Hendrickson smirked. "I might have known you'd defend him."

"What does that mean?" flashed back Jones, her colour rising, though she knew only too well.

This time Robinson joined in with a leer. "We all know he's your boyfriend, Wendy."

"He is not my boyfriend," she replied through gritted teeth, "I danced with him once and he gave me a lift home. Nothing happened. How many times?"

"Would that be a fireman's lift?" asked Hendrickson. He and Robinson cackled as Jones headed for the corridor.

"Piss off the pair of you."

"Please try and control your language, constable," Hendrickson shouted after her. "Your boyfriend might hear you."

As they headed for the car park, Aktar kept his eyes trained on Jones, waiting for the explanation. She ignored him for a few moments then, without looking at him, said, "Not a bloody word."

※

Brook pushed through the heavy metal door at the foot of the stairs and stepped into the artificial half-light. It was cold and dark, the chill winter's day having left a permanent freezing damp coating the ground. Brook shivered and pulled the collar of his overcoat up.

As was his custom, he stepped into the middle of the ramp to get to his car. He couldn't go near other cars. He needed space between himself and any obstacles. There'd been a rat once. So now Brook trod a path equidistant from both lines of vehicles.

He reached his old sports car, all the while scanning the floor for movement. He opened the creaky door and launched himself onto the cracked leather seat to avoid being nipped on the ankle by a stray psychotic rodent. He felt like a child launching himself into bed to escape the talons of the Bogey Man skulking below. He didn't care.

As he swung his battered Austin Healey Sprite out of the car park, Brook was appalled at its throaty din. The reverberations of the old car's straining engine clattered against the dark structures gathered around Derby's Police Headquarters and were flung back at Brook in a fit of pique by the empty office building across the road.

What a racket. He was aware of it now, once the bustle of the day had long departed. The roar he savoured with a connoisseur's pleasure on a sunny Sunday drive in the Peaks made him wince in the echo chamber of the night. It was a cacophony that could have shattered the walls of Jericho, had the biblical city been no more than a 50 mile round trip from Derby.

*

Brook picked up his takeaway and was home in a few minutes, one of the advantages of living in a city as small as Derby. A quick trip round the inner ring road past the Eagle Centre, skirting the new shopping precinct, and Brook was back at his down-at-heel rented flat on the Uttoxeter Road.

It wasn't much of a front but it was as good a place as any. And it was central. No Barrett home in a suburban development for Brook. No tasselled sofa and MFI flat packs. Brook was used to city living, where he could be quiet and anonymous: unless, of course, he was driving the Sprite home after midnight when everyone could mark his progress through the streets. Not that he cared about disturbing people. Like all insomniacs, he assumed everyone else slept like babies.

Brook slowed the Sprite to a crawl and carefully manoeuvred the delicate bodywork onto the pavement-cum-drive outside his ground floor flat. He killed the engine, heard the fan belt call a cranky halt to its day's work and stepped out of the driver's seat holding his Chicken Jalfrezi, listening to the pre-ignition running before the engine finally died. He closed the door gingerly, not bothering to lock it.

Instinctively he turned to the upstairs window of the flats next door in time to see the curtain fall. Brook nodded, satisfied. Old Mrs Saunders probably slept less than he did. He supposed she'd be having "a word" with him tomorrow about "all that noise in the middle of the night." Comforting really, having such a busybody keeping an eye on the place. Not that he bothered about security. He had nothing of value. But then again, he *was* a policeman and, as such, was as interested as Mrs Saunders in the "comings and goings," if only out of a kind of default curiosity.

Brook hesitated before going in. He wanted a cigarette. He'd gone without for two days. He extracted a dog-eared pack from the boot of the car and flipped open the box. One left. That was good. And bad. If he were still in Battersea, he could have gone for more, any time of night. But he wasn't. He was in Derby and it was closed.

Brook lit up and inhaled deeply, enjoying the sting and feeling an immediate and gratifying nausea. He stood by his car and looked out over the building site across the road and on, past the sweep of Derby's low horizon. There wasn't much to be seen. It was a dark, misty night and cold air was blowing down from the Peaks.

For the first time in the three years since his transfer, Brook was beginning to look at the skyline like an old friend. He hadn't chosen Derby as a place to live and work. He'd picked up the first available transfer out of London. If it had been to Baghdad he would have taken it. Just to get out.

And Derby hadn't let him down. It was a pleasingly unremarkable place to lose himself. An engineering town by tradition, which marked out the population as hard working and straightforward, it also boasted a large and well-integrated Asian population.

Frank Whittle, pioneer of the jet engine, was much honoured in a city where Rolls Royce was the main employer. Derby also had one of the largest railway engineering works in the world. It was a city built on transport, going nowhere. Obligatory retail parks ringed the city and much of the population and traffic had followed, making Brook's neighbourhood, if not any more glamorous, then certainly a little quieter.

And despite the inevitable decline of such an industry-dependent city, crime was not excessive and murder was rare.

But what really marked out this East Midlands backwater was the Peak District, a few miles to the north-west. Brook had fallen in love with it and took every opportunity he could to drive into the hills and soak up the peace of the countryside. Ashbourne, Hartington, Buxton, Bakewell, Carsington Water. All were favoured haunts, where he could dump the car and walk for hours alone, clearing his mind of all the clutter.

And now, as a bonus, he was discovering a sense of belonging. That was good. It would prepare him for the biggest challenge of all;

retrieving a sense of himself.

For the first time since joining the Met as a callow, yet confident twenty three year old, Brook began to believe that it might be possible to wash the garbage from mind and body. Now, here, he was only wading in the gutter. In London he'd been drowning in a sewer. There *was* hope.

Chapter 2

Brook took a final urgent drag and tossed the cigarette. He walked up the communal access road and unlocked the back door into the kitchen of his flat. He never used the front door as it opened into his living room, a quaint reminder of a childhood spent in a back-to-back terrace, with which he wasn't comfortable. Memories of strange, rubicund men collecting rent or insurance and breathing light ale fumes into his pram were still keenly felt forty-odd years on.

He looked briefly at the answer machine. For once it was flashing so he played the message. It was from Terri, his daughter, wishing "a happy birthday for tomorrow to my number one dad," her nickname for him since acquiring a second father. She'd moved with her mother and "number two dad" to Brighton after the divorce. Brook didn't wipe the brief message but left the machine flashing to remind him to ring her.

It didn't sit well with Brook that a father should need a reminder to talk to an only daughter and his unexpected good mood soured as a result. He looked at his watch. It *was* his birthday. He could see the single envelope on the mat by the front door. He left it there.

After picking at his curry and downing a celebratory glass of milk, he showered and went to bed. He remembered to leave a little food by the flap, in case Cat tired of its nocturnal foraging, and lay down to read in his box-sized bedroom, head grazing one wall, feet flat against the other for the warmth from the radiator on the other side.

For a change, sleep came quickly, though it rarely lasted beyond an hour. And too often it would be an hour of visions exploding across his brain. Some he could recognise, some he couldn't. Then sometimes, on a case, he would see something – a face, a crime scene, a piece of evidence – and recall an echo of it in a dream he'd already had. It bothered Brook at first until he'd been able to write it off to the Job.

The things he'd seen were enough to fever any brow.

Tonight even the concession of one fitful hour was withdrawn and he woke to the noise of the phone a few moments later. It was DS John Noble.

"Sir, you're awake."

A sigh was Brook's only answer. "What's up, John?"

"Murder, sir. A bad one."

"Bad as in poorly executed or bad as in not nice?"

"The latter I think," replied Noble, making a conscious effort to impress with his vocabulary. Eighteen months hanging on to DI Brook's coat tails had taught Noble three things. "Avoid swearing, John, in my presence at least. Try to speak proper English, if you know any. And most important, don't ever call me guv."

"DI Greatorix should be dealing but he's already on a call."

"So he is. Where are you?"

"ASBO-land."

Brook let out a heavy sigh of frustration. "John, if you're on the Drayfin, just say so."

"I'm on the Drayfin Estate."

"What's the address?" Brook jotted it down. At this time of night it wouldn't take him long to get to the rundown housing estate on the south side of the city, built in the sixties when Britain's city planners had decided that people were keen to live cheek by jowl in identical, low cost boxes. It was little surprise to Brook that residents in such areas attracted more than their fair share of Anti-Social Behaviour Orders. "I'll be ten minutes."

*

Fifteen minutes later the noise from Brook's Sprite ensured that those houses on the Drayfin Estate still in darkness were fully alerted to the commotion in their midst, and soon switches were being flicked and curtains twitched.

If he spent much more time driving around in the middle of the night, the National Grid would be inviting him to the staff parties. The idea brought a brief smile to Brook's lips. A pity he couldn't introduce such levity into his dealings with others, he thought.

Brook was mulling over the comedic potential of his future trans-actions with Sergeant Hendrickson when, without warning he jumped onto the brakes. The car shuddered to an unconvincing halt. Seconds later a black and white cat hurtled across the path of the Sprite and skittered away into the mist, a pink tail hanging from its mouth.

15

Brook exhaled heavily and, fully awake now, pulled over to the huddle outside Number 233 – a small red brick semi-detached – as an ambulance was pulling away. He killed the engine, aware of looks and smiles exchanged between the knot of uniformed constables attempting to keep warm on the verge outside the house. He could tell from the patterns of exhaled breath that his arrival had provoked words as well as restrained amusement.

He wondered if the earlier incident with Hendrickson had been thrown into the mix for general sport. Such disputes spread like wildfire amongst the smaller, close knit stations and D Division was no exception.

A young man stepped from the throng. Detective Sergeant Noble was a good looking, fit twenty-seven year old who took a keen interest in his own advancement. Apart from a regulation-stretching blond mop, parted in the middle, he was smartly presented, even at this late hour. The contrast with his own hurriedly assembled and shapeless clothing wasn't lost on Brook.

"'Evening, John – or rather morning." Noble nodded but Brook could tell he wasn't his usual ebullient self because he fidgeted with his latex gloves, not meeting Brook's eye. "Have you puked, John?" he enquired with a hint of mockery.

"No sir." A pause. "Not yet."

"Who was that in the ambulance?"

"PC Aktar, sir. He was first on the scene. He fainted."

"Causing great hilarity amongst his colleagues no doubt." Despite himself Brook took a little comfort from this alternative explanation for the smirks that had greeted his arrival. "Is it a puker John?"

"Not so much to look at. I've seen worse. It's just..." he tailed off and looked at the floor.

"Is the PS in there?" asked Brook.

"The surgeon's been delayed."

Brook raised an eyebrow then nodded. "Right, the other murder. And SOCO?"

"Same."

"A fresh crime scene. Talk me through it."

"The family's name is Wallis."

Brook narrowed his eyes in recognition. "Bobby Wallis. Yes. Petty theft and an ABH. General scourge if memory serves. Which one is it?"

"Well." Noble looked round as though he were afraid of making a fool of himself before turning back to Brook. "There are four bodies."

"Four?" Brook fixed his DS with a stare and began to be impressed. A long-buried echo sounded in the vaults of his heart,

16

quickening its beat. He ignored Noble's faint nod and ran his bottom lip underneath his upper teeth, a gesture of calculation that he hoped would mask his unease. "Go on."

"Bobby Wallis, his wife we're assuming, plus his daughter – Kylie – plus a baby. One survivor. The son. Jason Wallis. He was out cold and a strong smell of booze on him. Could be drugs as well. He's gone off to hospital." Brook turned to Noble with his eyebrow cocked. "He's under guard," answered Noble. "But there are no obvious blood-stains on his hands or clothes. And if he was in there..." Noble looked away.

Brook nodded then looked around as though a cigarette vendor might recognise his need and come forward with a pack. It seemed he was about to make one of those periodic visits to hell that he'd moved to Derby to escape. Months of stultifying boredom, interspersed with sporadic journeys through the entrails of the human condition, Brook a mute witness to the black hole of depravity and despair that sucked all virtuous emotion from him. Black. The colour of man's heart. The colour invisible in the night. The colour of old blood.

"Witnesses?"

"A neighbour across the street, Mrs Patel, says she saw a white van make a delivery. Around 8.15. There are pizza boxes from Pizza Parlour inside so it looks legit. She remembered a partial plate. I've put it out on the wire. No hits yet."

"Score one for the busybodies. Are you checking with Pizza Parlour?"

"They're closed but we're running it down. Do you think it's important?"

"Yes. The van's wrong. In my experience most pizza deliveries are done on a moped. If Pizza Parlour did have a van, they'd have their livery all over it."

"So why would our nosy neighbour not see that if she can remember a partial?"

"Exactly."

"I've been onto Traffic to be on the lookout on all the major roads."

"Good. Give it to the motorway boys as well though he may be long gone. And tell them we'll need to look at all the CCTV for our time slot."

Brook waited while Noble got on the radio to Dispatch, all the while scanning the uniformed officers for the chance to bum a cigarette. But no-one would light up until the senior officer had disappeared into the house.

17

Noble rejoined Brook. "Well, let's take a peek, John." And with that Brook attached his mental blinkers and concentrated fully on Noble's brisk summary as they walked towards the front door.

"The next door neighbour found them, sir. A Mr Singh. He came round at about half past twelve to complain about noise – loud music – the front door was ajar so he walked into the front room and there they all were. Apart from the son – Jason – who was flat out in the kitchen."

"How were they killed?"

"Throats cut, and, well, you can see for yourself. You won't believe it." Noble's recollection began to gnaw at his composure. His features adopted the pained squint of a man holding on to himself, so useful at funerals.

Brook stopped and almost to himself echoed his DS. "Throats cut." Then with a turn of the head he roused himself to keep step with Noble. "I'll believe anything where people are concerned, John."

"The weird thing is the victims were just sat there, facing the telly, like they were watching Big Brother."

"Big...?"

Noble looked at Brook with a momentary puzzled expression then looked away, realising his mistake. "Big Brother. It's a TV programme, sir. Very popular, with ordinary people, I understand."

Brook caught the undertone of Noble's gibe with a flush of pleasure. He was learning a healthy disrespect for superiors. It would make him a better copper. "Please don't explain the tastes of the nation to me, John, I'm tired. Sitting around the TV like a normal family, you say."

"That's right."

"Since when has it been normal for a family to sit down together – as a family. Not since the golden age of Ovaltine and Dick Barton."

"Dick Barton?"

"The radio. Or the wireless, to be strictly accurate."

Noble nodded. "You mean kids have a TV in their own room..."

"Or a CD player or computer. The point being, never fail to question what initially hits you as normal. Families rarely socialise as a unit these days." A sliver of personal grief deformed Brook's features for a second and was gone.

"So having the family in one place is part of the MO. The killer's staged it."

"It's possible."

"Well that would rule out Jason as the perp." Noble was conscious of his gaffe before he'd finished the word and prepared himself for Brook's disapproval.

Instead Brook smiled thinly and looked him briefly in the eye. "Perp? Have you got indigestion John?"

Noble smiled back.

They stopped at the Wallis front door. It was open. Noble handed Brook a pair of latex gloves which he pulled on.

"Was the front door forced?"

"No obvious sign of it."

"How many have tramped through already?"

"Besides myself, PC Aktar and the neighbour, Mr Singh. Also the ambulance crew had to stretcher Jason out from the kitchen."

"What about Aktar? Where was he?"

"He fainted out here."

"Did he? That's interesting."

"Delayed shock maybe."

Brook nodded. "Maybe." Avoiding the handle, Brook pushed the front door back with a latex finger. There was another door on the right off the hallway with red smears on the handle. The door was open just a crack and Brook noticed Noble make a conscious effort to suppress a shudder at the thought of what lay beyond. Ahead, in full view, lay the brightly lit kitchen, door wide open. The sink was visible, as was the lid of a cardboard pizza box lying open on the drainer.

"How many have been in the living room?" asked Brook, fleetingly aware of his unintended joke.

"Mr Singh went in and found them. Aktar had to go in to check for signs of life. He went in the kitchen to check on Jason too. I only looked in at the door. I didn't want to disturb anything."

"I don't think we can compromise the hall any more than it is but watch out for any obvious bloody footprints, John. Step right up against the wall." With that Brook picked his way past the murder room, towards the kitchen, Noble following in his superior's footsteps.

Once in the bright stark room, Brook knelt down to examine the linoleum. "What do you think that is?" he said indicating a small knot of dark red matter on the floor.

Noble felt his gorge rising. He managed to wrench out a, "Dunno," keeping his eyes averted from the offending unction.

Brook removed a pencil from his coat and prodded the floor then raised the red tip of the pencil to his nose. He sniffed, suppressing a smile, aware of the discomfort of his audience. This must be how the boy who ate earwigs at Brook's primary school had felt. He stood and turned to look at the open pizza box on the drainer. Two closed boxes were neatly stacked under the top one.

"Tomato sauce. From this pizza. Pizza Parlour's Quattro Stagioni

– Four Seasons – to you and me," he added with a smile. "And very good they are too."

"You know your takeaways," said Noble.

"I went to university, John. That's how I was able to read it off the box. Note two pieces missing. One cut from the ham and mushroom segment, the other torn from the pepperami. Jason Wallis was found unconscious here, this is where he fell, but the rest of the family are in the living er...lounge?"

"Right."

"Good. Remind me. Is PC Aktar heavy?"

Noble was taken aback but had become accustomed to not reacting to Brook's odd questions.

"Fairly heavy, yes."

"Right." Brook's expression took on a faraway look. There was silence as both men realised they'd used up all their distractions. Suddenly, with a full swallow of air for Dutch courage, Brook sought the eye of his DS and nodded towards the living room door. "Am I right in thinking the killer's left us a message in there, John?"

Noble's lips parted in surprise. "How did you...?" As Noble's voice began to falter, Brook, alive to his discomfort, tapped into one of his meagre seams of humanity – the mother lode had been exhausted long ago – and he threw Noble a straw to clutch.

"I'd like a peek at the scene before SOCO start bagging and tagging. You've already seen it, John, so wait outside for the surgeon. I don't want anybody else in the house until SOCO have done their stuff. No-one else comes through that front door." He paused before adding, "Okay?" The two men, normally cloaked in layer upon layer of emotional cladding, looked at one another as men rarely do. Noble's instinct was to turn away and adjust his protective layers but something made his eyes linger, the need to communicate his gratitude.

"There's a lot of blood on the floor. You might compromise footprints."

"I'm just going to look from the door not traipse round shaking hands and sitting on laps. If this has been staged I want to see it as the killer intended it to be seen. Atmosphere John, remember."

"Right. Get a feel for the crime before anything else. Mind the handle. There are blood smears on it."

As Brook prepared a finger to push open the bloodied door, he turned to Noble. "Get onto SOCO and the PS and give them a hurry-up. And get on to the hospital. They probably know but tell them they might need to pump Aktar's stomach. Young Wallis too. Just to be on the safe side."

It was the smell that hit Brook first. It wasn't new to him, the smell of death, the sweet smell of ageing blood, the excrement expelled by a body no longer able to maintain its integrity, the sweat no longer evaporated by the heat of its host. These things weren't new to Brook but the smell of a victim's terror was. Almost. Only twice before. In London. Brixton 1991. And the first time, 1990. Harlesden. *Harleshole of the Universe*, as his old DI, Charlie Rowlands, had dubbed it.

And the same thoughts were intruding then, as now. Did his own fear give off the same scent on those rare occasions his nightmares overpowered his reason?

Brook wondered – no he knew – this was the smell discharged as people watched their own deaths unfold. Yes, he knew, as he knew the other smell, the hint of perfume – Talcum powder. To keep sweaty palms dry inside latex gloves. He wished he had some now.

Brook stood to one side of the door and tried to take it all in. Bobby Wallis sat in his armchair, facing the TV. His body was contorted with effort, his fists clenched and spotted with blood. His head was tilted at an angle, as though puzzled by something. Brook peered at the half-closed eyes and turned to follow the victim's sightless gaze, squinting above and beyond the TV to the word "SAVED" daubed in blood on the alcove wall. Rivulets wept from all the letters except the D. This letter was fainter than the others though the writer hadn't been short of ink. A message from the killer. SAVED. Who was saved and from what? Brook was no nearer knowing. The Reaper was back. He knew that much.

The memories came flooding in and Brook was tempted to move around the room as if physical activity could quell the images in his mind. But one of those images was of stepping in a pool of blood all those years ago in Brixton so he managed to anchor himself.

He noted the poster on the chimney breast and nodded in recognition. Van Gogh's Irises. It didn't belong in this house. Rich, vivid colours stood out against the grubby walls. The blue and golden flowers, the single white flower. But now the picture was different, scarred by the slash of red, like a giant approving tick on a piece of artwork. He was held for a moment. Harlesden in 1990, Brixton a year later. And now Derby. Why such a long gap? It made no sense.

Brook forced his mind back to the present and returned his eyes to Bobby Wallis. There was a new orifice under his chin and his dark blue sweater was saturated black with blood. Arterial sprays were everywhere. Walls, clothing, furniture, the small silver Christmas tree in the corner, the dark carpet probably, though it was difficult to tell.

There would be blood all round the bodies and footprints in the blood – the neighbour's and PC Aktar's – who would have had to tramp around the room checking for signs of life. They wouldn't be hard to distinguish for today's Scene of Crime Officers with their digital imaging technology. The killer's footprints would eventually be isolated – for what it was worth. They'd still need a suspect before they could find a match.

Brook moved his head, trying to catch a look at the front of the man's face. Then he saw it, reflected in the dim light, a faint glimmer scarring his cheeks. It was there as before. The man's cheeks were encrusted with it – salt from tears. Something had made this man cry and sure as hell, it wasn't Big Brother.

Brook remembered him now. Bobby Wallis had form and Brook was willing to bet he hadn't cried since early childhood. He was a local hard man, a man's man, a petty criminal, who graduated from years in the system and drifted in and out of menial work. Sometimes he got drunk and beat up those who were sure not to fight back. Not his family though. They were part of him. He'd protect *his* kids. He'd protect his wife. Love was another matter.

Brook remembered his own dead father, a miner in Barnsley. Although as different from Bobby Wallis as chalk from cheese, Brook recognised the symptoms. A life built on small successes, hungrily sought and endlessly trumpeted to drown the background hum of failure.

With his father it had been his work as a union official and coaching the church boys' football club. With Wallis it would have been a good result at the bookies or the chance smile of a barmaid "asking for it."

Brook turned his gaze to the ample figure beside Bobby. Mrs Wallis – he seemed to remember they were married – was on the sofa comically dressed in a towelling tracksuit that stretched itself, with more than a hint of complaint, around her abundant flesh. At least in death she'd discovered irony, thought Brook, trying to suppress a grim smile.

A pack of cigarettes and gold lighter sat neatly beside her. They would surely have been knocked over in the death struggle so they had to have been placed there post mortem. If there was a reason apart from the killer's sense of order, Brook didn't know it. His eye lingered on the pack. He was sorely tempted to take one and light up.

Mrs Wallis had also cried. Her face was contorted with pain and effort, though Brook doubted whether she'd have been able to plead for her life. Like her husband, she wore the large, sopping bib of a blood-stain beneath telltale sinew, protruding like a bag of giblets from her throat. Another life to make no mark. Gone forever. Brook nodded. The same format. And the gore wasn't too bad. He could cope. Except. There was always "except." That was the same as Harlesden and Brixton too.

The girl lay face down on the fake animal skin rug. Brook was glad he couldn't see her face – an oversight on the part of the killer perhaps.

Her feet were bare up to her ankles where her pyjamas took over. The bottoms were relatively free of blood and were dotted with cartoon characters. Her top lay in tatters around her torso. It had been slashed open, exposing her back and shoulders. Something had been carved onto the smooth alabaster skin below her shoulder blades and Brook strained his neck to make it out. SAVED again. The lettering was cut in straight lines including the S. The blade had been thin and very sharp, as Brook could see no evidence of effort or hacking around the deep cuts; another cutthroat razor perhaps, or even a scalpel.

The area around the girl's torn neck shone dark with blood though not as much as might be expected for such a major wound. Nor was there much blood coming from the cuts on her back.

He decided these wounds were administered post mortem to prevent excessive bleeding. That fit the pattern. The killer wouldn't want his message obscured. Dr Habib would have to confirm it but Brook was sure enough and took some measure of comfort from the fact.

Now he scanned the floor. He could see no obvious sign of the weapon. The Reaper had taken it with him this time. The Reaper. Brook was annoyed with himself. How quickly he'd parcelled up the crime and assigned it to his old quarry. He had to keep an open mind.

He began to scan the room itself. For a family home there was very little mess. Some Christmas cards on a string had been taken down to make way for the Van Gogh poster but even then they'd been neatly stacked behind the little Christmas tree in the corner. If you didn't count the bloodstains, there was order. The killer had arranged every-thing, tidied everything so only the important things remained to catch the eye. Before or after death, Brook couldn't tell. A bit of both, probably.

A few crumbs of food on the carpet were the only other signs of disorder. Probably caused by the victims as they knocked over their meal in the struggle to understand what was happening to them. The pizza boxes were now in the kitchen, out of the way. They'd done their job and were now just clutter as far as the killer was concerned.

Everything was deliberate, put in place for Brook to see.

He shook himself to gaze again at the girl, trying not to imagine her ordeal. A few hours before, she would have been pink with life, the rug a deathly white. Now the roles were reversed. She couldn't have been more than ten or eleven. What had *she* done to deserve this? She hadn't chosen her parents. Brook could write off their useless existence with little guilt. But the girl should have had her whole life in front of her.

Next Brook glanced at the carry cot beside the TV, glad he couldn't see inside. It must have been the thought of the little mite that had eaten away at Noble's sangfroid. This was a new outrage for The Reaper: murdering a baby. He remembered what Charlie Rowlands used to say in London, *"The smaller the victim, the bigger the crime."*

Was that what started the tears for Bobby and Mrs Wallis? Or was it their young daughter's throat being torn open in front of them? He wished he could be sure it was one of the two but he knew not to take it for granted. Impending death could induce terrifying selfishness.

And the son, Jason, a petty thief and general chip off the old block, Brook recalled. He was alive and the girl and the baby were dead. Why? That didn't tally with the past. In Harlesden and Brixton no-one was spared.

For a split-second Brook was consumed by the hope that this was different, just a one-off, mindless slaughter, not the work of The Reaper but the drug addled frenzy of a teenage boy or a disgruntled neighbour pushed over the edge. He looked back at the Van Gogh poster and the bloody daub on the wall and the thought died in its infancy.

Brook wanted to step outside. His need for a cigarette was becoming almost clinical. He swept his eye round the room one last time. On the shelf of the fireplace above the gas fire stood a bottle of red wine with two half full glasses either side. "Nice symmetry," nodded Brook. He couldn't make out the label from where he was but suspected the killer had brought it. It looked too expensive for the weekly Wallis shop at Lidl.

To the left of one of the wine glasses what looked like a lipstick had been stood on its end. Brook glanced at Mrs Wallis to see if she was wearing any. It was difficult to tell. It had probably fallen out of her pocket and had been tidied up by the killer.

Brook turned and then looked back. Whatever impression the killer wanted to convey, the chances were he would want it seen as someone came through the door. Many serial killers enjoyed creating a tableaux. In this case, family life as it should be: gathered together to discuss the events of the day, then wiped out by a single act.

As Brook turned again to plot a path back to the cold night air a noise from behind halted him and his head snapped back towards the murder scene. He froze, not daring to move, listening for further noises. He stared at Bobby Wallis for a long time, watching for any sign of movement, examining the wound on his neck again to be sure he was dead.

He turned to leave but the noise returned. This time it was unmistakeable. A rustling of material. Someone or something was moving in the room. Brook stood like a statue for what seemed an age, his breathing shallow, his ear cocked, only his eyes allowed to move. The next sound was one Brook had not heard for many years. Not since Terri had been a baby. It was an infant gurgling, preparing itself to wake and scream for a feeding with that disproportionate power that robbed so many new parents of their sleep.

Brook stepped round the room as quickly and as delicately as he could manage before peering into the carry cot next to the TV. A baby wriggled, its eyes closed, trying to kick off its blanket. Tiny eyes flickered but instead of joy Brook's mouth fell open in horror. On the child's forehead – in small lettering – the word "SAVED" again. Brook narrowed his eyes and pulled the restrictive blanket away from the baby and felt around its torso for any further signs of injury. The baby wriggled even harder and began to kick out and cry. Brook plucked the infant from its swaddling, hardly daring to look at the disfigurement inflicted although there was something odd about it.

He walked towards the door holding the child but stopped suddenly. Then he bent down to sniff the baby. A second later Brook had produced a handkerchief, dabbed it into his mouth then wiped away a corner of the letter D from the baby's forehead. "Lipstick." Brook sighed with pleasure and relief and hurried out of the room.

"Sergeant!" he screamed at the top of his voice. "Get over here!"

At this terrifying noise, the baby opened its mouth and began to scream as loudly as tiny lungs would allow. Brook was unable to keep from laughing out loud and long at the baby's distress. In a bad mood, he'd once said there was, "No finer sight than a child in tears," and finally his words had found a more worthy setting.

He'd forgotten how to hold an infant and he marched the baby out of the front door at arm's length, as though he'd set the chip pan on fire. Noble flew to him and took the bundle, amazed.

"I thought..."

"Get the little sod off to hospital. If you can, get a shot of the forehead before it gets cleaned off. And when you've done that get this place completely sealed off. See to it yourself, John, and let's get it right this time."

Two hours later Brook stood at the gate of the Wallis house, pulling hard on a "borrowed" Silk Cut and stamping his feet to keep warm. It wasn't yet five o'clock but despite that and the biting cold a small huddle of interested bystanders stood shivering in the blackness on the other side of the potholed street, their faces glowing in the burnished light of flashing squad cars and ambulances. A Scientific Support van was parked next to Brook's Sprite, its back doors open. Noble pulled up and got out of a squad car and approached Brook looking sheepish.

"How's the baby, John?"

"It seems fine. No injuries."

"Did you get a shot of the writing…?"

Noble waved a disposable camera at Brook and nodded.

"…and was it lipstick?"

"It looks like it. The hospital's sending us a sample." Brook nodded. "Sir, I'm sorry about…"

"It's not your fault John. I'm sorry I snapped."

"I didn't check…"

"You had a crime scene to preserve. You had every right to accept what Aktar told you. It's his mess."

"Even so."

"Don't worry about it. I'm just pleased we found out before the PS arrived. That *would* have been embarrassing."

"How could Aktar have made such a mistake?"

"I suspect he was already feeling unwell."

At that moment, a scene of crime officer in bright protective clothing carrying one end of a carpet emerged from the house. The other end of the carpet followed supported by another officer. They placed it carefully in the back of the van.

"Do you want a look round before the bodies go, inspector?" he said.

"Please."

Brook leapt up to the front steps with Noble in reluctant pursuit.

Inside more officers in bright clothing were photographing the victims before bagging the hands, feet and heads to preserve any trace evidence adhering to them.

Brook stepped across the now bare floor to the girl still lying face down on the rug. He examined the cuts on her back but saw nothing new. Then he looked hard at her ankles and wrists and finally, the back of her head.

26

"No marks," he said across to Noble who was doing the same examination of Mr and Mrs Wallis.

"Same here. No obvious contusions or restraint marks as far as I can tell."

Brook nodded. "They were drugged." He went to look more closely at the wine bottle on the fireplace.

"You think the wine's drugged?" asked Noble.

"I don't think so. The girl wouldn't have had wine. The killer brought it for some reason. Maybe for himself – to celebrate a job well done."

Noble managed a chuckle. "Yeah, good health. Perhaps he's left saliva in the glasses."

"We'll see." Brook walked back to the door and looked again at the scene as a whole. The TV was pushed back into the alcove, the CD player against the far wall. Brook had checked. It was an old one. Not like Brixton. No entry there. It was the pizzas. They were the way in. He approached the CD player.

"This has been dusted, I take it," asked Brook of no-one in particular.

"Yeah," answered a SOCO kneeling down by the fireplace.

Brook turned the power on with his knuckle and ejected the tray. A CD of Mahler's Ninth Symphony lay there. There was no case nearby.

Brook smiled. Mahler: something to listen to, something beautiful. He pressed play. The tray returned to the body of the machine. Brook waited for the music. Nothing. The display told Brook that fifteen seconds of the first track had elapsed. He located the volume control and moved it round to the right. At once the low strains of Mahler's melancholic lament could be heard. He held the circular button and turned it further round. Shuddering horns filled the room.

Brook turned it to full blast and everybody stopped what they were doing and turned to the source of the annoyance. The sound was distorted. Brook returned the volume control to its original position with an apologetic smile then turned off the power.

As he looked round the room for the last time, Brook knew the killer was a man, *the* man. It couldn't be a woman. Course it couldn't. It wasn't just statistical. Women give Life – at least biologically – men take it. No need for offender profiling to tell him that.

"I've seen enough."

Chapter 3

As the pale light of a December dawn broke over the city skyline, Brook's weary eyelids began to close. Odd the way he always felt more tired when he was denied his eight hours of solid insomnia. He could lay awake reading and thinking – all night sometimes – and still feel viable in the morning, but if he wasn't horizontal he was unable to recreate himself and it drained him.

For the second time that morning the phone shattered his fragile peace. It was Chief Superintendent McMaster, before eight in the morning no less. She wasn't usually sighted before noon, what with all the courses, seminars and consultations she had to attend. She had an endless timetable of heavy-duty liaison to get through, but here she was, in her office, at the end of the criminal rush hour, wanting to speak to him.

Brook hadn't spoken to the Chief about a case in months, so little was she involved in criminal matters. The last time they'd spoken at all, McMaster had dialled the wrong extension. Brook knew that wasn't the case this time. Local TV and radio had already been sniffing round and she had to have basic facts to release.

"*DI Brook?*" She had a mellifluous voice, a crucial selling point at her promotion interview.

"Ma'am."

"*Can I see you right away, in my office, please? I need to pick your brains about last night.*"

"Right away, ma'am."

"*Thank God, you were on call last night, Damen. We can hit the ground running. I'll have a coffee waiting.*"

Brook replaced the receiver with a smile. Even at half past seven in the morning she felt able to play him like a violin.

Brook picked up his preliminary report and looked at his reflection in the mirror. He was a mess. He knew he had a good excuse but he also knew that the Chief Super would be immaculate, even at this early hour.

Brook stood outside her office, hand raised to knock, when Noble turned the corner carrying a plastic beaker of coffee. He had a large envelope under his arm. He hadn't slept either but at least he wasn't wearing a tatty polo neck.

"Are those the SOCO photos, John?"

He nodded. "I put a rush on them."

"Good. I'm going to brief the boss. You'd better join me."

Noble examined his watch and raised an eyebrow. "She's actually here?"

Brook hesitated. He was sensitive to snipes at the Chief Super. They were alike – outsiders against the rest – and a dig at her was a dig at him. He decided to say nothing, then knocked and entered.

"'Morning ma'am. DS Noble's with me to fill in some of the blanks."

If McMaster noticed Brook's dishevelled condition, she didn't let it show. "Fine," she beamed, emptying a cafetiere into two solid French coffee cups, complete with matching saucers. The woman's touch – a little strategy to make her male colleagues feel subliminally masterful and at ease. Brook knew the routine. At some point she'd feel compelled to water her spider plants. "I hope he's brought his own. Black with sugar isn't it, inspector?"

"Yes ma'am. The bitter and the sweet," he said after a brief pause. She glanced slyly back at him and Brook felt he saw the ghost of a smile crease her 45 year-old features.

Evelyn McMaster was short, with wavy blond cropped hair and a tidy figure. And yes, her general appearance, make-up and all, was immaculate. She was what the politer elements in the division referred to as a handsome woman. To the less polite elements, this meant that while her looks wouldn't make you vomit neither were they likely to induce an erection.

Brook liked McMaster. He enjoyed seeing somebody beside himself stir the simmering pot of resentment bubbling away in the division. But it was more than that. He admired the strength of the woman: not just the character she needed to drive her way to the top despite the Force's inbuilt sexism – but also the will and the energy required to keep her mask in place, to play her role to the hilt, all day, every day.

Everybody wanting to speak to you, soliciting your thoughts, goading you into newsworthy errors, forcing you to discipline every word and tunnel your vision to their agenda. Dealing with people who don't respect you, who don't want you there yet still retaining the self-possession to treat all comers in an even-handed way, was something Brook had to applaud. The effort would have consumed him. Brook's mind needed vast lumps of downtime, even during the day, to uncouple his thoughts from their moorings and set them adrift from the images of his past that tried, too often, to clamber aboard.

McMaster sat down and invited Brook and Noble to do the same.

"Well gentlemen. A busy night. DI Greatorix picked up a murder as well." Brook managed to exhume an interested expression. "Annie Sewell. Poor old dear killed in her so-called sheltered house, though I doubt it'll knock yours off the front page." She nodded sadly at the horror of it all, as she'd learned many years ago on her first counselling course. "Is that for me?" she said, indicating the sheaf of papers in Brook's hand. He handed it to her and watched her read it quickly and without emotion.

"Three deaths?" she enquired. "I heard four."

"No ma'am," Brook returned evenly. "You know how these rumours start – the first impression of the neighbour."

Brook and Noble exchanged a glance when McMaster resumed reading.

"Windpipes severed. Time of death between eleven and midnight. I assume that's preliminary," she asked with a glance at Brook. He nodded. "Very unpleasant," McMaster concluded. "At least from these bare facts," she added with perhaps a suggestion of criticism. "Thoughts gentlemen?"

"The only suspect we have is the Wallis boy, Ma'am. Jason." Brook offered. "He was drunk and may have been on drugs. It's just possible he may have gone berserk. He's still unconscious in hospital. We'll be seeing him later to question him and hopefully get the results of any tests." Brook sipped at his coffee.

"But you don't see him as our killer?"

"Unlikely."

"Why so sure?"

"The scene isn't disorganised enough for that kind of chemically fuelled slaughter," said Brook.

"And his clothes and hands show no visible blood stains, ma'am," added Noble.

"I see."

"Also there's no weapon. If Jason's our killer we have to accept that in his drunken and/or drugged stupor he killed his family, turned on loud music to attract attention, stumbled out to hide the murder weapon and stumbled back in to munch on a leftover pizza before keeling over."

"Stranger things have happened on drugs."

"True but there are a couple of other factors that diminish the likelihood."

"And what are those, Damen?" she asked.

Whenever she called him Damen, Brook knew she was trying to convey approval. He accepted it without ego. It was a compliment to his powers because it was her way of coaxing the most, and best, information from him. As she saw it, the more she knew, the better her ability to outflank any criticism from below or, more importantly, above. An in-control bad leader looks like a good leader under almost all scrutiny. Not that she was a bad leader.

"Well, Forensics will have to confirm this, but it's clear from the blood patterns that the family were killed where they were found. Even if we assume that Jason was in full control of his faculties, we then have to accept that he walked into the room and cut his sister's throat where she lay, without father or mother moving a muscle to intervene. Then he did the same to his parents, in which order I don't yet know, though I suspect it was ladies first. Again, little sign of physical struggle."

DS Noble's face betrayed a caveat to Brook's theory but he had trained himself, after several painful lessons, not to lay himself open to ridicule. That applied doubly in the presence of the Chief Super.

"Couldn't he have overpowered his father first, taken him by surprise," asked McMaster.

"The mother as well? No, we checked. Again, subject to forensic confirmation, there are no marks on any of the victim's wrists or ankles. They weren't tied up. There were no injuries or contusions on the parents' skulls so he didn't creep up and knock them unconscious."

"What's the second reason?" asked McMaster.

"Sergeant?" asked Brook, fixing Noble with a stare. He couldn't let him have it too easy.

Noble hesitated but knew not to wait too long. A swift error would pass notice much easier than a long anticipated one. "The baby?" he offered, trying to keep the question mark out of his response.

"Right. The baby completes the family. Its..." Brook looked at Noble for a prompt.

"It's a girl, sir. Bianca."

"...*her* presence on the scene is part of the killer's strategy. The baby was brought from her bed as part of a logical choice, as was the decision not to kill her. If Jason had done this under the influence of narcotics or alcohol, why bring the baby down? Surely, if it's a drunken mindless act, he would have killed his baby sister upstairs, where he found her. It doesn't make sense. Our killer sees it differently. He wants the baby in the family portrait but chooses not to kill it. Her."

"Why?"

"Perhaps he's showing us he has the intelligence and humanity to feel mercy. God knows. But he needs the baby there to fulfil his need."

"What need?"

"Maybe he's a Bernardo's boy, an orphan in search of a family. Whatever that is," Brook added, with an unexpected trace of bile that surprised even himself. "It's difficult to say."

After a suitable consoling pause, McMaster ploughed on. "What about writing SAVED on the wall and cutting it on the girl? What's that all about?"

Brook looked at the wall behind her head as though he were casting around for a solution to a question he hadn't yet considered. It didn't do to over-egg the pudding. "Some kind of religious claptrap I imagine. Maybe crowing that he's saved her soul from a life of sin and packed her off to Heaven."

"A God squadder," she nodded. "Why *he*?" she queried.

"The usual reasons," replied Brook.

"Statistically sound, I know," she countered, with a more confident edge in her voice. She was on her own turf. "But why so sure?" She stood and picked up a small water jug on her desk.

"Do you want the classic profile of the serial killer?"

She turned sharply from her spider plant, spilling a little water on the floor. "Is that what this is?"

"I think so. This has been planned for a long time. All that was missing for the killer were the right victims."

"And if it is a God squadder we're looking for a middle-aged male," nodded McMaster, "which rules out the Wallis boy."

"Why middle aged?" asked Noble before he could stop himself.

"Jason's too young to be appalled by the moral cesspool of society," said Brook. "That's more a function of my age group."

"Are you saying that whoever did this has picked the Wallis family out at random?" Noble asked.

"No. Our killer has sound reasons for wanting *this* family dead."

"Well," said Noble, deciding to risk humiliation in the hunt for brownie points, "if they weren't selected at random, surely the killer must know the family, or some members of it."

"I don't think so, John. He just thinks he does."

"This is idle speculation," rejoined McMaster, deciding she'd learned all she was going to learn. "I'm cancelling my course in Birmingham. I'll be briefing the press this afternoon so I'll need your CID/57's as soon as possible. I think DS Noble has a point. I don't like the idea of serial killings, Damen. This isn't London."

"That's what the Yorkshire Ripper team said. One of the reasons he was free to kill for years."

"Point taken," said McMaster, adopting her non-threatening, conciliatory body posture, "but I want all other avenues explored first. Use whatever resources you need. Bobby Wallis was a nasty piece of work – with previous. I want to know about enemies, neighbourhood feuds and so on. And check out this Mr Singh who found the bodies. Maybe he took his complaint about the noise too far. Maybe there was an argument about something. Who knows what people will do under stress? Have you run the MO through CATCHEM?"

CATCHEM, Central Analytical Team Collating Homicide Expertise and Management, a computer database introduced in 1992 which could build an identikit profile of any serial offender from the distinctive characteristics of the offence, one of the fruits of the review carried out after the Yorkshire Ripper debacle and an overdue response to the American violent crime profiling system, VICAP.

"We will but it won't yield anything new," said Brook.

"Why so sure?" she flashed back at him.

"Because this isn't a murder, it's an execution. This family's been punished." There was silence. Neither McMaster nor Noble understood his meaning and they waited for Brook to elaborate. He failed to take up their invitation. "Anything else, ma'am?" he offered finally.

"Yes. Be certain Jason Wallis is in the clear before you let him back into the community, assuming he has any living relatives. Better get someone onto Social Services come to think of it. Find out where he and the baby might go." Brook and Noble rose to leave. "And inspector. You report directly to me on this. And only me."

Brook nodded and ushered Noble out of the office. She knew. He could sense it in her demeanour. This was no domestic argument or spur of the moment killing. It was part of a series – the first as far as she was concerned. It made her uneasy, that was clear. And not just for the community at large. This could be a Godsend for the pack of hounds that dogged her every move.

Chapter 4

Back in his office Brook drained his coffee and massaged his eyes. He reached for the envelope left by Noble and flicked it open.

The top picture showed the pathetic, spindly corpse of Kylie Wallis, marble white, sightless eyes. It caught Brook momentarily unprepared and he recoiled as though from a red hot poker. Careless. Being tired he'd forgotten to erect the shield around his emotions, as much a part of his daily routine as pulling on his trousers.

Once his feelings were correctly attired, he looked again and began to sift through the evidence, these peep shows of insanity, with the detachment of the automaton.

He paused over a photograph of the wine bottle before putting it on one side. Then he extracted and retained a couple of others. Noble entered with two cups of vending machine coffee.

"We can land a spacecraft on Mars, John, but we still can't create a machine to deliver a decent cup of coffee," Brook grimaced, as he sipped the frothy liquid. "Have you got a cigarette?"

"I thought you'd quit."

"Cut down, John. There's a difference."

"Just quit buying," Noble said with a playful grin. Brook decided to deliver the chuckle Noble required as payment and accepted the proffered cigarette, inhaling deeply even before Noble had extinguished his lighter.

"Sir." Noble was suddenly uneasy. "I wanted to thank you..." – Brook glanced at Noble with a look of mild bemusement though he knew what was coming – "...for not mentioning my cock-up last night." Brook smiled.

"Forget it, John. It wasn't your fault. You had good reason not to enter the crime scene, especially as another officer had told you there were no signs of life. I'm not sure I can be quite so forgiving with Aktar though. Tampering with the evidence is a very serious matter."

"What do you mean?"

Brook searched for the relevant photograph. "Remember the pizza, the Four Seasons. Look at it. What do you notice?"

"Notice?"

"Be boring and factual."

Noble hesitated briefly, unsure of what was required of him. After a pause to verify Brook's serious intent, Noble took a stab at it. "It's a half-eaten..."

Brook raised an admonishing eyebrow to Noble who knew the signal well and corrected himself.

"...partially-eaten pizza."

"Better."

"It's had two pieces taken from it."

"Go on."

Noble looked at a loss.

"Describe the pieces, John."

"Well, one's a triangle cut out of the ham and mushroom bit..."

"Triangle," said Brook with heavy emphasis. Noble looked back at him, perplexed, trying not to laugh.

"The other piece," Noble smiled suddenly, "is torn from the salami segment. This pizza could have been eaten by two different people. Presumably Jason Wallis tore a piece off...and someone else took the trouble to cut a slice. The killer?" he said hopefully, before shaking his head the instant Brook shook his own. "Aktar. The...idiot," barked Noble with real venom, remembering to omit the adjective.

Brook decided not to string it out any longer. "And what happened to both of them?"

Noble nodded now, giving the appearance that he'd got there before his superior. "They both collapsed. The pizzas were doctored in some way. That's how the killer was able to cut the family's throats without a struggle."

"Right."

"That's why you asked me about Aktar's weight. Jason's just a skinny kid. He fell where he was eating, where there's tomato sauce on the floor, but the drug would take longer to be ingested by a heavier man so he would have finished his piece and still have been able to move around for a while. People would think he'd fainted after seeing the bodies."

"That's very impressive, John."

"What? Telling you what you already knew?"

35

"I only knew because I was looking for it."

"What do you mean?"

"Well...I've seen this MO before."

"When?"

"A long time ago."

"With throats cut and the blood on the walls?"

"Similar."

"That's how you knew there was a message for us."

"Yes."

"And the doctored pizza?"

"No. That's different. Things change each time – just enough to muddy the profile."

"But he immobilised and killed families?"

"Yes."

"Who was the killer?"

"We never found him, John."

"What...?"

"I don't want to say any more at the moment because the connection's not certain. And I need you to keep an open mind about things so you can pull me up if I start barking up the wrong tree."

"Whatever you say." Noble was annoyed but did a good job of not showing it. "So what now?"

"Now? Until we find the van we concentrate on the house."

"SOCO are still going over it."

"They won't find anything."

"They might."

"Not a chance. The planning that went into this. He's not going to take his gloves off and touch things, or get peckish and leave a perfect set of dentures in a lump of cheese."

"I guess not. He might have had a sip of wine though."

"Don't bank on it. What about the weapon?"

"Nothing so far."

"How many uniforms have you got looking?"

"Dozens."

"Get more, at least for a day or two, and widen the search. Fingertip. Get onto the council and suspend refuse collection in the area. Search all dustbins and grates on the estate. We're not going to find it but we need to have looked." Brook sighed and then yawned. This was the part of the job he hated most. Clearing away the debris, the procedural minutiae that delayed everything, prevented him bringing his skills to bear on the nub of the case. "There's so much garbage to organise."

"When do we speak to Jason?"

"This morning. But you're going to Pizza Parlour first. We need to know how the killer set this up in case Jason doesn't know."

"What do you mean?"

"Well if Forensics confirms that the pizzas were drugged, it means our killer must have delivered them…"

"So he's used them to make sure the family are unconscious which suggests he came back later, after they'd been eaten."

"Right." Brook paused, waiting to see if his point had hit home.

"But if he's delivered them, how can Pizza Parlour have taken the order?"

"Good question, John."

Noble thought for a moment then his jaw dropped open. "Christ! The bastard rang the Wallis family. He's taken the order pretending to be Pizza Parlour." Noble shook his head and squinted at the floor. "Hang on, you wouldn't order food from a takeaway that called out of the blue. Not unless they were giving it away." Noble looked up at Brook's expectant face and smiled. "Maybe they were. Of course – a free meal like a promotion or prize or something. Who's gonna turn that down? Was that the MO in the other case?"

"We thought so. Though we never had any survivors to confirm it."

"But not pizzas."

"No. A video recorder and a CD system."

"Like winning a competition," Noble nodded with a smile. "Neat."

Brook checked his watch and helped himself to another cigarette, looking at Noble for an objection. He lit up and took another huge pull. Soon the news would be hitting the streets of Derby. Not that he expected The Reaper to be within earshot. He was long gone.

*

Having roused his complaining car for the fourth time that morning, Brook dropped in at his flat on the way to the hospital. He needed to shower and change before meeting Noble there.

After showering he lay on the bed for five minutes and closed his eyes to relieve the stinging. Before he left, he rang the station to requisition a car for the afternoon. He couldn't keep traipsing around in the Sprite. The water pump wouldn't stand for it.

He booked a taxi to take him to the DRI. As he waited for the cab, he stared at the still-flashing answering machine, but decided against ringing Terri back.

Too often, in the last ten years, he'd danced around his feelings for his daughter, curtailing difficult conversations with phoney interruptions. Sod's Law dictated that the cab driver would honk his horn the moment he started talking to her. He didn't want another, albeit genuine, interruption to reinforce her jaundiced view of his love for her. Now he needed to talk, needed to spend some time with her, even if all he could embrace was a disembodied voice.

*

Noble was late so Brook left him a message at hospital reception, telling him to wait. He didn't want him seeing Jason Wallis on his own. Then he went to see PC Aktar. He was sitting up in bed reading The Sun. Fortunately, it wasn't visiting hour so he was alone, though clearly his family had arrived with armfuls of provisions earlier that morning.

"I hate to butt in on someone trying to improve himself." Brook was amused by Aktar's panic-stricken attempt to acknowledge his superior – lying horizontal in hospital-issue pyjamas – though he made sure he didn't show it.

"I'm sorry, guv. I wasn't expectin' yer, anybody..."

Brook noted Aktar's broad northern accent. Not a trace of Asian inflection. He kept silent while Aktar flustered, determined to make him sweat. There was an empty plastic bag on a chair beside the bed. Brook picked it up and pulled out Aktar's boots from the locker and slid them into the bag.

"Give these to Noble when he comes in. Forensics needs all the shoes from the Wallis house."

"Guv? Is there...?"

Brook put a finger to his lips and held Aktar's dark eyes in his own. "Don't ever call me guv, constable. If you're still in the Force after today, you'll call me Sir or Inspector, is that clear?"

"Guv?"

"Is that clear?"

PC Aktar was suddenly very abashed and Brook began to feel sorry for him. "Yes sir."

"That's better. Your career depends on the answers you give me in the next few minutes," said Brook, peeling one of the photographs he'd set aside earlier, from his jacket. "Look at this."

"Yes sir."

"What do you see?"

"It's the living room of Mr and Mrs..."

"What do you see, constable?"

"The CD player in the Wallis house."

"What do you notice?"

"N-Nothing, sir."

"Exactly. It's been turned off. DS Noble tells me that a Mr Singh went round to the Wallis household to complain about the noise. Do you understand?"

"Yes sir. I think so."

"Explain it to me then, constable."

"It was Mr Singh, sir. He went round. Said the front door was open. He went in and turned off the CD player. Said it was on very loud. I told him he shouldn't have but he said he had no idea, at that time, what had happened. Until he turned the lights on, he thought they were all asleep."

"The lights were off?"

"Yes sir. According to Mr Singh."

"Then how did he manage to turn off the CD player?"

"The display, sir. He said it was very bright, sir. He could see to move round the room okay and well…"

Brook's tone softened. "I see." He tossed the picture of the partially eaten pizza towards Aktar who examined it briefly before looking away. He wouldn't lift his eyes from the bed cover. He looked, and clearly felt, a fool. "You're very lucky constable. I think we may be able to forgive one mistake as your actions haven't compromised the case – this time."

"It won't happen again sir."

"It better not. And I wouldn't mention it to anyone unless you want the Force and yourself held up to ridicule."

"Don't worry sir."

"When are you out of here?"

"This afternoon, sir."

"Report for duty to DS Noble, he'll have some chores for you. Who's your partner?"

"WPC Jones, sir."

"Wendy Jones." Brook felt a tic of apprehension. "Good officer. Take her with you. This order is direct from the Chief Superintendent and you take your orders from DS Noble and myself. Understand?"

"Perfectly, sir."

Brook made to leave but turned back. "And constable. The next time you feel peckish at a crime scene, send out for a bag of chips."

Aktar's foolish expression returned. "Yes sir. Thank you, sir."

✼

Brook drained his third plastic coffee of the day and shuddered. He tossed the thin beaker into the adjacent bin. "What have you got, John?"

Noble flicked a notebook. "Pizza Parlour didn't send anyone round to the Wallis house with anything last night and you were right, they don't deliver in vans. I spoke to the manager. He said they did have an identical order to the one at the crime scene. A Four Seasons, an American Hot and a Seafood. All family size..."

"Let me guess. They were collected, not delivered and the customer paid cash."

"Right."

"What about CCTV?"

"They don't have it."

Brook smiled. "Our boy's determined not to make it easy for us. Description?"

"Nothing useable. A man. Middle aged maybe."

"That's it?"

"Nobody remembers who picked it up. They only look at the money – as you suspected."

"Yeah, it'd be nice to be wrong for a change. What else?"

"DC Morton took a formal statement from Mr Singh next door. Singh said he went round to the Wallis house about half an hour after midnight. The front door was open but he didn't suspect anything. The CD player was on loud so he turned it down and then off. He said he had no idea the Wallis family were dead because the lights were off. When he turned on the lights – bingo!"

"And the volume?"

"He said the music was distorted."

"So it must have been on full. Interesting. Okay. Have Forensics got his clothes and shoes?"

"They have."

"Prints?"

"Yep."

"Did we ask him about times?"

"He said he didn't go round straight away. He said he heard the music start earlier but it got really loud just past midnight – he looked at his watch. He stood it until half past before going round."

"So our killer turned the music up and left just after midnight."

"It looks that way."

"And Jason got home soon after and had his pizza."

"Wouldn't he have heard the music?"

Brook nodded. "Yeah it's a strange one. Even out of his head you'd think he'd hear it and investigate."

"Maybe he thought it was the TV."

"Even so."

"And there's the baby. Surely it would have woken up."

"Babies are funny, John. They can sleep through anything. Maybe it did wake up, maybe not. But unless she was screaming her head off who's going to notice? With Aktar struggling to stay conscious that leaves Mr Singh, who's in a situation for which he has no training."

"I suppose."

"What about the CD?"

"Sent for dusting. It was" – Noble checked his notes – "Symphony No. 9 by Mahler. I thought he was reggae."

Brook smiled at Noble. "Bob Mahler and the Wailers. You know your music, John. And the case?"

"No sign. Looks like the killer brought the CD and took the case with him. So we've very little chance of tracing the purchase."

Brook nodded. "Anything else?"

"Yeah. DC Cooper found a phone number for a Mrs Harrison at the Wallis house. Apparently she's Mrs Wallis' sister. A nurse. Divorced. Lives in Borrowash. She'd just heard the news and was obviously in a bit of a state. Says she hasn't seen the family for a couple of weeks, though Mrs Wallis phoned her two days ago. Nothing in her manner to suggest she was worried about anything. I sent a WPC round for tea and sympathy. She says she's willing to do the formal ID."

"Good."

"We got a fax from BT. Every call to the Wallis house up to two days before the murder came from numbers listed in Mrs Wallis' address book, except one. That came from a public phone the day before."

"So he could check out the menu before ringing to take their order. Is it close to Pizza Parlour?"

"Near enough. And it's coin-operated not card."

"Really?"

"Hard to believe they still exist, I know. Forensics is giving it a quick once over but there's no telling how many people have been in there since."

"What about enemies?"

"We asked Mrs Harrison. She says not. Bobby had an occasional *word* with a neighbour or someone down the pub at chucking-out time. But nothing out of the ordinary. Nothing on this scale."

"And nothing in his jacket about dealing?"

"Not even a sniff of drugs, no joke intended. He wasn't the type."

"Check with the Drug Squad anyway. Just to tick it off."

"A message from the Chief. There's a press conference at four, in time for the local evening news and she wants you there."

"Damn. I wish Brass could jump through these hoops by themselves."

"I reckon she needs a man there to give the public a bit of confidence."

Brook turned to Noble, this time without amusement. He had to stop letting these remarks slide, if only for the sake of balance. "That's right. Evelyn McMaster knows exactly what kind of small-minded bigots are out there, John. And to her credit she's big enough to swallow her pride and pander to their intolerance if it will bolster confidence in what we're doing. That makes our job that bit easier, don't you think?"

Noble was suitably abashed.

"Here," continued Brook, pointing to the photograph of the Wallis fireplace. "You'll have to follow this up now. I'll speak to Jason on my own. What do you see, John?"

"A bottle of wine."

"Not quite. It's a bottle of expensive wine. A Nuits-Saint-Georges to be precise. From Burgundy."

"How do you know that?" asked Noble, with a hint of suspicion. It was still an offence in most station houses to drink anything other than lager and cheap whisky.

"Because I spent my honeymoon on a barge in Burgundy and that was a wine we could never afford. We weren't well off, but I imagine it would still cost you at least £15-20 in a supermarket. Assuming you can get it round here. I doubt the Wallis family are oenophiles," he flicked a glance at Noble but his constable was maintaining the face of a stoic, "so get someone to find out where it was bought and by whom, if you can. Who else is on the team apart from Cooper?"

"DC Morton, DC Bull, DC Gadd."

"Jane Gadd? Good officer," said Brook evenly, ignoring Noble's quick glance. Jane Gadd was Noble's girlfriend. Brook wasn't supposed to know that – nobody was – but receding proximity to sexual relationships had sharpened his antennae in such things. More importantly she was young and hungry for promotion, as were DC's Dave Bull and Rob Morton. This was a big opportunity for them and he knew they'd toe the line and work hard.

"Try the big supermarkets centrally. They'll know if they stock it. When Aktar's discharged get him and Wendy Jones to help. Send them round the off licences."

*

WPC Wendy Jones was reading a magazine as Brook peered through a crack in the curtains. He hesitated. This could be difficult and Brook wasn't sure how to play it. That was nothing new. He hadn't been sure on any of the previous chance encounters since their little fling the previous New Year's Eve had left them both with a severe case of embarrassment.

Nearly a year ago. Brook could scarcely believe it. The power of alcohol had a miraculous power to transform behaviour. Brook could scarcely tally the demure, black-stockinged professional before him now with the reckless passion of that night. The energy and the urgency of her lovemaking had left its mark on Brook, a casualty of a more repressed generation.

It had been the best sex he could remember – and he had a good memory – and had offered him a glimpse of a happiness he thought he could never experience after his divorce.

He hated to admit it, but the touch of young flesh had thrown open the stable door on emotions he hadn't allowed free rein in a long, long time – lust, the poignancy of retreating youth, the urge to retrieve his wasted life. For the first time in years, Brook had experienced fleeting optimism. It was a very unhealthy period.

He coughed as he entered to allow her a few seconds to prepare. Her generous mouth dropped open briefly to reveal a glimpse of her perfect teeth. Her large dark eyes met his and she stood up. Brook was reminded of her long legs and stunning figure – what one of his poker-playing colleagues in the Met used to call a "Full House."

"Sir!" she said her eyes almost level with his. She was only a couple of inches lower than Brook's six feet.

"I didn't know you were riding shotgun, constable." Brook decided only at the last second not to call her Wendy.

"Only while PC Aktar's in here, sir." She fiddled with the grip restraining her long brown hair.

"I've just seen him."

Jones seemed very nervous and Brook was reminded of her acute awkwardness at waking up, not just with a senior colleague but in his hovel of a flat. She'd scuttled back to her riverside development as quickly as she could. "How is he, sir?"

"He's feeling a little sorry for himself."

"I daren't imagine what he saw to cause him to pass out like that."

"No. It was pretty bad," he added, deciding not to expand. "How's this one?" Brook enquired, nodding towards Jason Wallis who

43

was unconscious or asleep.

"The doctor says he'll be fine – unfortunately."

Brook gave her a quizzical smile.

"Sorry sir. But the little girl...I didn't see her." She looked to the ground, suddenly embarrassed, as though she'd let down her sex by not forcing herself to see such a sight. "And this...lowlife gets away with a headache and even more celebrity. There's no justice."

"Celebrity?"

"Young Wallis, sir. After that hoo-hah a few weeks back. He assaulted a teacher in a lesson at Drayfin Community School. Threatened to rape her."

Enlightenment creased Brook's features. "That was Jason?" He nodded with satisfaction. "Thanks for the reminder, constable. Has anybody spoken to him?"

"About last night? No sir. He's not really been conscious. Why?"

"So he hasn't said anything?"

"Not a dickey bird," she replied with an unexpected, if hesitant, smile. Her smile vanished before it had a chance to wrinkle the edge of her mouth. "Doesn't he know?"

"I don't think so. Given the state he was in, I'm pretty sure he couldn't have killed anyone and..." Brook tailed off, unsure of the words.

"Would you eat pizza if you've just found your family butchered?" concluded Jones with a nod. "Do you need me to stay?"

She seemed very efficient all of a sudden. There was also the merest whisper of affection in her voice and a small seed of pleasure took root in the barren soil of Brook's ego. He smiled, trying to imagine the question in a different context. "No, take a break, but keep yourself handy. Shouldn't there be a social worker with him?"

"She's gone for a coffee, sir. She'll be back in a minute." Brook nodded. She made to leave the cubicle then turned. "One thing. Jason's under technical arrest, as a suspect..." she hesitated.

"Go on."

"We emptied his pockets. He's got a hundred pounds on him. And a strip of tablets. Ecstasy I think. Might be helpful."

She left and Brook turned to young Jason. He stared at the child-like face for a moment trying to square his innocent expression with a threat to commit rape. He was just a kid. What had gone wrong with the world when little idiots like this felt they could threaten such violence?

Jason's mouth lay open and a small stalactite of saliva was hanging from his bottom lip. Brook frowned and shook his head. How old was he? Fourteen? Fifteen, same as Terri? Just a kid. Oblivious. Snarling defences taking a Time Out. Without the posturing, without his warped sense of self, Jason Wallis was just another scared little baby, needy and lost and dribbling.

If he was lucky – or unlucky – Jason might live another sixty years and Brook knew he could map out his sorry life now. From birth to death it was a story he'd heard many times before.

Drugs, booze, fags, the search for cheap thrills, school's boring, skip it, hanging out with friends, no qualifications, no future, hanging out with more friends, now petty criminals, stealing for fag money, destroying stuff, windows are good, milk bottles, bus shelters, phone booths, *yeah I did it, what you gonna do about it?*

He does what he likes. No-one to stop him. Jason and his friends aren't nobodies no more – they're big fish in a tiny puddle of piss. They've got power, the power to change things, not people, people can't hear them, people walk by them, unless it's dark, then they cross the road. Not people. Inanimate objects. They can't run; they've got to listen; they can be changed by the power, from one state to another; the alchemy of destruction.

And sex? Plenty of that. Sex with a minor, still at school, willing to bury her despair under his. No need to take precautions, that's the girl's job. So what if she's up the duff? Her problem. But wait. There's a baby, that's a nailed on income, your own place. Respect. Give it a whirl. I can walk away any time.

Shut the fucking brat up! I'm off out. Few beers. With my mates. Roll a couple of drunks. I've got to live, haven't I? They're insured.

I'm better off in pokey. I've learnt some good stuff. Get out. Get some dosh together. Go back in. Lesson learned. If only I'd listened in school, made more of myself. Too late now. Gotta tough it out. Can't admit I've gone wrong. What's wrong with driving a minicab? Life's okay. We're coping, waiting for those numbers. Doing fine. Kids have left. We'll get by. Is this it? All there is.

Brook looked at his watch. He had a lot to do. He looked around to see if anybody was watching then cocked his leg back to kick the bed but then thought better of it.

But suddenly the patient snorted and began to stir. Brook looked through the gap in the curtain for the social worker but saw no sign.

"What's happening? Where am I?" he croaked.

Brook went to the bed and looked down at him. "You're in hospital, Jason."

Jason sat up and blinked at his surroundings. He rubbed at the tube inserted in his forearm then looked up at Brook.

"I'm thirsty," he said in that whining voice children use to ask for something without the bother of having to ask. Brook poured him some water from a jug and he drank it down in one, occasionally darting an eye at his impassive visitor. The wariness of the guilty conscience was the first defence mechanism to be revived. He thrust the glass back at Brook for a refill and drank again, more slowly this time.

Thinking time, thought Brook. Eventually Jason cracked.

"Who are you?" he asked.

"Detective Inspector Brook." The answer didn't seem to surprise Jason.

"Fuck do *you* want?" he snarled. The routine fear of authority, accepted in Brook's distant youth, was now a faded memory – a museum piece of a reaction. Today the obligatory response of youth was contempt. Contempt for those who couldn't stop them doing exactly as they pleased. Parents, teachers, coppers.

"I can't talk to you without an adult present. The social worker…"

"What you on about?"

"I can't talk to you without another adult present. Those are the rules Jason. I'm sure you know the procedure by now."

Jason leered at Brook. "Oh I get it. It's that fuckin' teacher been spreadin' her lies again. I told you lot before, I never laid a finger on it. Get my dad in here."

"That would be difficult."

"You can't interview me without an adult."

"I just told *you* that."

"Then stop hassling me."

"I've gotta say, Jason, you've got this whole performance down perfectly."

"Fuck off! And who the fuck are you?" demanded Jason looking past Brook.

"My name's Carly Graham, Jason. I'm a social worker."

Brook turned and smiled at her. "Detective Inspector Brook." She was young and slim with long brown hair, attractive in a pale, mousy kind of way. She wore a tight brown sweater and a brown corduroy skirt down to her calves, where fur-lined brown suede boots took over. Jason looked her up and down thinking what to say next.

"Inspector. You shouldn't be interviewing Jason without at least one adult present. He's under age and vulnerable."

"I keep fucking telling him," spat Jason.

"No I keep telling you, Jason. I'm not interviewing him Miss Graham. I just got here and Jason just woke up and I've told him repeatedly I can't speak to him on his own."

"It's against the rules," she continued, to establish her firm grip on procedure.

"That could've been me talking, Miss Graham," replied Brook, a half-smile on his lips.

"I don't feel too good," wailed Jason, holding his recently pumped stomach.

"Under the circumstances, I don't think you should be taking things so lightly, inspector."

"No, I suppose not," replied Brook, making no effort to take things more seriously.

"What circumstances?" moaned Jason.

"It can wait until…" began Carly Graham.

"No it fucking can't. I want to know why he's here so keep your mouth shut bitch, until I tell you to open it."

Carly Graham glanced at Brook. She didn't show a flicker of emotion. Like Brook, she'd probably seen Jason's expression of scorn and hatred a thousand times. Finally she shrugged and waved her palm from Brook to her client.

"I'm here about a murder, Jason," began Brook.

"What's that got to do with me?" Jason sneered. This conversation had a well worn path and Brook wondered whether he could see it through. The Jasons of this world went out of their way to alienate. Unless they were spraying their scent over everything and everyone they weren't happy and Brook, in his fatigue, was tempted to jettison the script and give it to him straight. He fought the urge and tried to find his most sympathetic tone.

"We've got bad news," he said.

"Oh yeah. What is it?"

Brook smiled at Carly Graham. This was her field.

She sighed and took up the baton. "Jason, I'm afraid your father and mother are dead, your sister Kylie too. I'm sorry for your loss."

They both looked at Jason's uncomprehending face. After a moment Jason's face broke into a wide grin. "You lying bitch," he finally said. "That's bollocks."

"Jason…" began Brook.

"What are you trying to pull, you lying bastards? What do you take me for?"

Brook removed a crime scene photograph of Jason's father from his pocket and held it in front of his face. Jason's eyes widened then squinted in confusion. He made to grab the photo but Brook returned it to his pocket.

"They're dead. They were murdered last night." A tear began to dampen the corner of Jason's eye. The baby had returned. Brook wondered whether to be sorry for his loss but was unable to dredge up any sincerity.

Jason seemed unable to take it in. "Fuck off will yer. You're doing my head in."

"Their throats were cut. The baby was unharmed. I've got more pictures if you don't believe me."

"Inspector!" warned Carly Graham.

He'd gone too far but knew in his heart that the longer he dealt with this boy, the more he'd be glad he was able to affect him, to hurt him, to reach behind that curtain of aggression and find the heart of a child.

Jason's features crumpled and, like all but the newest men, he tried to hide his tears. Brook was pleased with the reaction despite the gnaw of guilt on his conscience.

"Me mum and dad?" he quivered.

"Yes."

"Kylie?"

"Yes."

"I don't believe you."

"Yes you do."

Now the tears began to fall. He sobbed for a minute, Carly Graham's hand patting his, before getting control of his emotions. "What's going to happen to me?" he sniffed.

Brook stared at the boy, then at Carly, trying to hide his disgust.

"Don't think about that now, Jason," cooed Carly. "Your aunt will be in to see you later. You should get some rest."

"And rest assured you'll be fully protected."

Carly Graham flashed Brook a warning look.

"Protected?" said Jason, almost to himself.

Brook wasn't proud of his satisfaction at seeing Jason squirm but knew it was the best guarantee of co-operation. "If you'd been home a little earlier last night we wouldn't be talking to you now. And it's possible whoever did this may see you as unfinished business."

Jason looked up, saucer-eyed. "Me?"

"Inspector. What good is this doing? Can't this wait?"

"Not if we want to catch the murderer quickly. Particularly as Jason may have been the main target."

"What you talking about? This is so gay. Fuck off and leave me alone."

"I'm talking about you, Jason. You're the celebrity in the family. There's a chance whoever did this was after you."

48

Jason began to sob again. A tear for his butchered father, a tear for his butchered mother, perhaps a couple for his torn sister and a bucketful for himself.

"We need your help," continued Brook

"I don't know nothing," he snorted, managing to resurrect a little aggression.

"That's a pity because the longer this man is free, the greater the danger to you." Brook's reassuring smile had the desired effect.

"You're doin' my head in. I don't know nothing," he insisted.

"So where were you last night?"

"Hanging."

"Where?"

"Around."

"Who with?"

"Some mates."

"I want names."

"Fuck that. I'm no grass."

"Where did you get a hundred pounds?"

"I won it on a horse," Jason sneered with the standard and-you-can't-prove-otherwise leer.

"Really. Well as you're too young to legally place a bet, that money will have to be confiscated."

"You can't do that..."

"And the Ecstasy?"

Jason's triumphant manner subsided. "I don't know what you're talking about. You've planted that on me. I've been out cold. Anyone..."

"Look," began Brook then paused for a deep breath to compose his thoughts, "I'm not interested in your...habits, Jason. If you want to pop a few pills to brighten your drab existence, who am I to care?"

Jason prepared to protest but was unsure how to go about it.

Carly Graham eyed Brook with concern. "Inspector, I don't think..."

"Under the circumstances, I can overlook possession. If you co-operate," said Brook, making an effort to keep to the script.

Jason withdrew his unformed objection and stared down at the bed, sullen but yielding. "What do you want to know?"

"Take me through what happened when you got home."

Brook took a few notes although it wasn't really his forte. Jason told him little that he didn't already know so he didn't have much to record. But he confirmed that his parents had "won" a competition at the local Pizza Parlour and that he'd nearly stayed in. He had no idea

what time he got home, though he had a feeling it was after closing time
– he was self-absorbed enough not to worry about admitting he'd been
in a pub. He'd got home starving and headed straight for the kitchen.
He tucked into the first pizza to hand. And then...nothing. Until now.
No, his parents didn't drink wine and no, they didn't listen to any of
that classical bollocks.

"But did *you* hear it when you got in?"

"Don't know, alright. I don't remember." Jason lowered his head
in despair at the thoughts and images crowding in. He sighed and
looked up at Brook. "I don't think I heard no music. Okay."

"Fair enough." Brook flipped his notes shut and stood up to go.
Jason was leaving a lot out but it could wait.

Suddenly the patient seemed animated, as though Brook's
imminent departure left unfinished business. Then his face brightened.
"What about the telly?"

"Telly?" asked Brook. "It's still there."

"No, you know. An appeal for witnesses and stuff. They can interview me and I can ask people for help to catch the bastard. I can handle
it."

Brook stood motionless for a second, unable to think of a suitable
response. He could see Carly Graham open-mouthed. "I bet you can,"
he said and walked away.

*

Brook passed Jones at the coffee machine. "What happened about
Jason's clothes?"

"Bagged up with his shoes and sent to Forensics, sir."

"Good. And you've booked in the money and the drugs?"

"Yes sir."

"Which means we've got Wallis on possession, possibly dealing.
We'll leave out suspicion of triple homicide."

"Sir?"

"He's a suspect, constable. Possibly dangerous. Cuff him."

"The doctor said..."

"Never mind the doctor. It's procedure. Cuff him."

Chapter 5

The press conference started promptly at four in the revamped media centre of D Division. Brook hadn't been in there since McMaster had been promoted. He knew she'd refurbished the place but hadn't realised how much. The last time he'd taken part in a press briefing, he'd sat at the end of a long table by the door, facing the window. The sun had slammed into his eyes throughout and he'd become bad-tempered and impatient with the stupidity of a local reporter, who took his dismay out on the Force in print the next day.

Being a consummate politician, Evelyn McMaster had spotted this handicap and had set about changing the layout of the room. The harsh colours were gone, the acoustics had been improved but, most significantly, the officers now doing the briefing sat with their backs to the windows and the journalists had any sun shining in *their* eyes.

The police had another advantage; the psychological benefit of a raised platform, boxed in to afford a view of head and upper torso only. They could now look down on the journalists literally, as well as metaphorically.

Brook sat stony-faced throughout McMaster's briefing-by-numbers, allowing his eyes to wander round the room looking at all the unfamiliar faces. A chord had obviously been struck with the nation's editors, because all the nationals were here, as were the BBC, ITV and other TV crews. The local media were all present, including Brian Burton from the Derby Telegraph, whose nose Brook had so firmly put out of joint a couple of years back. He was also the reporter who'd splashed important details of the Plummer rape case the year before, causing a great deal of damage to the prosecution, not to mention arousing suspicions between officers at the station about who'd provided him with key information.

McMaster drew to a close and invited DI Brook to add his own observations.

"I can only reiterate the comments made by Chief Superintendent McMaster," Brook began. "From the brutal nature of these murders, we know this man is extremely dangerous. Any information, relating to his movements in Drayfin last night, or any other suspicious occurrences, that could help us catch this man, will be gratefully received. All such information will be in strict confidence and will be followed up, no matter how insignificant it may seem."

"What progress have you made so far, inspector?" ventured one reporter, squinting to counteract the glare from the setting sun.

"Our enquiries are under way and no stone will be left unturned but at the moment we are awaiting the results of forensic and post mortem examinations. Until that information is available, it would be inappropriate for me to comment further."

"Have you found the weapon?" asked an attractive young woman with a microphone.

"Not yet."

"But you do know what type of weapon was used?" she said.

"As I say, it would be inappropriate to comment further at this time."

"Could somebody be shielding this man?" asked a man with a BBC microphone.

"It's possible," Brook nodded, unsure of the relevance of the question.

"You don't seem too sure," jumped in Brian Burton.

"I'm sure it's possible, Brian." Brook winced from a warning tap on the ankle bone from McMaster – another benefit of the enclosed panelling

"*I'm* sure that most normal people, inspector, find it hard to imagine that anyone could knowingly shelter such a monster."

"Then you don't know a great deal about people Brian."

"And you do?"

"One man's monster is another man's saint. The man we're looking for kills without pity, quickly, efficiently and for what *he* considers valid reasons, even if we can't understand or condone those reasons."

"You sound like you know him, Inspector Brook."

"It's my job, Brian, to get inside this man's head, to see what he sees, think what he thinks. It's not pleasant but that's the nature of offender profiling. And although our picture of this man is far from complete, we are able to extrapolate certain scenarios from the details of the crime. So in a sense, although I can't go into detail, we know things about him…"

"And when you've finished *extrapolating scenarios*, inspector, are you able to tell the public at large whether this man has killed before and if he's likely to kill again?"

Brook eyed Burton, barely masking his veneer of distaste.

McMaster, sensing the rise in temperature, stepped back into the fray. "Obviously this man is very dangerous, Brian. Certainly he could kill again which is why we need to catch him before he does."

"But is it likely he's killed before?" asked another reporter, spotting the omission.

"There's no possible way we can answer that until..." Brook rejoined.

Burton interrupted. "So, Inspector, your profile contains no mention of the similarities between the murder of the Wallis family last night and the unsolved Reaper killings of the early nineties, in which investigation you played a leading part when you were stationed in London?" The silence deafened Brook. He was vaguely aware of many faces looking at each other for assistance or clarification. "Well inspector?"

"We're not here to listen to wild speculation, Brian. Thank you for coming, ladies and gentlemen," McMaster said hurriedly, "and feel free to contact my office at any time." She stood, an amiable smile covering her face, and nudged Brook to leave.

"Are you going to answer the question?"

"We cannot give out specific details of last night's murders until the appropriate time..." began McMaster.

"Is there a connection between the killer using the blood of the Wallis family to write on the walls and the Reaper murders in Harlesden and Brixton in 1990 and 1991 and Leeds in 1993?"

Brook became aware of the low muttering of journalists, trying to gather scraps of information. He wanted to speak but McMaster had him by the elbow as discretely as she could and, ignoring the clamour for more sound bites, was pushing him through the door of the small antechamber at the back of the room. She closed the door behind them and turned on Brook.

"What the hell was all that?" she blazed, for once dispensing with the reflex niceties of her position. "Where has that hack got his information?"

"I don't know, ma'am."

"Don't know. That's not good enough. Now every crank and Edward the Confessor out there knows what we know." McMaster was silent. She strode to and fro, examining the floor, trying to regain her equilibrium. Eventually the pacing slowed and deliberation returned.

"The Reaper. Yes, I remember. Ritual executions. Families cut up. They never caught him."

"I never caught him," said Brook bitterly.

"You *were* on that enquiry?"

Brook nodded. "I was a DS."

"Is it true, Damen? Could there be a connection after all these years?"

"There are one or two similarities but, as you say, it's been a long time. All the same, I'd like your permission to go to London, check it out."

"You have it."

"Then I'll need a larger pool of officers here, ma'am. To help DS Noble."

"What do you need?"

"We need the computer manned for logging in any information. We need the Incident Room phones manned to sift through calls from the public. We need the murder book compiled. There's house-to-house to co-ordinate, the van and weapons search, family background..."

"How many?"

"I've got enough CID but I'd like to second the two uniforms who answered the call. If we keep them in-house, they're less likely to gossip..."

"Fine, fine," she replied putting up a hand.

"And authorisation for any overtime and unlimited uniform back up when needed."

"You have it." McMaster suddenly seemed very tired but her anger pulled her round almost immediately. "Where did Brian Burton get all that information?"

"He's local ma'am. He's got local contacts."

"But a crime scene is supposed to be sacrosanct, damn it. It's the Plummer rape all over again."

"There were a lot of people there last night, ma'am. Not all on the Force. He'd only need a couple of details and any decent internet search engine would have done the rest. It would have come out sooner or later."

McMaster narrowed her eyes at Brook. "It shouldn't have come out sooner than it was mentioned to me. Why wasn't I informed?"

Brook kept his gaze on the floor. "It's not definite, ma'am. I didn't want to jump the gun before I was sure."

"It's a bit flimsy but we'll gloss over that for the moment. When's the full briefing?"

"Eight-thirty in the morning."

"If I don't make it, I want you to read the Riot Act on this. Somebody in this station is feeding titbits to that journalist. I don't want anyone on the enquiry with loose lips. Clear?"

*

Brook was home late that evening. After the press conference he'd made a conscious effort to clear away some of the unavoidable foot-slogging attached to the case. First he'd read up all that was available on file about Wallis and son, including Jason's recent brush with notoriety in a back issue of the Derby Telegraph. There were few details and the teacher's name had been omitted. Brook made a note to chase up the information.

Noble was out checking a lead on the van used for delivering the pizzas so Brook rang the lab to check if they'd unearthed anything of use at the scene. They had nothing preliminary, which Brook had expected. Things would be gummed up for a while, what with staff shortages and the occurrence of separate murders on the same night.

Then he rang Dr Habib, the pathologist, and was encouraged to hear that he was performing the Wallis post mortems at that precise moment.

Finally, he made a brief visit to the Wallis house, this time driving to the Drayfin Estate in his shiny new unmarked Mondeo. On his way he listened to a recently purchased tape of Mahler's Ninth.

As he parked, a uniformed officer stepped towards the car to check out the occupant then nodded in recognition, if not respect, at Brook. It was a dark and cold night with a dusting of snow. A good thing. It discouraged the ghouls who gravitated to such gore. Even the reporters were absent, having been given bigger leads to follow by Brian Burton.

"All quiet, Constable...?"

"Feaver, sir. Yes, sir. All quiet."

"Dark round here, isn't it?"

"Yes sir. Most of the street lighting's been vandalised. Kids."

Brook nodded and bent under the police tape. He went into the dying room. It seemed bigger than his first visit but then it was virtually empty now. No corpses cluttering the place. He didn't go further than the doorway as a SOCO was still working in the room even at this late hour.

He'd seen everything he needed to the night before. He went into the bedrooms as he had before but, as then, there was nothing of interest. If he looked hard enough he knew he could probably find

55

something incriminating in Jason's room. But to what end? Brook had never been concerned about small time drug abuse or under age drinking. Even the unpleasant porn videos they'd unearthed under a creaky floor board were of no concern to Brook. All such matters fell under Brook's Law of Victimless Crime. Although the nation's legislators disagreed, Brook was unconcerned about citizens sitting at home drifting into a narcotic stupor and masturbating themselves to sleep. Best place for it.

And whatever Wallis and son got up to in the privacy of their home, legal or not, had not been the motive for their slaughter.

Eventually Brook sauntered away, like a tourist leaving a disappointing museum, and returned to his car. He paused as he opened the driver's door and looked across to the house next to number 233. After a moment's thought he reached into the Mondeo and pulled out the cassette tape of Mahler. "Constable Feaver," he shouted, waving him over. "Have you got a mobile?"

*

"Mr Singh. It's DI Brook. Sorry to bother you at this time. We've got a few more questions to ask you. May I come in?"

The slightly-built, middle-aged Asian man lifted a pair of bloodshot eyes towards Brook's warrant card. He wore an old fashioned dressing gown and pyjamas. His feet were bare. He hesitated briefly before turning away from the door and leading Brook into his neat living room, a mirror image of the Wallis murder scene on the other side of the wall. The furnishings were perhaps a little fussier and the colours a little brighter but the rooms were essentially the same, even down to the fireplace.

"I told the other detective everything I know. I'm very tired…"

"I understand." Brook noted a small but plump valise resting on a chair. "Going somewhere, sir?"

"My brother's house. In Leicester. I've…"

"You've had trouble sleeping after what you witnessed. I'm not surprised. But if you could find somewhere to stay in Derby it would be better. We need to be able to contact you…"

Mr Singh sat down on his plush sofa, indicating a chair for Brook. "I see."

"Do you live here alone?"

"My wife and daughters are in India for a few weeks. But yes, I'm alone…"

"A lot of worry, aren't they?"

56

"I beg your pardon."

"Daughters. A lot of worry. I've got a fifteen year old."

Mr Singh nodded. "Yes. They can be difficult." He wouldn't look at Brook, who sensed Mr Singh was probably picturing the *difficulty* Kylie Wallis had encountered next door. Finally his eyes turned to Brook. "What questions?"

"Just routine. Like how did you get on with the Wallis family?"

"Mr and Mrs Wallis are...were racists. And their son Jason. They were unpleasant people and we had nothing to do with them."

"So things were strained between you?"

"Not really. As I said, we had nothing to do with them. We kept out of each other's way."

"What about noise from next door? Was that usual?"

"Sometimes. Things got a good bit quieter when they had the baby though. Do you mind if I smoke, inspector?"

"As long as I can join you," replied Brook.

"Of course." Mr Singh took a pack of cigarettes and a lighter from his dressing gown pocket and lit up with a heavy sigh then studied Brook, wondering why he hadn't done the same.

Eventually the rupee dropped and Mr Singh retrieved his cigarettes, shook one out for Brook and handed him the lighter.

"Thank you. I left mine in the car."

"No problem. That's where I'll have to hide mine when my wife gets home."

Brook smiled but resisted the invitation for man talk. "What about Kylie?"

Mr Singh was puzzled. "I beg your pardon?"

"You said Mr and Mrs Wallis and Jason were racists. You didn't mention Kylie."

Mr Singh hesitated for a moment then smiled sadly. "She was a lovely girl. Lovely. They didn't deserve her, the rest of them. They were scum. I'm sorry to speak ill of the dead, but they were. They were trash and won't be missed. But Kylie was always nice to my girls."

Brook nodded. "When you went next door, you went into the living room first and turned off the CD player."

"Yes."

"You turned the volume down first?"

"Yes."

"Were you aware that Jason was in the kitchen at that time?"

"No. I turned the CD player off then turned the big light on at the wall..."

"You could see to do that?"

"Yes. The hall light was on."

"Then what?"

"I saw…" Mr Singh took a more urgent draught of tobacco and hung his head. "…then I went to the kitchen to phone 999."

"You didn't touch the bodies?"

"No!"

"Not even to check for signs of life."

"No. They were dead. Or I thought they were. I was glad to hear about the baby…"

"Then you saw Jason in the kitchen?"

"Yes."

"What did you do?"

"I called the police."

"You didn't check Jason's pulse."

"No."

"Why?"

"I don't know. I assumed he was dead."

"Then you went outside to wait."

"Yes."

"And you saw no-one and heard no vehicles?"

"That is correct."

Brook nodded and pocketed his notebook. "May I use your phone Mr Singh?"

"Please."

Brook drew out a piece of crumpled paper from a pocket and proceeded to dial. "Constable Feaver, it's me. Okay. Half way." He put his hand over the receiver and smiled at Mr Singh.

From the Wallis house a barely audible noise could be discerned. Brook listened, watching Mr Singh closely. Singh nodded. "That's how it started out."

"What time would that have been?"

"Twenty minutes to midnight."

"Why so exact?"

"When you're disturbed by neighbours you look at the time. In case…" He hesitated, then looked away, unwilling to finish.

"…in case you want to charge round there and have it out with them." Brook smiled politely.

"I suppose so. I wouldn't have. My wife…" Again he left the sentence hanging.

Brook spoke into the phone. "All the way up, constable." The music was no longer muffled. It pounded through the wall and crashed onto Mr Singh's floor which vibrated in tune. Then it died somewhat but that was more down to Mahler's composition. Before long the horns were hammering on the floorboards again.

"And it was midnight when it became that loud?" Singh nodded. "Okay. Thanks constable," said Brook into the phone. "Turn it off." Brook replaced the receiver and turned to Mr Singh. "I admire your patience. I would have gone straight round and hammered on the door."

"I was going to but they turned it off a couple of minutes later."

"Sorry. I thought you told DC Noble you put up with it until half past twelve before going round."

"I did. I mean I got my slippers on to go round but it stopped completely. So I went upstairs to get ready for bed then it started up again. Really loud. As you said, I stood it for as long as I could then I went to complain."

"And that would have been at half past."

"Yes."

"Why didn't you tell us this before?"

"I've only just remembered with you playing the music."

"And how long was the music off?"

"A few minutes inspector. Maybe five, no more than ten."

"I see."

"Is it important?"

Brook shrugged. "It could be."

"Is there anything else, inspector? I'm very tired."

"Me too. Thanks for answering my questions at this hour, Mr Singh."

Singh took the hint and set off for the front door. As Brook passed through the entrance Singh smiled at him. It was a bleak expression which Brook recognised as that of a fellow insomniac.

"When will my clothes be returned to me, inspector?"

"As soon as we've finished with them. Assuming you still want them. There'll be blood on the shoes and probably the garments too."

Mr Singh nodded. "Yes. I didn't think."

Brook left and returned to the Wallis house to retrieve his tape then set off for home.

*

After a hot shower, Brook lay on his bed to rest his eyes for a few moments. He nodded off but woke a few minutes later. Nonetheless he felt refreshed and rang Noble for a progress report.

There was news on the van. They hadn't found it but they'd had a hit from the partial plate. It had been hired locally. Brook had expected this. He made a mental note of the van hire company and told Noble to save the rest for the briefing.

Also, the bottle of wine hadn't been bought in a Derby super-market, Noble confirmed. They were checking French suppliers and off-licences the next morning.

Brook told Noble about the discovery of the drugs and cash on Jason. He also mentioned Jason's involvement in the near rape of a teacher at the local school to see if it seemed equally significant to Noble.

"Pity we can't leave him unguarded so the killer can finish the job then," said Noble.

"Maybe," replied Brook. "You know, his family are dead and all he could think about was getting on TV for his fifteen minutes of fame." Mr Singh was right. The Wallis family were trash. Only poor Kylie had ever held a thought for the sensibilities of others. Her death was the real tragedy. Suddenly Brook had a brainwave.

"John. Have you set up the ID with the aunt?"

"Tomorrow afternoon. Why?"

"Good. They're releasing Jason from hospital tomorrow. Have him brought there so we can hand him over to his aunt for safe keeping. His reaction might tell us something."

"We're not charging him with possession?"

"No. His family are dead, John. Let's give the kid a break."

Their conversation meandered on for a few more minutes then eventually there was silence and Brook could think of nothing else to say. He noticed the puzzled tone creeping into Noble's voice. Brook rarely spoke to him on the phone and had even chided him for it once. "Always better in our job to talk face to face, John," he'd said. "You get the full picture that way."

All possible distractions exhausted, Brook rang off, then, with a deep breath, dialled his ex-wife's number. He had to look up the code for Brighton and felt a pinprick of shame – it had been months since he last spoke to Amy and Terri. He told himself it was pressure of work but knew that was no excuse. Nor was it a lingering sense of awkward-ness – he enjoyed talking to Amy, better than when they were married, in fact. Even Tony, Number Two Dad, was okay. For a PR man.

"Hello stranger," said Amy smoothly. *"It's late."*

"Is it?" Brook was struck by the self-confidence his ex-wife had acquired since the divorce. Certainly her new husband was bland enough to make anyone feel worthy but there had to be something more to her new-found contentment.

Perhaps Tony was one of those weirdoes who refused to spend his waking hours telling his wife that the world was a sewer and that death was their constant companion and, ultimately, their friend. It was also possible that he was a better lover than Brook – unlikely but just possible.

His favoured theory was that Tony Harvey-Ellis had that most compelling attraction to divorced women of a certain age: the outward appearance of sanity.

Now, Brook could see the funny side. That time in London, he *had* been losing it. His obsession with a girl had wrecked his marriage. And, if anything, the fact that the girl was already a corpse when Brook met her made matters worse.

"How are you, Amy?"

"Never better."

A pause. "Is Terri there?"

"She certainly is. Would you like to speak to her?" she said with the suggestion of a tease.

"That would be nice."

"Ther-es-a! It's your dad. Can you hear me? Your dad. So Damen, on the telly eh?"

"Was I?"

"Yeah. A small bit on BBC and ITV. Very exciting. Just like the old days."

"Yeah. I'm getting an agent."

"Good to see you haven't lost your old detachment," she giggled.

"Ha ha," said Brook without rancour.

"Okay mum. I'm on the other line."

"Bye Sherlock. And happy birthday."

"Bye darling. How are you Terri?"

"I'm fine dad. To what do I owe this pleasure?" Brook was a little taken aback at this smokescreen. He was suddenly uneasy, sensing that she was under strain. Brook decided to play ball.

"Can't a father ring his daughter, whom he loves, without opening a public inquiry?" he breezed. Brook always managed to shunt declarations of affection into a subordinate clause. They were safer there. "I just wanted to see how you were." There was a click as an extension was hung up. As he didn't have one, either his ex-wife or her husband had wanted to know why he was ringing. Brook didn't like it. "What's wrong petal?" he asked with more urgency.

"Dad...I..." Brook heard a noise in the background that might have been a door. *"My mocks aren't 'til June."* The guard was around her voice again.

"Can't you speak, Terri?"

"*I'm afraid not dad.*"

"Can you ring me later?"

"*I don't see how dad but I'll try.*" The strain was audible in her voice.

"Is it something to do with mum?" he asked.

"*Oh no, no,*" she answered back with a feigned jocularity.

"Tony?" he ventured.

"*Mmm, yes. That's right.*" Brook's veins turned to ice and he found himself catching at a breath.

"What time does he go to work in the morning?"

"*Seven.*"

"Ring me here, as soon as he leaves. I'll be waiting. Any problems, you just bluff him. Tell him I know everything, whatever it is, and I'm coming down to sort things out. Okay. Got that, darling?"

"*I understand. Bye then dad. Nice to hear from you. And happy birthday.*" The line went dead but Brook was unable to replace the receiver for a few seconds. Problems with Tony. He didn't dare think. It was pointless jumping to conclusions. Terri was at a difficult age. It could be anything, he decided. Personality clash – he knew about those – or maybe she just needed some attention, needed to play the two dads off against each other for a while. That was the rational explanation.

He gleaned some surface comfort but a few fathoms down the fish were nibbling at his peace of mind. Tony Harvey-Ellis was a man. With men, at one level or another, everything could be reduced to sexual gratification. If that bastard had…

Brook sought solace with a familiar ally and made a conscious effort to return to the case so he trudged down the rickety steps to the dank and dingy cellar and from a rusty metal trunk recovered a large beige folder. He removed an antiquated rubber band, wiped off some of the dust, and what looked like mould, and returned to the discomfort of his living room.

The furniture in the room was sparse to say the least. Minimalism was the fashion but that implied design and expense. Most of Brook's *objets* could have been recycled from the council tip or unearthed in the furthest backroom of a teeming, hand-me-down warehouse.

There was a squeaky plastic sofa nestling along the wall next to the never opened front door. Just to ensure that the door was never used, Brook had placed a peeling formica-topped occasional table in front of it. In another corner, stood an old fashioned standard lamp which vomited its dingy flower-studded light onto a sturdier table, on which had been placed the phone and an ashtray.

The overall colour scheme, if scheme it could be called, for that again implied planning, was a grimy light brown, save for the once-white ceiling which had been gradually stained tobacco yellow.

Brook unwrapped the cellophane from the next coat, lit up with a sigh more relaxed than he felt, and sat down to inspect the folder. He tipped out a silver necklace and gazed at the heart-shaped links, remembering the dead girl, Laura Maples.

Eventually he dropped it back into the folder and pulled out various documents. A tightly wrapped plastic bag fell out with them. Brook held the plastic bag for a moment then took the small package back to the cellar and dropped it into the trunk then returned to examine the pile of documents.

He skimmed quickly through the chronological landmarks of his descent into hell and extracted the relevant photocopied reports, newspaper cuttings and the photographs Brook had taken with his own camera while on stakeout. Technically he shouldn't have taken photocopies of official documents, but the Met was fairly relaxed about procedure in those days. Now they would have had his warrant card on the fire before he'd have time to call the Police Federation.

There was a number, scribbled on the back of a report. He picked up the phone and pondered. It was a long time ago. He shrugged and dialled. Coppers rarely moved house unless they were transferring. They needed a familiar haven around them, like a favoured tatty shirt – a place to hide in safety and comfort from the hell of other people's society. The other end picked up on the first ring.

"*Hello.*"

Brook discerned more than a suspicion of alcohol in the voice. "Charlie. Is that you?"

"*Fuckin' 'ell. Brooky. I've been hoping you'd call. Wasn't sure you'd still have the number.*"

"How are you?"

"*I'm fucking shit-faced mate. How are you?*"

"Considering it."

"*You lying bastard,*" ex-DCI Charlie Rowlands laughed. "*That'll be the day that I die. You might lose a bit of that famous iron control of yours.*"

"It wouldn't be the first time, sir."

"*Well. I saw the press conference. Tell me, Brooky. Does that dyke with the brush handle up her arse have any idea what you're dealing with?*"

"The Chief Super? I don't know, sir."

"*Call me guv, not sir. And another thing. Don't call me guv. I've*" *been retired since the last ice age."*

"What should I call you, guv?"

"Call me Charlie, you daft sod."

"Charlie." It didn't sit right with Brook, even though he'd always hated calling him guv – too much of the professional cockney about it. "I need to see you."

"Is it true? Is it another?" An audible strain of foreboding suddenly surfaced in Charlie Rowlands' voice.

"I think so. Yes. Another." Brook waited. He knew the effect his call was having.

"Same MO?"

"Similar."

"Who was the target?"

"The son. He got himself in the news a few weeks ago. He was chucked out of school for assaulting and threatening to rape a teacher." Brook spoke softly so as not to excite Rowlands. He had a bad heart and had taken early retirement in 1994 at the age of 56. That was fairly late for today's career-minded desk jockeys, but Charlie Rowlands was one of the old school. He'd always said he'd never retire, that they'd have to drag him out kicking and screaming. The job was his life and that was very nearly the cost.

Given that, it was a surprise to Brook that he'd managed to hang onto life for more than a decade since. He'd been expected to keel over within six months. He wasn't exactly a health nut. He smoked and drank heavily off-duty – and on, for that matter.

"Good riddance. And he did all of 'em, did he?"

"All he could lay his hands on but the son got lucky and didn't turn up and he left the baby."

"Okay. Dad had form, did he?"

"Minor stuff but he was a thug."

"That's a comfort then." Rowlands sounded sober now. He was moving into the stage of melancholy clear thinking. *"Signatures?"*

"Music. A picture. And expensive wine." Brook knew what was coming, though Rowlands was putting it off.

Eventually he said, *"Was there a message?"*

"SAVED."

"In blood?"

"In blood." Brook was now scarcely audible so keenly did he feel the need to monitor Rowlands for signs of strain.

For what seemed an eternity the two men listened to each other breathing before Rowlands, with a huge sigh, said, *"Come when you like. I'm never out."* Brook confirmed the address and prepared to hang up. *"Damen,"* said Rowlands. He rarely called him that. *"Sorenson's a goner."*

The line clicked and Brook was left with the receiver in his hand, lost in thought until the whirring from the ear-piece brought him back. He replaced the receiver and went into the kitchen. He needed a drink. Actually he needed a drink in a public place to satisfy himself that a normal world still existed but he decided against it in case Terri tried to ring.

He rooted around in the kitchen. He knew he had booze somewhere. Eventually he pulled a dusty bottle of sweet martini – won in a raffle a couple of years before – from the highest cupboard. The cupboard had sixties sliding glass doors caked in grease and Brook kept everything he never wanted to see again in there. He glanced at the photograph albums but resisted.

He cracked the seal on the bottle and examined the rust coloured liquid. He'd only kept it in case of female visitors. Fat chance. There'd only been the one night with Wendy...WPC Jones, and she'd asked for a beer. Nobody but winos drank this garbage any more. Brook poured a large measure and drank it down with a grimace. He poured another and sat back down at the table to nurse it. He turned back to the yellowing file. Like it or not it was time to think.

He put his hand in the folder and pulled out the necklace again and draped it around his fingers. The silver hearts glistened in the half-light and Brook stared at them, seeing the face of the girl who'd worn it all those years before – what was left of it, after the rats had eaten their fill.

He returned the necklace to the folder and began to organise reports and photographs from The Reaper killings into one chronological pile.

Chapter 6

It was cold. Very cold. The air above the duvet was crisp enough to blue the two noses peeping out from the cocoon like a pair of stunted periscopes.

Amy Brook flinched at the intrusion of the phone and uncoupled herself from her groaning husband. She didn't need waking in the middle of the night in her condition; she woke plenty with no disturbance.

Delicately, trying not to take the full weight of the mass in her womb onto her stomach, she swivelled towards the offending noise.

"Sorry to wake you love. Can I speak to him?" Detective Inspector Rowlands, soon to be a DCI, spoke with unusual gentleness, as though a lowered voice was less irritating. To hear him, Amy Brook was forced to concentrate even harder, pushing sleep further away.

"It's for you," she droned, jabbing the phone into her bleary husband's huddled form. She swung her legs onto the floor without breaking the crust around her eyes. "Tea?"

"Don't bother gorgeous," Damen Brook replied, hand over the mouthpiece, his eyes resolutely closed.

"No bother, I'm suffering for two now." She rose gingerly, supporting her large belly in her forearms, clambered to her feet and waddled down to the kitchenette, yawning and shivering in equal measures.

"What's up, guv?"

"Murder. A bad one. Meet me at 67b Minet Avenue, above the laundrette."

Brook scribbled furiously. He'd soon learned to keep pad and pencil by the phone. "Where's that?"

"Harlesden." The phone clicked. Brook swung his legs onto the cold floor and dressed, though not as quickly as usual. The inclement weather had provoked him into wearing pyjamas for the

first time since his early teens and he fiddled with the outsize buttons and starched material, unaccustomed to such a test of dexterity.

Having dressed sufficiently he crept downstairs and cast around for the A-Z, sweeping it up as he clambered into his overcoat.

Amy stood by the door, one arm supporting their first child – their only child as it turned out though they'd planned four – one holding out a mug of tea.

Brook looked at her eyes, virtually closed save for a glimmer of pupil which shone between the lids. He took the outstretched mug and turned away, stifling a tic of horror. It was the same face, the death mask of a butchered prostitute he'd seen the year before. He'd noticed the face. She'd been stabbed repeatedly in the vagina and the killer had tried to cut off her breasts.

Brook took a sip of tea and kissed her on the forehead.

"Go upstairs before I go out," he said, one hand on the doorknob. "Don't want the baby catching its death."

"His or her death," she corrected him, obeying like a robot. Brook looked after her, aching to follow. He blinked at his watch. Gone three. A fine night to leave your warm bed and milky soft wife. She'd long since stopped asking him what time he'd be back. He'd long since stopped apologising.

Brook hurried through the spitting wind to his temperamental Triumph Stag, the usual will-it-won't-it knot pulling on his gut. He'd need something more practical in a month, he reflected not without regret. Another expense though. Another temptation to give in to the Kick Back Squad.

"It's only £50. Everybody else is in. You don't have to do anything illegal."

"What do you call this?"

No, they'd manage. He wasn't going to put himself at the whim of crooked businessmen and seedy night club owners. He'd joined the Force to catch criminals, not become one. The Brooks would get by without brown envelopes.

Besides, he was a graduate. He knew his Economics. He'd seen the way things were shaping. After the stock market crash, property in London was cheap – but not forever. If they could afford to hang onto the flat when they moved into their Battersea house, they'd clean up in a few years. Fulham was up and coming. There was money to be made. Not that he cared about money. Not as much as Amy. Brook worried more about choice, that's what money bought: freedom to choose. That was something they might need soon, especially as it was becoming clear to both of them that his current choices weren't making him happy.

He shook the worries from his mind and turned to more practical matters. He drained his cup and placed it onto the passenger seat with the others, before pulling on his carefree face and patting the leather clad steering wheel with affection.

Then he rotated the ignition key nonchalantly as though expecting no resistance. "Come on." The engine coughed a haughty response, complaining in injured tones at being disturbed at this ungodly hour. "Come on," he pleaded a little more insistently.

"Start please," he ordered with a hint of teeth beginning to grind. The Stag decided it had made its point and spluttered into life on the fourth turn and Brook swung off the kerb and north onto Fulham Palace Road, towards Hammersmith. Traffic was light though London was never deserted, even at three in the morning, something which never ceased to amaze Brook. His hometown, Barnsley, became a ghost town after what local publicans, without irony, called Happy Hour.

Twenty minutes later Brook pulled onto Minet Avenue. For a second the headlights illuminated a fox, nonchalantly nuzzling through shredded bin bags. It turned to face Brook, calm, at home. This was its patch, its time.

Brook killed the engine behind the flashing lights of a squad car and nodded to the constable on crowd control, though there wasn't much interest at that time of the morning.

"What have we got Fulbright?"

"A nasty one, sir."

"Brooky. Up here." DI Charlie Rowlands was leaning on the top of the stairwell that climbed to the first floor flat from the alley at the side of the grimy launderette. He pulled urgently on the inevitable Capstan Full Strength.

Rowlands was a tall, well-built man with the permanent flush of excessive drinking on his face. His eyebrows knotted in the middle above intelligent black eyes and a large, pockmarked nose. He had an air of the thinker, though, to Brook, he always seemed not to be wrestling with present problems but distant mysteries.

Unlike Brook he was in regulation dress for an officer of his age: dark grey suit, grey raincoat, flecked with moisture, and a tie that would last have had sartorial approval on VE Day. His brown suede brogues confirmed the impression of a man who cared nothing for his appearance save that it wouldn't be noticed.

At this moment, he was in imminent danger of falling through the flimsy iron rail on which his weight rested.

"Guv." Brook stepped carefully up the damp metal stairs and perched at the top, fearing the whole structure might suddenly tear itself away from its fastenings under their combined presence.

Rowlands' features seemed drawn and apprehensive and Brook felt his superior's unease was not selfish. "What have we got?"

Rowlands flicked his cigarette onto the wall across the alley and swept his nicotine-stained fingers across the thin wisp of grey hair he habitually trained across his bald head. It amused and comforted Brook that someone with so little idea of fashion could channel his vanity into such a hopeless venture. More hopeless than ever, now the rain had left the umbilical to Rowlands' youth matted against his crown.

With a heavy sigh, he turned to train his penetrating dark eyes onto Brook's. The smell of stale whisky defeated the stench of urine rising from the alley and infused the air between them. Rowlands' drinking had been virtually constant since the death of his daughter the year before. She'd been at university in Edinburgh and, despite being the daughter of a senior policeman, or maybe because of it, she'd succumbed to the attractions of heroin.

Brook was worried about him. He didn't need to be out on a night like this. Not with *his* heart. But Brook understood the self-perpetuating disease of police work. The more you saw in the job, the more you wanted to be away from it, but the more time you spent recreating yourself the more you dwelt on the terrible things you'd seen. The only answer was to keep working. Work was the only consolation, the only solution.

But there was a cost. Sooner or later something would have to give. Health, marriage, sanity. Take your pick. With Brook it would be two out of three. All he could hope was that it would be later rather than sooner.

"Sammy Elphick."

"Sammy Elphick? Oh dear, what's he been up to? Got himself in with the wrong crowd, has he?"

"It looks like it. Whatever Sammy's got into, it must have been pretty bad because they've all been done. And it's no robbery. There's a room full of stolen goods that's not been touched."

Brook screwed his face, sifting through scraps of memory. "Did he have kids?"

Rowlands nodded. "A boy. I've never seen anything like this, Brooky. In all my years..."

"How bad is it?" Brook replied, damping down the fear and excitement that swelled in him at the start of a case. This didn't sound like a routine refuse disposal.

"I don't know any more," Rowlands replied with a curt little laugh. "I need you to tell me." Brook caught the little look of envy thrown at him. Charlie Rowlands was on the final bend of the course and his emotional resources were spent. But he still saw scraps of humanity, of feeling, clinging to his DS and he needed it now to inform his own dead soul.

He ushered Brook through the door into a short hallway, in which it was difficult for both men to stand in comfort. It smelt of damp and stale beer and vomit. The walls were lined with peeling wallpaper, which was grubby and torn. There was a halo of worn grime around the outdated circular light switch.

A gilt-framed picture of Jesus hung on the back wall. It hadn't seen a cloth in decades. The incongruity didn't escape either man and they exchanged a bleak smile. Sammy Elphick in the House of God? Only if there was lead on the roof.

Ancient, ill-fitting linoleum clung to the floor, the pattern long since obscured by substances which tugged at the soles of Brook's Hush Puppies, announcing his every step with a squeak. The dim light was provided by a wall fitting, wittily shaped as a candle with a small bare bulb as its flame.

Brook took all this in, as might a man about to be executed, seeing everything, drinking in the banal details around him to assert his connection to life – the spider dropping from its web, the nipple of damp forming on the ceiling, the pounding of his heart.

Brook didn't enjoy this part of the job. Or rather he didn't enjoy the thrill it gave him. The adrenaline of dread. What was behind that door? He'd been told it was bad but that made it worse.

Would it be a study in scarlet? Would Colonel Mustard be prostrate on the floor of his library, smoking jacket wrapped around his tidy corpse, spotless lead pipe lying beside him? Unlikely.

At school Brook had dreamt of being a superstar detective grappling with unfathomable clues, crossing swords with fiendish criminals, saving the day. As a child he hadn't considered wading through pools of blood and vomit.

Rowlands pushed open the door and Brook began assessing the scene. The worst was over. The not-knowing. In fact, he was surprised by Rowlands' misgivings. There seemed to be order and purpose about the room with only the smell of faeces to gnaw at Brook's equilibrium, offset by a hint of perfume. Talcum powder, Brook guessed. There was another smell, intermingling. Hospitals.

As he took everything in he was aware of the distant mumbling of lowered voices, could see the flash of the police photographer adding another chapter to his Book of the Dead.

The boy hung from the ceiling by the light cord, his head to one side, purple tongue peeping through parted teeth. Brook's first thought was of Ariel in the Tempest, hovering above Prospero, awaiting instruction. He stared, expecting a horror that didn't arrive. It was okay. He could function. He paced around the body trying to gather facts and impressions, not moving his eyes from the boy.

Yes. The boy was Prospero's angel, floating, invisible, watching over his earthly charge. He had on thin nylon pyjamas and couldn't have been more than ten or eleven. He was very slight but even so the ceiling rose was hanging off at the unexpected burden it had been asked to support and looked like it might give way at any second.

Brook looked past the boy briefly, at the fireplace alcove and the daubing of "SALVATION" in blood red finger-writing. Trickles had formed at the base of some of the letters and Brook nodded apprecia-tively at this dramatic touch. Perhaps he was going to tangle with Professor Moriarty after all.

"Our boy fancies himself as a bit of a Stephen King," chuckled Rowlands.

Brook smiled in agreement and moved closer to the boy. His eyes were closed and sunken and his tousled hair fell in a heap across his face, a couple of strands touching the light bulb still in situ. They were singed.

"Was that light on when we got here?"

Rowlands looked nonplussed for a second then turned to enquire of the photographer who shrugged. "Not when I got 'ere, it weren't," he answered.

"Maybe the bulb has blown. Check that, will you, when you've finished?" Brook said to the man combing for fibres on the carpet. "It should have been on," he said to Rowlands.

"How do you know?"

"Just an impression. A good show needs lighting."

Brook moved around the corpse as though it were a maypole, being careful to avoid stepping in any blood. The only sign of violence on the boy was the congealed blood around the stump of his missing middle and forefinger. From the small lump above a slight blackening stain in his breast pocket, Brook deduced that the sliced off fingers had been placed neatly in there. Neat was the word. There'd been no major struggle here. This was highly organised.

Brook examined further, wondering why he wasn't appalled. Perhaps it was the neatness. Yes, that was it. He could focus. He could take it all in. Why was that? Was he just a good copper or had he become so hardened?

Rowlands was right. It was a bad one. Killing children was the last great taboo. Even regular criminals abhorred child killers. They weren't safe anywhere, least of all in prison where child killers were vital to the self-esteem of other inmates. Run-of-the-mill lags could feel good about themselves once they no longer clung to the bottom rung of the ladder. They were better than child killers and had a duty to inflict righteous retribution on any in their midst who'd abused, raped or murdered children. Society demanded it.

But despite society's abhorrence, Brook was unmoved, could look at this child without tears or nausea. Was it because he wasn't yet a father? Was it the absence of blood and gore? He didn't know. Rowlands, who had known fatherhood, also seemed calm but then he'd been "seeming" calm for thirty years.

"What do you see, laddie?" Rowlands eyed him closely looking for any sign of distress. Brook became aware of the scrutiny, grimaced to affect displeasure, and was sickened by the hypocrisy. He stared intently at the face of the boy.

"From the look on his face, I'd say he was dead before he was strung up there. I don't think that wire could support a struggle. It had to be a dead weight. There's no terror in his expression, he looks at peace."

Rowlands nodded declining to reveal if this was a revelation or a confirmation. "Go on."

"His fingers were removed post mortem because there's not enough blood from the wounds. The blood was already starting to congeal when the killer cut them off. The spots below his hand could indicate that they were sliced off where he hung. Impossible if he was struggling. Neat job too. I can't see any hacking. Scalpel maybe."

Brook wrestled with himself for a moment and the photographer paused, impressed, as did the officer now looking for fibres on the sofa.

"It's almost as if..." Brook looked around for the first time at the mute figures of the man and woman, agog on the sofa, tape over their mouths, their sightless eyes frozen in shock forever.

"What is it?" asked Rowlands.

Brook looked carefully at the position of the couple on the sofa. Both had been elaborately tied together and the rope around their ankles disappeared under the sofa and re-emerged over the back to be wound round their chests and hands. Their throats had been cut and blood caked their clothes, the rope and the sides of the sofa. Sprays from the first arterial cuts had even landed on the other side of the room.

They posed for another picture but yet again failed to say "Cheese." As the flash died, Brook caught the silver slug trail of their tears.

He went behind the sofa to take in the final terrible view afforded them.

"What's that doing there?" Everybody stopped and followed Brook's finger to a poster on the wall. He walked over to it and examined it. "This shouldn't be here. It doesn't fit."

"What is it?"

"It's all wrong. Take a look around, guv. I don't wish to sound like a snob but this poster is tasteful. "Fleur de Lis, oil on canvas at the Metropolitan Museum of Art," said Brook, reading from it. "This art doesn't belong here."

"What do you mean?"

"I mean Sammy Elphick is not going to have such a thing in his pokey little existence. He's not remotely interested in any art he can't fence." Brook turned to the couple on the sofa. "He just wouldn't be." The enormity of Brook's assumptions began to slow him down. He closed his eyes and tried to imagine the family's pain. He'd dismissed these people's lives as worthless.

"You think the killer brought it?"

"Probably," Brook replied softly.

"Why?"

"I guess to tell us something. To communicate his superiority over Sammy and his family and tell us he's not our usual, run-of-the-mill murderer. Look around, guv. This has all been staged. Sammy and Mrs Elphick...?" Brook raised an eyebrow at Rowlands who confirmed their union with a nod, "...have been...they've been immobilised here, facing their son to watch him die. I think the killer is taunting them."

"Okay."

"They've had to watch their son die, guv. And yet..." Brook shook his head.

"What?"

"Look at the boy. He's at peace. The killer hasn't made him suffer. He's been killed before being strung up so the parents can witness it. Look at their tears. Maybe the kid's been drugged and smothered, then strung up in front of his mum and dad." Brook put his nose up to Mrs Elphick's. "Chloroform. Guv, he's put them out and revived them. Perfect. What's the first thing they see? Their son. Is he dead? Possibly. But they can't be sure. They cry. The killer is pleased – the desired effect. He's not had the heart to kill the boy in front of them. That would be too hard on him, he's young. But once he's dead, he has no scruples about brutalising the corpse, cutting off his fingers, showing them off to the parents to make *them* suffer, to increase *their* misery."

"So he wants them to think their son has died in agony even if he hasn't. Interesting."

"You don't sound convinced, guv."

"We're just talking. Go on."

"They've been drugged and revived to see the fact of their son's death. They've been punished for something and their son is the method. But they haven't been tortured either. There's no frenzy here. They've been killed quickly, almost as an afterthought to the main event. It's not their physical pain he's after but their mental torment. He wants them to cry, he wants them to see their son dead and know they're going to die. He doesn't relish the actual killing, just the fact that his victims will no longer exist. In fact, I bet he almost wishes he could let them live."

"Why the fuck do you say that?" asked Rowlands.

Brook pondered for a moment then turned to Rowlands with a half-smile. "Because they've learned their lesson."

Chapter 7

Brook was jolted awake by Cat rubbing herself against his legs. He lifted his head from his arms and squinted down at the squirming, affectionate fur ball at his feet. He felt a little dizzy so he returned his head to his arms for a moment and instead tried to move his lips but they seemed welded together, caramelised almost, by the stale sweet alcohol. His first drunken stupor for years.

He lifted his head again and was surprised to feel only a dull ache. He drank so rarely these days, he expected heavier punishment. For a few months in the nineties he'd tried to hit the bottle but soon tired of it. His insomnia wouldn't be denied by alcohol-induced coma.

Brook stood and winced in unexpected pain. His back muscles were tight from the wooden chair. That's what came of getting a plush new car. No sooner had he experienced the pleasure of a cushioned seat than his back protested about having to accept second best.

He padded off to the kitchen taking the empty bottle and brimming ashtray with him. The linoleum was icy on his bare feet and he hopped from foot to foot before jumping onto the hall carpet for relief. He slipped on his loafers and returned to the kitchen to turn out a large tin of mush into a bowl.

Cat ate remorselessly until the bowl was empty then sauntered past Brook as though he didn't exist, to seek out the hottest radiator to doze under.

"Enjoy that, monkey?" Cat ignored him and trotted off to the living room. "Don't mention it." He smiled. There was a time when Brook would have preferred dogs. He still did, but over the years, as his job took him full pelt away from childhood, he'd noticed the resemblance the dumb mutts had to victims of crimes – battered wives and abused children, in particular.

Cats were different. Nothing was unconditional. If you played ball you'd be given the appropriate amount of love and affection. But if you didn't feed and house them properly they'd find somewhere better to live. Their demands provided a behavioural straitjacket from which you couldn't deviate.

Dogs were too innocent for this world. They belonged in boyhood, in a past of hot endless summers and English sporting supremacy.

Brook flung open the back door to clear his head and ventilate the flat. He didn't believe in aspirins. The freezing morning air felt good so he stepped out to have his last cigarette. It'd been many months since he'd smoked in the morning but as it was the last in the packet...best to get it finished. Already he was thinking like an addict again.

Brook lit up and exhaled towards the heavens. The sky was still black but the occasional early bird drove by.

On one such pass, a car's headlights picked out a figure standing on the other side of the Uttoxeter Road. Brook narrowed his eyes, curious. People didn't stand around in this weather, at this time of the morning.

From the shock of long blonde hair, it had to be a girl and she appeared to be staring back at Brook standing in the communal alley at the side of his building. He must look odd, outside in the bitter cold in shirtsleeves.

Brook continued to glance over, glad of the cigarette as pretext for loitering. There wasn't a bus stop nearby so her presence was mildly interesting and he continued to observe her. Perhaps she was a prostitute or someone waiting for a lift into work.

She wore a dark blue padded jacket, buttoned up to her chin, faded blue jeans with horizontal slashes in the knees, brown boots and a pair of garish pink ear muffs, the sort of garb only young people seemed able to wear and not feel self-conscious.

One thing was clear. She was cold, jogging up and down in an effort to keep warm. Brook, in shirt and trousers, was reminded of the bite of winter morning and shuddered. Flicking his cigarette against the wall for the satisfying spray of orange, he turned to go inside.

As he did so, he noticed the girl crossing the road towards him so he tarried a moment longer. Perhaps she wanted directions.

She walked steadily towards him, her gaze locking onto Brook's face so blatantly that he felt no embarrassment about staring straight back at her.

She was young, twenty perhaps, and had straggly unkempt hair, parted vaguely in the middle. Brook noticed a touch of darker root. She was medium height with a pretty face and a button nose. Her complexion was clear and soft and her grey eyes were large, with a hint

76

of Eurasian slant. She moved well on her slim legs, like a model, aware of her attractions.

When she was a few yards from Brook, she hesitated, as though she'd remembered something, and rummaged in a generous, fleece-lined pocket.

"Good morning," she smiled, revealing a full set of teeth in a large, slightly protruding mouth. There was no trace of an accent, which Brook, rightly or wrongly, always took as a sign of a middle class upbringing.

Brook returned her smile, resisting the urge to start flapping his arms around his freezing torso. She consulted a piece of paper from her pocket. "Could you tell me where the Casa Mia Hotel is please?"

"The Casa Mia?" Brook knew it well. He could've taken her there blindfolded so many times had he been called in to deal with the unfortunates who fetched up in that DSS fleapit. Sergeant Hendrickson joked that it would be cheaper to have an officer permanently stationed there, to save on petrol. He wasn't a natural comedian.

"Why would you want to go to that dump?"

She seemed slightly nonplussed by Brook's frankness but she smiled, her grey eyes fixing him. "I'm staying there tonight. I've got an interview at the university, tomorrow."

"For what?" asked Brook.

"To study there," she replied. Her expression carried a semblance of reproach, as if Brook had suggested she looked like she'd be applying for a cleaning job.

Brook was tempted to challenge her further but he was shivering so he gave directions and darted inside after watching her retreat.

He looked at his watch. He had an hour before Terri could call so he nipped inside to pull on a coat and went back out into the cold.

A couple of minutes later, he was staring up at the menu board in the steamy warmth of Jimbo's Café, known to regulars as Jumbo's because of the girth of its proprietor.

Brook sat down with his mug of tea to await his Farmhouse Special, having helped himself to one of the tabloids on the counter. He wasn't feeling hungry, as a purely functional eater he rarely did, but he knew he hadn't eaten for over a day so he had to take on board some fuel.

As he smirked at the nursery school alliteration of the Page Three caption, he suddenly became aware of a tightening of lips and stomachs amongst the only other customers, two stout lorry drivers tucking in to two oval plates of saturated fat, at the table in front of him. Brook turned to follow their gaze and saw the girl. She closed the door and smiled at him as if she'd just spotted him.

"Hello again." She passed Brook and ignored the other table with its four eyes moving up and down her body like a barometer in a British summer. She ordered a cup of tea and painstakingly counted out the change from a small beaded purse.

"Nothing to eet, meese?" enquired Jumbo, in his broken English.

"No thanks." She returned to Brook's table with a smile and a nod at the chair in front of him.

"Please," said Brook, folding the paper away. She put her cup and saucer opposite him and took off her coat. Full House Brook noticed, trying not to stare. To his amusement, and the dismay of Jumbo and the other table, she then proceeded to pull the baggy patchwork sweater she was wearing over her head. This was accompanied by synchronised intakes of breath, as she almost pulled off her flimsy T-shirt with it. Having revealed a bare waist, the T-shirt, to mixed feelings from her male audience, clung to her unfettered breasts, allowing the sweater clearance.

Eventually she sat down, pulling her T-shirt back over her midriff. Heavy sighs were released around the room and Brook almost expected a round of applause to follow. He tried to ignore the looks of exquisite pain directed at her from the other table and hoped his own expression didn't betray the same yearning. Unattainable pleasures were to be avoided at all costs. The emotional epidermis of this male was pocked with enough wounds.

Still, it wasn't easy for Brook to find a place to rest his eyes. Even looking directly at her face couldn't hide the dark rim of her nipples goading him into a lingering gaze. Fortunately his breakfast arrived to distract him and he tucked in with more gusto than he'd felt a moment earlier. "No joy, then?" he mumbled, through a mouthful of toast.

"No, you were right. It wasn't a very nice place," she replied absently.

Brook looked up to try and fathom why she'd need to lie. He saw her looking at his plate and realised that she didn't have enough money to buy herself any food. Come to think of it, when he looked again, her cheeks did seem a little hollow, gaunt even. He was savvy enough to avoid wounding her pride by offering to buy her something so he just rolled his two sausages to the side of his plate and shook his head.

"I told him no sausages," Brook complained. "I hate sausages. Look, I've paid for them already. Would you have them? I can't stand waste."

She seemed to perk up a little. "Well if you're sure you don't want them?"

"I'm certain," he said and before the last syllable was out, she'd fallen on them as delicately as she could manage. Watching her mimic fellatio, Brook wished he'd offered her some toast instead but they

78

were gone in a trice and she smiled gratefully at him.

Brook returned her smile but was puzzled. What did she want? She hadn't had time to get to the Casa Mia and back and he knew, as a graduate himself, there was little likelihood of entrance interviews in the week before Christmas. She looked far too classy to be on the game but you never could tell; it wasn't the exclusive preserve of pressured single mothers and granite-faced fortysomethings. She wouldn't have been out of place in better parts of London but this was the rough end of Derby.

"Where will you go now?" he asked trying to get to the bottom of it. He didn't have long to wait.

"I've tried everywhere else. All full," she said unable to look at him. "I'll have to go back there, I suppose."

Brook scrutinised her, chewing both his food and his thoughts. "How old are you?"

"Twenty-two." She looked at him for the first time without the discomfort of deceit so Brook decided it was the truth. He had nothing to lose, certainly nothing valuable in his flat, except Cat.

"Look. I go to work at eight. I'll leave a key under a brick near the back door, right." She feigned surprise quite well. "It's a bit shabby but if you can't find anywhere else at all, there's a sofa for the night, if you want it? No strings and no charge."

"That's very nice of you," she said with mock uncertainty. She felt she ought to put up some attempt to ask for a motive, and her manner became more worldly. "Why would you do that? For a complete stranger, I mean."

"Why? Because I was a penniless student once, for all the good it did me, and because you're not much older than my daughter and I'd hate to think of Terri wandering around a strange city without a place to stay. Also I'm a policeman, so it's my job to prevent crime." He looked hard at her for signs of a flinch to betray that she was on the make in any way. There was none.

Instead recognition flickered across her features. "You were on the TV last night," she said, open-mouthed, pointing at him, "about those murders." Brook nodded his confirmation, basking ever so slightly in his new-found celebrity. Top of the world ma. "Well, I'd feel much safer under a policeman's roof than some of the hotels I've seen. Thanks very much for the offer."

She stood up to leave and held out her hand to shake his. "I'm Vicky."

"Damen." Brook shook her hand and shot her a mechanical smile, trying to mask his fresh doubts about her age. If she thought being a policeman was a guarantee of moral rectitude, she must be more naive than he'd assumed.

She reassembled her layers, drained her cup and headed for the door, throwing a beautiful smile over her shoulder at him. This time four pairs of eyes took the tour around her southern hemisphere.

Brook turned back towards the occupants of the neighbouring table who were radiating a mixture of resentment and respect. He shrugged his shoulders modestly and pulled his best 'Yeah-I'm-a-babe-magnet' face before resuming his breakfast.

*

The phone rang just after seven-thirty. Brook picked up before the end of the first ring.

"Terri?"

"Dad."

"Talk to me."

"Dad, stop panicking. There's nothing wrong."

"What do you mean?"

"I mean there's nothing wrong. I just got worked up about some silly thing, that's all."

There was silence as Brook wondered what to say. He wasn't able to square away his daughter's reassurances with her barely contained anxiety of the previous day. He decided to gamble.

"Has Tony been making… sexual advances towards you?"

"No dad. It's nothing like that. Everything's fine."

Bulls-eye! She'd failed even the simplest interview technique. From nowhere, beads of cold sweat studded Brook's brow. His darkest fears were confirmed. His daughter and that… She was only fifteen. *Fifteen.*

Nowadays kids were au fait with these…matters, but what Brook had suggested was appalling, even by today's standards. A fifteen year old girl – his daughter – sleeping with her stepfather. And yet there was no high-pitched squeal of shock, no incredulity that he could even think such a thing, no startled denial – *"I can't believe you said that dad."* Nothing. It could mean only one thing. Such thoughts had already been assimilated in her mind. The concept was familiar. Not shocking or unthinkable, but fact.

Brook swallowed hard but no tears came. Instead a volcanic anger bubbled in the pit of his stomach. His baby. And that bastard. He hung up without another word and stared at the wall, unblinking, almost catatonic.

Chapter 8

Brook rested his elbows on the desk and propped his head in his hands. His eyes were stinging so he closed them and massaged the lids. His head now throbbed and his mouth reeked of stale tobacco and bacon-flavoured sweet martini.

With an effort, which to casual observation would have suggested disability, he hauled himself to his feet and shuffled to the door. He didn't want to face anyone so he locked his office door, hoping that no-one needed his attention. Fortunately he wasn't included in station banter and most people left him alone, although Hendrickson had given him a passing sneer as he arrived.

Brook checked his watch. Ten minutes to briefing. He pulled a Greater London Street Atlas from a drawer and turned to the double spread of his old beat to reacquaint himself with it. Fulham, Shepherd's Bush, Hammersmith and, of course, Harlesden. He stared at Minet Avenue in Harlesden, scene of the first Reaper killings, as though it might offer up new clues. On an impulse he flicked over the page to check how to pick up the A23 to Brighton before closing the tome decisively.

*

DS Noble, DC's Morton, Cooper, Gadd and Bull, PC Aktar and WPC Jones gazed back at Brook from the sanctuary of their plastic chairs. All tried to remain still but each fidgeted in their turn, aware of their exposure. Usually there'd be a table to cocoon them but Brook had removed it. He'd been to enough briefings to know that such comforts discouraged concentration.

He tore the cellophane from a new pack of cigarettes and lit up, leaning against a desk. Crutch in hand, he was finally able to raise his red-rimmed eyes to the assembled company. He let smoke drift up into his face, hoping to offer his audience an alternative theory for their condition.

Brook usually enjoyed leading briefings but he wasn't looking forward to this one. At least McMaster hadn't put in her threatened appearance.

"Okay," he said to the floor before fixing his eye on an indeterminate point behind Noble's head. "Let me give you the watchword for this enquiry: discretion. What happened in Drayfin two nights ago is not a regular occurrence. Not in Derby. Not anywhere. People are going to want to know about it. People, clever people, are going to pressure you, offer you inducements to talk about what we have seen and what we're doing about it.

"The Chief wants me to make this clear at the outset. We can't afford anyone on this enquiry who feels they can't resist that pressure. And that includes pressure from fellow officers and those close to you. Say now if you feel you're not up to it. We keep the facts of this case close to our chests otherwise careers are going to be in the balance.

"The nation's media will be watching so this case is priority number one and the Chief has given me a free hand to authorise any additions to the team," Brook nodded at Jones and Aktar, "and we'll have as many bodies from uniform as we need to do any legwork." Brook glanced up but couldn't detect any offence taken by Aktar or Jones.

"So to details. There are three corpses in the mortuary – Mr and Mrs Wallis and little Kylie Wallis." Brook nodded towards the pictures arranged around the white board behind his head. Aktar and Jones were already mesmerised by them, a reaction Brook recalled from his early years in the Met. "Their throats were cut. No forced entry. No apparent motive. Before we go over what we know does anyone have any ideas, thoughts or observations of any kind about the nature of this crime?"

There was a silence that only Noble seemed eager to fill. "It's not random. Our killer has planned this for a long time."

"How do we know that?" asked Brook.

"Because he telephoned the family the day before, telling them they'd won a competition, a free meal courtesy of Pizza Parlour," continued Noble.

"Okay." Brook waited. "Why has he gone to all that trouble? Why not just turn up and start slaughtering them?" He could see that Jones knew the answer but had decided not to play teacher's pet.

Brook decided to press on. He had better things to do than

shepherd these novices through such an intense investigation. A second later, he realised that he hadn't. "Well. This way he can fix the whole family's location at a given time. Or so he believes. They've won something for nothing. Who can resist collecting their winnings?" Brook surveyed the outbreak of nodding. "And so it begins. John."

Noble flipped open his notebook. "On the morning of the murder, our man, wearing dark glasses and a black baseball cap, hired a white transit from Euro Van in Allenton. He paid cash and gave a false name and had a licence to match. Name of Peter Hera."

"Hera?" said Jones.

"Yes?" Brook queried.

"I don't know. It seems familiar. Something from Greek mythology."

"Hera was a goddess of some kind," replied Brook. "Married to Zeus, I think."

"Maybe this guy thinks he's a god," offered Rob Morton.

"Could be," nodded Brook, trying to sound impressed. Clearly nobody else in the room had ever bothered with crosswords or simple anagrams. He motioned Noble to continue and returned his eyes to the floor as if thinking about the case.

"The van he hired was the same van seen outside the Wallis house on the night of the murders. It hasn't been seen since. An alert neighbour, Mrs Patel, remembers seeing the white van outside the house and the fact that the driver delivered several flat boxes. She jotted down what she could see of the number plate, it was dark and foggy, remember."

"Why would she do that?" asked Aktar. "I mean, getting a pizza delivered is hardly suspicious, is it? Even in ASBO-land." He permitted himself a satisfied smile at this.

Noble knew better and kept a straight face even though DI Brook didn't appear to be annoyed. In fact, Noble wasn't even sure he was paying attention. He looked as though his mind was elsewhere. "To those law-abiding citizens who live on the Drayfin Estate, everything is a potential crime, particularly at night, constable. Let's just be thankful Mrs Patel is nosy enough to jot down a partial. We had enough to trace it to Euro Van. Uniform haven't yet found where it's been dumped but it shouldn't take long. We've had Traffic review all the relevant footage and there was no sign of it leaving Derby on any of the major routes. It should still be here. We've put out a national alert just in case it slipped out on a minor road. Locally we're concentrating on bus and rail stations..."

"Good thinking, John," chipped in Brook. "I don't think our

killer's local but he's not going to risk driving home in the van. Nor is he going to dump it anywhere there's obvious CCTV, so look further afield." Noble nodded and made a note.

"Do we have a description at all?" asked DC Bull.

"Nothing useful," Noble continued. "He was dressed in black overalls, the baseball cap and glasses hid his face. One thing. The neighbour thinks he was small and slim but it was hard to see and there are few working street lights in the area. Euro Van would seem to confirm the description. So we're looking at around five-six, five-seven, and 140lbs. Age unsure, but the guy who hired out the van says not young. At least middle aged. But that's very roughly. He didn't take much notice.

"We know the mileage of the vehicle when it was hired out but until we find the van, we don't know how far he's driven. Nor do we know where he took the van until he was ready to commit the crime. All we know for sure is that at 7.25pm, on the night in question, he drove to the Pizza Parlour on Normanton Lane, being careful to park away from the restaurant, and bought three large pizzas, paying cash. According to the till roll that was at 7.36 exactly..."

"I know you'll think this is a daft question, sir," ventured Aktar, "but why take pizzas to the Wallis house? They seem a bit cumbersome. In fact, why take food at all?"

Brook paused, gathering his thoughts as though he'd been following proceedings. "It's a very good question, constable. Yes, food's cumbersome but it has certain advantages. First, because he's handling food, it allows him to wear disposable gloves without arousing suspicion. I'm certain there'll be no fingerprints..." Brook shrugged.

"I see." Aktar nodded mechanically.

"He also knows that the whole family will eat hot food immediately," added Jones. "So whatever drug he's added to the food will be ingested straight away. That's good for his schedule. If he brought round drinks as a prize, he can't be certain the whole family will consume at the same time, never mind that it would be easier to see if it's been tampered with. You'd be suspicious if a coke bottle had a broken seal."

"And people have different drinks, I suppose," added Bull, getting into the swing.

"That's right," said Brook, holding his eyes on Jones. "He might have to take beer for the parents and coke for the kids. Maybe the mother doesn't like beer. He can never be sure. With a pizza, it's a sure shot for the whole family. It's relatively bland for a start. He can't risk curry or Chinese in case somebody doesn't care for it. And don't forget they'll have ordered their favourite toppings when they *won* the competition."

"He's thought about this a lot, hasn't he sir?" said Morton. "The cunning bastard."

Brook would normally have stamped on such displays of emotion, they were counterproductive to logical thought, but he remembered his own first encounter with barbarous slaughter and let it slide. If Morton was very lucky he might not lose the rage that had been painstakingly squeezed from Brook, year on year.

"Go on John."

"Mrs Patel remembers the van pulling up just after 8pm. It's only a five to seven minute drive from Pizza Parlour so he's used the intervening time to doctor the food. The killer thinks the whole family will be there, but he's wrong. Jason Wallis has gone out. Our killer delivers the boxes and then, we assume, he leaves to let the family tuck in. We don't know if he knows about Jason's absence but he may have found out."

"How?" asked DC Gadd.

"Steering the conversation to check if everyone's there, pretending the boxes are about to spill if he doesn't put them down inside the house. There are ways," answered Brook. He nodded at Noble.

"Mrs Patel remembers looking again at 8.20 and the van was gone. By then the family are tucking into the pizzas. We'll find out from Forensics this afternoon what each of them ate.

"Our killer is confident that he can return later and get in without a struggle. The front door has bolts but at that time of night the door would only have been on the latch and any criminal worth their salt can get past an old Yale lock. It's cold and dark and late when he returns, so he's unlikely to meet many people. We don't know if he pulls up to the front of the house in the van. Probably not. Certainly no-one sees him.

"Our best estimate of the time he returns is between 11.00 and 11.30 because the music the killer puts on starts at 11.40 according to the next door neighbour, Mr Singh. Around that time the victims were killed – the PM's may fine tune that but don't bank on it – and the music is turned up to full volume around midnight so it's quite a small window with all he has to get done. At half past midnight the neighbour's had enough and goes round to complain and finds the bodies."

"One thing John – it may be nothing – but Mr Singh said the music was turned off some time between twelve and half past, then turned on again which means our killer may have left later than midnight."

"Why would he turn it off?" asked Jones.

Brook shook his head. "I don't know."

"Maybe he turned it down when Jason came back?" said Aktar.

"That's a good thought, constable. It would explain why Jason heard nothing when he got home." Aktar was thrilled with his contribution so Brook tried to let him down gently. "There's just one problem with it."

"If Jason came back why didn't he get his throat cut?" said Jones softly. "It wouldn't have been difficult in his condition."

"Right!" said Aktar, trying not to look crestfallen.

Brook smiled at Jones. "Go on John."

"So having returned, our killer probably has a small case or bag carrying a bottle of wine, two glasses, a corkscrew – in case the Wallises don't have one – the murder weapon and – given the careful arrangement of the victims – possibly a camera," continued Noble assuming credit for his superior's observations. "He may have a change of clothes as well as the Van Gogh poster and a CD of Mahler's Ninth Symphony. And before you ask, it's not Bob Marley," he added with barely a glance at Brook. "Mahler's a classical..."

"He wrote nine symphonies, his last being the most famous. He was dying and knew it. He wrote it as his own requiem," continued Jones. "My dad's a big fan," she explained, examining her shoes missing Brook's approving smile.

Noble, chastened, looked at Brook who raised an eyebrow. "Thank you, Constable Jones," said Noble. "Okay. Our man re-enters the Wallis household. And if he didn't know before, he knows now that Jason isn't there and could return at any moment. So he has to hurry.

"We think he brings the baby downstairs and puts it in the cot. The girl is out cold where she lay, face down on the rug. He cuts the girl's throat..."

"Not yet, John."

"Sir?"

"Not straight away. He revives Mr and Mrs Wallis before he kills the girl."

"He does?" exclaimed Noble.

"Oh yes. That's vital. That's what the wine is for. Remember the tear tracks. It's important that mum and dad watch their daughter die. You can't teach someone a lesson if they're not paying attention," he added. "They watched her bleed out in front of them and knew *they* were next. That was supposed to be their final sight on earth. That and the Van Gogh poster."

"You're kidding," said Aktar to nobody in particular. Jones also betrayed an exclamation of disgust although the undertone of anger was what hit Brook. He was impressed with WPC Jones.

"I suppose they couldn't listen to the music or taste the wine if they were unconscious," she observed.

"Exactly. Constable." The temptation for Brook to call her Wendy was becoming difficult to resist and he saw that she'd noticed it as well. Brook became self-conscious and decided to move things along.

"To finish off for you, John, the killer goes about his work quickly. He's annoyed because Jason's not there. And it's spoiling his vision, his creation, and he doesn't know when or if he's coming back. He can't appreciate his work of art fully. He puts up the poster…"

"What's that in aid of?" asked Aktar.

"Probably to tell them he's better than them because he appreciates art," Brook said. "Though it's more likely he's telling us. Anyway, he revives the parents. It's not easy because he's had to use enough juice to put them down and keep them there. He manages it but they can't stand or call out. Perfect. All they can do is watch as he slices across Kylie's throat."

"Doesn't he revive the girl?" asked Noble.

"I don't think so. She's small and she'll have felt the effects of the drug more than her parents. And he doesn't need her to suffer, that's for the parents. She's an innocent. But she still has to die. She's an essential tool for our killer who has no qualms about killing her or desecrating her corpse. So, to rub it in, he cuts her top down the back and cuts the word SAVED below her shoulder blades, while her parents watch." Jones and Aktar continued to listen but with heads bowed. The others simply stared at a convenient point on the wall.

"The baby's been brought down and he uses one of mum's lipsticks to write SAVED on its forehead. By now Bobby and Mrs Wallis have started to cry and struggle but can do no more than wriggle and empty their bowels. If he hasn't put the music on before, he does so now.

"He enjoys the music, but probably not the wine – he's too intelligent to give us any useable saliva. Then he turns to the parents. I think he does Bobby last. He deserves to wait.

"He cuts the throat of Mrs Wallis and watches Bobby's reaction as she chokes on her own blood. The spray from her arteries hits Bobby, the carpet, the killer, everything. Maybe he steps back and takes photographs of the last moments, I don't know. I'm just speculating but that's what I'd do." Jones looked up at him sharply, but Brook was lost in thought. She glanced at the display behind his head, imagining what the killer's own album might show.

"Finally he turns to Bobby. He watches him struggle and smiles.

87

He waves the scalpel, cut-throat razor, whatever it is, in the air, like a conductor with a baton, and closes his eyes to savour the music. Maybe he talks to him. *Listen. You'll like this bit. Close your eyes. Have a sip of wine. It's a Nuits St George."*

Brook stops for a moment as though frozen. Silence. Nobody moves. Nobody speaks. Nobody breathes. It's dangerous to rouse sleepwalkers.

"And after he cuts him?"

Brook snaked his eyes towards Noble. "He waits. Watches. Listens. To life ending. Then he dips his finger into the blood and writes his message on the wall. And it's done."

"But because of Jason, he has to hurry."

"That's right Wendy." Brook was unaware of the slip. Jones was acutely aware. "He'll need to change into fresh clothing or, more likely, take off protective overalls which are covered in blood. He wraps the weapon in his overalls, stuffs everything into his bag, turns the CD up and leaves before the commotion starts. Whoever finds the bodies will see a neatly organised execution posing as a cosy family scene. Minus Jason." Brook looked round. "Questions?"

Nobody could think of much to say at that moment. Finally DC Cooper made his first contribution. "How does the killer know the Wallis family have a CD player?"

"He doesn't. Maybe he's got a small cassette player and a tape as well, just in case. But he can do without the music if he has to."

"And why kill the girl if she's innocent?" Jones asked, taking her hundredth glance at the photographs.

"That's his MO, constable. Her death will serve his purpose because it makes the parents suffer so much more. Not only do they have to watch her life end, but they know they'll be joining her."

"I don't get it, sir." Aktar's broad accent made him sound plaintive.

"I'm not sure you're supposed to." Brook kept silent for half a minute. He'd sped through the briefing, feeling the need to get it over quickly so he could be alone but now he felt it necessary to leave a pause for the full impact to sink into his team.

"Now we have a puzzle. There are two survivors. Jason Wallis, who should have been there..."

"Lucky bastard," muttered Jones.

"...and baby Bianca who was. Question. Why take the trouble of bringing the baby down from its..." Brook looked at the ceiling in self-admonishment, "*her* bed, to complete the family gathering and yet not kill her?"

Noble glanced at Jane Gadd. He knew that Brook would already have the answers but he sensed an opportunity to impress her. "It could be an act of mercy on the part of the killer to show himself in a better light. Make us think he's not an animal." Noble paused, trying to appear spontaneous. "And also he knows the baby can't identify him."

"True," nodded Brook. He put his hands in his pockets and allowed discomfort to linger to remind his audience of the need to think. He became aware that Jones wanted to fill the vacuum.

"Sir," she said hesitantly. "I know this might sound a bit weird but...I get the impression that he doesn't enjoy the killing. Even the parents."

Noble kept silent but drew in a mocking breath. Aktar felt obliged to smile weakly so he could keep a foot in both camps. Morton, Cooper, Bull and Gadd turned to Jones with varying degrees of confusion etched on their faces.

Brook just stared. "Go on, constable." The inquisitive tone removed the smile from Noble's mouth.

"Well sir, they all died quickly and relatively painlessly, after they'd served their purpose. You said the girl died first and was probably unconscious when he cut her throat. Her purpose wasn't to suffer but make the parents suffer. He wants them to suffer a lot but even then it's mental torture. They die just as quickly as the girl. Their real ordeal is to watch their children die."

"But the baby's alive!" protested Noble, looking at Brook for support that didn't arrive.

"Okay. But if he's already killed the girl, they'll think he's going to kill the baby as well," continued Jones. He only has to pretend. He bends over the carry cot to make it look like he's going to cut the baby, just to turn the screw. But they can't see. He doesn't *need* to do it to make them suffer, so he doesn't. That's why he brought the baby down and that's why he didn't kill it. Her." Jones halted suddenly uncertain. "Is that too simplistic, sir?"

Brook smiled. He wanted to clap but for Noble's sake he had to be non-committal. "An interesting idea, constable. Worth thinking about." He arched an eyebrow at Noble, who registered it with satisfaction. Brook hoped Jones wouldn't see but his hope was in vain and he saw her colour rising.

"As you've got your thinking cap on, constable, answer me this. Why this family?" His attempt to throw her a bone failed. The damage was done. Blank faces greeted Brook's hardest question. Jones just looked at the floor, her face a mix of emotions. All strong.

"It was thanks to you, PC Jones. You put me on the right track."

She perked up a little but Brook could see she wouldn't forget his slight for a long time. "I realise motive is hard to fathom for this sort of crime but believe me, although we can't see it, serial killers have strong reasons for apparently random killings."

"Serial killer?" PC Aktar exclaimed. "In Derby?"

"You're right, constable. They're rare in this country but they exist. Shipman, Sutcliffe." He turned to Noble next. "How do we know it's a serial, John?"

"The organisation," Noble said.

"And?"

"The selection of appropriate victims." Noble looked pleased with himself but not with Brook's response.

"Well remembered. Although the Wallis family seem to be randomly selected, they're not. I think Jason Wallis was the reason for this crime. Constable Jones pointed me in the right direction." Brook continued to check her demeanour for signs of forgiveness. There were none. "Ironic then that he should escape his fate."

"Why is Jason the main target, sir?" enquired Aktar.

"He's made enemies, constable. I think our killer has seen him on the news or in the papers in connection with the threatened rape of a teacher. He's decided that the world would be a better place without him."

"But he kills the rest of the family even though his main target didn't turn up?" Noble's scepticism was clear. "I'm sorry but that tells me he enjoys it."

"I know it's hard to fathom, John, but PC Jones has a point. He has to kill the family. He wants to, if only to disguise the fact that Jason is the real target. Don't forget he's been planning this for a long time and Jason could turn up at any minute to collect his just desserts."

After a pause, Jones found her voice. "Presumably the writing is something religious, about saving souls."

"Probably," shrugged Brook.

"Then why write it on Baby Bianca despite not sending her soul off with the others?"

"Good question..." conceded Brook.

"And why not cut it onto mum and dad? Presumably if he's a religious nutter, he's saved their souls as well," she added.

Brook shook his head. "I don't know – pressure of time, perhaps." He was becoming fatigued with his team's attempts to comprehend things he'd been grappling with for years.

Brook glanced as inconspicuously as he could at Wendy Jones and made his mind up. All that remained was to deflect Noble's ego from the insult he was about to inflict.

"No doubt you're all aware from the press conference that there are some similarities in this case with a murder I investigated in London..."

"You mean The Reaper killings," nodded Rob Morton.

"I do. It was a long time ago and it's a bit of a long shot but it needs to be checked out. I want to speak to Forensics before I go but then I want to know I can leave somebody of your calibre in charge, John. You've got the best CID team in the Midlands to back you up," beamed Brook at the assembled DC's who glowed with all the modesty they could muster. "And Aktar can assist." Brook felt Wendy Jones's subtle change of expression. Was this a further snub?

"We won't let you down, sir," replied Noble, suddenly radiating all the pomposity of a French mayor. Brook was pleased with his ability to manipulate, but irked at Noble's gullibility.

"Good. Liaise with the Chief, but this is what I want. Keep going house to house. Talk to the neighbours again. I want to know when exactly our killer returned and, if possible, when Jason got back to the house."

"Right."

"Speak to Mr Singh again and get a more detailed statement about the half hour before he discovered the bodies. We want precise times about when the music was turned on and off. It may be that the volume was up high the whole time and Jason didn't hear it because the music was at a quiet section. Mahler blows hot and cold doesn't he, constable?"

"He does. Sir," replied Jones, not looking up.

"Get on to the media. I want to know how far Jason's moment of infamy was scattered. What papers was it in? Did it get onto local or national telly?" Brook continued to reel off tasks so Noble wouldn't have time to think about his demotion. He jotted them down furiously.

"Check the hotels and B & B's. I want to know of any men alone who checked out of their rooms on the morning of the murder or the day after. Names and addresses, reasons for visit, all that stuff. Cross reference with the height and weight of our description. And start checking people out as soon as you get names. Keep it to hotels within five miles of Derby to start with. I want a list on my desk when I get back."

"What about cabs, sir?" suggested Noble, picking up the mood. "He may have done a reccy of the killing ground. We could check any fares to and from Drayfin a couple of days beforehand."

"Great idea," purred Brook. "And find that van. It's unlikely but he may have been careless and left us something. When you do find it, go house to house around it. I want to know where he went from there. Did he have another car waiting? Did he call a cab? Did he walk? He might not be in disguise at that point so any sightings will be more significant. Check all parking tickets issued up to two days before the murder in case he had another car and got sloppy. Get as many bodies as you need to help. But mum's the word remember. The Chief wants this watertight. The media already know more than they're supposed to."

"Right."

"I'll get back to Jason in due course. There's more to come from him but for now we'll let him sweat. Where's the aunt's house?"

Noble flipped to the back of his notebook. "Mrs Harrison. 41 Station Road, Borrowash. The baby's going there too."

"Good. It goes without saying I want the house watched round the clock for the time being. Set it up John. That teacher Jason assaulted, constable?" Jones looked up.

"Mrs Ottoman?"

"I assume she has a husband."

"Yes." She seemed wary.

"I think it might be worth us paying them a visit, John." There was a pause as Brook gathered his breath.

"What do you want me to do, sir?" Jones enquired with a note of excessive deference. She was very ready to take offence, which made his reply all the more startling.

"You?" Brook was halted for a moment, trying to find the right approach, before deciding there wasn't one. "You're coming to London with me." Brook tried not to assess her reaction too closely and was impressed with her poise. She was smart. Her intelligence could be very useful on this trip. At least that's what he told himself.

Chapter 9

Brook pushed the handle of his cup around the saucer and stared into the dregs like a gypsy who's forgotten how to read the leaves. There was so much to organise and delegate to his team, so much to consider from his past as well as the present, so much to try not to think about concerning his daughter. But none of that was bothering him at this moment.

Brook was thinking about Wendy Jones. Was he doing the right thing, taking her with him to London? She had made a good impression in the briefing. She was sharp and intuitive and wouldn't be out of place in CID. Taking her with him could be justified. But that's what was gnawing at him. His instincts were generally spot-on when it came to police work but disastrous when it came to personal relations. Which category applied here?

She'd certainly seemed pleased, if taken aback, when he'd pulled her to one side after the briefing. Her surprise appeared professional, that he should take her on such an important assignment. He knew she was ambitious and the glint in her eye showed she saw a big opportunity looming. For the moment she seemed to have forgotten their night of passion. That would be temporary though. Things could still be awkward.

He glanced at his watch then around the station canteen trying not to catch eyes. It was filling fast with packs of rowdy males, ribbing each other, eager for their something and chips – salad was for girls. Then a quieter group would latch onto the queue and Brook knew it would always contain a female officer. He sat at his usual seat at a corner table, facing the wall. He could only see the back of the lunch queue but it was enough – not for him the gunfighter's seat, facing the room, scanning for potential opponents. He had no interest in his colleagues, or they in him, required no knowledge of who was in the room or who was coming in. Even Noble had been given special dispensation by Brook. "I know you've got your reputation to think of, John," he'd said. "I'll expect you to nod politely, but you don't have to sit next to me. You see enough of me as it is."

But today would be different. Today, as people drifted in, Brook felt the urge to change seats to monitor conversations that normally would have passed him by but now pierced him.

There it was again. Things were being said, things about him. What things? He wished he'd taken the wall seat but now he was stuck, too self-conscious to move. All he could do was listen, aware that for once the invisibility he nurtured so keenly was gone.

People resented Brook. He didn't mind. The less people liked him the less attention they paid him. He liked his life better that way. But today was different. Today he could hear "nudge nudges" and "wink winks" being launched in his direction, though he couldn't be sure he was the target.

He listened to a familiar source; Hendrickson. What was he saying? He hoped he was still crowing over Brook's climb-down the other night but feared there was a new focus for his comic gifts. Wendy.

Brook pricked his ears but couldn't catch the drift. Perhaps they were signalling, pulling faces at him, pointing. He had almost dredged up the courage to change seats and face his tormentors when his fears were confirmed.

An upsurge of coughs and giggles and muted whistles began and he turned briefly to see Jones enter the canteen. They knew already. His impending trip to London had spread around the station and details of his fling with her the year before were now being resurrected for recent arrivals.

Brook pushed his cup away and began to rise but before he could lock his knees, DI Greatorix was at his table, tray of pie, chips and beans in hand. "Hello Damen. You look a bit rough round the edges."

"Do I?" Brook retorted without surprise.

"But then you often do," Greatorix beamed back. Brook looked back without expression. His fellow inspector was such a sartorial disaster area that Brook accepted such admonition in the interests of balance. "Got a minute?"

Brook wanted to leave but didn't know how to put Greatorix off. He hesitated then sat down again, at least grateful that he wouldn't have to listen to any more banter.

"Chip?" Greatorix nodded at his plate and folded a laden forkful into his mouth.

"No thanks. Make it quick, Bob. I'm due at Forensics." Greatorix smiled as best he could, indicating his inability to respond through his food. Brook waited and watched.

Greatorix was about ten years older than Brook. And about eighty pounds heavier. He had a sagging face – misshapen by heavy jowls – which was constantly covered by a film of sweat, visible even through his thinning head of slicked back hair. He was a healthy – or should that be unhealthy? – perspirer and his clothes always appeared to be in a state of accelerated condensation.

It didn't help that he overdressed his ample frame to a ludicrous degree, the main culprit being the thick worsted overcoat, which he never removed, even in summer. His stained nylon shirt, which still had another couple of weeks to run, clung to a warm undergarment and, when the weather got really cold, below 20 degrees centigrade for instance, he had a tatty grey cardigan with overworked wooden buttons, which he wore to keep himself moist.

The curious thing was, he didn't smell. Everyone remarked on it behind his back. It had puzzled everyone at the station for years. Finally, Brook deduced that Greatorix wore so many layers precisely to keep the sweat and odour under wraps: a clear case of putting the coach before the horses.

"I was wondering if you'd like to swap cases. By rights the Wallis murders should have been mine, you know." Greatorix looked gravely at him before cracking into a bean-skinned smile. "Not a chance, eh? You wouldn't want to plough through my boring old croaker. Poor old dear" – pause for another mouthful, two mouthfuls by Brook's standards – "but I was thinking you might need some help."

"Oh? Have you closed yours then?"

"No. But it shouldn't take long, if it *can* be closed. Burglary gone wrong. We haven't got a lot to go on," he shrugged. "No, it's just...you seem a bit short of experience in your team. Apart from you obviously."

"That's the way the Chief wants it." Brook could smell something, something that surprised him though he knew it shouldn't; jealousy. Brook had drawn the glamour case, the one with all the exposure. Greatorix was left with the dud, a no-hope case of murder, an old biddy killed during a robbery – a common crime, of little intelligence and little interest to anybody. Nobody cared about Annie Sewell, least of all Detective Inspector Robert Greatorix.

Brook smiled suddenly. He could see the joke. The Wallis case was the last thing he wanted, the last case he would have chosen. He didn't want to rake over his past or work under the glare of public interest. Unlike Greatorix, Brook didn't see an opportunity for advancement, more a trapdoor to disaster.

But it was too late for regrets, too late to worry about jeopardising his rehabilitation. He was stuck with the Wallis case and now he couldn't let go. Not because he wanted it but because he was the only one who could crack it. He'd cracked it before, after all. He was destined to catch this killer, he knew that. And Fate had intervened to confirm it, sending Greatorix on a routine burglary gone sour, leaving the way clear for Brook to fulfil his date with destiny. A disturbing thought which had been kicking around in his subconscious mind for a while chose that moment to surface but he was unable to attend to it.

"Listen, Damen. There's been some muttering about the way *she's* handling things."

"There's always muttering, *Bob.*"

Greatorix held up a placatory hand, flicking chips onto the floor. "Don't get me wrong, inspector. I just want to help. I could be very useful. I've got contacts."

"That's the point – the Chief doesn't want the wrong people being contacted, getting their snouts into the trough and spreading alarm."

Greatorix stopped cutting and chewing. Brook had found his target. "What's that supposed to mean?"

Brook smiled and clambered to his feet. Bulls-eye! "I'll make a deal with you, Bob. You tell me what Brian Burton wants from you and I'll put in a word with McMaster." Brook walked away.

Greatorix glared at his back. "You're a real prick, you know that, Brook?" he spluttered towards the retreating figure. Brook turned.

"Of course I know."

"You'll never have any friends in this nick, you fucking toffee-nosed know-it-all. I was nabbing villains when you were still working out how to undo bras." Greatorix was standing now, shouting, almost apoplectic in his sudden rush of anger, but Brook had already gone. The canteen was hushed, waiting for Greatorix to come to his senses. Other people's problems were meat and drink to the social whirl of station life and nobody wanted to miss a thing.

After a few seconds, Greatorix flicked a glance round the room and sat down to contemplate the rest of his meal. When it was clear there would be no more gossip fodder, a likely lad at the front of the queue bawled out, "Encore!" to gales of laughter and derisive hoots.

Greatorix, who had a penchant for *le bon mot*, became even hotter under the collar and eyeballed the heckler. "And you can fuck off you big-nosed fucker!" he spat through a shower of greasy sputum to the accompaniment of even more hooting and the clutching of invisible handbags.

Chapter 10

It had started to rain by the time Brook and Noble arrived at the mortuary. They hurried inside and walked the short distance to Pathology.

A short man with a chubby, cheerful countenance and round pebble glasses hailed them. Although nearly sixty, like many Asians, Dr Habib's hair was still brown and his eyes soft and without wrinkles.

The green apron he wore sported dark stains as did the cranial blade of the saw he carried slightly behind his back, having just realised it wasn't the done thing to greet people holding an implement for cutting heads.

"Inspector Brook. And the faithful Sergeant Noble," he exclaimed, removing a face mask, unaware that his archaic turn of phrase had provoked the usual glance between the two officers. He went to shake hands before realising the potential hygiene risk and withdrew with a shrug. "How are you?"

"As well as ever, doctor."

"Oh dear. I'm sorry to hear it, inspector," he replied with a glint in his eye. "Still no improvement, eh?"

Brook let out a polite laugh. The jokes didn't get any better. "What have you got for us, doc?"

Habib tossed his bloodstained gloves into a disposal bin and turned into a small office. He washed his hands vigorously in a small sink before turning to rummage through a sheaf of papers. "The Wallis family. Bad business. Bad business. Do you want to see the bodies?"

"It can wait until the formal ID unless you've something you need to show us," answered Brook.

"Not really, not really. Fairly straightforward." He picked up some papers and skimmed through them before glancing up at Brook. "I think maybe you're looking for an Asian gentleman for this, no?"

Brook looked across at Noble and turned back to Habib. "Why do you say that?"

"Just a thought, inspector, but these killings seem to me very ceremonial, like the Halal ritual slaughter." Habib pierced him for a reaction.

"It's not figured in our profile yet. Interesting thought though."

"Statistically speaking, the majority of serial killers are white males, doctor," offered Noble.

"So they are," nodded Habib. "Just an idea. Well, let's see." Habib peered up from the manila folder. "Hmm. You're not going to like it, inspector."

"Try me."

"This gentleman must be the cleanest killer in history. He knows what he's doing. It's too early to be conclusive yet, we're still working on some things," he said shooting an apology towards Brook. "We're not exactly overstaffed, don't you know?" Brook smiled his under-standing.

"Well, let's see. Assuming it was a man," Habib glanced up at Brook in case of a rebuttal, "we're looking at a right-handed individual. Difficult to assess height as none of the victims were standing, though from the angle of the incisions on the two adults, I'd say the killer was medium height at best. No more than 1.72, 1.74 metres. Around 5-8 if you prefer old money. Possibly smaller.

"The weapon was very sharp with a thin blade, probably a scalpel because the incisions are too precise for most knives."

"Could it have been an old cut-throat razor, doctor?"

"Indeed yes, inspector, as long as it was well maintained. Now if I can just show you," he said, adopting the posture of the killer. "He cut from behind each of the victims from the left ear, through the trachea – the windpipe," he beamed at Noble, expecting his lower rank to be in possession of a lesser education, "and finishing at the right ear. Only the girl's windpipe was completely severed. The parents would have taken several minutes to lose consciousness as they still had partial breathing.

"There is... no sign of any sexual assault in either female or the male for that matter." Brook caught the hesitant note in Habib's voice and narrowed his eyes. "Interesting thing. There was no struggle from the victims at point of death and yet they weren't restrained or struck unconscious – I'll come back to that in a minute – and nothing under the nails, unless you include enough dirt to grow a field of potatoes."

"Most of us don't feel compelled to scrub up every fifteen minutes," observed Brook.

"Indeed it is so. What else? There were no alien fibres on any of the victims, no skin, no foreign hairs. He's been very careful. Assuming he has hair. Lots of people don't, you know."

"Most people have skin though," Noble chipped in.

The good doctor could only shrug. "Maybe your own forensics people can find something on the clothing. The parents had drunk a little wine before they died, if that helps. The killer must have drunk the rest. Not a surprise, it looked expensive..."

"How do you know he had a drink?" interrupted Brook.

"Because of the bottle." Brook and Noble showed no signs of enlightenment so Habib continued. "There isn't enough wine left, inspector."

"What do you mean?" asked Noble.

"I'm guessing, of course. I saw the bottle at the scene. Going by what was in the glasses and the minute amount ingested by the victims..."

Brook nodded. "If we add what's in the glasses to the bottle, some will be missing. More than Bobby and Mrs Wallis can account for." Habib smiled his assent. "Just because he left no trace of having drunk any wine, doesn't mean he didn't raise a glass of his own to celebrate then take it with him."

"Christ," muttered Noble.

"Only a small one. He wouldn't want to contravene Her Majesty's drink driving laws," added Habib, with a guilty chortle.

"No," agreed Brook. "He wouldn't want to get himself in *too* deep." He was pleased to see Noble taking offence. "Go on doctor."

"Well. Let's see." Habib adjusted his glasses. "The blood on the wall, the writing, is from the girl I think, AB negative, quite rare. Your lab people will have to confirm that as well but the smears on her neck indicate that someone has pushed their fingers into the wound."

"Have you got anything we can use to catch this man, doctor?" asked Noble impatiently.

Dr Habib smiled back at him. "Yes, yes. Of course. Two things, don't you know?" Habib removed his glasses and looked grim. "Bad business, bad business," he said shaking his head. "How old was the girl, inspector?"

"Eleven. Why?"

"Well, when I said there was no sign of sexual assault that wasn't strictly true."

"You mean she was raped."

"Oh no. I mean. Well yes. How can I put this?"

"Any way you like, doctor. As long as it's quick."

"Yes. The girl's hymen was no longer intact." Again Habib turned to Noble to spell it out for him. "She wasn't a virgin, sergeant."

"The bastard raped her!" said Noble, through gritted teeth.

"Yes, sergeant. As a minor, legally speaking, she must have been raped. But..."

Brook nodded. He knew where this was going. "But not last night."

Habib pointed his forefinger at Brook. "Exactly, Inspector Brook. It is just so."

"You mean...?" Noble was taking his time. He hadn't been around as long as Brook.

"Yes John. That's what he means."

"Who could do that?"

"Assuming the girl wasn't in a consensual sexual relationship..."

"She was eleven years old for Christ's sake," pleaded Noble.

"Well then."

"You mean her father...?"

"It fits John. There was a girl in one of the Reaper killings in London. The father was a pimp. She'd been sexually abused. Fathers and daughters John – it's an old song." Brook thought of Terri and just as quickly pushed it out of his mind. "And it would explain where Jason gets his own violent inclinations."

"I suppose," agreed Noble softly.

His incomprehension touched Brook, reminded him how young he was. Work. That was the only protection. "What was the second thing, doctor?"

"The second thing?" Habib had been momentarily distracted by the bad business. "Yes. You're looking for a medical man. An older, medical man, I would say: someone who may have access to a dispensary and has a sophisticated knowledge of drugs. Remember there was no struggle? There was a good reason. All the victims were poisoned – Scopolamine, sometimes called Hyoscine. It's a narcotic and mydriatic. It induces sleepiness and dilation of the pupil..." he added for Noble's benefit. "...in the eye."

"There are also traces of morphine. Doses are very difficult to get right so he'd have to know what he was doing. We've found traces ingested by all the victims. It could have been administered in powdered extract on top of the pizzas. It would look a bit like parmesan cheese or salt. From the stomach contents I'd say the girl ate from only one pizza, the parents had pieces of them all – they had pepperoni, prawns, ham – in their stomachs."

"Anything else?"

"There was enough to kill, which is rare with Scopolamine, but I'm supposing this wouldn't be too big a problem for him. They wouldn't have been able to ingest it all before they started feeling unwell, so the parents didn't receive a fatal dose. However, it would take a lot less to kill the girl and she would probably have died whether her throat was cut or not."

"And would it paralyse them?" asked Brook.

"Most likely. If conscious they'd find it quite difficult to move, though not impossible. They'd be seriously disorientated, somnolent and delirious."

"Why do you say an older man?" asked Noble.

"Because of the history of the two drugs. Scopolamine used to be combined with morphine as an anaesthetic but that was many years ago, before the Second World War. It induced an effect known as Twilight Sleep. The same procedure was used in childbirth in the sixties but it fell out of use because the patient would be conscious but unable to feel or move which often caused complications. The parents had a larger dose than the girl. It's almost as if he knew which pizza they were going to eat."

"He did," said Noble. "He rang to take their orders."

"Blimey! This gentleman's very good."

"Would it affect the vocal chords?"

"Indeed it is so, inspector. How would you know that?"

"They weren't gagged."

"That's right. They would have been suffering from laryngeal paralysis." Habib turned to explain himself to Noble but was halted by a raised hand.

"I understand," he countered.

"Quite so, sergeant," Habib nodded. "Although in this case, suffered is the wrong word." Brook was broken from his thoughts. "They wouldn't have felt much. A mild discomfort, perhaps, even when they were cut open."

"They didn't suffer?"

"Very unlikely."

"Well done Wendy...PC Jones," Brook muttered in appreciation before glancing covertly at Noble to see if his carelessness had registered. It appeared not. "Anything else, doc?"

"Not for the moment. I'll let you have my report as soon as it's typed up. We're short-staffed..."

"Thank you doctor. We'll take a break before the ID. Let you get on with things."

Brook started to follow Noble before turning back to the doctor.

He hesitated and looked to the retreating Noble, who held the door for him before realising Brook wasn't behind him.

"Get me a coffee, would you John? There's a machine round the corner."

Brook waited for him to disappear before facing the expectant Habib. "Doctor." He hesitated again. He was about to commit a severe breach of protocol. If he wasn't careful he wouldn't have any friends left in the Force. "Inspector Greatorix asked me to run my eye over the Annie Sewell case, if it's ready. I know you're short-staffed…" he interjected to forestall yet another airing for Habib's favourite topic.

"Bad business, inspector. Bad business. Do you want to give him the report? I've got it here," he said rummaging for another folder.

"Well no. He said to take a photocopy and to be sure not to tell him that I'd got one." Brook spoke as emphatically as required and lifted his eyebrows into a quizzical half-smile. Dr Habib stopped and looked at him carefully to make sure he hadn't misunderstood. Then he broke into a broad eighteen-carat grin.

"Inspector Brook, you're such a naughty boy, very naughty indeed. Take this one," he said shaking his head in amused disbelief. "I have other copies. But if he finds out…" he shouted at Brook's back.

Brook raised a hand to acknowledge.

"Problem sir?" Noble gingerly held out the hot liquid in the too-thin cup.

"Not at all, John. Just thought I'd better tell the good doctor not to suggest looking for an elderly Asian medical expert in his final report. We wouldn't want him ending up in a cell, would we? Throw that garbage away, John. Are you trying to give me heartburn?"

They walked back to the main entrance and stepped outside. The rain had stopped for the moment though the sky was still leaden. Brook looked at his watch. "Young Wallis is due in half an hour. Who's with him?"

"DC Gadd, sir."

"Right. And Mrs Harrison?"

"Coming under her own steam. She knows the way, she's a nurse."

"Fine. We'll wait. There's a chuck wagon in the car park. We'll have a proper cup of tea. My treat."

*

Brook walked next to Habib, followed by DC Gadd, petite and pretty with short, bobbed blond hair and pert features, guiding a handcuffed Jason Wallis with one hand. His aunt, a portly woman in the mould of her dead sister, walked on the other side of Jason. She seemed preoccupied but, being a nurse, was inevitably calmer than most faced with such an ordeal. Noble brought up the rear, next to the social worker, Carly Graham, and the duty solicitor who had picked up Jason's case.

Brook glanced over his shoulder at Wallis with a mixture of satisfaction and pity. The cockiness was gone and he was concentrating hard on the floor. The baby was back, trembling below the surface, ready to bawl.

Carly Graham detached herself from the back and quick-marched to speak to Brook. "Inspector…"

"Nice to see you again, Miss Graham." He held out his hand to shake hers.

"Inspector, can I speak to you?"

Brook slowed to listen. "No problem."

"Is it necessary that Jason be handcuffed?"

Brook looked aghast then smiled appreciatively at Miss Graham. "Miss Graham, I hadn't realised. Thank you for mentioning it. Constable Gadd. Why is Jason handcuffed? I don't think that's necessary. He's not going anywhere." DC Gadd raised an eyebrow and looked over at Noble who looked away. Then she removed the handcuffs from Jason who massaged his wrists in time-honoured fashion. "I'm sorry about that Miss Graham – crossed wires somewhere along the line."

"Thank you, inspector."

"No thank *you* for pointing it out, Carly. May I call you Carly?" She flushed and Brook beamed at her. "Sometimes official procedures can be quite heartless."

Brook turned and caught Noble's amused eye. Then he looked at the boy and felt a pang of guilt. This was tough on him. Perhaps, no matter what he was or what he'd done, he didn't deserve what had happened to him. Then Brook remembered the face of hate from the hospital, remembered the ordeal of the teacher threatened with rape. Unless something was done, Jason Wallis would end up like his father.

The thought of Bobby Wallis – and Kylie – brought Terri and her stepfather to mind. Brook tried to clear it away. Then something else drifted into his mind. He thought of Laura Maples again – for once outside of his dreams. Perhaps seeing her necklace again…or perhaps being in a mortuary with grieving relatives…

*

103

DS Brook stopped at the end of the corridor and stood in front of the door, barring the way, arms outstretched like a bouncer outside a nightclub. "This isn't necessary Mr Maples. Your wife…"

Maples turned his heavy-set face to Brook and fixed him with his bloodshot eyes. The silence was massive here. No longer the distraction of footsteps clattering around the white-tiled walls. No more the need for monosyllabic clichés to divert the mind. There was nothing now to drown the well-mannered snuffling being suffocated behind Mrs Maples' handkerchief – it was rude to impose grief on others where they came from. Grief was private tragedy, not public embarrassment.

Suddenly aware of the genteel noise being suppressed by his wife, Maples turned and hugged her to his chest. She was tiny, diminished against her husband, who wasn't tall himself. It was as though she were folding in on herself to touch the parts that mattered. Her spirit. Her womb.

Then Maples held his wife away from him and bent his head close to hers. "It's okay love. You stay here, Jean." She didn't reply, or couldn't, so he guided her to a nearby bench and eased her down. The sobbing was hushed a little, as though the prospect of not seeing revived hope. Perhaps their daughter was still missing. Alive somewhere. Happy.

Maples stood up to face Brook as best he could. His forehead was creased in pain and confusion. His greying hair was wilder than the rest of his appearance. Even for this, or perhaps especially for this, Maples wore a neat, slate-grey suit with a pale yellow shirt and dark green tie, knotted harshly into his flabby chin.

"Not necessary, sergeant? Not necessary? Do you have children?"

Brook nodded. "A baby girl, sir. Theresa." Brook felt a sudden rush of shame. His daughter was alive. Laura Maples was dead. There was no call to goad the poor man with his good fortune.

Maples nodded back. His eyes pierced Brook and a bitter smile sympathised with him. They shared the look that spoke of secret dread, the dread that gripped all fathers of daughters.

Words weren't required for Brook but they were for Maples. "We haven't seen Laura for over a year. We can't stop the images unless we see her, I see her. She's all we have and whatever condition she's in, we want to talk to her. Then we want to take her home with us. Lay her to rest. Does that sound unnecessary?"

Brook acquiesced with a prolonged blink of his eyes. He understood very well. Her dental records couldn't bring comfort. Her parents might. They could be a family again.

Brook opened the double doors to the tiny Chapel of Rest,

tucked away in one corner of the sprawl of Hammersmith Hospital. The technician, who had stood apart during all the heart-wrenching, head bowed, hands clasped in front, the professional invisible, moved forward at Brook's nod and eased himself between Maples and the cheap coffin perched on the plinth at the far end of the chamber.

With practised ease he removed the lid and stood back, head bowed, into the shadows. Brook watched from the door as Maples inched forward.

A few feet from the coffin, he staggered slightly then fell forward onto the container. He turned away then looked back. His shoulders began to shudder and his head began to shake. Brook heard, "Why did you leave us love?" and stepped outside the door. He beckoned the mortician to join him. The mortician obeyed without looking up or unclasping his hands.

Eventually Maples walked out of the chapel, his face blank, eyes like small planets. "Mr Maples, I'm very sorry. If there's anything I can do..."

Maples turned, wild-eyed, tears trickling down his face. He nodded, emitting a bitter laugh. "There is. Lock your daughter in a room and keep her there until her wedding day."

*

Brook stepped over to Jason and took him by the sleeve. "That's far enough Jason. You and Miss Graham can wait here until we're done." Jason heaved a sigh and leaned back against the wall. He continued to look at the floor until the attendant arrived and opened the double doors of the mortuary. Unfortunately Brook had positioned Jason a few feet too near the entrance and when the doors opened his head lifted towards the sudden shaft of bright sunlight from the high windows which streamed across three sheet-covered mounds. His lip began to quiver and Brook motioned Gadd and the duty solicitor to stay with Jason, while he, Noble, Mrs Harrison and the attendant slipped quickly into the bright room, closing the doors behind them.

Dr Habib had returned to his office. The mortuary attendant stood ready. Noble and Brook hung back, looking at each other rather than towards the bodies.

One by one, Mrs Harrison, head bowed, was shown the bodies. No words were exchanged, just a look from the attendant and a nod back from the nurse towards Brook.

Only when the smallest mound was revealed to Mrs Harrison did her composure begin to crumble. She turned towards Brook and nodded then she bowed her head again and began to sob gently. "Poor Kylie," she gulped. "She didn't deserve to die like that."

Brook opened the door before Mrs Harrison rejoined them. Jason was still outside so Brook pulled the door back as far as he could to let him see the re-covered corpses. "Jason, why don't you wait outside in the fresh air?" If Jason heard, he didn't react. Instead he stared, saucer-eyed, beyond Brook towards the stainless steel trolleys, eyes wide but not appearing to see.

Then Jason clamped his eyes shut and began to pant. Brook grabbed his arm and held it tight, feeling him trying to peel away. He felt Jason shivering beneath his grubby jacket and guided him away from the piercing winter sunlight back towards the gloom of the corridor. Then the boy started to sob. Carly Graham appeared at Jason's other arm to help support him.

Out in the cold air, Jason could hold his stomach no longer and he ran behind a parked car to vomit hard and heavy. Eventually he was able to stand upright. DC Gadd produced a bottle of water and helped him locate his mouth around it.

Brook offered him one of Noble's cigarettes, which he accepted and smoked urgently. From time to time he would spit to expunge any stray morsels of his last meal. He wouldn't, couldn't speak.

Brook watched him, guilt tugging at him. He felt sorry for the lad now but was still pleased with the result. That was the reaction he wanted. The reaction that showed him not only had Jason not killed his family – which he knew – but that in there, somewhere deep inside his layers of hatred and mistrust, Jason was hiding a proper person, someone who could distinguish right from wrong, someone who knew how to treat others and could be a useful member of society. Perhaps it wasn't too late for Jason. Perhaps he could be saved. Saved? Brook nodded. Saved. The writing was on the wall.

Gadd and Noble stood by the car talking in low tones. Brook directed Jason to it. DC Gadd prepared the cuffs.

"There's no need for that, constable. He's no longer under arrest. Take Jason and Mrs Harrison home."

"Yes sir." She opened a door for the stricken youth and he scrambled inside. Carly Graham got in beside him, clucking and patting and talking in low tones designed to bring comfort.

As DC Gadd drove away, Brook looked after her. "Nice girl that. You should ask her out, John."

"Not my type," he replied. "So young Wallis is off the hook?"

"Not completely, John. We may still need to interview him. About the drugs and the cash. But it'll keep."

Brook walked up the path towards the neat red brick semi, admiring the garden as he went. The house was for sale but it was clear from the loving care that had gone into the garden that the move was a reluctant one. He glanced next door at the two decaying cars perched on piles of bricks in the front yard, a large black and white cat watching Brook and Noble from the bonnet of one.

Brown paint peeled from a front window. A grimy curtain blocked the view into the house, sparing further blushes, if shame the residents felt.

The contrast with the house Brook approached now was stark. The Ottomans were clearly proud of their little empire and had done a lot with what they had, a corner house with a larger than average garden.

The small lawn was manicured and the flowerbeds were free of weeds. The hedges were trimmed, save the one that adjoined the neighbouring property, which had been allowed to grow tall to blot out the view. The garage was in a good state of repair too, with newly painted doors. A shiny Nissan snuggled between the open doors and a Volkswagen sat on the drive, minus its badge.

Even the gate, which Noble was now closing behind him, had been carefully maintained. It opened and closed without a sound save the click of the latch. As Brook neared the house, a slight man, about five-six, mid-forties, was scrambling to his feet with a small basket of weeds, pulled from cracks between the stone flags of the path. He looked round at Brook's approach.

"Mr Ottoman?"

The man narrowed his eyes against the wintry sun. He nodded as he spoke. "Ay. And you'd be the police I suppose."

"DI Brook, and this is DS Noble," said Brook offering his ID which Ottoman took longer than was polite to examine.

"You're here about the Wallis murders."

"What makes you say that, sir?" inquired Noble.

"Well you showed bugger all interest in what that bastard, Jason Wallis, did to my Denise so unless you've come about some other..."

"Quite right, sir," Brook interrupted. "We've come about a crime that's been committed, Mr Ottoman. Not one that's been threatened."

"Threatened? That bastard..."

"Can we go inside, sir?" asked Noble with counter-balancing charm. "We shouldn't be discussing this outside."

Mr Ottoman hesitated and then gave in to a lifetime's training. "I'm sorry. Yes. It's been a difficult time. Come in. My wife's making tea. She hasn't...she's been under a lot of strain."

"Of course she has, sir. We understand."

"She's not been back to work then?" inquired Brook, still looking around. He glanced at the upper storey of the house in time to see a curtain fall.

"She's signed off until after Easter, inspector. She's had a nervous breakdown. You've no idea what that's like." Brook allowed himself a thin smile and snaked a glance at Noble to check his reaction. There was none.

Ottoman showed them through a small spotless kitchen and into the equally well-ordered lounge then went to the bottom of the stairs. "Denise. We've got visitors."

Brook and Noble sat and waited. Denise Ottoman evidently came down the stairs, Brook could hear the descending chord of each step, but she declined to come into the lounge. Instead she went into the kitchen to her husband. After some hushed conversation, she emerged a moment later behind Mr Ottoman, carrying a tray of four cups.

She was a plain woman of about forty, a little taller than her husband. Her hair was dark and long with grey flashes and was swept to the back of her head to be held by a grip. She wore slacks and loafers with large socks crumpled around her ankles and wore a very baggy woollen polo neck, which completely swallowed any figure she might have had.

All the while her husband's eyes followed her progress, like a new parent monitoring the first faltering steps of an infant.

Denise Ottoman placed the tray on a coffee table, declining, at first, to look up from the floor. Until she discovered her cigarettes were missing. Then her face became frantic and she cast her eyes around the room for them, a rising panic bubbling to the surface of her emotions.

Brook recognised the symptoms. The shock of innocence removed in one brutal corruption, her vision of the world soiled and crumbled to dust at her feet. She now had "victim" written all over her, though not in red lipstick. Brook had seen it all too often and reached swiftly into Noble's pocket to offer her one of his cigarettes.

She looked up at him now with her red-rimmed eyes, grateful. "Thank you." She lit up and they all sat at Mr Ottoman's bidding. Denise Ottoman coughed up smoke as elegantly as she could. She was not a smoker.

"What can we do for you?" asked Mr Ottoman. He looked at Brook and then at his wife in turn. Brook stared back at Ottoman and waited for Noble to speak.

"Well, sir, we just wanted to..." Noble's pre-arranged hesitation worked perfectly. Brook was a fine teacher.

"You want to know if I'll confess to the Wallis murders. Am I right?"

Brook smiled. "Not at all."

"Then why are you here?" asked Mrs Ottoman. Her voice was little more than a squeak.

Brook turned his gaze to her. His voice exuded a detachment he didn't feel. "We're here to eliminate you from our enquiries, Mrs Ottoman." She looked away and Brook felt her pain. He didn't enjoy this but it was his job. To be sure he got the truth he always pushed people as hard as he could, even when convinced of their innocence. "Although you have a powerful motive for wishing harm on Jason Wallis, and possibly Mr Wallis, we're certain you or your husband didn't commit murder. But there are formalities. We'd like you to tell us where you both were on Monday night so we can close the book on it."

"We were here, inspector."

"All night?" chipped in Noble.

"Of course all night, sergeant. Where would we go on a Monday night in winter, in Derby?

"Just the two of you?"

Ottoman looked at his wife who resumed her examination of the floor. "Just the two of us."

"And what did you do?"

"Do, inspector?"

"Yes."

"We watched television."

"All night?"

"All night. Every night."

"What did you watch?" asked Noble.

Ottoman smiled for the first time. For Noble it was an odd thing to do. But Brook recognised the impulse behind it.

"I haven't the faintest idea. You see, when I say we watched television, what I mean is my wife sits on the sofa sobbing herself to sleep, unable to let me near her. And I sit here staring at the TV, unblinking, not listening, not taking notice of what's on, not even realising it is on. It's just white noise to me but more comforting than hearing my wife cry or the sound of blood throbbing in my ears."

Denise Ottoman ran from the room. Brook heard the soft gulping noise trail into the kitchen before giving way to a more vivid wailing. Noble stirred to go after her but Brook stopped him with a motion of his hand.

"Do you understand? There's nothing else we can do. We can't go out, we can't have friends round. We can't have a bloody life. I can't even go to work without Denise ringing me to say she's heard a noise..."

"I see..."

"No you don't see, inspector. You don't know what that animal did to her."

"She was threatened sir," chipped in Noble, at once seeing the reproving look on his superior's face.

"Threatened? My wife is on tranquillisers. That bastard got her by the throat and pushed her back onto the desk. Then he forced himself on top of her, laughing, running his hands over..."

"I'm sorry." Noble's attempt to retrieve the situation was in vain.

"My wife was terrified. She couldn't move. She could feel him...lying on her...ready..." Mr Ottoman looked down at the floor and wrung his hands. His voice had softened as though he were confessing to a priest. He looked up briefly. "He would have, you know, if..."

"You don't have to relive this, Mr Ottoman. You've told us where you were. That's all we came for."

There was a long silence before Ottoman could manage, "Sorry."

"Don't be. When things like this force their way into your life it can be a shock to the system. You will get over it. Trust me."

"Get over it?"

Brook looked at Noble, inviting him to get up but Ottoman's voice made him pause.

"Do you know what the worst thing was?"

"Tell me."

"When he was on top of...my...wife...he turned to the other kids, kids Denise has known and helped, some of them for four years, and said, *"Who's after me?"* And you know what they did? They laughed. They laughed and cheered. They thought it was *funny*. Even the girls. Maybe they were just glad it was her and not them, I don't know but...what's happening to people, inspector? At the risk of sounding Victorian, things...it didn't used to be like this. What happened?"

"I don't know."

All this time Ottoman had been staring into space. Now he engaged Brook's eyes. "She can't go back you know. Twenty years of her life and she can never go back. Never. Can you imagine it? Standing in front of that bunch of animals, trying to help them. Can you imagine the message that sends? Can you? Yeah. Fuck me over any way you want. I'm a teacher. I'll take it because I'm worthless." He paused for a second and ran his fingers through his hair before looking back at

Brook. "Sorry. There's no excuse for that language."

"Don't be. We're not nuns."

Ottoman laughed without mirth. "Do you want to know another thing? That piece of shit could be back at school the week after next if the appeal goes his way, which it will, after what's happened. Sympathy vote."

Brook stood with an air of finality, Noble following suit. "I see no reason to trouble you again, Mr Ottoman. I'm sorry for the intrusion. Thanks for the tea."

"Inspector." Ottoman remained seated, looking at the floor. "Is it true what the papers said? About poor Kylie, I mean. Having her throat cut."

"Yes but she didn't…" Noble was cut short by his superior's interruption.

"Didn't stand a chance. It was a terrible sight." Mrs Ottoman was standing by the door now, wrestling a handkerchief around white knuckles. She gave a little whimper. Mr Ottoman was grave and narrowed his eyes in a good approximation of suffering. "She begged for her life but it didn't do any good. I shouldn't be telling you this." Brook hoped that under their current level of stress the Ottomans wouldn't spot such an obvious lie. They didn't show it if they did.

Mrs Ottoman looked at her husband who shook his head. "Poor kid," he said with a sigh. "She didn't deserve that. Not when her brother is still alive. Her classmates are devastated, absolutely devastated."

"Classmates?" inquired Brook with an arch of the eyebrow.

"Yes. I'm her teacher, as you know. *Was* her teacher." He corrected himself. Brook glanced at Noble without expression. Noble was less able to hide his surprise. "Well one of them. Not her form teacher. She's in my literacy group. I teach at Drayfin Lane Primary, when I'm not on leave to look after my wife." He held out an arm for her to slip under which she did after the briefest indecision.

"Yes." Brook nodded. "Devastated."

※

"What do you think?" asked Noble in the car.

"Ottoman teaching Kylie Wallis? Interesting coincidence. Though that's probably all it is."

"There's something wrong about those two, don't you think?"

"They're married, John. What could possibly be right?"

Noble emitted a curt laugh. "I don't mean that, sir. I mean…"

111

"I know what you mean. You mean the house and the garden."
Brook nodded absent-mindedly.

Noble covered his blank look well but when Brook refused to
elaborate he had to concede his ignorance. "What about them?"

"So neat. Well organised."

Chapter 11

Brook closed the door to his flat with mixed feelings. On the one hand, he was grateful for the chance to cut himself off from the world, on the other, secretly dreading the invasion of private thoughts. Poor Terri. He'd barely thought about his daughter all day, cut his emotions off at the knees, absorbing himself in his work until he could do no more. What kind of father was he?

But now he was home, alone with nothing else to distract him, at the mercy of images of his daughter and her stepfather. His daughter, little Terri, in bed...

Brook pressed the play button on the flashing answering machine. Someone had called but there was no message. He tried 1471 and recognised the Brighton code although it wasn't the Harvey-Ellis home number. He dialled and waited.

"*This is Hall Gordon Public Relations. Our office hours...*"

Brook rang off and re-dialled. "Who's that? DC Morton. Can you get me an address? It's in Brighton. Hall Gordon Public Relations. I'll hold." He grabbed a pen and paper. A few moments later he jotted it down and replaced the receiver.

He thought for a moment, staring at the address then made a decision. He looked round for the folder he'd been reviewing the night before and suddenly realised, with a jolt, it was gone. He'd left it on the table, next to the phone. There was a note instead.

> *Thanks again for your generous offer. I've nipped out for some food (you've only got penicillin cultures in the fridge) and I'll do the cooking. My treat.*
> *Vicky.*
> *P.S. Love the cat.*

Now Brook saw the girl's carpetbag on the sofa. He'd forgotten about his spur-of-the-moment offer that morning. Stupid! Or perhaps he'd been shrewd. Perhaps he'd invited her to share the lonely hours, deflect him from himself and thoughts of his daughter. And it wasn't all bad. She loved Cat and she was intelligent. She could spell penicillin and use apostrophes. Most young people whose writing Brook encountered, petty criminals and fresh-faced coppers, ground out statements like they were pulling teeth. Even then Brook would have to skip through them and correct all the text message spellings. Apostrophes were something to sling on any word ending in S. Just in case. In a few years the English language would be dead. Ageing rappers would be the new English teachers. 4 shore.

Brook saw the folder on the floor next to the sofa and leapt over to it. A cursory check revealed nothing missing – as far as he could tell. There'd been a lot of loose stuff in there – he might have forgotten. At least Laura's necklace was there. He took it out of the folder and put it in his trouser pocket, then slipped the address he'd jotted down into the front of the straining folder.

Brook felt ashamed. He was getting old. Paranoid. Of course she'd moved it. She'd shifted everything but the phone, ready for a meal. There were Brook's two spoons and forks – from odd sets – two glasses, one with a stem, the other a tumbler, looking as though they'd been cleaned, of all things. She'd also brought in the salt and pepper, a cheap, if matching set he'd filched from the Police canteen.

Brook went to his room and threw the folder onto his bed then pulled a small suitcase from underneath. He opened it and tossed in sufficient clothes for a two or three night stay. For once he took a little more care over his selection without really understanding why. Finally he closed the case, took it out to the Mondeo and, with a guilty glance over at the Sprite slipped it into the boot along with his bulging file. The old thing wouldn't have made it down the M1. Not in a million years. He wasn't betraying the old bucket he was saving it.

He smiled at this justification. Only children attributed personality to inanimate objects – like a little girl with a doll. The image returned him to Terri but, just as quickly, he pushed her away again.

Before he closed the boot, Brook took out the two slim folders from Dr Habib and put them in his room – a little light reading for the early hours.

There was another folder from the Forensics lab. He left it where it was. He'd already had the potted version. The wine glasses were clean and too common to be traceable to a particular shop. Serology confirmed that there were no traces of saliva in the wine, other than the Wallis parents.

There were no fingerprints in the blood on the wall and no glove prints. The killer wore latex gloves, which on rare occasions can be identified by the microscopic imperfections built into them during manufacture. But, of course, they needed the gloves to obtain a match.

Minute traces of talcum powder, to stop hands becoming too sweaty, were found around the room and on the victims, confirming the use of gloves. If delivering food, nobody would notice the difference between those and looser, food-handling gloves.

The story was the same with other fibres and hair. There was an abundance of foreign samples and several hairs different to the victims, but without fibres or hairs from the killer, a match couldn't be made. It would take weeks just to separate and identify the many different samples, with no telling how long ago they were deposited on the victims or in the house. Until a suspect was identified or an arrest made it was just a case of bureaucratic evidence collection and going through the motions.

Footprints were the same. There were dozens – so many marks across the film of blood particles on the carpet that they were almost indistinguishable. There were blood traces in the downstairs corridor and the path but these too had been compromised by other shoe patterns.

One of the SOCOs told Noble they were going to sort them out with an Electrostatic Mat borrowed from Nottinghamshire but although Brook didn't say it, he didn't see much point. Eventually they would find a usable footprint, but they had no suspect to match it to and Brook had no doubt that everything the killer wore at the Wallis house would have been destroyed by now. If they found the van they would be able to distinguish which set of footprints belonged to the killer more quickly but that would only get them a shoe size and just maybe some identifiable fibres, but to compare against what? No suspect, no comparison. And given the care and planning that had gone into this, Brook thought it highly unlikely there'd be fingerprints in the van.

The hospital report on Aktar and Jason's stomach contents matched the forensic examination of the pizzas. Habib had been right. All the victims had scopolamine poisoning with traces of morphine. It was all beginning to chime. A well-organised and sophisticated killer had struck in Derby. Apart from that they had nothing.

He looked at his watch – nearly seven. He decided to shower and shave quickly before Vicky returned from wherever she'd gone to pick up food. It was dark and cold and, in spite of himself, he worried about her being out alone in a strange city. Brook recognised the irony with a bitter narrowing of the eyes. He worried about other people's daughters while not daring to think of his own.

*

Brook emerged from a tepid shower fifteen minutes later. Still no Vicky. Despite wet hair, he threw on a flimsy T-shirt and a pair of jogging pants and walked out to the main road, hoping to catch a glimpse of her. She strode into view almost at once, waving one of her shopping bags and smiling broadly. The taxi that had dropped her off screamed away. Brook caught a flash of baseball cap pulled low. He followed the car with his eyes as discreetly as he could. Most minicabs in central Derby were P-reg saloons, but this had a recent plate and looked shiny and powerful.

"Are you mad?" she said, catching sight of his attire.

Brook grabbed one of her bags, glancing inside. Pasta sauce, spaghetti, wine, breadsticks. There was a bill in there, which he pocketed without her seeing. "I was born in Yorkshire which makes me a couple of notches tougher than anybody else," he beamed back at her. "Or just plain stupid."

"That'll come in handy when you taste my cooking then." As she laughed she threw back her head and moved her jaw up and down as though she were attempting to sink a yard of ale. Her hair shimmered in the half-light thrown onto her from the street lamps and her teeth sparkled like distant galaxies. Brook found it a gladdening sight after the tensions of the last few days and, for a few seconds, he felt light-hearted, without a care in the world, like a teenager on a date, his sole worry, how to impress a beautiful girl.

*

Vicky pushed her fork to the side and let out a sigh. She was a very poor eater even compared to Brook, who'd finished five minutes before. She threw down her wine, however, and Brook recharged her glass for the third time and went to open the second bottle of Rioja.

He returned having quietly slipped the cash she'd spent at Sainsbury's into her beaded purse. They talked for a while longer. Jones was picking him up to go to London at six in the morning but Brook found it hard to terminate pleasant human contact and he got the impression she felt the same way. She seemed to carry the same submerged pain as Brook, the same hunger for companionship. And

116

thus far, she hadn't tried to steer the conversation around to the case, which he'd half-expected. Perhaps she'd had a look through the file and that had been sufficient.

"I almost forgot, Vicky," said Brook, raising his glass. "Congratulations. I assume." She smiled vacantly for a moment, unclear as to his meaning. "I'm assuming you've been offered a place... at the university."

Light dawned. "Oh...yes. Thank you. I was but I turned it down." She smiled thinly. After a moment's hesitation she added, "I didn't like the campus."

"I'm not surprised," nodded Brook. "All that red brick."

"Horrible, isn't it?" she replied, thinking she was on solid ground. She'd failed the simplest bluff.

Brook smiled. "Truly horrible." Now he was curious. What was the girl doing in Derby? She hadn't been to the university that was clear. "Where will you try now?"

"I don't know. I'll go home first. Think about my options."

"Where's home?"

"London."

"Whereabouts in London?" Brook tried to sound interested and not pushy.

She hesitated, appearing to realise Brook was trying to hurry her, stop her thinking up more lies. "Fulham."

"Fulham. That's North London, isn't it?"

"South-west – though north of the river."

"Is it? I don't know London very well, I'm afraid."

Brook didn't quite know where he was hoping to go with this. He only knew there was now a tension about her which was making the atmosphere awkward. Perhaps she knew he was lying. After all, she claimed to have seen him on TV, at the press briefing, and Brian Burton had mentioned Brook's link to the Reaper's London killings. Had she remembered? Had she made the connection?

And Fulham. How big a coincidence was that? Not very, he surmised. The Brooks had left Fulham a few months after the slaughter in Harlesden. She couldn't have been very old in 1990, even assuming she was lying about her age now. There was nothing to tie her to any of the Reaper murders. Except that she was here now – in Derby. Why?

Brook yawned. Leave it. "Well. Thank you for a lovely meal."

"You're welcome. Thanks for letting me stay." She drained her glass once more and reached for a refill, the awkward moment past.

"I have to be up early for work tomorrow." He stood with an air of finality, gathering crockery.

"Would you wake me up? There's an early train I'd like to be on."

"No problem." Brook pondered offering Vicky a lift back to London but decided against it. He wanted to brief Wendy Jones about the case and about the first Reaper killings in London, before they arrived. He might also have to tell her about his intention to visit Brighton to see his daughter and it would be difficult with a stranger in the back seat.

"Are you sure you won't let me wash up?" After the best part of two bottles of wine, she was beginning to slur her words. She gave Brook a very sexy and submissive smile, which he managed to ignore. Just.

"A deal's a deal," he smiled back and trotted off to the kitchen.

*

Brook took his time with the washing up. He was determined to finish only when all the pre-sleep bathroom noises had finished.

Twenty minutes later, all was quiet. Having dried and put away the dishes for the first time in years, he brushed his teeth and went to bed. As he opened the door to his bedroom, he was drawn by a crack of light from the living room. That door had never been easy to close. He reached for the handle softly but before he could pull it closed, a movement caught his eye and he lifted his gaze, just for a second. It was a second too long.

His trained eye took in all there was to see before he knew he was looking. The sleeping bag lay on the plastic sofa. Vicky wasn't in it. She sat naked on the edge of the sofa, her back to him, framed against the light, brushing her long blonde hair, which fell between chiselled shoulder blades. Brook could hear the rush of the hair through the bristles as she stroked. This Venus de Milo had arms.

He gazed for what could only have been seconds but felt like hours. If the chronometer timing the ache in his chest were anything to go by, he could have been watching this girl, performing her centuries-old ritual, since the beginning of time.

Brook wanted to break away but couldn't. Life stood before him. Life as it should be. Naked, innocent, just being, acting not thinking, not wasting a second on anything other than its own glorification. No worries, no problems, no artifice, no past, no future. Life, her life, bathed in cheap light and burnished it, allowed it to caress her, rejoiced in it as though it were the light of Heaven.

Brook watched, out of himself, as though watching himself watch her. It seemed he was part of her performance and she knew he was

118

there. As God needs the Devil, she needed him. There could be no light without shadow. She was life. He was death, waiting in the dark, outside looking in, an observer not a player, wanting, yearning to sully, to corrupt, to kill innocence and feed guilt.

Brook exhaled a querulous sigh from the depths of his soul. Suddenly he felt his misery deeply. He could taste the stale breath of unhappiness leaving his lungs. If only it were that easy to expel. But it could never be. Were he to exhale his pain, he knew he couldn't survive for he breathed little else. It was the only fuel his body knew.

A second, a minute, a day, a year, a lifetime later Brook felt a tear roll down his face. It caught the upturn of his upper lip and meandered toward his cheek before turning into his Rioja-stained mouth. His hand still held the doorknob but lightly. The sweat was loosening his hold so he let go ready to move away. A draught cooled his hot palm.

Where he prepared, she acted and a single alabaster breast turned its proud profile to Brook, its peach-fuzz curve trapped against the luminescence beyond.

He could stand it no more.

He wiped the rivulet from his face and turned. Time to return to his sarcophagus. He summoned a "Goodnight" from somewhere, trying to sound bland over the spluttering, and pushed into his room without switching on the light. He tore off his clothes down to vest and underpants and jumped into bed, clamping his eyes firmly shut as his mum had taught him in his sun-kissed infancy, lest the Bogey Man came to call. Within seconds he was asleep, or what approximated sleep for Damen Brook, a twilight existence of mumbled nightmares tearing at the fabric of his brain.

But even unconscious, Brook could still dredge a measure of solace from the case. His case. Nobody else could have it. It was up to him now.

Chapter 12

Detective Sergeant Brook checked the address in his pad – 12 Queensdale Road – and nodded. Very smart. And not divided into flats either. Whoever owned this pile was sitting on a small fortune.

Brook counted four storeys. Below stairs a small front garden gave way to a neat basement room. It had a freshly painted grill over the window and Brook could make out polished wooden floors through the glass. To his right, at ground level, a tiny balcony, home to dozens of pot plants. It guarded a large bay with lace-curtained French windows. Ivy clung to the stone above, hanging down to obscure Brook's view through the lace. He could just make out the folding screen, which further cocooned the occupants from the outside world.

Two large sash windows looked out from the floor above. Again, both seemed freshly painted and were surrounded by ivy.

The top floor was harder to see but he could make out a circular window, rather like a porthole, only larger. The top half of the window had been opened into the room beyond.

Brook raised a hand to the old-fashioned brass bell-pull but hesitated a moment for no reason he could think of, and stepped back. This was a big house in a pricey area, just off Holland Park Avenue. It didn't make sense. This sort of house had never been on Sammy Elphick's CV. He was seriously small time and this was way off his turf. All the stolen goods recovered from Elphick's flat had been traced, where possible, to small properties in Harlesden and Willesden Green.

Brook shrugged. It was the last call on the list. After this, all the long shots were played out. The enquiry was dead. It had been running on fumes for weeks, as it was. They had no forensic, no witnesses, no motive and no suspects.

Suddenly Brook could hear faint strains of music coming from the circular window. He listened. Opera. He knew it. La Wally. An aria, the famous one, where Wally refuses to marry her father's choice and announces she's leaving. He lost himself for a moment. It was so beautiful. He'd heard it first a couple of years before, in some pretentious French film – all neon lighting, obscure dialogue and designer violence. The song was the only thing memorable.

Brook waited for it to end. When it did, he held the bell pull but remained motionless, listening for what was to come. Nothing. He yanked down hard and heard a clanging within. No music before his arrival. One song in isolation. As though the song had been played especially for him. Ridiculous. Still, Brook couldn't suppress a feeling that his visit was...anticipated. Because a place like this and a small time thief like Sammy Elphick. It was risible.

The solid oak door swung open unexpectedly. Brook had a good ear and had listened for the noise of footsteps bounding down the stairs but there were none. A neat, middle-aged man – the records had said fifty-two – with receding red hair stood before Brook. He was medium height, about five-seven, Brook surmised, though his slight stature gave the impression of an even smaller man. He was slim to the point of being wiry, and wore the anonymous clothing commensurate with his generation: white cotton shirt with a thin check, woollen tie with a light tartan design, grey slacks and light brown suede brogues.

He was possibly the most unremarkable man Brook had ever come across. The sort of man guaranteed to sell large amounts of life assurance to the elderly. The sort not to be noticed entering or leaving a murder scene.

But one thing marked him out – the eyes, the windows to the soul. He had the blackest eyes Brook had ever seen. They were black as pitch, endless, all-enveloping black like the sea at night. So black that Brook felt himself lose his bearings in them. Their hypnotic quality held Brook. He stood gazing, locked into an absurd stupor, not knowing his purpose. For a moment he was transported back to his youth, sitting in front of the old black and white in his pyjamas, hot milk in a glass beside him, watching Bela Lugosi hamming it up as Dracula.

Whenever he looked back on this day, Brook realised that if he hadn't known before, he knew now. The Reaper killings were not ordinary crimes and this man standing before him was no ordinary criminal. He had found his Moriarty.

Yes, Brook knew a great deal in those seconds. Not why someone like Victor Sorenson might feel the need to slaughter a family he couldn't possibly have known but he knew with absolute conviction that this man had murdered Sammy Elphick and his wife and son in a grubby flat in Harlesden. And he knew that he'd done it without a second thought.

Brook smiled politely, at last able to swim to the surface of those eyes. The man smiled back. His eyes didn't join in.

"Mr Victor Sorenson."

"Professor Sorenson, in fact. How can I help you?"

"I'm a police officer, sir," said Brook flashing his warrant card. Sorenson peered at it then looked back at Brook as if there'd been a mistake. "May I come in?"

Sorenson stared at Brook for a few moments, still unable to comprehend. "Of course," he gestured across the threshold, "Detective – Sergeant – Brook." Sorenson lingered over the middle word with distaste.

Brook stepped inside and followed Sorenson into the hall. It was dark and he had a little trouble adjusting to the gloom after the sharp winter light outside. He had to screw his eyes to see his host, who gestured for Brook to follow him up the stairs.

As he climbed he tried to take in as much as his senses would allow. He was aware of plush carpet beneath his feet and the presence of numerous pictures neatly fixed to the panelled wall.

"It's a couple of flights, sergeant," Sorenson threw over his shoulder. For a fifty-two year old, he was remarkably sprightly and he bounded up the stairs two at a time, challenging Brook to keep up. At the top of the stairs, Sorenson strode through a bright threshold and waited, like a footman, for his guest to enter. He closed the lacquered door behind Brook and swept a regal arm at the room. "This is my study."

Brook looked around the vast room, adjusting once again to the change of light. It was a festival of air and brilliance after the melancholy of the hall. The low sun streamed through the porthole window catching the orbit of dust in the atmosphere. "Lovely," said Brook before he could stop himself.

Sorenson smiled. The flattery touched off a hidden corner in his icy personality, as if he approved of Brook's manner and, in spite of his rank, perhaps even his suitability for the task ahead.

"That's nice of you to say. May I offer you a drink, sergeant? I don't know if you indulge on duty but I've got a sublime Lagavullin. Double distilled. A monarch among malts." His manner had changed swiftly. He now seemed eager to please, attentive, as though Brook's appreciation had ushered him into a secret brotherhood over which Sorenson presided.

"Thank you. I'll have a small one." Brook was shocked by his answer. It was out of character. He wasn't a big drinker and never on duty. Something he couldn't explain seemed to draw him into compliance with his host. Or perhaps he was just buying a little surveillance time, if that was what was being offered.

Brook looked around as Sorenson opened a polished walnut cabinet and cleaned two chunky glasses with a white cotton cloth. It was a beautiful room, large and airy, the longest wall of which was lined, ceiling to floor, with books. He stepped closer to gain some clue to his host's mind.

Brook could see this wasn't the library of an old fogey, there were no dust encased leather tomes, no brimming ashtrays or chaotic desktops. This was the working room of an academic, slightly dishevelled and lived in, but generally neat and ordered.

He examined the shelves trying to affect an absent-minded interest. No book had lain untouched and Brook sensed that each had been read – nothing was for show. And what a variety: philosophy, religion, psychology, anthropology, astronomy, geography, metaphysics, chemistry, wine, art, music, pathology and even heraldry. All life was here. And death. Death and history. The Third Reich, The Great War, The Birth of Israel, The Spanish Inquisition, The Cultural Revolution, The Great Plague, The Vietnam War and, most intriguing of all, An Encyclopaedia of Torture.

Anyone else might have thought the possession of so many volumes on death ghoulish, but not Brook. The greatest history entailed the greatest sorrow. That's what made it so fascinating, so involving.

Death was a given, Life a treasure, a bauble to be snatched away, a nourishing oasis but always in the distance, something to struggle for but never reach, a mirage, a chimera, a rotten trick. The legerdemain of God. Now you see it, now you don't. C'est la vie.

Brook continued to examine without interruption. More books. All neatly clustered into subjects: languages, architecture, medicine – endless books. What impressed Brook the most was that all the books were offering some kind of knowledge. There wasn't a single piece of fiction in the entire collection.

He glanced over at the desk. A book on Italian opera lay open on the opulent leather. Every object his eye surveyed reeked of money and carefully understated taste. There was a ledger with a gold fountain pen beside it, beyond that a silver-framed photograph of two children in old-fashioned clothing – two boys who were almost identical. The picture held Brook for a moment. The smiles were there as you might expect, but one of them barely covered the look of anxiety on one young face. There was an atmosphere between the two, a tension visible.

Another picture showed Sorenson arm in arm with a man who was also Sorenson, clearly his twin. The two had been snapped in early middle age. They were the same, yet different. Sorenson's brother seemed more thick set, a little taller perhaps, and most striking, had a confident air about him, which contrasted with the strain in Sorenson's expression. It was as though he had his brother's arm up behind his back, and was instructing him to look happy. The black eyes were the same though. Black as tar and equally lifeless.

In the corner stood the stereo, one of the few sops to modernity. A record span round, the stylus suspended above.

"I enjoyed the Catalani, professor. A beautiful aria." Brook wasn't sure he should have confessed his knowledge but he felt he was being drawn into a game he could only play once his credentials had been thoroughly checked. He didn't know how he knew, but this piece of music could be his passport to the next level.

Sorenson turned from the cabinet. His features cracked into a wide smile. This time his eyes took part. "Isn't it?" He surveyed Brook and nodded with contentment. "Unfortunately his only great piece."

Brook turned to continue his reconnoitre of the room as Sorenson removed the seal from a stout green bottle. The wall opposite the bookshelves was dotted with oil paintings, all old and tastefully framed in wood and gilt. No Fleur de Lis but a hefty quota of portraits and landscapes and what looked like a Van Gogh, though Brook hadn't seen it before. It was of a table with a half-eaten meal of bread and cheese and a pitcher of wine next to it. He walked over to examine it more closely.

The light was interesting. Half the table was in harsh sunlight with Van Gogh's characteristic broad strokes, and half was in the shadow thrown by somebody standing nearby, unseen.

"What do you think?" whispered Sorenson in Brook's ear, offering a glass. Brook was startled by his host's sudden proximity. He certainly had a delicate footfall. "Wonderful, isn't it?"

"It is," agreed Brook, taking a sip of his drink. He gazed into the heavy tumbler with approval as the harsh, smoky liquid flowed over his tongue. "Delicious."

"The Van Gogh I mean, sergeant."

"Yes. Very fine. But I haven't seen the original before."

A slight pause for effect and then, "You have now." Sorenson beamed with a hint of poorly concealed glee. Like a schoolboy with a champion conker.

Brook turned to him and smiled back but he was disappointed. It was a stupid lie and had broken the spell that had fallen over him. Nobody could keep a picture worth millions in an unguarded townhouse, particularly as that same house had recently been burgled by an untalented thief like Sammy Elphick.

Brook put down the glass and fumbled for his notebook, keen now to get on with things. "You're probably wondering why I'm here."

"I probably am," said Sorenson, still beaming.

"Well, sir, you'll be pleased to know that we've recovered the video recorder you reported stolen."

"Have you?" Sorenson's attempt at surprise was woeful. "After all this time." The black eyes didn't waver. They watched Brook, probing his reactions.

The truth slammed Brook in the chest. He had nothing to offer but surprise but managed to conceal it. "Yes sir. We were a bit surprised. It's not usual for thieves to hang onto a top-of-the-range video recorder for several months."

You took it with you, thought Brook. *You took it with you to gain entry and left it in Sammy's flat so we'd find you, so you could gloat. What a piece of work. The poster, Fleur de Lis, was a calling card. Art. The song you just played for me. What are you trying to tell me? What's the message?*

Sorenson grinned back at Brook as if he'd heard his thoughts.

Brook tried to ignore the goading expression and pressed on. "Is that the VCR's serial number you gave the officers who dealt with your case?" asked Brook, showing Sorenson his notebook.

"If you say so, sergeant. I couldn't be expected to remember that after so many months." The black eyes bored into Brook, mocking the puny attempt to wrong foot him. "Where on earth did you find it?"

"In Harlesden, sir, in the flat of a Sammy Elphick, a small time criminal. He's known to us – burglary, theft, shoplifting. Minor stuff."

"Then, I'm very glad you've caught up with him. I hope you put him where he can't do any more mischief."

"Someone's already taken care of that, sir. He was murdered."

"Murdered?" Sorenson was trying a bit harder now but the glint in his dead eyes betrayed the artifice, as did the barely controlled smile. "Dear, dear. Still, that's justice, Sergeant Brook..."

"Justice?"

"If you commit a crime you can hardly complain if you become a victim."

"Sammy Elphick was a criminal, sir. And a habitual one. He caused a lot of misery, that's for sure..."

"There you are then..."

"But he wasn't a violent man."

"Wasn't he?" Sorenson's features were suddenly severe.

"Not to our knowledge."

"I disagree. Most criminal acts involving a victim perpetrate some kind of violence, sergeant, if not always physical."

"A death sentence still seems excessive." Sorenson shrugged but was unable to maintain eye contact. "His wife and young son were also killed." Brook had dropped the "sir" in an attempt to offend Sorenson's superiority complex. But if he noticed he didn't register it. Nor did he register surprise at what should be even more shocking information.

"Is there anything else?" asked Sorenson, dispensing with Brook's title in turn. He seemed tired all of a sudden. The loss of his appreciative audience had perhaps irked him. Brook wondered whether it was a good time to press him, provoke an incriminating error.

But Sorenson's coldness returned and he insisted that Brook wind up quickly. He wasn't sulky, as some became when they lost the upper hand, just matter-of-fact, as though the first round were over and it was time for the players to retire.

Brook handed over the appropriate forms for the reclamation of stolen goods, which were received with barely a glance, and followed Sorenson back down to the front door. There was something which didn't quite fit, which nagged at Brook, and which he knew he had to dredge up before he left if it were to be of use.

"Have you a record of the serial number on your television, professor? Just to be on the safe side. You never know..."

"A television? I don't own one, sergeant," he replied with a reproachful sniff, before he realised what he was saying. "I've got better things to do."

Brook smiled. "Then why would you need a video recorder, sir?" he asked, with the kind of excessive politeness guaranteed to annoy.

Sorenson grinned but not with embarrassment. Then he nodded at Brook with genuine pleasure. He seemed pleased with Brook's question, as though it were a valuable reminder not to underestimate his opponent.

After a pause designed to show Brook that he was concocting some flippant but unshakeable lie, he said, "It was a gift for a friend."

Brook raised an eyebrow to question Sorenson's claim to friend-ships then decided to leave it. It was a dead end. With a nod, he turned on his heel and left.

Chapter 13

Brook woke with a start. His heart was pounding. A nightmare? He'd never had nightmares about The Reaper and that's what he'd been thinking about when he drifted off. He lay back in bed, gathering himself, breathing deeply.

Had he heard a noise? It seemed so. Strange. He was rarely disturbed by noise. Usually his eyes just opened as though waking gently from a coma.

He roused himself, lifted a grimy curtain and peered into the crisp gloom of the night. Maybe Cat had been ferreting around in Mrs Saunders' bins.

He licked his lips. The red wine had given him a thirst. He cursed, remembering his young guest. It was his habit to make tea when he first woke but, for obvious reasons, he didn't want to disturb her. It wouldn't be healthy to face such repressed yearnings twice in one night.

Recalling the earlier peepshow with a lurch of pain, he groped around on the bedside cabinet and smeared a tissue with spittle, then wiped the dry-tear tackiness from his cheeks.

Brook flicked on his bedside lamp and leant down to the floor for the two slim files. Work. That was the key. He could rearrange the deckchairs while the ship of his soul sank into the inky depths.

He read the Wallis file again but could find no fresh inspiration so he turned to Annie Sewell. Dr Habib was right. It was a bad business. Annie Sewell had died between 7.30 and 9pm, a few hours before the Wallis family. But the manner of her death diluted any thoughts Brook might have had about The Reaper being involved.

The poor woman had been beaten with a blunt object before being strangled with the flex of her bedside lamp. According to Dr Habib, at least two assailants had been involved because of the way the victim had been held down while the life was being choked out of her.

One odd thing. Traces of cocaine had been found in and around the victim's nose as well as on a nearby table. Also, her nasal passages were torn and bruised. It seemed her killers had snorted coke in her flat before she died and had forced Annie Sewell to do the same. Apart from this final humiliation, there were no similarities to The Reaper's style.

But Brook was still troubled. There was something about the timing. He couldn't rid himself of the thought that had struck him during his conversation with Greatorix, that there could be a connection between Annie Sewell and the Wallis murders. Surely it was too big a coincidence that Greatorix should be called out on another murder on the very same night, leaving Brook free to pick up the case that only he could solve, that only he could recognise as the handiwork of The Reaper.

It seemed too neat, too much of a coincidence. Two different murders in one night. This was Derby, after all. Not London. Or even Nottingham.

Once again Brook felt the hand of The Reaper guiding him, moving him around the chess board like a pawn, ensuring Brook was on the case – nobody else would do. Somehow he'd engineered the death of this anonymous old woman to clear the way for his old adversary. The Reaper didn't want an unworthy plodder like Greatorix getting his clumsy mind around his work of art. He wanted a foe that he could respect. He wanted Brook. Brook was the only one capable of getting close, the only one capable of understanding.

Brook smiled. The Reaper had overestimated him. At least that showed a lack of judgement. That was one weakness. Years of wrestling with the facts had got him no nearer. A killer who murders families but takes no pleasure in it. Why? Vigilantes know their victims and are driven by hate. They enjoy the killing at least while they're doing it. If The Reaper was a God squadder, appalled by the behaviour of petty criminals, why kill the children as well? What were they being "SAVED" from or for? Brook had speculated for years about religious imagery and biblical notions of sin and retribution, but it took him no nearer a solution that fitted the facts. Wendy Jones had got as close as Brook in five minutes. One reason he wanted her on the case.

And other questions still nagged at Brook. Why had The Reaper stopped for so long only to resurface in Derby years later? There was no logic to it. Most serial killers can't control what drives them. They continue until they're caught. Subconsciously, many want to be caught so they can unveil their masterpiece to the world and revel in their newfound status.

But The Reaper was different. He conformed to no profile. He *didn't* want to be caught, didn't want recognition. It seemed he wanted only Brook to see what he'd done, to be his audience. He didn't crave attention, didn't want the world to worship him as a serial killer *nonpareil*. Such publicity shyness shattered the profiling mould.

Brook returned the folders to the floor and turned off the lamp. He stared into the blackness, unseeing. Charlie Rowlands said Sorenson was dead. Sorenson was The Reaper. The Reaper had killed in Derby. Sorenson couldn't have been The Reaper. Brook shook his head. He'd been so sure...

A faint noise disturbed him again. This time there was no mistake. This was no cat foraging, no external presence. His bedroom door was opening.

Brook didn't move. His hands were behind his head. He tried not to make a noise or change his breathing though he didn't know why. Wasn't it best to show the intruder he was awake to scare him off?

Brook flexed his fingers ever so gently, inclining his head towards the door. All was black. But he hadn't imagined it. He could feel a change in the air currents.

He didn't know how he knew, perhaps it was the imperceptible changes in leg tension that signalled movement, but whoever it was, inched closer.

"Daddy," whispered a voice. Brook guessed it was Vicky a split second before she spoke. He could still faintly remember the scent of a woman. Soap. They always smelt of soap. They like to wash.

Brook shivered as she pulled back his duvet and thrust her cold hands under his vest. "Hold me, daddy."

She was naked. To check Brook quickly ran his hand between her shoulder blades down to her downy buttocks, and just as quickly pulled it away.

"What are you doing, Vicky?" It was a stupid question because her hand was already on his pants, massaging him into an aching erection, one which had been waiting in the wings for months, and which now emerged with the eagerness of the understudy given his big chance.

"Stop it!" Brook's voice carried a collapsing authority that she must have detected because she continued to move her thumb and forefinger delicately around his straining manhood. "Vicky. Stop it!"

"Do you like that daddy?" Brook liked it. But he had to put a stop to the fireworks exploding along his thigh. It had been so long and Vicky was so soft.

Brook grabbed her hair and leant across to the lamp and flicked it on. "That's enough." He looked down at her eyes which began filling with tears. He tried not to look at her body, her breasts pointing at him, the perfect curve of her groin down to her pubic hair.

"Do you like my teeth, daddy? I've been to the dentist."

"I'm not your daddy, Vicky. Now snap out of it!"

"Don't worry, daddy. I won't tell. It'll be our secret," she looked nervously at the door. "Mummy's gone shopping." She closed her eyes tight and lay back, inviting him to her.

Brook shook his head. "Vicky. This is wrong."

"Please daddy. I won't tell. Promise." She opened her eyes again and looked at Brook and the despair in his face.

He loosed a groan from way down deep and closed his eyes to shut the door on his loneliness and self-loathing. "I love you daddy," Vicky sobbed, putting her arms around his buttocks and pulling him towards her.

"Vicky I can't," whispered Brook, his voice dripping with distress. "It's not right. Please go."

"But I'm scared daddy. It's dark. I don't want to be alone."

"I'm sorry. But this can't happen."

Brook held her away, trying not to look at her soft warm body. Vicky stopped struggling to reach him and her body relaxed. She looked at Brook. "Just hold me then? Keep me safe." The little girl voice had gone and she gazed up at Brook with large sad eyes.

Brook looked back at her for what seemed an age. Finally he nodded. "I can do that."

Vicky lay down next to him and closed her eyes. Brook placed a strategic pillow between them and lay down to enfold her slight frame with his arms. She was cold now and he stroked her forearms to warm her up. She in turn rested a velvety cheek on his hand.

"Am I still daddy's special girl?"

"Daddy's special girl," he muttered, half into the pillow, and reached over to turn out the lamp.

*

When Brook woke, it was because of noise again – this time a pounding on the kitchen door. He glanced at the display of his alarm radio. He never used the alarm. Why would he? It was ten past six. Wendy Jones was late. Brook loathed tardiness but decided against mentioning it to her. He extricated himself from Vicky's glowing embrace.

She didn't wake. Brook was glad. Perhaps he could leave before she realised he was gone. That would be the simplest way. He didn't want to lie – he wasn't good at it – but right now he knew he'd have said anything, done anything to cover his tracks with Wendy.

*

"Morning sir." Wendy Jones raised an eyebrow at her superior knotting his dressing gown belt severely. She was accustomed to his being dishevelled but being unprepared was a surprise. Brook bore little resemblance to the man who prided himself on his attention to detail, to cold logic and control. This was more like the man at whom she'd thrown herself, last New Year's Eve. The recollection brought a blush to her features, but the embarrassment was tinged with pleasure.

Brook waved her to sit at the kitchen table. No need to go through to the living room. He obviously didn't want her revisiting the site of their furtive passion and Jones was grateful for his thoughtfulness.

Brook was uneasy, unsure what to do. If he made tea, they'd be delayed. But if he hurried her out, Wendy might suspect something.

At least it gave him a problem to solve – take his mind off what had happened, stop him wondering if he'd done or said anything to cause Vicky to come to his bed. Maybe she'd seen him peeping at her. She would think he was a pervert. The sewer he'd been trying to flee for nearly twenty years had taken root inside him. He was its prisoner. There was no way out. He could see that now. Pointless trying. In an odd kind of way, the knowledge was quietly liberating. But that was what worried him, what was causing the dull thud in his head.

He tightened the tatty towelling robe around his diminishing waist still further. He must eat more. He could see the clench of his genitalia through the material and turned back to the corridor to avoid exposure.

"I won't be a minute. Help yourself to...something." Brook darted to the bathroom, showered in one minute and dressed in three. The note to Vicky could take twice as long but he didn't dare permit himself the time. He had to get Wendy away before Vicky woke. He couldn't heap public humiliation onto private suffering.

*

Jones looked in the fridge, expecting to amuse herself at its desolation but was mildly surprised to see food and wine, albeit sparse, on one shelf. She then noticed that the sink contained no piled plates and the drainer was empty, unlike her last visit.

She had just about decided that Brook had tidied up for her benefit when she saw the two glasses on the side, red dregs still moist at the

131

bottom. Lipstick clung to the rim of one of the glasses. To her surprise, she felt a rush of something approaching jealousy and was ashamed. She knew she had no right. After all she'd spent nearly a year trying to ignore both him and the jibes from her colleagues. Until the murder of the Wallis family and her involvement with the case, she'd almost persuaded herself that nothing had happened between them. And then he'd walked through the screen at the hospital and her heart had lurched in a way she hadn't experienced since her childhood sweetheart had first brushed her breast with the back of his hand. And now she'd missed her chance, assuming she still wanted one.

*

Brook emerged from the hall in a plain grey jacket and trousers. He had suits, but he'd forgotten to keep them together and often wore different combinations of the same two suits on consecutive days, causing much hilarity behind his back.

As he walked in, he noticed the wine glasses before Jones looked up. There was nothing to be done. Perhaps she hadn't spotted them. He smiled at her in a business-like fashion and she returned it with something approaching warmth.

"Shall we go?" he said, indicating the door.

"Have you said goodbye to your guest?" said Jones, with what she hoped was a playful smile.

The acidity of her insinuation crushed Brook and he couldn't hold her look. "I left a note," he muttered to the linoleum, in a voice that declared the matter closed.

Jones stood, feeling very foolish, and brushed herself down. She hadn't wanted to wound him but she had. Then again, he'd humiliated her at the briefing and she was able to take a measure of comfort from a debt paid. However, the way things had started wasn't good. They had a long journey in front of them and things were already awkward.

Brook glanced up at her as she stood up. She looked very good in a flowing, rain-flecked gabardine covering a dark pin-striped trouser suit and a white silk blouse, open at the neck. She opened the door and prepared to step out into the dark morning.

"Daddy. Where are you?"

Brook looked at Jones. He tried to smile but could only manage a weak grimace which he felt sure was about to tip over into hysteria. It was still a good effort given that his world was crumbling around him. What would Wendy think? What would she say? Any moment a young, naked blonde would come stumbling into the kitchen wiping the sleep from her eyes.

Brook handed Jones the two folders from Dr Habib and bolted towards the bedroom. Vicky stood at the door. She smiled and seized him into a naked hug. Brook pushed her away, gripping her elbows in his hands.

"Stop! Vicky. Stop! I've got to go, I told you. I'm working. I won't be back for a few days."

"I see. Yes I remember." She seemed confused for a moment.

"Vicky. About last night..." Brook didn't know what to say. "I...you'd been drinking..."

"Don't worry." She gave him a caring peck on the cheek. "You were very gallant."

Brook looked at her, a warmth burning inside him. The anvil had been lifted from his heart. "You said things."

She looked away from him. "I always do." Vicky turned back to him with doleful eyes and gently covered his hand with hers. "Thank you for last night, for thinking of me." Then she smiled and the little girl was gone again. In her place, the mature student said, "I'll feed the cat and put the key through the letter box."

Brook nodded and held her eyes for a second. "Goodbye," he said, then turned to leave.

*

Brook walked Jones to the Mondeo in something of a daze. He didn't notice her stare, her wish to apologise with a look. He removed the case from her car and put it in his boot. He put all the files and folders on the back seat for ease of access and backed the car out so Jones could park her car in his space.

Eventually she climbed in beside him, still trying to engage him. She removed a long blonde hair from his shoulder and tried to catch his eye with a smile. When she could stand the silence no more, she said, "So your daughter's staying with you. How old is she?"

Brook emitted a tiny, mirthless laugh. "Daddy's special girl?" He paused and looked into the distance. "She's fifteen."

133

Chapter 14

"Forget it Brooky, you've got nothing. No prints, no fibres, no DNA and no witnesses. Nothing. Just a purple tart sitting in a field full of purple flowers."

"Fleur de Lis by Robert Lewis Reid. Oil on canvas."

"I thought it was a poster."

"I mean the original, guv."

"So this professor is into art in a big way. Big deal. It won't get you a warrant, Brooky, so put it out of your head."

Rowlands removed his feet from his desk and inhaled deeply on his cigarette. Tobacco smoke was oxygen to him now, the essential lenitive to deaden nerves and allow him to function. A few seconds later, having spread its soothing balm, the smoke began its return journey from lungs through mouth and nose, into the flask being raised to lips. Rowlands took an urgent draught before holding it out to his subordinate. He hated drinking alone, particularly in the morning, and Brook felt compelled to offer all the support he could, until his boss could put his daughter's death behind him.

So DS Brook accepted the flask and tilted it, making sure his tongue was covering the neck. The whisky burned the tip and fell back.

Brook stared out of the window at the rooftops sprawling across West London and popped a sly mint into his mouth. He could see the snake of sighing cars on the elevated M4, sidling impatiently towards their destination, and it held him for no particular reason. So many people going nowhere.

He turned to Rowlands, summoning all the gravity he could muster. "He did it, guv. I know it. He knows I know it. And what's more," he said raising an impressive finger, "he made sure I know it."

"You're talking in riddles, Brooky."

"He knew I was coming, guv. He played me some music. Opera.

It was another calling card. He's sending messages with art." Brook flinched as he said it. That which seemed so certain sounded absurd when voiced.

Rowlands shook his head. "People like Victor Sorenson don't go around murdering lowlifes like Sammy Elphick no matter what they may have nicked from him. They've got too much to lose."

"But Sammy didn't nick anything don't you get it, guv? Sorenson took the VCR with him and left it there. Just so there'd be something to connect him to the Elphick murders. He doesn't even have a telly."

"Irrelevant old son. He might have been about to buy one."

"You don't need to tell me the legal objections. I know it makes no sense and I know it'd be laughed out of court. But I know he did it. And we've got to stop him."

"Brooky." Rowlands paused. He didn't want to offend. "Putting aside the complete absence of physical evidence, if we accept that this man..."

"Sorenson."

"If we accept that this Sorenson did take his own VCR to Sammy's as a way in, you lose the only motive you've got."

Brook laughed. "I know."

"You do?"

"Yeah. There is no motive – at least not one that you can recognise."

"But you would?"

"When I hear it. Look, guv, I'm not sure there even is one. That could be the point. I know it sounds flimsy. But you'll see."

"I see a wealthy retired businessman with no reason to commit multiple murder..."

"And the burglary at his house?" argued Brook, clutching at a straw.

"A burglary which you say never took place. According to you, this Sorenson buys a video for a TV he doesn't have, notes the serial number, claims he's had a break-in so he can report the thing stolen, then months later takes it to a flat in Harlesden to gain entry, kills Sammy Elphick and his family, and leaves it for us to find and return to him so he can give us a hint that he's the killer. Flimsy ain't the fucking word, Brooky. The word is non-existent and don't tell me that's two fucking words, you toffee-nosed, fast-track twat." Brook laughed.

"And tell me this," Rowlands continued. "Why the fuck would this guy go to all the trouble of leaving absolutely no trace at the scene of the murder and then confess to the first copper who turns up on his doorstep?"

"He didn't confess. He wanted me to know. There's a difference.

He doesn't want us to prove it, guv, he wants to keep doing it. He's laughing at us."

"Bollocks!"

"It's a classic case of super-ego. This is the first of a series, guv. He knows we wouldn't finger him for The Reaper in a million years, unless he gives us a nudge. He's killed three people and we can't touch him for it. But he can't have his fun unless he can watch us running around like headless chickens trying to pin it on him."

"But we're not trying to pin it on him, Brooky."

"I am."

Rowlands began to pant. His breath came quickly these days. Even the mildest difficulty enervated him. "Give it up, son. You'll get nowhere with it. Our best, our only chance to catch this bastard is when he does it again. If he does it again." Rowlands spoke softly, deliberately. Brook saw the sign. His superior had nothing more to say on the matter, even if he could summon the necessary breath

"He will, guv. And when he does, I'll be ready."

There was an awkward silence between them and Brook wasn't sure why. There hadn't been many. They were friends as well as colleagues since Elizabeth's death. Brook had nursed Rowlands through that dark time. He was still nursing him. There had been some difficult moments. These matters were usually suppressed, emotions weren't easy – their job had no use for them. They were a hindrance, an encumbrance to efficient function. Extreme events were often turned into humour to make them easier to deal with. Even Rowlands' de rigueur divorce had been a source of thin amusement to Brook and his boss. But the death of a child...

Rowlands pushed a piece of paper towards Brook. "Here, take your mind off things. Go for a drive in the sunshine."

"What's that?"

"An address near Ravenscourt Park. Uniform have found us a body to check out. It's probably just a derelict with an exploded liver..."

"I'll take a look."

"And stop worrying so much about Sammy Elphick and things you can't change. It's not good for your health."

Brook glanced at the cigarette and the flask, then at Rowlands and raised his eyebrows. They grinned in unison.

"Point taken." Rowlands broke into a tarry chuckle. "I'm serious though. It'll cost you if you make it personal, Damen. That way lies madness. Take it from me. Besides," Rowlands searched for a justification and came up with one that guilt would only allow him to mutter under what passed for his breath, "it's only Sammy Elphick. When all's said and done, who's bothered?"

Brook paused, mulling over something, then nodded. "You're right, guv. It's only Sammy Elphick. He won't be missed." Then quieter, "You're right."

A sudden cloud glided over them, as though both men were confronted by something they'd rather not face. Save for the distant ringing of telephones there was nothing to disturb the moment.

Brook was the one to break it. "Do you remember that night, on the stairwell? When I asked you if it was a bad one and you said you didn't know. I think I understand what you were saying."

"Do you? I hope not."

Brook ignored the warning and stared at the wall, conjuring the scene. "I saw what you saw. I saw Sammy. I saw his wife. I saw the boy. *This is a bad one,* I thought. *This is a brutal, heartless killing of man, woman and child, and every right-thinking person in this world should be appalled.* And do you know what, guv? I didn't care. I didn't give a damn about those people. I looked into that boy's face and all I saw was a case – a problem to solve. I didn't see a family. I didn't see a history – work, play, life, death. I saw three corpses and a challenge. I didn't see a brutal killing and I wasn't appalled." Brook looked hard at his boss. "Do you understand what I'm saying?"

Rowlands raised a bloodshot eye to Brook and nodded.

Brook missed the attempt at closure. "I thought it would hit me later. I'd have nightmares. But it hasn't. And I know it won't."

"No," agreed Rowlands. He took another tincture and thought for a second. "How old are you, Brooky?"

"Twenty-seven. Why?"

Rowlands nodded, a bemused look spreading across his countenance. "Christ. I was twenty-seven," he glanced up at Brook as though to reassure him of the relevance of this information, "when I stopped."

"Stopped what?"

"Giving a shit."

Chapter 15

Wendy Jones closed the folder and turned to Brook. "I see your point. Bobby Wallis and Sammy Elphick could have been brothers."

Brook talked straight ahead, focusing on the motorway. "They were both small-time villains, though there was never any evidence of child abuse in the Elphick case. That doesn't mean it didn't happen."

Jones pondered for a moment. "You know, if it weren't for the children being killed as well, I could almost imagine it was a policeman or somebody striking back..."

"A vigilante?"

"Right. I mean, who's going to miss Bobby Wallis? Or Sammy Elphick?"

"We went down the same road. If it weren't for the children..."

Time gathered around them and Brook waited. He could sense Jones thinking hard about the case, forming her ideas, identifying questions. He was pleased she didn't feel the need to fill silence.

"Why the name?"

"What?"

"The name. Why was he ever called The Reaper?"

"That was my fault. I'd seen a lot of violent crime before Harlesden. Bad things. Killings, gangland executions, domestics, overdoses. You've seen corpses?"

"Not many. My mother. In the hospital."

"Sorry."

"There's no need."

"Any violent deaths?"

"I was first to that tramp a couple of years back. In Markeaton Park."

"Beaten to death?" Brook remembered. Jones nodded. "What did you notice?"

"Sir?"

"When you stared at him longer than was necessary, hoping that no-one would think you were being ghoulish, what did you notice?"

Jones pondered for a moment. "Everything."

"In particular?"

"The face, his face," she corrected herself, "it was all out of shape, his mouth was open but not like people open their mouths. It was like...a caricature of what the human face should look like."

"Anything else?"

"The body. Every muscle, every joint seemed to be in the wrong position. It put me in mind of that game Twister, people used to play at parties years ago."

"At Christmas," Brook smiled and looked away.

"It was like a grotesque game of that, only worse. Think of the most difficult position to hold the human body and then freeze it. That's what I noticed."

"Violent death does that – throws up all sorts of weird and wonderful positions. That's what spawned The Reaper. When I looked at the Elphick family that first night, the violence was missing. The boy was hanging from the ceiling but he didn't seem unduly troubled. The parents were tied and killed quickly. They'd suffered more from seeing their son die, they'd cried, same as Wallis and his wife. But in the end they were just sitting there, dead, their throats cut. They looked quite normal – apart from a look of surprise.

"And talking about it later with Charlie Rowlands, I said it seemed less like a murder, and more like the Grim Reaper had just breezed in and removed their lives. No fuss, no bother, no struggle. Three less people in the world. Who's next?"

"And Brixton?"

Brook hesitated before saying, "Same." There was nothing to gain from elaborating further.

Jones nodded. "Brixton. December 1991. Dark evenings again. That's why he does it round the turn of the year, isn't it?"

"And bad weather, to discourage witnesses."

"Floyd Wrigley, West Indian origin," she read from the file, "his common law wife, Natalie, and their daughter, Tamara. Aged eleven." Her verbal tremor was not lost on Brook. She leafed through the file for the pictures and stumbled through them. "Did you see the scene?"

"No. Yes. I mean, not really. It wasn't my case but they asked me in on a consult. It was the same as Harlesden. Parents tied up, throats cut, watching their daughter die – all to the accompaniment of Mozart's Requiem. This time the girl's throat was cut, unlike the Elphick boy.

139

And she'd been drugged like young Kylie, I assume to limit her suffering." Brook turned towards Jones to ensure she saw his approval. "She was innocent you see – as you spotted the other day." Her colour darkened.

"It says here that the man, Floyd Wrigley, had a deeper cut than the woman and the girl. The blade hit a bone and the cut didn't run from ear to ear." She turned to Brook. "That's different."

"Maybe." Brook was sombre now. Jones caught his mood and stopped herself, thinking she might be digging up unhappy memories. He, in turn, recognised the change in her and tried to lighten up. "He worked out in a gym. Had strong neck muscles which were difficult to cut."

"Wouldn't he have been hard to overpower then?"

"He was also a junkie. If you can believe the two go together. Heroin. He was high as a kite. They both were."

"Any hint that race was significant?"

"I don't think so. Just the criminal tendencies. Wrigley was a thief and a violent man. All round scumbag. Had a couple of ABH's on his CV, and a Wounding, some guy he knifed during an argument about paying for sex with Tamara. The things people do for their fix."

"He pimped his eleven year old daughter?" Jones looked into the distance, her voice little more than a croak. She was aghast. Brook was annoyed with himself. He'd been carried away. Such embellishments were out of character. Unnecessary. It rarely happened with him, the adrenaline rush of the showman. Perhaps, unconsciously, he'd been trying to degrade her a little – all her sex. A little payback for, well, where to start?

He looked across to see the mark his words had left. Too often he forgot that even fellow officers hadn't waded as deeply into the sewer as he had. They could all identify and acknowledge the stench of society's entrails, but *their* clothes didn't need a boil wash at the end of each day.

His inability to gauge the emotional threshold of others was a terrible weakness, and he was ashamed. Wendy Jones was still an innocent abroad, a provincial girl with an endearing ignorance of the world as dung heap. He tried to soften the blow.

"Actually that was just a whisper. Probably not true, otherwise they'd have had him on toast, wouldn't they?"

"How did The Reaper gain entry?" asked Jones.

"Brixton? Same as Harlesden and the other night – bearing gifts. A VCR in Harlesden, though you won't find that in the file, and an expensive new Compact Disc player for Mr Wrigley and family. Once inside he had the element of surprise. Not that he needed it with Wrigley and his girlfriend doped up to the eyeballs."

"He still tied them up?"

"Sure. Adrenaline at the point of death can be a powerful ally."

"But he didn't tie up Bobby Wallis and his wife."

"No. He's had a long time to polish his act. He'd found a way to disable them without force."

"The last one was 1993 in Leeds. Although I couldn't see any..."

"Don't bother. There's nothing in there on Leeds. I could only photocopy Met documents. Besides, I've never been convinced about Leeds. It was a copycat and a pretty ropey one at that."

"Did the Leeds Force speak to you?"

"Sure. They were taking no chances after the Yorkshire Ripper. It was just wrong. As far as I could see it was a gangland thing. Drugs. Professional job. But the Leeds boys wouldn't have it, I don't know why. They insisted on chalking it up to The Reaper. You'd think they'd have been pleased to know a serial killer *hadn't* struck on their patch."

"Why so sure it was gangland?"

"The victim was Roddy Telfer. He moved to Leeds from Glasgow in 1992. A real slime ball whichever way you look at it: junkie, pimp, thief, small-time, same as the others, but someone disliked him enough to put a sawn-off in his mouth and blow his head off."

"A shotgun? That's not The Reaper's MO."

"No. Far too messy."

"Then why think it was The Reaper?"

"Because, using what was left of Telfer's brains and a gloved finger, a leather glove I might add, he wrote "SAVED" on the wall. Actually, he only got as far as the E when he was interrupted by Telfer's girlfriend..."

"Interrupted? Wasn't she there from the start?"

"No she wasn't. She came home during, or straight after, Telfer's murder. It doesn't fit. That sort of chance occurrence wasn't, isn't, a feature of The Reaper's method. He's too careful. He would have had them both there at the start."

"So what happened to her?"

Brook hesitated but decided that he couldn't avoid cast iron facts. "He strangled her, which wasn't easy. His hands were covered in Telfer's blood, so it was hard to get a grip. She wasn't easy to manoeuvre. She was eight months pregnant and..."

"Oh God!"

"You didn't know that?"

"No, why would I?" Jones put her own leather-gloved hand to her brow and then her mouth. She closed her eyes composing herself the best she could.

141

"I'm sorry…"

Brook said nothing. It would serve no purpose telling her the rest. Even the hardened Yorkshire CID officers who'd briefed him had blanched at the memory.

They were approaching a service station and he pulled into the inside lane. He was pleased in a way that she was so sickened by this detail. The death of an unborn child should sicken. Once Brook would have felt the same way. Now Brook's distress could only ever be vicarious. After the Maples girl, all deaths could be squared away – even that of Roddy Telfer's unborn child. The offspring of a criminal – rough justice certainly, but life goes on.

*

Moments later Brook pulled the car into the slip road of the service station and parked. "Open the window."

Before he could soothe her further, she leapt out of the car and ran across to a clump of bushes. Brook listened to her retching. He picked up a packet of tissues and got out. "Here," he said offering a tissue as she emerged finally, brushing herself down. She wasn't too ill to check her shoes for telltale splatters.

"Thanks."

"Come on," said Brook, taking her by the elbow and leading her across to the restaurant.

*

Ten minutes later they sat over their coffees. Brook had drained his and was watching Jones for signs of returning nausea. But she simply stared into her untouched beverage, stirring superfluously at the sugarless black liquid. Brook knew what was coming. Ground that had been raked over many times by Amy.

"Doesn't it bother you?" She lifted her head to look at him. "The stuff you've seen."

"You sound like my ex…"

"Doesn't it?"

Brook was forced to appear to be addressing the question – another unlamented technique from his marriage. "Yes. But not in that way."

"Then how?"

"Can we leave it, please?"

"But…"

142

"I don't want to discuss it, Wendy."

Her Christian name brought her up sharply. Brook smiled at her. Perhaps this frank exchange would destroy the barrier that was between them.

"I'm sorry." She roused herself now in a gesture of full recovery. "I've got no right."

"Forget it."

She smiled weakly at him. "I'm sorry about the delay."

Brook smiled. "My fault. You haven't seen what I've seen." He looked full into her eyes. On an impulse he put his hand on hers and was pleased to feel it yield in welcome. "Don't ever lose that."

"What?" She cocked her head to one side and quizzed him.

Brook found it very attractive. "The capacity to feel." She nodded, though she seemed uncertain of its value.

*

They had driven a few more miles in silence before she spoke. "Can I ask one more question, about the case?" she said disarmingly. "Then we'll drop it, sir."

Brook saw his chance to finally bury the harm he'd inflicted at the briefing. "Look. First, don't call me sir when we're on our own. Second: I brought you along for your intelligence and your deductive powers, Wendy. You don't need to ask permission to get the information you require or to make an observation, no matter how trivial it may seem."

She maintained her equilibrium well but Brook could see she was pleased. She reached into the file and produced a glossy photograph of Professor Victor Sorenson leaving his desirable residence in Holland Park. It had been taken by Brook during what the division counsellor had called "a period of obsessive stalking as a result of guilt transference." Brook must have been the only officer who'd understood Dr Littlewood's jargon because nobody else had ever pushed him over his couch.

"Who's this middle-aged bookworm?"

"Him?" replied Brook as blandly as he could. "Oh, that's The Reaper." He fixed his gaze and his mind on overtaking the lorry in front. He knew that if he saw her jaw drop, he'd be unable to keep a straight face.

*

Later that morning, Jones was surprised when Brook pulled the car

143

into the entrance of the Kensington Hilton, though she tried not to let it show. It had been a surprising day. First the Reaper file. Then hearing the story of Brook's first meeting with Sorenson and how he'd decided he was The Reaper – though she tended to side with Brook's boss, Charlie Rowlands. There was no evidence.

Then they'd listened to a tape of Mahler's Ninth Symphony at close to full volume to see how many times and for how long the music became so quiet that anyone listening in Mr Singh's house next door might have thought it had been switched off altogether. And certainly there were passages when Mahler's crashing cymbals and thumping horns gave way to more reflective melody, particularly during the Adagio, but nothing substantial enough to encourage Mr Singh to believe the CD player had been turned off for up to ten minutes.

Next DI Brook had taken her on a detour to Harlesden to see the site of the first Reaper deaths – like a pair of ghoulish tourists. They hadn't left the car. Brook simply pointed out the metal stairwell running up to Sammy Elphick's old flat. According to Brook little had changed except the launderette was now a betting shop.

And now this final surprise, staying at the Hilton Hotel, no less. It seemed unbelievable to Jones. That McMaster would okay such an extravagance, and an unnecessary one at that. There must be half-decent hotels for a lot less.

She darted a glance at Brook who, it seemed to her, was aware of her confusion and was trying not to acknowledge it. For some reason she had the impression that he'd stayed here before. It was something about the ease with which he negotiated his way onto the hotel's forecourt. It wasn't possible to turn right into the Hilton's drop-off zone but, with barely a second beat, Brook took a circuitous route round a one way street and emerged back on Holland Park Avenue travelling in the opposite direction, pulling up outside the main entrance a few seconds later.

Then, without a glance at his companion, Brook had gathered the evidence folders from the back seat and popped the boot. He handed the cases to a spotty faced, eager youth and dangled the car keys at the doorman before ushering Jones to the entrance.

*

"Two adjacent en suite singles please," Brook mouthed at the attractive receptionist with just the right amount of superior boredom. Another day, another capital city. "Top floor if you have them."

"Certainly sir. How long will you be staying with us?"

"Just the one night." Brook handed her a credit card and yawned, this time with genuine fatigue. It'd been a long night and a stressful day. A part of him began to wish he hadn't brought Jones. Relaxation would be impossible in her company. The awkwardness had receded but it was still there, and the effort he was required to make in front of her was draining his reserves.

He turned round to squint at the Piano bar, which was busy, even at 11.30 in the morning, though most people were waiting rather than drinking. Killing time. That was a skill he envied.

*

Jones divided her attention between Brook and the board on the reception wall with its gilt letters picking out the room rates – £210 per night for a single room. No way. She couldn't square that with the penny-pinching grind of justifying even the smallest amount of overtime back in Derby. Also, they were staying only one night but Inspector Brook had told her to pack for three. It didn't make sense unless they were going to be camping out the other two nights.

A thought struck her. She'd heard rumours even before her night with him. Afterwards, when the gossip had started to spread, Sergeant Hendrickson had joked about it – she remembered going crimson – had said that if she could overlook all that was wrong with Brook, she'd be making a very good match. *"He's rolling in it, I'm telling yer. Up to a million, they reckon."* She'd shrugged it off at the time. Anyone with that sort of money wouldn't be working in the Job, and they certainly wouldn't live in the dump Brook called home. She liked the car, the Sprite, it showed class, personality even, but...

"There you are sir." The receptionist handed Brook two card keys. She called out to the boy who was holding the lift and he nodded.

Jones followed Brook into the lift. She was bursting to say something but didn't. She couldn't predict his reaction in front of a stranger.

*

Brook continued to avoid her look. He assumed she was on to him. Would she be insulted, think this was to impress her? With a sinking feeling he suddenly realised that staying at the Hilton might look like a tawdry effort to get her into bed. It was too late to explain now so he resolved not to think about it.

With the business of the porter out of the way and the £1 tip dispensed to a look that implied the porter had been handed the contents of Brook's nose, Jones marched back into Brook's room to clear the air.

Brook was at the window, concentrating hard. His case was open on the bed and he had a pair of binoculars in his hands, gazing down at the gardens of Royal Crescent, across Holland Park Avenue, and beyond that to the chimneys of Queensdale Road.

"Do you mind telling me what's going on?"

Brook started. "Wendy. Problem with the room?" He hoped that was all it was.

"The room's fine, sir, very fine. *That's* the problem."

Brook nodded. Things could get...No. He had to stop being negative. Things *would* be awkward forever if he didn't buck up his ideas. "This is my old room, you know."

"What?"

Brook laughed and sat on the bed, which made Jones even more uncomfortable. The parallel escaped him. He handed her the binoculars and motioned her to the window to take in the view. If in doubt, concentrate on the case. "You can almost see his study from here."

Jones stared at him. "What are you talking about?"

Brook waited, assembling his thoughts. "You asked me today if what I've seen affects me. I think you deserve a response. I can't answer yes or no – I can only tell you what happened, what I did."

"You don't have to."

"No. But I want to. One of the reasons I brought you." She didn't argue. Her interest was aroused. She waited but Brook said nothing. For several minutes he stared at the wall, thinking. Jones began to think he'd forgotten her and was about to speak when Brook broke the silence. "I've told you how I met Sorenson. I haven't told you what happened afterwards. To be honest, Wendy, I'm not that clear about it myself. Do you mind me calling you Wendy?" Brook's sudden piercing glance into her eyes raised the temperature between them. She shook her head, not wanting to staunch his momentum, though it was more a disinclination to hear how the tension, some of it sexual, affected her own voice. Fortunately he looked away again almost immediately.

"For six months after my first encounter with Victor Sorenson, I hardly saw my wife and baby daughter. I admit I became obsessed. I'd found The Reaper, for a time the most wanted man in Britain. People hated him. People feared him, as they'd been taught. And people wanted to know who he was, wanted him caught so they could see him and understand him. Given a face, the monster could be removed from their nightmares.

146

"But he wasn't caught, couldn't be caught. There was no evidence, there was nothing. Here was a monster that was invisible, a ghost who killed without pity, without emotion. Who was he? Where was he? Nobody knew. Only I knew and I couldn't speak. Not legally. I had no proof. The only reason I knew Sorenson was The Reaper was because he wanted it that way.

"Rewards were promised, by the papers, by the police, for information leading to a conviction. But, as with all these things, the real information, what people wanted more than his capture, was the gore, the visceral thrill of knowing what The Reaper had done and how he'd done it – you forget now the impact the first murders had in the tabloids – and for that they needed me.

"It was my case. I had the inside track, the details they wanted. But, of course, they couldn't have them. Not from a police officer. Charlie Rowlands, my old DI, and I couldn't be touched, or pressured – the press knew that. Criticised, yes, but not hounded like ordinary civilians. *We* were trained. *We* could handle it. But we have families, Wendy. And what we know, what we've seen hurts *them*." He looked back at Jones with sadness. "One day you'll understand."

She smiled back at him, trying to radiate comfort. "I see it every day. It's not news. Officers taking their moods home with them." She had an urge to put her hand on his arm but resisted.

"My family, my wife and baby daughter. How can you share...?"

"How can you share The Reaper's work? No-one can describe what he did."

Brook was puzzled for a moment then chuckled. "The Reaper? What he left for us to find was nothing..."

"Nothing?"

"I mean, not nothing, obviously, but not the worst by a long way."

Jones waited, puzzled, not wanting to ask but not wanting to be denied. "What was the worst?"

Brook smiled and gazed out of the window and began the journey back. "A silver necklace with hearts," he breathed. He glanced at Jones but couldn't sustain it. She looked confused but it couldn't be helped. There were limits to be observed. He couldn't pour himself out too soon. There might be nothing left.

"I envied my DI, Charlie Rowlands, after The Reaper. Before, I'd always pitied him, his dependence on booze and fags, deadening his senses to get him through. I hadn't realised he was the lucky one. His family had already gone. His daughter, dead at nineteen from a heroin overdose. His wife remarried. It was my turn. And he knew. He tried to warn me but I thought I was...invulnerable."

"But you found The Reaper."

"Sure, but Sorenson and I were the only ones who knew that. It was like his private joke. Even Charlie wouldn't wear it. He was like my own father but he just wouldn't believe it.

"There was nothing I could do. Nothing I could say. It would've meant my job. My biggest case. It would make or break me. In the end, it did both. And neither. Does that make sense? It was my greatest success and my greatest failure, Wendy. I'd found The Reaper. *I'd* worked it out. Nobody else could have got close. Nobody ever did. Sorenson knew I'd got him. And yet I hadn't. I'd failed."

"What happened?"

"I hit the streets. Or rather I hit his street. I couldn't do anything clumsy. I knew that much. None of the usual tactics would've worked..."

"Usual tactics?" enquired Jones.

"Harassment at work, endless search warrants to go through his belongings, take his life away in bin bags, that sort of thing. Not that I could have got a search warrant. I had no probable cause. He was a wealthy and respected man. I was on my own. But even if I had, he would have...I'm not explaining this very well. Look, I told you about our first meeting, the music and the whisky and the painting and all that..."

"Yes."

"Well the longer I've had to think about it, the more I've come to realise that he was...playing me."

"I don't understand."

"You weren't there, you didn't meet him. He wanted someone, needed someone capable of understanding what he'd done, what he was going to do for as long as he chose. Something special. Something remarkable. Murder, but with a difference – the taking of lives but not for personal gain or kicks. He was a soldier. He wanted me to know that somehow.

"He hadn't killed out of fury, out of passion, but for a reason that no-one could possibly comprehend. But he needed someone to at least try. He couldn't tell the world unless he was caught, which he didn't want, but he could show me; I could be his audience. I could be his muse."

Jones stared back at Brook. He saw that she was having trouble taking it in. "Are you saying he was killing for you?"

Brook laughed and stared hard at her. "In a sense, I suppose I am."

"And if you'd started harassing him, you think he would have stopped including you?" Jones said.

"Exactly. Then nobody would have got close. There'd be nobody to point a finger, to know that Victor Sorenson was The Reaper. Of course, there was a selfish element as well. I didn't want to be excluded, you see. This was the big one. The case that was worthy of me, that excited and thrilled me. The case I'd been waiting for all my life. I was hooked."

"So what did you do?"

"What could I do? The case was dead. There were no leads to follow. So I waited and I watched." Brook stared at the floor, aware that this sounded pretty limp.

"For what?"

Brook looked up at her and felt his powerlessness. "For the next one."

Jones fell silent, tense, but not with the run-of-the-mill awkwardness that sometimes crackled between them. This pause was natural and unforced. She concentrated hard. "So the Wallis family were killed for you. The Reaper came to Derby because you were there."

"I think so." Brook was experiencing a calm he hadn't known for many years. Middle age had shown him that tightening the lid didn't work and the more he poured himself out, the better he'd felt. Discretion may be the better part of valour but for Brook, it was also the greater part of self-destruction.

"But you said Charlie Rowlands told you Sorenson was dead."

"I know. I can't explain that."

Jones nodded. "Why is this your old room?"

"I'd end up in here sometimes. Not often. A few nights when I'd had too much of his whisky. Sorenson didn't want me sleeping over for obvious reasons."

"You stayed at his house?" Jones couldn't keep her voice down at this.

"No. I just said."

"But you drank with him."

"A couple of times, yes. After a week of watching his house, he came over to the car and invited me in."

"And you went?"

"Why wouldn't I? He was my prey. I could stalk him more easily at close quarters, perhaps force an admission, an error."

"Are you sure you weren't *his* prey?" said Jones sombrely. She was sitting now, fixing him with her big eyes.

Brook smiled back at her – a smile of warmth and tenderness and affection that he hadn't practised in years. His cheeks muscles strained at the effort. "Now you see why I brought you along. That's a subtlety

149

that would have escaped DS Noble's attention."

Jones ignored the flattery. "What did you talk about?"

"Things. Philosophy, religion, politics."

"The Reaper?"

"Sometimes, though not directly. He'd ask about the case, as though he were an interested observer."

"Did you question him? Accuse him?"

"I didn't have to. We both knew."

Jones was silent now, thinking. "You drank with him a couple of times but stayed here a few nights. Why was that?"

Brook smiled his appreciation of her powers of reasoning. The shift in their relationship, no matter how temporary, hadn't escaped him. She was now *his* superior and he was forced to justify his actions to her. "I couldn't go home, Wendy. I was scared."

"Scared of what?"

"You mean for whom?"

"Okay. Scared for whom?"

"For my family, for myself."

He looked at Jones with a mixture of apprehension and sudden exhilaration, his expression pleading for her to stop mining this deep stratum of emotion, yet willing her to go on so that he could finally exhaust himself of the burden. Jones urged him on with an eyebrow.

"I was confused. There was another case. A teenage girl, Laura Maples, was murdered. And I wasn't sure what kind of...person I was becoming."

"Meaning?"

"Sorenson. When I spoke to him, it was a gradual thing, and one I'm sure he was bending over backwards to achieve..."

"What are you talking about?"

"I began to envy him. I know it sounds incredible. You've got to remember the state I was in. My life was beginning to unravel. And...Sorenson had what I needed. Complete control over his emotions, his destiny. It was only natural." Brook tried to think of a way to dress up his next utterance, make it more ambiguous. He failed. "I liked him."

*

After a moment, when the only noise to disturb them was the distant hooting of horns muffled by double-glazing, Jones realised there was nothing more to say. To introduce the question of who was paying for the rooms, and why, would have been absurd after such a

150

conversation. She rose to leave.

Brook was alerted to her presence again. "I'm tired. I need a nap."

"Good idea."

With a supreme effort, Brook looked at his watch. "I'll see you in the bar at two." And with that he fell back onto the bed with a sigh and closed his eyes.

Within five minutes, Wendy Jones was changed and on the street. She had a couple of hours to kill and she needed some air and time to think. She'd not been to this part of London before so now was an ideal time to take a walk, look around.

She strolled west towards Notting Hill, taking in what sights there were, the fine restaurants, the novelty of a tube station, the opulent houses sitting grandly back from the road, aloof among the mayhem of traffic, remnants of a more civilised age.

Chapter 16

As DS Brook arrived at Ravenscourt Gardens, the hottest day of the year was drawing to a close. The temperature, up in the low thirties in the middle of the afternoon, had eased to a more comfortable 22 degrees, as the sun began to fall over the horizon.

If Brook had any doubts about the directions he'd been given, they were soon dispelled when he approached the street. The lights of three panda cars flashed at the end of the road, intersecting with Ravenscourt Park.

Brook pulled up to the melee and stepped from his car. After a brief conversation with one of the constables, Brook followed him to the railing above a basement flat.

He descended the few steps to the litter-strewn yard and trained a torch onto what passed for a door. He took a step forward and skidded on the vomit of the young PC who had found the body. Uniformed arms grabbed to steady him.

"Easy sir," said a voice. It was a nasal voice, its owner pinching his nostrils to defeat the stench.

Brook wretched as the odour hit him but managed to stuff a handkerchief in his mouth and over his nose. From the entrance to the building came the stench of old putrefied meat. It mingled with, yet dominated the other smells – as royalty fraternised with lowly subjects – lording it over the damp cardboard, the sick, the dog shit and the urine.

"You don't have to go in there, sir. It's not pretty. We think it's a young girl. She...You should wait for the police surgeon."

But Brook had to see. There was something he had to find out. He had to know if Charlie Rowlands had been right about Harlesden. Had Brook lost all feeling, all sense of the suffering of others? Was he out of reach at twenty-seven? He had to see.

"Just a quick look, constable. While it's fresh." He caught the ironic grin of the PC and pulled back the warped hardboard that doubled as a door, then shone in the torch. A rustling was taken up inside. Brook puzzled for a second, assumed it was the wind, and squeezed his slender frame through the gap and under the police tape. More rustling – early autumn leaves caught in the draught from a broken window perhaps.

He took his first step into the chamber. The smell was worse now and Brook clamped his nose tighter. He made his way carefully towards the interior room, picking his feet over various lumps of indistinct detritus. A scurrying in the corner wheeled him round and his light fell on a whiplash tail. Rats. Brook grimaced. He agreed with Winston Smith. He hated rats.

But he thought of Harlesden, imagined Amy beside him, as he had several times since, looking on as he examined the boy, watching him as he strolled from place to place, unconcerned, stroking his chin in contemplation and smiling when a theory suggested itself. What would Amy think of him? What kind of monster was he? He had to press on, prove to himself he could still be affected. Prove it for her sake.

A moment later he was at the entrance to the murder room. He lifted the light from his feet and swept it round the space.

Brook was surprised. Even in this squalor, efforts had been made to create a homely atmosphere. Off in one corner was a tiny, one-ring stove, a screw-in gas canister still attached. A small pan sat on top. Behind the stove there were a few unopened tins. It was quite orderly.

An old pair of curtains hung across the window and a few sticks of furniture, rescued from skips, were arranged around the room. A house-proud squatter – was there anything sadder than this self-delusion? The victim had tried to create a sanctuary, a place away from confusion, impose a pattern, a personality on her environment. Pathetic really.

Brook knew then this girl was not from London. He knew because he'd had the same reaction when he first arrived from Barnsley. Fearing the encroachment of others in this massive city, his first instinct was to construct boundaries. So Brook had bought the poky flat in Fulham to have a place to shut himself off, barricade his thoughts from all the distractions, all the invitations to self-destruction. It was the only way to survive in such a place.

But the attempts at civilisation only threw the spectacle on the mattress into sharper relief. Having taken in the periphery, Brook finally moved his torch to illuminate the corpse then span away, his gorge rising at what he saw. But he didn't puke. His heart thumped and his mouth cracked with sudden dehydration but he didn't puke.

After a few seconds to compose his nerves, he knew he had to look again. He opened his watering eyes and took quick urgent breaths. He tried to keep the smell out but flimsy linen was no match for such perfume.

He turned again to the face of the girl, inclined towards him, head slightly raised by the makeshift pillow on her deathbed. Her eyes were gone or at least invisible in the blackened sunken orbs where they once belonged – eaten away by bacteria, maggots and rats. The hair had survived though, short and blond with red highlights, as did that part of the ear adorned with indigestible studs. Some of the nose was also intact, some flesh still clinging to the cartilage.

There wasn't enough left to show Brook that this had been a pretty girl, but the teeth confirmed she was young. They were clean and straight, no absentees even at the back of the jaw.

Brook took a step nearer but hesitated. That fluttering sound again, this time emanating from near the body. It was the same noise he had dismissed as the wind a moment before, louder now, and clearly made by some corporeal creature.

Brook noticed a pile of tattered clothes by the bed that the girl had removed or had removed for her. Perhaps some animal had made its home there. He peered at what looked like a shirt and a sweater. They weren't scattered and torn but dropped into a pile implying that the girl was able to take them off on her own. Whether this was under duress or not, Brook couldn't say.

He moved the light down. The shard of a beer bottle protruded from the girl's throat at a right angle. Marks showed where several attempts had been made by the killer to force it in. He'd finally succeeded to such a degree that the neck of the bottle was nearly level with her chin.

A pair of grimy panties dangled from the bottle. The killer's final act had been to wipe off his prints with them. Such presence of mind would guarantee Life if they ever caught him. If.

The fluttering again. Brook swung his torch sharply onto the pile of clothes. Nothing. No movement. Perhaps he was imagining it.

He continued his appraisal but the noise returned. He looked around now for something to work with. He found a stick and crept closer to the body and the pile of clothes. He had to put his handkerchief away to have two hands free but the smell wasn't as bad. He'd acclimatised.

He took the stick and, holding the torch in front of him, gingerly stabbed at the material. Nothing.

He stepped back, troubled. He turned to the body and moved his light over the lower half of the girl's torso. The knees were together and the legs were raised into the foetal position, presumably in a futile gesture of self-defence. Brook imagined a noise behind the girl and guessed there could be something nestling in the mattress.

He moved round and shone the light on the girl's legs. Immediately the noise increased. It was the sound of animals panicking and though he tried to withdraw the light, the damage was done. A flurry of activity drew his attention and he saw something furry and quick move under the girl. As it did so, her right leg, which had been locked into the rigor mortis of sexual prurience, swung away from its neighbour.

A dozen wary eyes returned Brook's horrified gape but wouldn't be deflected from their meal. The rats were big, bigger than when they'd started their meal. But they were still hungry.

Brook was appalled. Appalled at this desecration, yes, but more by the attention the rats were suddenly paying him. He wanted to run but was frozen, unable to break away from the feeding rodents, cloaked in blackened viscera. He couldn't move, he dare not move and to point the beam elsewhere would mean not knowing, not being sure where the rats were. Would they continue to gnaw at the humiliated corpse or transfer their interest to him?

Hours passed in a few seconds. Still Brook was rooted. After what seemed an age, the rats seemed to lose interest in Brook as they became accustomed to the beam. They liked its unexpected warmth and bathed in it. And they became blasé about the threat posed by Brook.

One by one they returned to their business, no longer munching with their eyes darting at him, but ignoring him so completely that Brook decided it was time to take his chance.

He reversed through the doorway into the outer room, still not daring to turn the beam onto his exit. Nearly there now. He was being an idiot. Rats didn't attack human beings unless they were stricken in some way, and then only in the most extreme circumstances. It would be like a shoal of mackerel having a go at a shark.

Finally Brook came to a halt. He couldn't look any longer at the girl. The more he'd drawn away, the more he could see the bigger picture. This girl had died. Here in this hell. And what was left, what her parents would want, would need to take away for proper grieving, was being defiled by these monsters.

A panic washed over him and his breath seemed to be rushing from his body. He had to get out. He turned and fixed his torch on the entrance but as he did so he heard a terrible screeching from the direction of the girl. He wheeled round and caught the full horror of the rats tearing out of the torso towards him.

He dropped the torch, hoping that was all they wanted, and ran.

155

He ran for all he was worth, no longer caring what he stepped in or kicked over. To be outside, in the clean night air, was all Brook wanted from life now.

Nearly there. He was quicker even than the filthy animals. But as he got to the entrance, to his horror he found his way barred. He'd gone the wrong way. Or something had fallen across the makeshift door and Brook was unable to shift it. He tried again but it wouldn't budge. He was trapped.

Brook span round in terror to see the pack of slick-haired rodents teeming past the rocking beam of his torch towards him. Then he couldn't see them, he could only hear the scratch of their claws on the concrete, tearing closer and closer. He tried to speak but could make no noise save for a gentle whimper of despair.

Brook pushed against the wall and braced himself. All he could do was look to the ceiling, try to block out what was happening. Then maybe he could protect his face, his eyes.

The first one was on him, then another and another. He screamed and kicked out wildly, but it was no use. They were on his trousers, ripping at the material. Then one was on his ankle, his sock. It must have smelt the fetid gust of heat wafting down Brook's leg because it squirmed into the narrow opening of his trouser leg and began hauling itself up towards his crotch, slicing through his flesh as it went.

Brook put his arms to his thigh to prevent access but realised that he was being driven nearer the ground so he stood up straight. If he went to ground he was done for.

But the rat was in his pants now – Brook could feel its snout nuzzling away at the gusset.

And then the pain. Pain like he'd never felt before. Searing, blinding. "Please get them off me, get them off me, get them off me."

*

"Get them off me!" DS Brook woke with a start and took a deep breath. His face was drenched with sweat, his hands clammy. The drone of police chatter on the radio brought him back and he sat up to open the window and adjust the driver's seat. The cold night air revived him. He drained his Styrofoam coffee, now cold, and began breathing normally again.

Soon he was flipping his notepad open and shut to stave off boredom. He knew all the tricks to enrich his life.

He glanced at the crossword on the passenger seat but decided against it. His brain was overheated enough. Instead he closed his eyes to ease the sting of too little sleep.

His shift had finished hours ago. He could have been at home now, with his family, arm round his wife, enjoying a spot of synchronised gaping at their brand new daughter, a small pink parcel of helplessness and need, the better part of him poured into that vulnerable vessel.

Brook thought of baby Theresa and smiled briefly. But then he saw the Maples girl. Her empty eye sockets glared at him. Black holes that pulled in all Brook's happy thoughts, all his hope for the future.

He remembered her face, a contortion of pain, that strange grin of pleasure that sudden death can bestow on lifeless features. But she wasn't lifeless. There was movement...

Brook shuddered but kept his eyes shut tight. It was no use. He couldn't separate them. He couldn't think of little Theresa without the girl, Laura, intruding. Theresa, who came into the world as Laura was being butchered. They were the same in Brook's mind. Indivisible. To Brook it was a rebirth, the girl had been reincarnated, savagely taken from the brutality of the world to start again as Brook's daughter. But it was no second chance. Brook knew the world now. His daughter was doomed. Doomed to repeat the cycle of innocence corrupted. And it was all Brook's fault. He'd brought another victim into this terrible world.

Brook wanted to open his eyes but the ache endured so he focused on the case. Forget little Theresa, think of The Reaper – Brook's name for him. How to catch him? How to win?

The lure of detection calmed him, drew him away from those immobilising minefields of emotion and allowed him to go on.

The moisture too returned to soothe pupils that felt as if they'd had a vigorous rubdown with a harsh towel. A tapping on the window jolted him back.

"It's Sergeant Brook, isn't it?"

The mocking tone irritated Brook. He wound down the window and contemplated Victor Sorenson's expression of forced bonhomie. If anything his demeanour seemed even more triumphal than it was the last time they'd met.

"What can I do for you, sir?" Brook replied with just the right amount of feigned respect.

"It's an unpleasant evening. I thought you might like a drink. Unless, of course, you're on a case."

Brook looked back at his prey, sifting the pros and cons. His eyes were even more impenetrable at this late hour.

He had the same clothes as their previous interview, or very like them, and clutched an umbrella in his bony talon to keep off the rain.

"I'd be delighted," Brook beamed back, trying to ape the tone of phoney good manners. He stepped from the car and followed Sorenson's meagre frame across the road and into the hall of his imposing home. The ivy dumped several large droplets of water down the back of Brook's neck, causing a shiver as he crossed the threshold.

"Don't be afraid, sergeant," grinned his host, catching the reflex. Brook smiled back and removed his raincoat, which Sorenson hung on a wrought-iron coat rack. He deposited the umbrella in the porch and closed the front door. All extraneous noise was now silenced and Brook could hear sombre melodic voices floating down from above.

"Mozart's Requiem. Do you know it?"

"I've heard it."

"A fitting epitaph, wouldn't you say? Please."

Unlike their first meeting, lights burned brightly, so Brook stepped quickly ahead of Sorenson, meaning to take his time reaching the study. He needed to examine what he saw, try to get a better feel for his opponent. He got the impression Sorenson wanted the same thing. So Brook trudged carefully up the stairs, Sorenson fell in behind.

As they climbed, Brook tried to take everything in. He examined the decor of the hall as well as the pictures on the walls – muted colours, soft rich carpets, marble steps, old oak banisters, discreet lighting. Everything was supremely tasteful and orderly. The set designer had done a magnificent job.

One or two of the pictures seemed familiar and conformed to Brook's evolving image of The Reaper and his obsessions.

"Do you know this work?" asked Sorenson, nodding at a large triptych framed in carved wood, at the top of the first flight.

"The Garden of Earthly Delights by Hieronymus Bosch, isn't it?"

"Quite right, sergeant."

"Don't ask me how I know that," Brook added with a self-effacing expression.

"Being a policeman, I suppose you're bound to know it."

"Am I?"

"Of course. Apart from lending his name to a selection of superior power tools, Bosch was obsessed by man's inclination to sin, in spite of his fear of God's punishment. And sin is your raison d'etre, is it not?"

He was being teased. But Brook was that rare breed, a copper who'd taken the time to think about his role. "Not at all. My concern is the law."

"Is there a difference?"

"A huge one as I'm sure you know. I lock people up when they break the law. That's my job. I don't arrest a man for coveting his neighbour's wife, or for being slothful, or proud, or vain." Brook gave his host a piercing look, which Sorenson greeted with an appreciative nod.

"A good answer, sergeant, though not quite correct. You lock people away *after* they've broken the law."

Brook entered Sorenson's study and sat down in the high-backed leather chair indicated to him. The embers of a coal fire glowered in the grate and Brook stretched his legs to allow small blue flames to nibble at his damp feet. "Don't you ever question what use you are if you can only act in retrospect?" Sorenson asked from the drinks cabinet, his back to Brook.

"That's a perennial frustration of police work, agreed. I suppose the best I can hope to achieve is the protection of the innocent from those who would steal from them or do them harm."

"But that can't happen unless a crime has already been committed."

"True. But part of protecting the innocent is also seeing that they can't be punished for something they haven't done."

"A philosophy the guilty use to their advantage."

"Maybe. Nevertheless, arresting a killer, after the fact, can and does prevent further crimes."

Sorenson turned and handed Brook a heavy glass containing a generous measure of the same whisky he'd had on his first visit. The name escaped Brook and he couldn't make out the label. He took a sip and recalled the delicious smoke of his first tasting. For a second he speculated whether it might be poisoned and noted, with an amused twitch of the lip, his indifference to the prospect.

Sorenson sank into an identical chair opposite Brook and beamed at him. "Doubtless, that will be a great comfort to Mr Elphick and family."

Brook's answering smile was thin. He was in the home of a child killer, after all. "Unfortunately our after sales service seems to be more in-demand these days." Sorenson chuckled at this. "We can only hope to learn from what we see and be ready next time." The significance in Brook's voice was not too clumsy.

"You think there'll be a next time? For this killer you seek? For this Reaper?" Sorenson's eyes answered his own half-hearted question. "I mean, it's been a year now."

"I'm sure of it."

"And where do you think this killer might strike?"

"Somewhere local. He's not a young man."

Sorenson chuckled again. "Isn't he?"

Brook's attempt to ruffle his opponent's ego didn't appear to have hit home. Perhaps Sorenson's vanity applied only to his work.

There was a marked silence after that slingshot though it didn't seem to be the result of any souring of the mood. Perhaps it was tactical, so Brook waited for his opponent to open the next door on their tussle.

When Sorenson did speak he had some difficulty phrasing what to say.

"Do you ever dream, sergeant?"

"Dream?" Brook shifted in his seat. This was a road down which he didn't wish to turn. It was an odd question and one that provoked another. How could this man home in so accurately on Brook's weak spots? It was unnerving. He became uneasy but tried not to show it. There was something about Sorenson that disturbed. It should've been his crimes but wasn't – Brook had been unaffected by his handiwork. It was his mind, his thoughts, his questions, his probing. And what he said to Brook without speaking made even the silence between them seem like an interrogation. Sorenson was a man who could say more with his eyes than his mouth and when he did, when he looked at him with that mocking stare and amused superiority, Brook imagined himself being stripped bare and paraded for amusement, like some conquered chieftain through the avenues of Ancient Rome.

Those black eyes. They saw all. They had a power that enabled Sorenson to see through people. Through skin and bone and carti-lage, right through to the essence of being. Several times Brook had experienced the feeling that events in his past, his feelings and even his soul were available to Sorenson for examination. Everything that made Brook tick, and more importantly, threatened to stop him ticking, was as accessible to Sorenson as a daily paper.

Again those eyes were doing their work. Boring into him. As they penetrated, Brook felt his whole life being downloaded, taken from him and placed on file in the brain of his opponent. If knowledge were power, Brook was at Sorenson's mercy.

But how would he use the information, the psychological insight? Would he use it? Did he just want to know Brook or was there another motive? What did Sorenson want from him apart from stimulating conversation? An audience for his vanity? Someone to manipulate? Certainly Brook had no fear that Sorenson meant him harm.

But what did he want? And how did he know about what came to Brook in dreams? If he did know. Perhaps he was guessing. Perhaps Sorenson had merely stumbled onto the thing that was eating away at Brook's mind, taking his rest, threatening his sanity. Did he ever dream? Christ! Brook hadn't stopped dreaming since finding the Maples girl.

160

"I see that you do."

Brook mulled it over, not knowing how to continue. "In my profession you see things..."

"Of course." Sorenson made no attempt to prompt Brook further. He merely nodded sadly and gazed into the fire. Brook was wrong-footed by this sudden glimpse behind the curtain, a glimpse of affection for humanity, a glimpse of regret for Brook's pain. He suddenly found himself willing to tell all but unable to articulate it. The moment passed but Sorenson wouldn't be denied.

"Tell me."

Brook looked into the fire and remembered. It hadn't been that long since they'd found her. Six months. Less maybe.

Brook hesitated then set off. Perhaps he could offload his burden onto someone who deserved it. "There was a girl. Laura Maples. She died a few months ago."

"Ah yes. Not far from here. I read about it. Ravenscourt Park. Who was she?"

"Who was she?" Brook was unprepared for the simplicity of the question. He spoke as though he hadn't been thinking about it constantly. "She was nobody. A routine murder victim. Another street girl meets a sticky end."

"But she was more than that."

"She was a... No. To her parents perhaps." Brook stared blindly at the bright eyes and toothy grin of the schoolgirl smiling up at him from the fax tray – everything shiny and young. Her hair, her skin, her silver necklace with little hearts on it, strategically placed over her shirt and school tie to flag up her gentle rebellion.

"She was seventeen when she arrived in London, and quite pretty in a fresh-faced kind of way. She'd left her comfortable, stifling existence in the country and headed for the golden paving stones of London. No reason. No family strife, no abusive father, no lack of love or prospects. It was just that, for some, that's not enough. For some" – Brook managed not to add "of us". Sorenson had enough psychological crowbars – "the sheen of optimism, the embrace of life departs early."

"So she headed for a better life." Sorenson's smile didn't offend.

"No. Just a shorter one. You know the story from here. She's homeless, her money runs out, she ends up on the streets. She's young and healthy, she can make good money. Only the street isn't a shopping mall for the exchange of goods and services. It's a jungle. She stands out a mile. It's her first time."

Brook stared into the fire, unable to blink. His eyes began to complain once more. "She's picked up by a punter who goes back with her to her squat in Ravenscourt Park. She's got an old mattress and a small camping stove and a few candles..."

Brook took a sip of his drink. "We can't tell if he ever intended to pay but once they're inside it becomes clear he doesn't have to. He's in a derelict house with a naïve girl. It has a piece of urine-soaked hardboard for a door. There's nobody to stop him. Nobody.

"And what can she do? This pretty, nervous girl with little idea of the rules. So he decides. Why pay when it's more fun to take?"

"He rapes her."

"Why not? He's a strong man. She's a powerless girl. It's an old formula. But it doesn't stop there. Maybe she's crying, she gets upset and provokes him in some way, he's hurt her, violated her, torn off the necklace she's been wearing for years, a keepsake of his conquest. It cuts into her neck and she starts to scream.

"Or maybe, finally having such power over someone, even this gauche, stupid girl a long way from home, awakens something in him.

"He's never had power before, he's nothing, no-one respects him, no-one is in awe of him, no-one is aware he even exists. But this girl knows. She sees his power, fears it and he revels in it. He sees her fear and feels his power over her and it feels good. He wants more. He has the power. He feels it welling up inside him, the ultimate power over life and death. Suddenly he's a god. He is God. He can choose. He has the power to transform her into something else: a lifeless monument to his power."

Brook halted on that crescendo and took a moment before going on. "And so, that night, her insignificant life ends. There's an old beer bottle on the floor. He breaks it and uses it. Gently does it. Don't rush it. Feel the fear, her fear, feeding into him, leaving her weak, making him strong..."

Brook screwed his eyelids shut again, having forgotten to blink for a while – that, and the fire, has desiccated his eyes. If he keeps them closed perhaps he can imagine himself in the light and the warmth of an empty place – empty of all but Amy and little Theresa. And the girl Laura – shiny, full of life and hope.

"And you haven't caught him?"

"No. And we won't."

"How long was she there before you found her?"

Brook looked at his host. Bulls eye again.

"At least a month, maybe six weeks. We found her in summer. The smell..." Brook couldn't hold Sorenson's gaze. His mouth tightened around the rest of the story. Sorenson's eyes probed, waiting. Waiting until Brook became uncomfortable, not long. He felt obligated to finish but couldn't get past, "There were rats...I..."

"I see." Sorenson nodded in contemplation but little evident sympathy. "And was your horror confined to your visceral disgust at what the rats had done to her soft young flesh?"

Brook blinked as though smelling salts had been administered. "Sorry?"

"Yes, but for whom?" Brook looked into the fire, seeking solace. Sorenson continued to bore into him. "Regrettable though the death of Laura Maples may be, the horror that you feel is not for her ordeal but the physical desecration inflicted post mortem. Am I right?"

"Perhaps." Brook continued to gaze at the fire, aware of the mistake he'd made. Sorenson couldn't be affected by anything Brook, or anyone else, had seen.

"Surely the greatest pain or humiliation or mental torture has to be dispensed while still alive, while able to feel, to sense. The dead don't suffer, my friend."

Brook raised his eyes to engage Sorenson's, fighting the triumphant smile beginning to crease his lips. Suddenly he was close. "Or cry."

Sorenson smiled back, unperturbed at the excitement in Brook's eyes. He looked away and nodded, then back at Brook. "Did you cry for Laura?"

Brook stared back. "I will."

Sorenson emitted a sharp laugh. Brook saw that his host was pleased with the reply. "And did you cry for Sammy Elphick?"

A pause. "No."

"Because there were no rats?"

"Because he was nothing. A blight on the planet."

"But did that mean he deserved to die?"

"No. But it means he won't be missed."

"And the child, sergeant?"

"Who?"

"Sammy Elphick's son."

"What about him?"

"Will he be missed? Did you cry for the future that was taken away from him?"

Brook was unsettled. Don't answer.

"Did you?"

Brook drained his glass and stood to fetch a refill sanctioned by a wave of his host's hand. Sorenson remained unmoved as Brook poured and returned to his seat. Brook stared once more into the fire that was all but out. He took another long pull at his glass and gasped at the wrench on his throat.

He swirled the warm brown liquid around the glass and watched crystals dance against the dim glow of the ashes. Anything but look at Sorenson. Eventually he spoke, in a murmur he hoped would be difficult to distinguish but which instead seemed to echo around the room like a gunshot. "No."

And there they sat. Hunter and hunted, in no particular order, occasionally drinking, rarely moving or even looking at each other. At one point, Sorenson revived the fire with some dry fibrous logs and the two busied themselves inspecting the progress of the flames. From time to time the dull cracking of the logs would turn to spitting and Sorenson would nimbly jump up to return a hot ember to its place.

The heat blazed now and began to scorch the right side of Brook's face so he forced himself up to stroll around the study, inspecting books and paintings and record collections again. He looked back at Sorenson whose eyes had closed. His head remained upright, however, and Brook guessed that he wasn't asleep. Perhaps he was being invited to leave – or provoked into some indiscretion.

He drained his glass and placed it carefully on a coaster on the writing desk and picked up a piece of blank A4 paper that had been folded and stood upright. On closer inspection he saw it was a home-made birthday card, indecipherable apart from the childish crayon sketch of someone who could be Sorenson.

"From my nephew. Very talented, don't you think?"

"Nephew? Your brother's son?" Brook asked, remembering the photographs of Sorenson and his twin.

"Not any more, sergeant. My brother Stefan died." For once Sorenson was unable to meet Brook's eyes for fear of revealing too much. The hurt was clear in his expression.

"I'm sorry."

"Don't be. It's been two years. I'm over the worst. Losing a twin, they say, is like cutting off a limb. For once, *they* are not wrong. Twins are aware of each other from the moment they're born. Did you know that? Fifty years with a different person who is in fact you. A person who knows what you know, feels what you feel, says what you were about to say. Fifty years.

"And then nothing. No more. You're alone. You stand by the bed and watch as your own being withers and dies. All that you took to be a reflection of yourself changes into a caricature of what you are and becomes a kind of sick celestial joke. No rats, sergeant. Just cancer. Eaten, yes, but not post mortem. My brother, part of myself, eaten alive, from the inside, knowing it will not stop hurting, ever, until everything stops.

"And God does it hurt. To see the agony in his eyes, fear cloaked by the lion's smile, pierce you, beg you to help, to do something, to put a stop to it. Then when you don't, when you can only stand and watch and shrug and smile back, see the look in the eyes turn to

164

hate. Why me? Why not you? Do something. Are you enjoying this? Did you cause it? Do you want me to die? Help me!

"That's the worst thing I've seen, sergeant. That's what I dream about. You're not leaving?" This time it was a question suffused with human warmth, revealing a loneliness that mirrored Brook's. It put Brook on his guard.

"It's late."

"Perhaps it is. I've enjoyed our talk. Thank you for coming." He rose to show Brook out. Brook watched him walk across the study to open the door. What a piece of work Sorenson was. Easy company. Brook was rarely at ease, even at home. Perhaps he was home.

"My pleasure."

"You can see yourself out, I'm sure."

"Of course."

Sorenson returned to his chair and this time slumped down in a manner guaranteed to show his fatigue. Brook wasn't convinced. Was he really going to sleep or was this an invitation? After a moment's thought he decided he couldn't pass up such an opportunity.

"Goodnight." Brook closed the study door behind him and clumped noisily down two flights to the front door. He opened and slammed it shut with exaggerated force.

For a few seconds he stood completely still, waiting, listening for the noise of the study door opening. When a moment later, nothing had registered he picked his coat from the rack and kicked off his shoes. He wrapped them in his coat and set off back to the first floor, all the while listening for movement from the floor above.

The first door he tried opened into a small room dominated by a large wooden chest with slim drawers, the kind used by artists and architects to store sketches and paintings. Brook flicked on the light and inspected a couple of drawers at random. They were full of neat sketches and plans separated by tissue paper and appeared to be designs for some kind of building. Notes on the designs were in a foreign language Brook assumed was Swedish. Sorenson was a dual national, Brook had discovered, and had moved to London from Stockholm in 1960 as part of his father's chemical company expansion.

Brook extinguished the light and moved onto the next room. This time the door creaked slightly but after a moment's panic on hearing footsteps from the study, Brook was relieved to hear the strains of music once more, followed by footsteps, presumably returning to the chair. He waited a moment longer.

No door opened but there was something – another noise, closer to home, in the room he had just entered – and the hairs on the back of Brook's neck began to tingle. Somebody was whistling quietly, behind the door he'd just opened. Brook stiffened, assessed his alternatives, then realised what it was. The light was off. Somebody was sleeping.

He listened for a sign that he'd disturbed the occupant but the breathing remained regular and deep. Who was in there? Brook was sure from his skimpy file that Sorenson was a bachelor who lived alone. Then again the file wasn't very up-to-date. But married? No. There was nothing in Sorenson's manner or lifestyle to suggest that he'd recently found his soul mate.

Brook decided he had to risk a look. He inched his way further into the room and peered tentatively round the door clutching the bundle of coat and shoes in his moistening palms.

What he saw made him stand erect, relaxed, forsaking the tension of defensive readiness. A small nightlight softened the gloom and in its glow stood a bunk bed with two small children fast asleep, contorted into positions only young physiques can master.

The girl was on the bottom, her face turned to the light for comfort. Her eyes were screwed tight but her mouth lay open allowing its liquid contents to seep along her cheek and into the pillow. Her light brown hair was matted and she gripped a glassy-eyed teddy bear to her throat.

The top bunk was much darker and quieter than the girl's. Brook fancied that its occupant was male but he couldn't be sure. If he'd had a sister, he'd have bagged the top. The girl looked about five or six. He couldn't see the boy but he looked smaller.

Brook felt the need to linger, to see that no harm came to them. He had no idea how long he watched the children sleep. He realised, when he thought about it later, that he had forgotten where he was for that moment in time, that he was in the house of a suspected child killer.

And as he gazed at the sleeping infants, Brook remembered that he himself was a father and for the first time the thought moved him. He had responsibilities now. And until he could get home to his own family, to protect and care for them, he felt the need to safeguard these surrogates.

Finally, he closed the door as softly as he could and crept back down to the ground floor. Either he'd misjudged Sorenson completely or he'd been set up. Was it possible that he was meant to see the children to shatter all the presumptions Brook held about Victor Sorenson – The Reaper?

Yes it was. But that still didn't account for the fact that two young children, possibly his brother's orphaned children, felt so safe in Sorenson's midst, so able to abandon themselves to sleep, under his roof.

Even if it was a set-up, Brook knew one thing had changed in his perception of Sorenson. He didn't hate children, not enough to kill without reason, at least. That had been the hardest thing to square away in Harlesden – the Elphick boy – and it was clear now that Sorenson hadn't killed him out of some pathological loathing for young people – if he'd killed him at all. Brook began to harbour his first doubt.

He stood by the front entrance and contemplated his next move. The front door beckoned to him. He wanted to go home to his family. He wanted to fall into the arms of his wife and make everything right. He wanted to sneak with her into Theresa's room and watch their new baby sleep, that foolish smile, exclusively patented for new parents, deforming his face.

Instead he stepped through the door that led off the main hall, snapped on the light and closed the door behind him. He was in a spacious living room, sparsely furnished. It wasn't as cosy as the study and Brook guessed it was rarely used. What furniture there was, seemed thrown together as though this room contained all that was left of the pieces that didn't belong in other, more organised rooms.

There was an oddment of a suite. A winged chair, in a dark blue material, sat on one side of the cold black fire grate with a two-seater sofa, in faded brown suede, on the other. There was nothing on the walls but a large mirror over the fireplace flanked by a pair of ornate wall lights. The screen he'd seen from the road on his first visit guarded the lace-curtained bay window.

Brook was already retreating through the door and was about to switch off the light when he spotted something that made his heart leap. In a corner of the room, partially covered by curtains drawn across French windows, sat a pile of sturdy boxes.

Brook put down his bundle and scampered over to examine them. The delivery note on the top box, revealed that the boxes had been dispatched nearly three months ago and yet, the seal on the boxes hadn't been broken – a brand spanking new Compact Disc player, top of the range, and not even unpacked. The most expensive new technology not even opened or examined.

Brook's eyes narrowed. He knew. It was time. Time for No. 2 and this was the Reaper's entrance ticket. For video recorder to Harlesden, read Compact Disc player to the next family of victims.

Brook swung round at the sound of the door handle being turned. He looked feverishly for a hiding place. He didn't dare slip behind the curtains for fear of them moving, opting instead to leap into an alcove, where he pushed himself back against the wall and held his breath. He closed his eyes briefly, then, recognising the

167

absurdity, opened them at once.

He listened for the door opening but heard nothing. Then he saw and his heart fell into his socks.

Slowly, very slowly, and without a murmur, the door was swinging open. He saw it, frozen, in the mirror above the fireplace, which meant he could be seen in it, by whoever walked in.

Move, his nerve ends told him. Move. Slide down the wall, pull the curtain across your face, do something.

But he couldn't move. He couldn't wrench himself away. His eyes were locked on the door's progress and he could do nothing but watch, his mouth dry, the moisture having fled to his brow which had erupted in beads of sweat.

Then it stopped. The door moved no further. It hadn't swung open and he couldn't be seen. But what was happening? Who was on the other side of the door? Was it Sorenson? What was he waiting for? Brook's heart was about to implode. Still no movement. The door wasn't opening, wasn't closing. Why?

Brook couldn't move. He couldn't breathe. He could feel though, feel the springs of sweat, now galvanised into rivulets, cascading down his face. He'd had too much whisky.

The whisky? Perhaps it had been poisoned. Or drugged. His pores were trying to tell him something. He was in a bad way and if he didn't pull himself round...

Brook made a vow at that moment. If he got out of this house with his job, his liberty and his life intact he was going to clean up his act. No more stalking, no more nights away from home. He'd get help. It wasn't too late. He could still be a husband, a father.

With a sharp and unavoidable intake of air, which sounded like a passing steam train, Brook watched Sorenson's bony talon reach through the aperture between door and wall and flick off the light. Brook was caressed by the darkness.

The bar of light stumbling in from the hall narrowed to a shard and Brook began to regain his senses. But a sliver of light remained and Brook could hear no sound of Sorenson moving off. Then again, he hadn't heard him arrive either. The man's footfall was non-existent.

Brook waited for what seemed an eternity before moving. When his lungs were functioning properly again he tiptoed to his coat and slipped on his shoes. He moved to the door and put his eye to the crack of light.

His every fibre screamed as he stared directly into Sorenson's baleful eye and he leapt back from the door with the yelp of a startled puppy.

He reached out a hand to the light switch and flooded the room with light and grabbed the knob to pull open the door, swaying back slightly for safety's sake.

There was nobody there. Nobody. No sound of someone on the stairs, hurtling through the house. All was quiet save the wheezing from Brook's overworked lungs. He must have imagined it. A trick of the light. Or the product of his over-stimulated imagination. Whatever it was, Sorenson wasn't there. He was in his study. Brook could just hear the comforting muffle of classical music. What was happening to him? He was losing it. He had to get out.

He slipped his coat back on and, in one bound Brook was through the front door, closing it swiftly but with only a faint click. He ran to his car without looking back, not seeing the wind, if it was the wind, ripple at the curtains of Sorenson's study window.

Only when Brook was hurtling through the deserted streets of Kensington did his equilibrium start to return. Finally he was able to slow the car to a more respectable speed. He began to feel again, began to be aware of things, sensations, noises. With a start, he looked down at his left hand and saw the delivery note from the unopened boxes lodged there, becoming smudged from the sweat of his palms.

At the next red light, he squinted at the document. With a sigh of pleasure, he found what he was looking for and nodded. The serial number of the CD player.

Brook forgot his promise. He was safe now. He didn't need help any more, didn't need to go home to his family. He had all the help he needed right there in his hand. "Gotcha!"

Chapter 17

"What do you think?"

Rowlands shrugged and looked over at his colleague in the driver's seat, weighing his response with care. "I think I need a drink." Rowlands closed the folder and fumbled for a cigarette, lighting it with a trembling hand which he then held out for inspection. Three times he tried to cure the shakes with no more than an act of will. He failed each time.

"About the file, I mean."

"How long are you going to keep this up Brooky?"

"Guv..."

"I mean it. It's been a year now and yet you won't face it. This is nothing. We've got nothing on Sorenson and we never will have. I'm sorry lad. I can't cover for you much longer."

"What do you mean? I'm not asking you to. I get my work done."

"Do you think I give a toss about your work? This is the Met, Brooky. No-one gives a flying fuck as long as the villains are killing each other. I'm talking about Amy, lad. Remember her and your baby. I'm talking about your wife ringing me to complain to me about your workload and me having to pretend that it's my fault you're never at home."

"Guv..."

"No, Damen, it's got to stop. You've got to give it up. You're still young..."

"But he lied, guv. You accept that at least. His twin brother, Stefan, we talked about him. He told me he died of cancer..."

"So what? So he didn't die of cancer. So he was beaten to death in his home. Big fucking deal. It's a touchy subject to some people."

"Guv!"

"All right. What do you want me to say? He lied to you. What of it?"

"So it got me thinking. Stefan Sorenson was beaten to death in 1989, two years ago, disturbing an intruder who's never been found. Don't you see? Sorenson didn't want me to know that. Why? Because he found him. He knew I'd guess. That intruder was a burglar and maybe that burglar was Sammy Elphick..."

"Maybe, maybe, maybe..."

"It's motive, guv. He waits for his revenge. He finds the man who orphaned his nephew and niece. He's going to kill him and what's more, to pay back the suffering inflicted on the Sorensons, he decides to take out Sammy's family as a bonus. And what better way to do it than to make Sammy watch, make him suffer the way Sorenson's suffered?" Brook cast his eyes around, looking for a way to continue. "Do you know losing a twin is like losing a limb?"

"I do now." Rowlands sighed and ran his sleeve over the condensation on the windscreen. He stared out at the rain, avoiding Brook's entreaties. He affected a dry cough and pulled out his flask to treat it. Brook took the offered flask and feigned a drink in his usual way.

Five minutes brooding later, Brook tried to resurrect a reasonable tone. "I just need two more weeks, guv. I know he did it and I know he's going to strike again soon."

"Why? If he's got his revenge."

"I think he's got a taste for it," Brook offered, weakly. "All I know is he's planning it."

"How do you know?"

Brook pulled the delivery note from his pocket and thrust it at Rowlands.

"What's this?"

"A delivery note."

"What's it for?"

"It's for a £600 Compact Disc player. Look at the date. It was delivered to Sorenson over three months ago. It's still in the box in his house." Brook smiled at Rowlands. "Remember the VCR we found at Sammy's."

"Yeah."

"That was his way in to Sammy's flat. The CD player's for the next victims. And we've got the serial number. When he leaves it there, we've got him." Brook couldn't keep the victorious grin from his features and regretted it at once.

"You seem keen for The Reaper to kill again, Brooky."

"'Course I'm not but he will. And when he does..."

"How did you get hold of this?"

Brook paused and stole a glance at his boss. He hadn't expected Charlie Rowlands, of all people, to wave the Book at him.

"During an illegal search," he conceded.

"You're telling me..."

"Yes, it's inadmissible, but if we have The Reaper, when we have him, we'll get round it. I promise."

Rowlands sighed. Brook waited but he knew he had him. The longer his boss kept silent the more he was unable to conjure objections.

"Two weeks Brooky. Then I'm pulling the plug. That means Amy as well as work. Got it?"

"Thanks."

"Do you need anybody else?"

"He won't move unless it's just me, guv. Don't ask me to explain it."

Rowlands got out of the car and turned to Brook as though about to speak. In the end, he shot him a weak smile and closed the door.

Brook watched him hover outside the pub, looking slyly back at the car, so he engrossed himself in tuning the radio to let Rowlands slip in without guilt.

He checked his watch. 2.30. A couple of hours of daylight left. If he went home now, he could take Theresa round the park, give Amy some time off.

He started the car and arrived at Queensdale Road twenty minutes later.

No sooner had he killed the engine and kicked off his shoes, than Sorenson emerged from his house. He brandished an umbrella over his head, though it was barely spitting, and walked the hundred yards to Holland Park Avenue.

Brook knew from painstaking observation that Sorenson travelled everywhere by black cab so he restarted the car and crawled along the kerb after him. Not once did Sorenson look round. He was either oblivious to the way Brook had dogged his steps for so long, or he simply didn't care.

He climbed into a cab a couple of minutes later and set off to the west towards Shepherd's Bush Green, Brook in pursuit two cars behind.

The traffic was building and progress was slow. Only a handful of cars were getting through the lights on each cycle and Brook was tempted to get closer, to avoid being left. He resisted. If push came to shove he could always bang on the portable siren to make up ground.

As he feared, Sorenson's taxi driver scooted through the lights on red and the car in front of Brook pulled to a halt.

Brook slapped the wheel in frustration and was about to reach down for the siren when he noticed the cab pull over on Goldhawk Road and stop.

172

For a second, Brook thought Sorenson had stopped to be sure Brook didn't lose him – that really would have been taking the mick – but instead his quarry leapt from the cab and into an adjacent hardware store. The cab's hazard lights came on. It was waiting for him.

When the lights turned in Brook's favour, he overtook the stationary cab and parked fifty yards beyond. A moment later, Sorenson emerged with a plastic bag and hopped back into the cab. Brook sank onto his side as the cab pulled round his car and then sat up to continue the pursuit.

Two minutes later, Brook glanced over at the neat park on his left. Ravenscourt Park. In another hundred yards they'd pass Ravenscourt Gardens, the street in which Laura Maples had lived the last part of her brief life and died the first part of her eternal death.

With a surge of panic, Brook realised that's where Sorenson was going. The knowledge gnawed at him, as surely as the rats had gnawed at young Laura.

Sure enough, the cab pulled into Ravenscourt Gardens and Victor Sorenson stepped out carrying his plastic bag. Brook waited round the corner giving Sorenson enough time to find the right house. There was no hurry. Brook knew where it was, he could have walked there with his eyes closed. Especially with his eyes closed.

After an appropriate pause, Brook pulled off the main road and walked towards the basement flat where Laura Maples had perished. Nothing had changed much. There were no onlookers being held back now, no flashing lights and no convulsing uniforms. Otherwise it was as he remembered it.

Brook stopped and put his hands on the railings as he had that warm summer night. They were cold to the touch. He gazed down at the yard. It was still full of detritus, most of it saturated into cardboard soup by winter rains. Only the discarded plastic bag was shiny and new. The smell was the same. Decay.

Brook descended into the depths and picked up the bag. Inside were empty packages for a torch and batteries. He dropped it to the ground. Perhaps he could haul in The Reaper for littering with intent to commit serial homicide. Charlie Rowlands had once done something similar to a sneering Yardie, after he'd thrown his McDonalds carton on the floor. "If you can't catch 'em," he'd said to Brook, "piss 'em off."

Brook looked at the boarded window and then at the door. The hardboard had gone, replaced by a sheet of corrugated iron that had been pulled aside. The stench of urine and faeces still pervaded. For once, Brook hankered after a pull on Rowlands' flask but had to be content with rapid deep breathing. He tucked his trousers into his

173

socks and then he was in.

It was pitch black so he waited by the entrance to accustom his eyes. If he hadn't given up smoking for the baby he might have had a box of matches to light his way. It would be a splendid irony if, having quit smoking for health reasons, Sorenson crept up on him now and cut his throat.

Eventually Brook felt confident enough to inch toward the feeble glow, emanating from the room in which the girl had died. At the thought of her, he saw again the bloated, blackening corpse of Laura Maples and felt a surge of nausea rising in him.

A noise from the next room distracted him and he pressed on, aware of rustling and nuzzling in nearby rubbish. Grazing rats probably. Brook wasn't sure he could go any further. He wanted to run back to the light, breathe fresh air.

"They're more afraid of you, than you are of them," he muttered, though he knew it wasn't true.

Brook clenched a fist. He had to go on. Sorenson was waiting for him. This could be the final test. And passing it could get him the ringside seat for Reaper 2 – The Reckoning. This time it *was* personal. So he inched forward, scuffing his feet across the floor to ensure he didn't tread on a scavenging rodent. He cursed Sorenson for leading him here and himself for being so squeamish.

Where was Sorenson? If he was in the next room he was certainly being very sparing with the torch. Perhaps this was a trap after all, Sorenson's solution to a year of harassment, but before he could ponder this theory further his blood curdled at the sound of a deep and baleful howling, emanating from the entrails of the house.

He had no time to decide whether to run or freeze because a shadow fell across the faint light of Brook's destination. It was moving fast and, before he could dive out of the way or even raise an arm for protection, the shadow had hurtled into him with a sickening thud of skull on skull.

Brook went flying in the dark and landed on his left shoulder, with a distasteful skid through something rotten and slimy.

But the shadow wasn't resting. Although knocked back by the collision, it rose quickly and charged headlong through the door, slithering to a halt before taking the stairs two at a time. Brook clambered to his feet. He caught a glimpse of a hairy face and filthy coat, shiny with wear, and made to follow but instead slipped on something that gave way under his foot and he sank back to the ground.

A foot from his head, a torch flicked on. The light startled the rat poised to sniff Brook's face and it scuttled away, hastened by Brook's scream of terror. He flailed his arms around his head for a moment to stave off any further invasion and scrambled onto his haunches, eyes wide, mouth set in a grin of fear.

The light turned to Brook and brought him some relief for his nerves though his stomach wasn't pleased to see the dog shit he'd fallen in.

"Are you alright, sergeant?" Sorenson declined even to feign surprise at the sight of his opponent.

"I will be when I get this stinking coat off," said Brook, taking the unexpected offer of Sorenson's hand. Brook was yanked to his feet by a powerful arm. "Thanks. Who was that?" he asked tearing off his reeking coat, nodding at the exit.

"That, I assume, is the new tenant," replied Sorenson.

Brook held his coat at arm's length, between finger and thumb, his face puckered until he burst into the fresher air. Outside he shuddered at the sight and smell of his clothing and sucked in much needed oxygen, all the while eyeing Sorenson with a look of mild annoyance. "You certainly spooked him."

"Yes. I don't think he heard me. He got a bit of a fright."

"I bet he did." Brook shot a glance at Sorenson's suede shoes. There wasn't a mark or a damp stain on them. The man's agility was remarkable. He must also have fantastic night vision to walk in there without his torch on. "What are you doing here, professor?"

"I could ask you the same thing," he replied with an accusing smile but Brook wasn't to be charmed off the subject and glowered at Sorenson. "Shall we visit the scene of the crime, sergeant?" Without waiting for an answer, Sorenson snapped the torch back on and marched back into the derelict flat. Brook made an instant decision to follow and leapt after him to make sure he got full value from the light.

When they reached the killing ground, Sorenson began to move his head around, looking, sensing.

"It was here wasn't it?"

"Yes."

He nodded. "I was moved by your story of the girl's plight. I thought I might be able to help."

"Help? How?" The undercurrent of Brook's scorn was ignored.

"With suggestions."

"Such as."

"I assume the Metropolitan Police are utilising the miracle of DNA fingerprinting, sergeant?"

"It's becoming a useful tool, yes."

"So you know what it is."

"It's the use of tissue samples to obtain a DNA profile of a person, a unique signature from the DNA molecule, which can be

175

visualised like a bar code. And no two are the same."

"And did you know that you'll eventually be able to get a profile, no matter how small or old the tissue sample is?"

"This is pie in the sky at the moment, professor. It's only just operational."

"Sergeant, the first patent in the UK was only issued four years ago. Yes, this technique is in its infancy but it will become ever more sophisticated. Samples that seem too small or old to give up their DNA secrets today will be easy to test in five or ten years. Did you find samples of young Laura's killer?"

"There was a lot of semen. But it was old and compromised."

"It looks like he's got away with it then..." said Sorenson with a knowing smile, "...unless you kept the samples."

"The file's still open," Brook replied, puzzled. Sorenson didn't fit Brook's identikit of a concerned citizen.

"I'm glad to hear it. Murderers are going to have to be ultra careful in future. Why, even a hair follicle falling to the ground could be their undoing." Sorenson beamed, for once without a trace of mockery. "Of course you'll need an idea of who to profile to see if you've got a match."

"How do you know so much about it?"

"Former contacts in the business. My father founded Sorenson Pharmaceuticals. I'm sure you know."

Brook looked at him, uncertain how to proceed. "Why have you come here, professor?"

"Like I said. To help."

"And how will this help?"

"Atmosphere, Sergeant Brook, never underestimate the power of atmosphere."

"Your brother Stefan was murdered during a break-in. Was it Sammy Elphick?"

Sorenson flinched for a second and Brook wasn't sure his experiment had worked. He was pleased to get such a reaction from Sorenson, to know that he could be affected, but his move was at odds with the way the game was supposed to be played. This crude stab at his quarry's underbelly might get Brook disqualified from the final round.

He needn't have worried. The smile returned at once.

"If you'll excuse me, I have a number of things to take care of." With that he set off back to the entrance, Brook at his heel to be sure not to get left in the dark.

Having ascended the slimy steps, Sorenson marched away. Brook watched him go. Suddenly he turned back, training the torch on Brook's face. With a look at the skies, he said, "It looks like it could be a wild night tonight." With a smug smile, he added. "There's going to be an electric storm and sparks are going to fly. Won't that be something?" Sorenson sniggered, looking very pleased with himself. He turned and walked away to hail a cab on the main road.

Such self-congratulation was an unpleasant sight and reminded Brook of his purpose. "Catch you later," he heard himself calling at Sorenson's retreating frame. The time was near.

*

Brook drained his coffee and dialled the hotel switchboard for an outside line. He felt good after his nap. He'd only been asleep for an hour so, perhaps, that wasn't the reason. They say confession is good for the soul, which heartened Brook because his present upbeat mood might be evidence that he still had one. How might he feel if he'd told Jones everything? No. There were some subjects that couldn't be broached – for her sake as much as his.

"DS Noble, please. Inspector Brook. Yeah, I'm having a fine old time Harry. Just connect me, will you?" A moment later. "John. How goes it?"

"*Okay, sir. We've found the van.*"

"About time. Where?"

"*Opposite Derby Station. Looks like he may have got a train out of town.*"

"Opposite? Then why the hell wasn't it found days ago?"

"*It wasn't on the road. It was on a private drive. Turns out the couple living there have just got back from a skiing holiday. They reported it as soon as they got through the door. We've got Forensics going over it now.*"

"Anything yet?"

"*No but there's a fair bit of blood around.*"

"It won't be our boy's, you can be sure."

"*We've got a footprint.*"

"What size?"

"*Eight. From some kind of sports shoe.*"

"That's something. Get onto Midland Mainline..."

"*In hand sir. Aktar's reviewing all the CCTV but we'll keep it for you to look at.*"

"Good. Anything else John?"

"*Yeah. We got a call from the hospital. They've done more tests on what was in Jason's blood. Apparently he was on something the night of the murder. Thought you'd want to know.*"

"We know he was on something. He had Ecstasy tablets on him."

"It wasn't that."

"What then?" Brook's heart quickened as he listened. He nodded. "Keep the surveillance on him. We want to know where he is at all times. Anything else?"

"Yeah. Jason's shoes have got no blood on them and there are no footprints of his in the front room. He's in the clear there."

"So it seems. What about his clothes?"

"Forensics is still working on them."

"Okay. Just a thought, John. When you go house to house around the van, ask if any other cars were on that drive over the last week. Maybe he had another car waiting. In fact, while you're on it, check the house. If the killer knew the residents were away for a while he might even have stayed there."

Brook put the phone down. He looked at his watch. He had half an hour before meeting Wendy.

*

Five minutes later he was strolling down Queensdale Road, hands in pockets, fingering the delicate metal with his left hand. He withdrew his hand and inspected the necklace with its small hearts. Why had he brought it? It was in the past and he should have left it in the file in the cellar. His heart was sad for the girl but she was in a better place now. Perhaps he should just send the necklace back to the Maples family. There was little justification for keeping it. Her parents might be glad of it – assuming they were still alive.

On the other hand they had plenty to remember her by and Brook still felt a responsibility towards Laura. He'd keep it for now, but he resolved to return it to the folder for good. No point trailing it everywhere, reminding him.

He strolled on. Yes, he ambled now. Like any tourist might. Not like before. Once upon a time he was in a hurry to get to Sorenson's house, mind racing, in thrall to the chase.

He hadn't been here for many years. Not since that last night in '91. The night of the storm. Now it was like he'd never been away. The house was exactly the same. The same ivy, the same porthole window on the second storey, the same screen behind the lounge windows, the same brass bell pull.

Brook lingered in front of the house, though on the opposite side of the road. He stood under the shadow of a tree, which hung over the fence of a small circular garden for residents only.

The night of the storm...

Chapter 18

It was tonight. Brook knew it. The preliminaries were over. The time was now.

And Sorenson was right. The weather was filthy – enough rain to make even Noah reach for his saw. It was a wild night, an end-of-the-world night. No-one would go out of their way to interfere with The Reaper on a night like this. It was down to Brook. No-one else mattered.

It wouldn't be easy. Visibility was poor. If it weren't for the ivy, he couldn't have picked out Sorenson's house through the rain beating down onto his windscreen.

He considered parking closer but rejected it. There were no spaces. Besides, Sorenson didn't want to give him the slip. Not after all that had happened, all the tests Brook had passed. This was the final showdown and Sorenson needed him.

Brook glanced at his watch. It was getting late. Past nine. Not late by his standards, but late for most families to take delivery of a brand new, top-of-the-range CD player.

Brook rested his eyes for a moment. He listened to the rain lashing against the car and felt it rocking under the wind's assault.

He opened his eyes at the sound of a vehicle approaching from the rear. A white two-seater transit van passed by. It had a sign on the door that Brook couldn't see. A hire van maybe.

It slowed to a halt in front of Number 12. A figure hopped out. Impossible to see who it was. About Sorenson's height and build certainly, but if it was Sorenson he wasn't in his usual garb. The man was dressed head to foot in black. A black one piece, overalls probably, black gloves, black sports shoes and, most striking, a black balaclava. Black to hide the blood.

The figure opened the back doors of the van and skipped up the step to Sorenson's house. Obligingly an outside light was turned on and, just to make sure Brook hadn't missed his entrance, Sorenson pulled off his woollen helmet.

Even at a distance of fifty yards, in poor light, Brook could see it was Sorenson. But what a difference. The version stood before Brook now was as bald as a billiard ball and, just to emphasise the point, Sorenson ran his hand over and around his shiny pate, feeling the rain on his skull, before disappearing into the house.

"...even a hair follicle falling to the ground could be their undoing."

The challenge had been thrown down. DNA sampling. Sorenson had told Brook how he might be caught, that very afternoon in Ravenscourt Gardens, and had shaved his head to prevent it.

Brook turned his attention to the van. There were things in the back but he could only pick them out in silhouette. One shape could've been a coil of rope. He was tempted to nip out and take a closer look but decided against it. Sorenson wouldn't be long if he were leaving the doors open. And there might be a limit on the latitude Brook was allowed. He could take nothing for granted.

Sure enough, a second later Sorenson reappeared, his black helmet back in place, arched under the weight of the boxed CD player Brook had seen on his previous visit.

With the boxes safely lodged in the van, Sorenson returned to the driver's seat and drove away. The rain began to beat down harder as Brook pulled the unmarked squad car out into the road and sped after his prey, trying to maintain discreet distance. It would be difficult. Traffic wasn't light in such weather. Fortunately Sorenson didn't drive as fast as most Londoners, perhaps unaccustomed to driving, perhaps to be sure not to lose Brook.

They headed south. Progress was steady. Across the A4 on the Earls Court Road, on over the Fulham Road then left onto the Kings Road. The van now heading east turned south again towards the river, right onto Beaufort Street and Brook's pulse quickened as a secret dread began to pull on his gut.

The van crossed Cheyne Walk and, as Brook had begun to fear, went straight onto Battersea Bridge. No. He wouldn't let himself think it. Sorenson wouldn't be so stupid.

Over the river now and on into the night. Still south. Latchmere Road. Not far now. He hoped he was wrong. He wasn't.

Through the lights Sorenson slowed and turned left onto Knowsley Road and drew to a stop outside Brook's new house. Amy's house really, he'd spent so little time there.

With some difficulty, Brook found a parking space a few cars behind the van. It was all he could do to leave it at that. His every fibre screamed at him to pull across the van, drag Sorenson out and beat him to a mush.

He didn't. He couldn't. All he could do was sit, paralysed, his fear mounting. He watched the van but no-one got out. Sorenson was just sitting there, waiting. Waiting for what?

The rain pulverised the bonnet of Brook's car and his wipers were on top speed. It was hard to see what was happening. And then a panic began to grip Brook. Was Sorenson still in the van or had he got out somehow, using that delicate touch for sneaking around he'd demonstrated before?

Wild ideas suggested themselves. Was there a hatch in the van, which even now Sorenson could be crawling through, before dragging himself along the blind side of the parked cars to the track which led to Brook's back garden? Was it possible he was even now in the house?

Brook couldn't think straight. He was suddenly hot and panting heavily. Sweat burned his eyes but he brushed it away quickly to avoid lowering his lids. Where was Sorenson? What was he doing?

Brook tried to keep his eyes on the van but he had to look at the house, just to be sure. He darted an agitated glance at the warm glow behind the living room curtains and suppressed a shiver. There was nobody outside the house. He was sure. But had The Reaper got out of the van? Was he already inside? What was happening to Amy and baby Theresa at this minute? Surely Sorenson wouldn't...

Even as he rationalised Sorenson's behaviour Brook knew he was making a massive assumption. Sorenson was The Reaper, a cold-blooded killer, a man who could execute a child without a second thought. Brook had forgotten. He'd been sucked into Sorenson's world and had lost sight of what he was, what he'd done. Perhaps that had been the plan. To lullaby Brook so he could put his family under the knife.

He had to get out of the car. He had to look. This was his family. He must go look.

But he couldn't. Brook was numb, burned onto the seat, drained of energy, of will, his eyes locked onto the van in which he hoped and prayed Sorenson sat. All he could do was hang on. Hang onto that kernel of faith that had taken root in his gut.

He likes me. We have an understanding. He wouldn't do that to me.

Then it hit him and his face contorted with self loathing. He'd betrayed them. His own seed. His family. The wife and daughter he was willing to sacrifice to his faith – his faith in Sorenson's need for him and his own hunger to be embraced by Sorenson's grand design, to be there at the death, literally or metaphorically, it didn't matter to Brook.

With a Herculean effort, Brook managed to raise his arm to the door handle and pull it towards him. It opened but as it did so, Brook saw the tail lights of the van cast their crimson fire over his hand.

Sorenson was on the move again, pulling out and round the corner, in no particular hurry.

Brook switched on his ignition but at once turned it off. He slumped forward, head bowed, eyes closed. His faith had been rewarded but at what cost? He was finished as a viable father, husband and human being – at the end of his tether. Rowlands had seen it and tried to warn him. Amy too.

The thought of his beautiful wife forced Brook to sit up. He started the car and set off. As he pulled level with the house he sounded the horn. Once. Twice. Nothing. He made to step out but Amy's face at the window, peering through the condensation, stopped him. She was safe. The Reaper hadn't called. Nor would Brook. He couldn't. He'd forfeited his wife and his daughter to the game. He'd lost them forever.

He sped away and followed the road back to the main street. He looked right and left. Nothing. Sorenson had lost him. Why? Why had he done that? That wasn't part of the plan. Think.

Going south. Always south. Brook turned left and gunned down to the lights just turning red. He slammed his foot to the floor and hurtled across the front of a startled black cab, which came to a skidding halt in the nick of time. Brook looked back in the mirror to be sure only the cab's horn had sustained damage.

On he sped. Onto Clapham Common. South. Keep going. Brook knew now why Sorenson had stopped outside his home. The game had softened Brook. He'd been civilised by it, by the genteel adherence to proper behaviour, to rules. That's why Sorenson had been to his home. To remind him what could happen if he forgot what he was dealing with – The Reaper.

Brook was angry – angry at the dance Sorenson had led him, angry with himself. He'd been a fool and Sorenson wanted him to know it. That was good. He needed that reminder. It could help him stay sharp. And focused. And hungry. Now he could win.

Chapter 19

Brook turned to walk back to Holland Park Avenue. He was going to be late meeting Wendy. Then an impulse overwhelmed him and he crossed the road and hauled on the brass pull of Number 12. He held his breath and listened.

No music. No sound. Nothing. He was about to turn away when a noise from within made him linger. The door opened.

"Can I help you?" The woman peered at Brook dubiously. Her voice had a heavy Scandinavian lilt. She looked about fifty years old with short blond hair, tinted to disguise any grey, wide, clear grey eyes and a clear complexion. She was still a handsome woman and must once have been a great beauty. She held a hand over her eyes to shield them from the low sun.

"Is this Professor Sorenson's house?"

"It is."

"Right." Brook was hesitant. He hadn't expected the house to still be Sorenson's. "I...used to be a friend of his...it was a while ago. I heard the news and came to pay my respects."

"That's very good of you," she said without gratitude. She was suspicious, uneasy, gripping the door with one hand. "It's a difficult time."

"Yes. Are you Mrs Sorenson?"

She hesitated. "Yes."

Brook nodded politely. She didn't trust him. Why would she? He didn't trust himself. It was time to get personal. "I hadn't realised Professor Sorenson...Victor had married. He certainly kept that quiet." He unfurled a smile that implied her husband had been a lucky son of a gun.

At the mention of his name, Mrs Sorenson seemed to thaw and she smiled back. "Oh no. I'm not Victor's wife. I'm his sister-in-law. Victor never married."

"Of course. I'm sorry. You must be Stefan's wife then. Widow," added Brook, glad he'd reviewed the file a couple of days before. His tone was regretful and he bowed his head in the appropriate manner. "I knew Stefan only slightly," he lied. "A terrible business..."

At the mention of Sorenson's brother, the frost returned to his widow's face.

"Yes." She dropped her eyes and a hint of remembered pain clouded her features. Brook was surprised. She hadn't got over it in all these years. There *were* others like him.

"How are the children taking it?" asked Brook, immediately realising that Sorenson's nephew and niece must be *her* children.

"Badly. Victor became a father to them."

"I know." Brook had nowhere else to go with this and wished he hadn't bothered. He looked at his watch, keen to be away from the awkwardness. "Well I must be off. Please accept my best wishes."

"Thank you." She held out a hand, more cheerful now that he was leaving. "Mr?"

"Brook. Damen Brook." He shook her outstretched hand.

To Brook's amazement Mrs Sorenson's face lit up in a warm smile of recognition, that changed her completely. She looked different now, different and yet, somehow familiar. Had he met her in the old days? He didn't think he had.

"Mr Brook! Why, of course. Victor used to mention you all the time. He was very fond of you, you know."

"Was he?"

"Yes. You were always in his thoughts and prayers."

Brook smiled back with as much warmth as he could manage. "And he in mine."

"Where are my manners? Won't you come in and have some tea?" She was positively gushing now and Brook found it unnerving. What had Sorenson said about him? The mention of his name usually had the opposite effect. Perhaps he should send Harry Hendrickson and a few others round for a reappraisal.

"I can't. Thank you. I have an appointment." Brook took a step back to try and close proceedings.

"What a pity. Well, thank you for coming. If Victor were..." Her lip began to wobble and tears filled her eyes.

"I understand," Brook nodded and turned to walk back to the hotel, not noticing the curtain twitch at the porthole window on the second floor.

"Interesting," he muttered. His impulsive act had thrown up an intriguing question. Why had Victor Sorenson been handed the responsibility of looking after his brother's two children after his murder in 1989, when the mother was still around? Or had they just been visiting the night Brook had crept into their room all those years ago? He resolved to find out.

*

Wendy Jones looked at her watch as Brook stepped into the piano bar. He caught the gesture and smiled at her not to be embarrassed.

"You're right. I'm late. Sorry."

"No need to be. It's just, twice in one day. It's not like you. I mean...they say..." Jones blushed.

Brook raised an amused eyebrow as he called a waiter over. "Really? And what do they say exactly?"

"That you're always punctual," she replied softly, looking at the ground.

"Anything else?"

Jones paused, then looked up and smiled back. She stared at an invisible list on the palm of her hand. "Rich, arrogant, clever, obsessive, no sense of humour, likes old sports cars, difficult to get along with."

Brook threw back his head and guffawed. "No sense of humour? I resent that."

She laughed and her face brightened. It was a heartening sight. Brook was reminded of their night together, recalled having never seen anyone giggle as much as her. Though he'd assumed that was Breezer-induced.

Jones continued her own reassessment. She'd been misled. He's just different to other people, she thought. Nothing wrong with that. And the things he'd told her, the things he'd seen. It would make anyone difficult to get along with. It wasn't surprising he carried the scars. In fact, he should have been more damaged. She felt a brief twinge of desire. He was lost and maybe she was the one to find him.

"So you are rich," she accused.

Brook's grin faded to a smile as though he was ashamed. "It depends how you define rich."

"Why don't you define it for me? Harry Hendrickson reckons over a million."

"Does he? Well, he's way out. If you really want to know, I sold my flat in Fulham when I got divorced. It made £180,000 profit all of which I gave to Amy and Terri. Last year I sold the house in Battersea for a profit of nearly £800,000, would you believe?"

"Which you gave to your wife and daughter."

185

"No. She's remarried so we split it. Okay?"

"And you're paying for the hotel yourself."

"Exactly."

"Just to take another look at this Sorenson's house?"

"Right." She didn't seem convinced. "Atmosphere, Wendy. It was important to get back the old feeling. No matter how painful. I hope I didn't embarrass you earlier?"

"No. I understand how you must have felt. This Sorenson sounded very charismatic and you were young."

"I felt better telling you."

There was a lull as both drank their coffee but the awkwardness had gone.

"So what now?"

"Now? It's too late to see Charlie Rowlands. We're going to check in with my old station, put out a few feelers and then I'm going to buy you a fantastic dinner."

"Sounds good. But as you're down to your last four hundred grand, do you mind if we go Dutch?"

*

Brook sat naked on the edge of the bed and pummelled his wet hair as he talked into the phone. DS Ross, a wide boy from Hammersmith nick, was on the other end.

"That's right," said Brook. "Married to Stefan Sorenson. He was bludgeoned to death in his home in Kensington '89. Right. How are you spelling that? S-O-N-J-A Sorenson. Got it. Belle Vue Park Retreat. What is that? Interesting. Four years? Sounds like a sick woman. Yeah. Thanks a lot. Don't worry I'm sure it's nothing but you'll be the first to know if I turn up a connection." An impatient pause. "I know I'm out of my jurisdiction," said Brook. "That's why you'll hear the moment I find anything. You'll have to take that up with my Chief Super. Yeah. Yeah. Thanks again."

Brook slammed down the receiver. "Moron." He'd forgotten the contempt the Met had for "Hillbillies," one of the many insults they hurled at coppers stationed outside the M25.

Still he had his information. Mrs Sonja Sorenson had spent four years in a "retreat". From 1988 to 1992. Retreat – a sugar-coated name for a mental institution, according to Ross, though attendance was voluntary, not to mention expensive.

Her mental problems pre-dated both her husband's murder and her brother-in-law's subsequent atrocities. Natural then that after

Stefan Sorenson's murder, responsibility for his children would devolve to Victor.

And perhaps it was feasible that she knew nothing about Victor's activities. But four years was a long time. Perhaps she knew what Victor had done. Maybe her husband's murder, and her brother-in-law's obsessive search for his killer, and his brutal revenge on Sammy Elphick and family, had prolonged her illness.

But that still didn't explain why such a young mother, with two very young children, should check into a glorified mental hospital the year before her husband's death.

Brook knew he should have delved deeper into Stefan's murder at the time, but he'd been so preoccupied with the Harlesden killings, and so thrilled to uncover a motive for them, that he hadn't felt the need to be exhaustive. Perhaps he'd been right. Perhaps there was nothing in it.

But now he had a bigger problem. He had a dinner date with Wendy Jones and he wasn't sure what to wear.

*

Wendy Jones chewed her final mouthful of baklava with her eyes closed. She swallowed, with an extravagant moan of pleasure, and resisted the temptation to lick the film of honey from her spoon. Instead she sat back, contented, and opened her eyes. Brook watched her, his chin resting on his knuckles, a half-smile playing around his lips. It was good to watch people, young people, enjoying life, satisfying their appetites with no thought other than self-gratification.

First Vicky, now Wendy.

The memory of his desperate night with Vicky, brought home to Brook the possibility of carnal pleasures.

"What are you smiling at?" asked Jones.

Brook filled her glass with wine. "Thinking how nice it is to see you eat."

"Don't. I'm supposed to be watching my weight."

"What for?"

"I'm getting...stocky."

Brook took the opportunity to inspect her. It was less embarrassing than showing her he could rely on his memory. "You've nothing to worry about Wendy."

"Don't be too sure. I need more exercise." When she realised the implications of what she'd said, she flushed. Brook pretended not to notice. He ordered two large cognacs and the conversation dried.

Finally Jones broke the silence. "Sir?"

"Please call me Damen."

"It wouldn't feel right…"

"Just for tonight." Again she went red so Brook followed up hastily. "You don't mind me calling you Wendy?"

"I prefer it."

"There you are then. What were you going to say?"

"I was wondering how strong a connection there is in London, with the Wallis killings."

"Only the MO."

"Then why are we here for three nights? There must be more valuable leads to follow in Derby."

Brook shrugged. She was probing in that clear-thinking way she had. She was right. Unless they unearthed a concrete link soon, they might as well go back tomorrow. He wondered whether to mention Brighton but decided against it.

Two large cognacs arrived. Brook drained his glass and called for the bill. Jones went for her purse but Brook insisted on paying.

"One thing puzzles me. It's a bit personal…"

"Go ahead Wendy."

"Well. If you're so well off…"

Brook opened his mouth to raise an objection.

"…relatively speaking," she added. Brook smiled his agreement. "Then…I don't know how to put this."

"Just say it."

Finally she found the words. "Why don't you live properly?"

Brook stared at her wondering if she was serious, then realised it was a good question, with no easy response. In the end he could dredge up only one answer.

"I don't know how."

Chapter 20

Brook slept as well as he had in years that night – his mind clear and clean. No guilt. No pain. It was the best therapy having someone to speak to, someone he could trust, someone he knew now he could spend time with.

When he slept that night his dreams didn't drift into visions of feeding rats, or porcelain corpses, but to Wendy and his longing for her. Hope invaded him. He'd seen his desire reciprocated and it had taken an effort of supreme will to decline the offer of a night-cap. Such an effort that Wendy could see his refusal was not another snub but the gesture of a man thinking of her sensibilities, in case the morning awakened forgotten embarrassment.

Brook woke refreshed, infused with a rare energy. He jumped out of bed to busy himself. He wanted to be at Charlie's house before noon. The sure way to get sense from him before the booze took hold.

After making tea and knocking gently on Wendy's door, he packed with the efficiency of the single man and went down to stow his bag in the car.

*

Two hours later, Brook and Jones swung into the drive of a medium-sized detached house in the leafy suburb of Caterham.

There was no immediate answer to Brook's pounding on the door and just when Brook had begun to think his old boss had gone out, the door opened.

"Brooky! How the bloody hell are you?" growled a voice laden with tar. There was also the tell tale aroma of mints. Charlie Rowlands stepped into the pale light and grasped Brook by the hand.

He felt the warmth of the greeting with a lump in his throat, swiftly gulped away. Brook was unused to the affection of a friend. "Not too bad," he replied after a second's thought. He never mouthed platitudes when asked even that simple question. "You?"

"Couldn't be better." Rowlands grinned at Brook. It was an obvious lie. His old boss had shrunk in the years since he'd known him. He had once seemed so tall, dominating the space in a room. To the young DC's of Hammersmith he was an intimidating figure – authority as well as physical presence. It was a potent brew. Charlie Rowlands had been a God.

But now he was diminished. Once he'd looked down into Brook's eyes. Now they were level. His back was no longer straight as a ramrod but curved and compressed. He'd lost weight as well as the last of his hair, and he was painfully thin. His face was bright and robust, however, as the faces of drunks often are. The red tinge around the high cheekbones and nose mimicked a rosy sheen of health.

But the eyes had it, as always. That look of sunken pain, which repelled slumber, the look Brook had seen staring back from the shaving mirror many times.

Rowlands continued to smile unsure how to continue. He snaked a glance at Jones.

"This is WPC Wendy Jones, sir."

"I can see she's a W, Brooky. I've still got some of me marbles. How are you Wendy?"

Jones stepped forward to shake his outstretched hand, blushing with pleasure at a remark she might have admonished from a junior rank. "I'm fine sir."

"Please. I've been retired a long time, luv. Call me Charlie. Got that, Brooky."

"Yes guv,"

Rowlands began to cough. His breath came in rasping bursts now and he held up his hand in apology.

"Where are my manners? Come in out of the cold."

"That'd be a first," smiled Brook.

Rowlands laughed without getting the joke and led them into a bright, modern kitchen.

"Still with the smart remarks, eh Brooky. And it's Charlie, remember."

"Right." Brook had only been to the house twice before – once for dinner, with Amy, to celebrate Charlie's daughter Elizabeth's eighteenth birthday. Then again a year later, alone, to put his boss to bed after her funeral had driven him to the brink.

That was a night not to be repeated. The two of them sat up

together the whole night, Brook waiting for his boss to pass out into the safety of coma, Rowlands waiting for Brook's vigilance to wane so he could destroy himself.

That night they drank and sobbed and drank and howled and drank and sometimes even laughed, before drinking some more. It was the laughter that signalled ultimate surrender, the laughter that kept the world at arm's length – for a short time.

Near dawn, Brook, way over his limit, had passed out on the sofa, his arm clamped round his quietly shaking host. When he woke, his first blurred vision was the sight of his boss, his friend, sitting at the dinner table, drink in hand, staring saucer-eyed at Elizabeth's doomed smile in the picture frame. His old Webley service revolver lay on the table but there were no bullets for it. By default, Charlie Rowlands had chosen life.

And now, perhaps, Charlie hadn't lied. *"Couldn't be better"* was the truth because now he was nearer death. Nearer his Elizabeth.

It was the first time Brook had been back since that terrible night and as he glanced through the house, he realised he hadn't expected the place to be in such good order. He'd assumed it would be more of a time capsule. Everything the same since Mrs Rowlands had given up on Charlie and left him to it. The pictures of Elizabeth still took pride of place but the parts of the house he knew were different. The kitchen was new and expensive. The lounge had also had a makeover. It was sparsely but tastefully furnished with none of the clutter wives felt obliged to scatter everywhere – objects accrued that told not of a life lived but an ambition to be someone else, someone better.

No flying ducks, barometers, carriage clocks. Give Charlie credit. Not everyone stopped trying. Not everyone gave up on creature comforts once their spirit was extinguished.

"Breakfast anyone?" asked Rowlands, plonking down two mugs of steaming hot tea.

"Yes please...Charlie, if it's no trouble. We didn't have a chance first thing." Jones sounded a little tentative and searched out Brook's face for signs of disapproval. Charlie turned to him.

"I could eat," nodded Brook.

"But only because it keeps the body going, eh Brooky? Nothing changes."

"Some things do," replied Brook rolling his eyes around the decor.

"This? Yeah." Charlie suddenly seemed uneasy and busied himself laying rashers of bacon onto a grill pan. "My new hobby. I say new. I started the DIY when I retired. It keeps my mind off...things. I'm sure you understand lad."

"You took a while answering the door. Did we get you up, sir? Charlie."

"No lass. I was sitting in the garden reading the paper." His tone didn't convince. "Where did you stay last night?"

Brook hesitated. "The Kensington Hilton," he finally said, looking intently at the bacon spitting under the grill.

Rowlands laughed. "Jesus Brooky. Not the Hilton again. What the fuck for?"

"Just to get the old scent back."

"I hope you were paying lad."

"Of course."

"Can I use your toilet, Charlie?" asked Jones.

"Course love. It's the first on the left," Rowlands called after her, running a surreptitious glance over her retreating frame. "You've got a beaut there, Brooky."

"She's a fine officer," Brook nodded, resisting the temptation for man talk.

Rowlands chuckled into a cough. "*A fine officer.* Yeah. Full house an' all." Brook nodded to condone Rowlands mocking. He'd earned it.

*

After breakfast, Jones got her case from the car to have a shower and change her clothes. While Charlie washed up, Brook stood on the patio and looked around the large sloping garden. It was slightly overgrown but generally in good shape. Charlie had been busy. But then he had a lot of memories to deaden.

The pine trees at the rear were mature and took most of the pallid sun out of the equation, even near noon. Most of the lawn was still covered in frost and emitted a satisfying crunch under Brook's foot. It was cold out of the sun so he returned to the patio. He took out Jones's mobile and dialled. While he waited, he checked that Charlie was still washing up then ferreted around the patio furniture.

He found the whisky bottle under the blanket draped over the sun lounger. It was a quarter empty. The mints were there too. Charlie's full English breakfast.

"John."

"*Sir. Where are you? The Chief Super wants to know.*"

"Still in London, John. What's happening there? Any developments?"

"*We've got a list of about forty single men who stayed in Derby hotels the night before the killings. We're checking reasons for visit,*" *which ones left the morning after, nothing so far."*

"Okay. I'll be back tonight. And for my sake, don't say anything about my calling. I'll brief McMaster when I get back. Got it?"

"But the boss wants to know where she can reach...?"

Brook turned off the phone and returned to the house. Rowlands was in the kitchen drinking coffee. A half finished brandy bottle stood on the table.

"Any news?"

"Not really. The Chief Superintendent wants to hear about progress so I didn't speak to her."

"How do you get on with that dyke?"

Brook gave Rowlands a look which he pretended not to see. "She likes me, as much as anyone in her position can afford to."

"It's all about image these days Brooky. The top brass won't stand for egg on their faces. Being a copper is all about politics. I'd barely get above DC if I had my time again."

"Maybe."

"Drink?"

"Of?

"Something to keep the cold out. Don't worry. It's after twelve. You used to be able to fake drinking strong liquor pretty well, as far as I can recall."

"Was it that obvious?"

"Blinding laddie. I didn't mind. You kept me company, in more ways than just that."

"Just doing my job, Charlie."

"Fuck off, Brooky. It was far more than that. You were doing both our jobs." Rowlands tipped a little more brandy into his coffee and looked at the floor. "I never had the chance to thank you. Not properly. Please let me finish," he insisted. "You saw me through that time. If it hadn't been for you I wouldn't have made it, I wouldn't have wanted to make it. You gave me the strength..."

With a cute sense of irony, Rowlands' rasping cough returned and Brook stood to clap him on the back. He poured himself a small measure of brandy and raised his cup to Rowlands. "Cheers Charlie."

"Cheers Damen. Here's to you and that lovely girl. I hope you make a go of it, I really do."

"What do you mean?"

"Come off it, lad. You deserve a chance at happiness." Rowlands was beginning to well up. "I blame myself, you know, for Amy..."

"What?"

"If I'd been able to look after myself at work..."

"Forget that now, Charlie. Don't even think it. There was nothing you could have done to save my marriage." Brook took a drink and winced at the unfamiliar heat. If he was to drive in the afternoon, he could drink no more so he put the cup back on the table. He looked at the floor. He didn't know how to say what he wanted. He wasn't even sure he wanted to say it. He decided, as usual, to keep it simple. "How long have you got?"

Rowlands looked up and smiled. He shook his head in wonder. "The best damn detective I've ever seen, Brooky, I swear to God. How did you know?"

"You haven't had a fag since we arrived. Not by choice I assume."

"You're right. Physically I can't handle them. One puff will have me on the floor, bringing me guts up. Lung cancer. Both barrels. Six months. More likely three."

"I'm sorry."

"Don't be."

Jones walked into the kitchen. Her hair was still wet from the shower. She wore a pair of dark trousers, baggy at the ankles but figure hugging at the high waistband. She placed an empty cup and plate in the sink. "That was great. Thanks."

"Don't mention it love."

"Constable, we're hitting the road again. You'd better dry your hair."

"Sir?" She looked round at the two of them but their eyes were glued together, waiting to be left alone. "Right." She took the hint and went back upstairs. The blast of the hair dryer followed moments later.

"Tell me about Sorenson, Charlie."

"What do you want to know?"

"When did he die?"

Rowlands grinned. "Around the same time as me."

*

Driving or not, Brook needed another pull on the brandy. "You said he was dead."

"I said he was a goner."

"So he's alive."

"Not really. Like me. Cancer. Getting in line."

"And how did you find this out?"

"He was in hospital, same time as me. He came over to speak to me."

Brook stared at the floor, eyes like flint. "Did he?" he said softly.

"I didn't know you knew him."

Charlie hesitated. "I didn't know him. He knew me though. Knew I was your boss from the old days. He wanted..."

"I know what he wanted."

"Do you?" Rowlands smiled. There was pleasure in his expression but it was buried under a mask of pain. "Do you really?"

"He wanted to know where I was."

"Yes."

"And you told him."

Rowlands paused, examining Brook's face. "Yes."

"When?"

"A few months ago."

Brook nodded. "And a family in Derby dies."

"You don't know there's a connection," said Rowlands.

"Don't I? So why speak to him at all, Charlie?"

"Because he's dying Brooky. He said..." Rowlands halted, unsure how to continue. His eyes began to water and Brook was eaten by guilt. He was giving his old boss a hard time but he had to know.

"What?"

"He said he had a bond with you – a friendship almost. He said he wanted to speak to you one last time. I understood." Rowlands darted him a look. "He said he had something to give you."

Brook nodded. "What was that?"

"Purpose. He said you needed purpose."

Brook laughed bitterly. "And that's what he's given me, Charlie. Problem is he's had to kill an innocent young girl to do it."

"You don't know that."

"Come off it Charlie. Don't tell me about Sorenson. You don't know the way he operates, the games he plays. Christ, I spent a year breathing the same air as him."

"If you say so."

"I do say so."

"So you don't want to see him then?"

"No, I damn well..." The venom in Brook's retort took Rowlands aback. Brook took a breath and softened his features. "No I don't. But what choice do I have?"

Rowlands smiled in sympathy. "None. Not if you want to be sure, son."

"I'm sure. He did it. He did the London killings and now he's killed in Derby."

"How can you be so certain?"

Brook locked his gaze onto Rowlands. Odd. For a second there was something...something in his old boss's voice that suggested he was probing. Probing not for impartial clarification, but for information he needed. Brook wondered whether to give it then answered softly.

"Peter Hera."

"Say what?"

"Peter Hera." Brook nodded. Back on the case he could put his baggage down and revel in the gratification of detection. "It didn't take long. You see Sorenson thinks I do crosswords. I was doing one the night he first invited me into his house for a drink."

"So?"

"It's an anagram, Charlie. Not difficult. Peter Hera. The Reaper. It was the name on the fake license given to the van hire company in Derby. In case I was in any doubt."

"Just that?"

"No but that was the clincher."

Rowlands nodded. "So The Reaper is back."

Chapter 21

"So will you see Sorenson?" Jones looked up from the map book to study Brook's face. It was fixed on the road ahead.

He sighed, showed some signs of having heard her. A few minutes later, he said, "I can't avoid it. When Victor Sorenson wants something he usually gets it." Brook pulled over to the kerb and killed the engine. "We're here."

"What time does she get out?"

"I'm not sure. Three-thirty?"

As if on cue, a stream of uniformed girls disgorged from the double doors of the handsome building at the end of the avenue and streamed towards the gates where the Mondeo was parked.

Brook took the time to run his eye over the beauty of the surroundings, the immaculate cut of the grounds, now covered in a patchwork layer of frost. As on his previous visit, he had to douse the fires of resentment against a system which allowed some children, through no merit of their own, to grow tall in these Elysian Fields, while others, through no fault of *their* own, huddled against the radiator of a dog-eared prefab.

Brook stepped out of the car, motioning Jones to wait, and walked to the gate. He tried not to appear careworn. He didn't want to burden her with more of his woes. She might get the idea he was too much effort in the long term.

The first gaggle of girls passed him, pulling on coats and mufflers against the chill seaside air. They were utterly carefree in their privileged cocoon. He was struck by their energy and zest, that sense of unabashed expectation that clung to them. They screamed and strutted and giggled and teased, some fingering cigarettes, longing, anxious, anticipating sufficient cover to don the cloak of adulthood, some chewing gum like it was going out of fashion.

And like all of their generation, they were afflicted by that selective blindness which prevents the young seeing anyone of Brook's age, even someone standing so self-consciously, staring in their direction, wondering what he must look like, a man in his forties loitering outside a girls' school on the last day of term.

They walked past him as though he wasn't there. He didn't exist, at least not until a middle-aged woman with a tight bun came out of a side door and proceeded to march to the gate, all the while her eyes boring into Brook.

"Daddy!" screamed a voice from within a pack of high-pitched banter and a slender dark haired girl came out of the crowd to fling herself at him.

"Terri." Brook raised his arm with a glance at the matronly figure who, somewhat reassured, slowed her approach to her duty position. There would be no abductions on her watch, after all.

Terri threw herself into Number One Dad's arms and he swung her round with less ease than he used to. Still, this bridge to the past was important to him. She was the best thing he'd ever done with his life. Perhaps the only thing. In spite of his trepidation, Brook's tension vanished and he cracked into a wide smile.

"Daddy. What are you doing here? I can't believe it." She was breathless and a little more self-conscious now, as a couple of her friends had planted themselves against the escaping tide and were looking on with interest. "Daddy, this is Cynth and this is Marsha."

"Hello Mr Brook," said the one identified as Marsha, sheepishly.

"We've seen you on the telly," added Cynth with a sidelong leer at Marsha. Ah, he was a celebrity. Now he was visible. Brook smiled back, unaccustomed to star-struck fans.

"Can we have your autograph, Mr Brook?" added Marsha.

"I can do better than that. Give Terri your address and I'll get my agent to send you a couple of signed photos."

"Cor! Would yer?"

"Take no notice Cynth. He's teasing you..."

"'Course I am. I don't have an agent yet. Now where do you want me to sign, girls? A body part perhaps..."

"Dad!"

"Or a piece of underwear?"

"Stop it!"

"Or would you like some of my DNA? I've got a sample in my pocket."

"DAD!"

"Well...we've got homework Tel, we'll see you later, yeah." They rushed away.

"That's got rid of them," observed Brook.

Terri turned to her father still open-mouthed. "How could you embarrass me like that, dad?"

Brook laughed in disbelief. "Well, for God's sake, Terri. My autograph? Doesn't the real world touch young people? I'm a policeman. The reason I'm on *the telly* is I'm investigating a triple homicide, and the man I'm after kills girls younger than that and doesn't turn a hair doing it. Does it all boil down to fame and money for girls like that?"

"And why shouldn't it? I'm a girl like that. We're only young once. Maybe we don't want the real world to touch us yet, dad. Is that a bad thing?" She was calm but furious.

Brook looked at his daughter. He hadn't seen her for so long. She seemed tall. And beautiful. And intelligent.

"That's a good answer," he conceded. He was very proud of her, suddenly.

"*I'm* a young person, don't forget. It touches me."

"Sorry."

Terri fixed her eyes on Brook. Her attempt to stop her lips curling up was in vain and she burst out laughing. "Their faces though. You're *so* bad." She punched his arm and shook her head in wonder and Brook laughed with her. "*Would you like a sample of my DNA?* That was really naughty, dad."

"I know. Will they be okay? I mean..."

"Those two? They'll be fine. That's nothing to the things they come out with."

"Spare me."

Brook took her hand and led her towards the car, he beaming at her, she chattering away. She was so...mature. Fifteen and so old. The outside world encroached too quickly these days, like it or not. But then it had to if they were to be kept safe. Brook, of all people, knew that.

"Why are you here, dad?"

Brook opened the car door for her and introduced her to Wendy Jones. He didn't register his colleague's puzzled expression as she eyed Terri's auburn hair. "Come on. I'll take you for a coke."

*

The cafe on Brighton pier was dingy and the coffee was bitter and expensive. Terri twirled her ice around the bottom of her glass with a straw and Jones merely stared at the table.

199

When Terri stood to go to the toilet, he took his chance. "Wendy, I've got to have a word with Terri, in private. Do you mind?"

"Not at all. I'll go." She kept her eyes on the table. Her voice was clipped and formal but she'd dropped all pretence to acknowledge his rank. Something was wrong.

"No please. Stay here in the warm. I need the air."

"Fine. Here comes Daddy's special girl now."

Brook's hair stood on end his mouth fell open. Vicky. His heart sank as he realised his blunder. How could he have been so stupid? Vicky's blonde hair. And Terri...

Brook swallowed a deep breath. He didn't have time to wallow in the embarrassment. He had harder emotions to deal with.

"Wendy..."

"Please don't call me that sir."

Brook nodded. Her anger made things easier. "I don't have time to explain. I will later, if you want to listen." His cold tone gave Jones pause for thought but she still couldn't look at him.

Brook stood as Terri returned to the table and escorted her outside.

"Isn't Constable Jones coming with us?"

"Not just yet. I need a word." The wind swept in from the sea, cold and refreshing, and the pier was close to empty.

"Terri."

She stopped and turned back towards him, searching his face for an explanation. He looked suddenly serious and in pain as though he had a toothache. Something in her realised the reason for his visit and she looked away.

"Terri. What's going on?"

"I don't know what..."

"You had something to tell me. Something you couldn't say in front of your mum. What is it?" She opened her mouth to speak but her expression caused Brook to dive in. "I want to know what's going on between you and your stepfather. I want to know now."

A cloud passed over Terri's eyes as she sought the words to pacify her father, but they wouldn't come. Instead she walked over to the rail and looked out over the foaming sea. Brook paced after her.

"Terri, please. Talk to me."

She looked up at him, then down at the boardwalk. "We're in love."

"You're what?" Brook's expression may have been uncomprehending but his heart was in the know. "Say that again."

"I love him dad. And he loves me."

"My God, you're only fifteen, Terri."

"I'll be sixteen in April."

"There are laws…"

"The laws are like borders, dad. They're artificial constructs. There's no…"

"Did Tony tell you that?"

"Dad we're in love. Deal with it."

"Deal with it?" Brook stared, still processing the information. A million questions crowded in – questions which were noble in their concerns for others. What about your mother? What about the legal issues? How long has this been going on? But one question burned above all others. The visceral ache that no father of a daughter can deaden. The only question that matters.

Brook's palms were sweating despite the cold. "Have you…? How does he love you?" he said softly.

Terri looked at the deck of the pier again. She couldn't find the words perhaps realising there weren't any. She looked every inch the schoolgirl now, despite her height, despite the make-up. She might have been in the Head's office, being told off for throwing water in the labs. At last she mumbled her excuse but instead of blaming another pupil and saying 'It won't happen again, miss,' Brook heard, "He loves me like a man should love a woman."

Brook looked away, a strange wheezing noise emanating from him. It was his breath leaving his body as though he'd been punched in the solar plexus. He could see the brown water seething between the boards. It made him feel dizzy. "But you're not a fucking woman," he spat at her.

Terri flinched at the obscenity and then her eyes glazed over into that shocking, hard-faced certainty patented by all-knowing teenagers who think it conveys experience but instead betrays only insecurity and selfishness. "I'm both of those things," she informed him, coldly.

Brook's heart fell into the icy sea. The penny dropped with it and, before the last syllable was out, he'd gripped her by the shoulders, and was shaking her violently. He closed his eyes and the moisture in them was forced onto his cheeks. Heads began to turn but Brook was oblivious.

"Dad, you're hurting me," Terri wailed, trying to prise off his whitening knuckles and wheeling around like a wrestler trying to break a hold. She looked around at the desultory passers-by who were assessing the free entertainment. A stall keeper took a step towards the dance. "It's okay, he's my dad," she panted. The man hesitated, deciding to wait for developments.

"Dad!" Terri shouted, shaking him in return. "People are watching."

But Brook shook her and shook her. The man who ran the sharp shooting stall took a further step but Brook was unaware of everything, save the rushing in his ears. He was mumbling incoherently, spinning her round. He could see and hear nothing. He was unconscious, drowning. His life zipped across his mind and was gone and Brook hoped that would be the end of it.

But suddenly there was calm – an impression of stillness. Brook could feel the warmth of the sun on his face. Nothing else. He was in orbit, flying towards great heat. His body was weightless and his head felt like it was on a stick. He was very tired and his head slumped to his chest. He became aware of his legs. They felt heavy and unwilling to hold him upright. With an effort of supreme will he opened an eye to see the water swirling below his disobedient feet. Then the noise of the waves rushed in and he was able to locate Terri's face. She looked at him. She was sad. Her eyes pleaded with Brook. Her mouth was moving but Brook couldn't hear. She seemed to be crying, pulling at him.

A numbing cold grabbed Brook a second later and other senses came rushing in. He heard, "Your mother. Your mother," and realised he was speaking.

Terri still struggled against his grip. "Dad! Let go!" Brook tried to let her go, to unfasten his fingers but couldn't work out how to do it. Then a soft mouth from behind touched his right ear and then a voice.

"Inspector Brook! Stop it. Let go."

All was noise and bustle now. Brook heard the panting and snorting of those struggling around him. Wendy Jones had an arm squeezed into his neck, choking him. Don't stop Wendy. You don't mind if I call you Wendy?

"Sir. We've got to leave now," she insisted.

Brook looked to the heavens and saw the grey sky above. He relaxed his muscles to signal his defeat and slumped into Jones's arms. She loosened her grip, just holding his shoulders to keep him upright.

"He wants locking up, he does," observed the sharpshooter.

"He's a fucking lunatic!" ventured an amateur psychiatrist, toffee apple in hand.

Finally Terri broke free and stomped away to the rail, sobbing. Brook turned his eyes to look at his hands still held in front of him like a novice bullfighter. He let them fall to his side as his knees gave way and collapsed to the floor. Jones lifted him up by the armpits and put her arm round him.

"Come on sir. Let's go." She held his limp frame and walked him through the throng.

"You should call the police, luv. 'Streets ain't safe with nutters like 'im roaming around."

"I am the police," she spat back, "and if you want a night in the cells, just stay there shooting your mouth off."

The potential have-a-go-heroes were aggrieved but wandered away, that's-the-thanks-you-get expressions glued to their faces.

*

"Sir?"

"Who is it?"

"Wendy Jones."

"I've told you. Call me Charlie. Everything alright?"

"No sir. It's DI Brook. I think he's had some kind of breakdown."

There was a pause though not a long one. *"Right."*

"We got down to Brighton, no problem. Then we picked his daughter up after school. From what I could gather she's having a relationship with a man. I think it might be her stepfather."

"Oh God. Not little Terri. How is he?"

"I'm not sure. He seems physically and mentally exhausted. I can't get him to talk. I can't even get him to look at me. He just stares into space."

"I know the symptoms. Where is he?"

"Lying down. I booked us into a B & B. I didn't know what to do."

"You did the right thing."

"It's like he's in a trance. Should I get a doctor?"

"No. He wouldn't do anything. You did the right thing. He just needs complete quiet. Try and get him to sleep, that's the main thing. Hot sweet tea and sugared rum. That's the stuff. He's in shock."

"You say this has happened before."

"It was a few years ago now."

"Was that down to The Reaper?"

"Amongst other things. You see, luv, Damen's got this brain – haven't we all? But his...it never stops unless he switches it off. But he has to take the trouble to do it. Most of the time he can but this case, it's got him thinking again and he's clever, he can't accept he hasn't caught The Reaper. I'm not explaining this very well. Suffice to say the last time it took away his marriage, his home and part of his sanity."

"He told me about Sorenson. About his relationship with him."

"*Did he? He hasn't told anyone else, luv. I think he really trusts you, Wendy.*"

"Do you?"

"*I do.*"

"What should I do?"

"*Look after him. Stay with him and keep feeding him hot, sweet tea and sugared rum. He'll be okay. If he drank more he might not be in this state now. By the way Wendy, your boss tracked you down to here. She's hopping mad you haven't kept her up to speed. I said you were working hard which took the wind out of her knickers for a while.*"

"You didn't have to…"

"*I know. I did it for Damen's sake. She also said if she didn't hear from him tomorrow, he'd be reprimanded.*"

"Shit."

"*Don't worry about that. Damen wouldn't. Look luv, forget all that 'til tomorrow. Just stay with him tonight. Ring me tomorrow morning, will you?*"

"I will Charlie and thanks." Jones replaced the receiver.

✻

Half an hour later she returned to the Seaview carrying two Sainsbury's bags. She retrieved her key from the tight-lipped landlady who made a point of glaring at Jones' shopping. What an insult. To buy one's own provisions, when even now a dozen contented residents were sitting down to a hearty meal of vitamin-free slop, was truly a slap in the face for Mrs Purley. Mr and Mrs Jones indeed – a likely story.

✻

Jones pushed open the door to their room with a bag then dropped both to the floor with a chink of glass on glass. She winced but Brook didn't move. He lay prone on the bed, fully clothed except for his shoes, snoring gently.

Jones decided not to disturb him. She ate her sandwich in the chair by the window and watched. Occasionally she crept to the toilet or made a cup of tea. Brook's cup sat waiting – rum and sugar – waiting for him to stir. On she waited, listening to the steady rhythm of his breathing, wanting to climb on the bed next to him, but resisting.

He needed her and she needed to be needed so she sat on, keeping her motionless vigil, satisfying herself with the lightest stroke of his

204

forehead, a taunt to the urgent physicality of their previous night in bed together.

And so the evening passed into night and night into early morning and still he slept. It was the sleep of the dead. His life, everything he'd worked for was gone, spoiled forever, and there was nothing left for Brook to do but concede and start from scratch, from the womb. Clear of all thoughts, all worries, all preconceptions and all conventions. Now he could sleep. Now he was nothing. Nobody. No job, no career, no family, no future and, for once, no past. None of it mattered any more. To worry about any of it, never mind try to influence it, was futile. He had landed on the longest snake in the game and it had crushed and swallowed him. He'd been so close but now he was back at the start. If he wanted to go again he had to throw a six. If he wanted to go again...

*

South. Always south. Brook checked his watch. He'd been driving around for over an hour since he lost Sorenson. Why had he let that happen? There had to be a reason. After all Brook had been through, to be discarded like this.

Disconsolate, he pulled up to the red light on the South Circular, at the crossroads of Brixton Hill. An hour ago he would have run the lights but now the urgency was gone. It was late. Near midnight. The tension of the chase had evaporated, the search fizzled out. Even the rain was stopping.

Brook had lost the game. He'd lost to Sorenson. He'd lost to The Reaper.

The lights turned and Brook drove on. He hung a left towards the city, intending to take a long loop through Brixton, back up to Clapham and home. It was over. Time to let go.

Home. Then a thought – an icy hand of dread squeezed his heart. What if he'd been tricked? Sorenson had lost him and then doubled back towards Amy and baby Theresa. They were alone. Helpless.

Brook blinked to gather his thoughts and get his bearings. Which way? He'd just missed the turn-off by Brixton Town Hall. Now he'd have to turn up by the Academy and gun it down there.

Brook changed down and floored the accelerator. As he did so, something caught his eye and he jumped onto his brakes and slithered to a halt. On the opposite side of Brixton High Road, Brook stared dumbstruck at a street sign. He gazed at it. Electric Avenue.

"There could even be an electric storm. Very rare. Yes, sparks are going to fly."

Brook stared on, his mind churning. A cabbie pulled past, glaring and gesticulating.

Finally Brook pulled into the outside lane and swung right, up towards Brixton Market, now deserted except for discarded fruit and vegetable boxes. He parked underneath the arches opposite the eastern end of Electric Avenue.

Brook's family were forgotten. The hunt was back on. He leapt from the car and padded down the street.

Chapter 22

Jones woke from her third uncomfortable night in the armchair to the sound of the gulls feeding on dawn crabs. It took her a moment to realise where she was, before the pain in her back reminded her. She'd spent the whole weekend in vigil, watching Brook sleep, feeding him rum when he roused briefly, sneaking out for half an hour of exercise in the evening or a bite of toast in the morning. Now it was Christmas Eve and, like it or not, she'd have to try and find a doctor. This couldn't go on. She couldn't endure another night in that chair.

She looked at her watch. Gone eight. She shifted her position but it didn't help. She sat forward and pulled the curtain aside and a finger of grey light crept into the room. Then she saw the crumpled bed. Brook wasn't on it. She sat up, wincing at the pain in her lower back and stood to stretch her legs. Where was he?

The noise of the shower offered first comfort, then anxiety.

She lifted a hand to tap on the bathroom door then stopped. There was an unusual noise coming from the bathroom. It was so commonplace, yet so unexpected, that Jones could only stand and listen, a baffled expression creasing her face.

No. There was no mistake. Someone, presumably Detective Inspector Damen Brook, was whistling. In fact, more than that, he was breaking into song as well.

Jones was worried. She raised her hand again but, as she did, the water stopped. A second later the door opened and Brook stood before her, one towel round his waist and another being rubbed vigorously through his thinning hair.

"Morning, Wendy. Shower's free." He beamed at her.

"Thanks." She continued to examine Brook for signs that all was not well. "Are you alright, sir?"

"Never better, Wendy. Never better."

"Good. It's just that for the last few days…"

"I know. I'm the weak silent type." He smiled as he came over to hold her shoulders then stooped to kiss her on the cheek. "I can't thank you enough. In fact, I can never repay you for what you've done for me. Now hurry and get cleaned up. I'm starving."

*

Brook buttered his fifth piece of toast and devoured it with the same gusto as he had the others. He poured himself another tea and sat back to enjoy the view out of the window and lick the butter from his fingers. The food on the table had been annihilated. Two full English breakfasts, both eaten by Brook, had followed two mini-packs of cereal and several unsanctioned refills of economy orange juice.

Brook purred as he picked at his teeth.

"You eat like a condemned man."

Brook smiled. "On the contrary, I've been reprieved."

Jones drained her tea and excused herself for a few minutes. When she returned to the dining room and sat down, Brook followed her progress, not hiding his attraction. She smiled back at him, still puzzling over the enigmatic grin, now a permanent fixture on his face.

"Let me guess. Charlie?"

"Still the great detective."

"It wasn't difficult. Navy rum with sugar. Doctor Rowlands' Miracle Cure All. I suppose he said I don't drink enough."

"He says you're in denial."

"He may be right. But if so I recommend it."

"The Chief Super rang him. If we don't get in touch, we're off the case. That was two days ago."

"*I'm* off the case. I won't let her tar you with the same brush." Jones pulled a face. "What? I can handle McMaster. Trust me Wendy."

"So you're going to speak to her?"

"Eventually, but not on the phone. I've got an errand to run in town then we can head back to Derby." Without irony he added, "Home."

*

Brook turned to give Jones a final reassuring wave then pushed his way into the smoked glass of the revolving door.

On the fourth floor he was ushered into a swish outer office and asked to wait. Leather sofas, soft lighting, tinted windows, tasteful, understated Christmas decorations. PR was clearly a good business to be in.

A colour co-ordinated brunette strode confidently towards him, default smile in place. Her hair was flawless, her teeth blue-white and her make-up without blemish.

"I'm Mr Harvey-Ellis' secretary. Can I help you?"

"Yes I'd like to see him."

"Is he expecting you, Mr…?"

"Detective Inspector Brook. By now, I would say, yes. Ms Gibbs," beamed Brook, scrutinising her nametag.

Ms Gibbs seemed unsure. She disappeared for a moment then returned. "I'm afraid he's in a meeting at the moment and can't be disturbed."

"You astonish me."

"We're closing at lunchtime, we're very busy. It's Christmas Eve. But if you'd like to wait…"

"No. I'd hate that. I'm easily bored. You trot along and tell him to disturb his meeting or I'll come along and disturb it for him."

Ms Gibbs stood open-mouthed, darting her Siamese eyes around the reception area in the vain hope that someone would come to her assistance. "I…"

"Still here?"

At this Ms Gibbs turned and scuttled away. Brook followed her into another office.

Unaware of him, she paused to compose herself outside a large pair of doors sporting the sign "Conference One." She brushed herself down, as though in the twenty seconds between the reception area and the conference room she'd been strewn with litter, and knocked timidly on the door before entering. Brook marched in behind her.

Perhaps a dozen people sat at the long polished table. Twelve pairs of eyes moved their curious gaze from the flustered Ms Gibbs to the encroaching Brook.

Only one person was standing, furthest from Brook, a burly man, an inch or two shorter than Brook, with a heavy-set face, partially obscured by thick wavy black hair. The jacket from his expensive suit had been discarded onto the back of a chair and he stood in shirtsleeves and loud braces. He had a pointer in one hand and stood to the side of a Data Projector. It was Tony Harvey-Ellis.

Only *his* eyes didn't engage Brook with curiosity. Only *his* eyes didn't bore into Brook's granite expression with a mixture of annoyance and interest. In fact, he didn't look at Brook at all. Terri must have poured it all out to him and now Tony stood on the scaffold of his own folly, resigned to his fate. Humiliation? Violence? Arrest? Perhaps all three. Resignation flowed from his every pore. No fear, just a hint of sorrow perhaps. Sorrow for the end of self-esteem, the end of a persona carefully constructed for others.

In those few seconds Brook almost felt sorry for the man. Then he remembered Amy. Poor Amy. Her world would fall apart again. Only one thing was a consolation to Brook at that moment – the thought that soon, perhaps today, his star would begin to rise in Amy's eyes again. It was an unworthy thought but it caused him no guilt. In fact, he liked the idea. Without wishing to, Amy would have to reassess her previous marriage in the light of damning new evidence against her current arrangements. There was no way back for Brook and Amy but it was nice to think of their history together being rewritten, if just a little.

A distinguished man in his fifties, with thick grey hair, stood to take charge of proceedings. "Can I ask what the hell you think you're doing?"

"No you can't." Brook beamed at him in such a polite manner it caused an immediate tremor of unease.

"Look here…"

"Sit down."

"Ms Gibbs. Call the police."

"The police are here, PR man," said Brook. "Tony Harvey-Ellis." He looked at Brook now, a grim smile glued to his face. "I'm Detective Inspector Brook. I'd like to speak to you in connection with several serious offences, including the corruption of a minor and rape."

Gasps exploded round the room. Tony's smile faded. He nodded at nobody in particular. He certainly didn't acknowledge any of his colleagues, now turned towards him, jaws sagging.

"Must we do this here, Damen?" His voice was calm.

"Do what?" Brook's air of bewilderment was over the top, as was his subsequent embarrassment. "Oops. Silly me. Have I been indiscreet? Have I said the wrong thing? Me and my big mouth. Then let's go to your office, Tony." Brook turned to the throng as he made to walk out. "Everyone just forget I said anything."

Brook waited for Tony outside the conference room and let him pass. Tony led Brook to another door and they went into his private office. As Tony closed the door behind Brook, a dozen faces looked on from the safety of the conference room.

When they were alone Tony turned to face Brook, flinching at the expected blow but not preparing to defend himself.

"Do you think I've come here to hit you, Tony?"

"I don't know. I only know I've been a shit. I deserve it."

"You want me to hurt you, don't you?"

"No, I..."

"'Course you do. You think you'll feel better. You'll think you've had your punishment."

"No."

"Well I'm not making it that easy for you. Not a chance. Nothing you can say will make me hurt you."

"Listen Damen it just happened, I didn't plan it this way..."

Brook took a one step run up and kicked Tony in the crotch. He collapsed to the deep shag carpet like a slaughtered cow, doubled in agony. His breath came in harsh rasps. And Brook circled him without expression.

"Now look what you've made me do. That's not what I wanted at all, but you're too clever for me. And now you're feeling a lot better and I feel like a fool." Brook ambled to the window and looked out across the bay. "Nice view."

Tony was still panting hard but not as violently as before. "Do what you want to me. It won't change what's happened. We still love each other."

Brook pursed his lips, his body rigid with effort. "Does Amy know?"

"No, and she's not going to, not from me anyway."

"She'll find out Tony. Sooner or later. Terri's a young girl. You took her virginity. She can't lock that sort of thing away forever. Not from her mum."

Tony started sobbing. Finally he said, "I've ruined everything."

Brook smiled and pulled him up onto a chair, patting him on the back. "Yes you have. But you see, that's self-knowledge right there. That's a good thing. I've discovered, and you'll find the same, that if you can acknowledge your mistakes, if you can put your hand in the air and say, *"I screwed up,"* it only takes ten, maybe fifteen years to get over it.

"Now here's what you're going to do, Tony. When I leave, you're going to pull yourself together and you're going to ring Amy. You're going to arrange to meet her in town for lunch at your favourite restaurant. Tell her you've got a promotion or a big salary increase, she's bound to believe a slick salesman like you..."

"I couldn't. I couldn't face her after this."

"That's good, because you're not going to. While she's out, you're going to slip back home, pack your bags and leave Brighton. Today."

"What?"

"That's right. Today. And you're not ever going to come back."

"What about Amy?"

"You'll never see her or Terri again. And don't worry. You've seen how well Amy gets over failed marriages. She can look after herself. She's got her own money. And some of yours."

"Where will I go?"

"I don't care, Tony – as long as you go for good. Clear?"

"But my life's here..."

"Not any more."

"It was an accident. I'll talk to Terri. She'll understand..."

Brook grabbed Tony by the collar and forced his face into eye contact. "No, you have to understand, Tony. If you don't leave I'll have you arrested. You've broken the law and you can go to prison. You wouldn't like prison, Tony. It's not for people like you. Especially if people get the idea you're some kind of nonce. And believe me they will. You'll feel like you've had a Giant Redwood shoved up your arse."

Brook released him and he slumped onto the floor. After a long pause for thought, Tony sighed with resignation. "Alright, I'll leave." With that, his face crumpled and he cried like a smacked child. Brook picked him up and patted him again.

"Good. That wasn't hard was it? And don't ever come back. Not ever. Understand?"

Brook gave Tony a friendly slap on the face and stood to walk cheerily out of the office, being sure to leave the door ajar for inquisitive spectators to get a clear sight of Tony's humiliation.

"Merry Christmas."

Chapter 23

Brook sat in his kitchen, drinking coffee and watching Cat vacuum his way through a plate of prawns, the traditional peace offering after being left to survive on the cheap cat food provided by Mrs Saunders while he was away. It had been five days since his return and one since his subsequent suspension – a month, on full pay.

"The least I can give you," McMaster had said. "It's out of my hands. DI Greatorix has taken over the Wallis enquiry."

She'd seemed genuinely sorry, though it was difficult to be sure. Perhaps the best indicator of her state of mind was the telltale signs of neglect in her beloved spider plant.

"Don't worry ma'am. I understand. I need to get away."

"A holiday?" She looked him in the eye to check he was serious. "That's fine Damen. I envy you. Have a good rest and we'll see you soon, fit and well."

A holiday. Hardly that. But no matter. Now he was free. Free to dig deep. Free to do what he should have done all those years ago, what he would've done had he not been so blinkered, so certain.

All that remained was to be sure Jones was untainted by his folly and, by the time he left the Chief Super's office, McMaster was in no doubt that WPC Jones had acted properly at all times and had even tried to object to some of DI Brook's decisions.

As a result, Jones didn't even receive a reprimand, just a quiet word, "one girl to another," as McMaster had put it.

But that was as good as it would get for Jones. Brook knew she could expect a harder time from colleagues. Nothing could stop the avalanche of comment from the rest of the station about their missing nights together in a seedy Brighton guest house.

It began for Brook as soon as he walked through the front door. He'd slipped into the station early that first morning, hoping to avoid the worst. But Harry Hendrickson was at the front desk when he arrived and his face broke into a malicious grin.

"Well if it ain't Romeo. Juliet still in bed is she, lover boy?" he'd said with a smirk. "She loves me, she loves me not. She loves me, she loves me not," he crowed at Brook's retreating back, before turning to PC Robinson for approval.

And this time Hendrickson wasn't the lone source of barbs. Everyone in the division felt they had a contribution to make and lost no opportunity to present their material. A group of fresh-faced constables sang *Dirty Old Man* under their breath before subsiding into a hum. Others, WPC's in particular, not wishing to lower themselves to crudity, just giggled.

Even Greatorix had joined in, going out of his way to deliver the odd wisecrack, though for the most part he was content just to be smug. And why not? It didn't get much better for a low-flyer like Bob Greatorix. Revenge was rarely so swift and so sweet and he wasn't about to pass up the chance to twist the knife – revenge for Brook's superiority, revenge for his insinuations in the canteen, revenge for all Brook's advantages – his money, his brains, his healthy glands.

But, to the annoyance of his detractors, Brook was at peace with the world. Once he would have recoiled from such attention, everybody knowing his business and talking about it. He still didn't enjoy it, but since that day on the pier with Terri, he'd changed. He'd lost his daughter, the only thing of value to him. Now, nothing mattered. Now he was able to cope with the jibes, all the more since discovering that cheerful forbearance of the baiting diminished the pleasure of his tormentors.

Brook wasn't worried for himself. He could handle it. He *had* handled it for years. But Wendy. The thick skin he'd acquired didn't extend to her and he knew she'd been reduced to tears on at least one occasion.

It was easy for Brook. He'd only been in the station for a couple of days before his suspension kicked in. Wendy would have it tougher for a while. She'd get through it, he knew that, but at what cost to their relationship? Assuming they still had one.

She'd phoned him after her talk with McMaster – that was a good sign – but then the conversation had turned to *Daddy's Special Girl* and that morning at his flat when he'd passed Vicky off as his daughter.

Even so, such was his new-found serenity that he couldn't hold back a smile after putting down the phone on her frosty tone. Never before had one of his infrequent relationships been threatened by the notion that he was a womaniser.

Brook extinguished his cigarette and went to the bedroom to finish packing. He stowed the suitcase under the table and picked up the phone, dialled Directory Enquiries, noted the number and dialled again.

"Belle Vue Park? Yes. I wonder if you might help me. I don't know how to begin. Yes. Yes. I'll try." With a theatrical sigh, he managed to control his emotions. "It's alcohol you see. I've been having problems. Yes. Well, not yet, but I think I'm weakening. It's New Year's Eve tomorrow and I...I'm sure it's a busy time. Yes, I'll hold. That's great. Yes, tomorrow for three nights. Thank you very much. Brook. Damen Brook. B-R-O-O-K. You were highly recommended by a friend. Sonja Sorenson. Well it was a few years ago. Okay. I'll see you tomorrow evening."

Brook replaced the receiver and left the flat. He walked through the grey streets to Jumbo's, pulling up his collar at the morning drizzle. Noble was already there nursing a cup of tea. He looked up at Brook's arrival and, before he could think, shot an involuntary glance at the clock.

"Morning sir."

Brook ordered his Farmhouse Special and sat down with a mug of tea.

"I know. I'm late. It's not like me and I'm not a millionaire," he added.

"Right." Noble handed over a folder and indicated a Tesco bag half full of video cassettes.

"Is that everything, John?"

"Everything of use. The list is on top. I can't let you keep it."

"What about the videos?"

"Greatorix won't miss them but I'll need them back at some point. The list contains all men on their own who checked out of local hotels a day either side of the Wallis murders. There's no Peter Hera though."

"Did you think there would be?"

"I've no idea. Is it important?"

"We'll see. Even if he didn't stay in the area, this is where we might trip him up, John."

"How?"

"Because he was off his turf. Derby isn't his town John, so he had to take risks. He had to deal with people to get things – vans, accommodation, pizzas. If we're lucky..."

Brook flipped open the folder and worked down the list of names.

215

For a moment he paused but then resumed before snapping the folder shut.

"Nothing jumps out. Pity." He handed the folder back to Noble.

"Should we extend the search?" asked Noble. He was embarrassed at once.

"It's not for me to say, John." Brook smiled to wipe away Noble's faux pas.

"Maybe he'll be on the tapes."

"Maybe. Any other developments?"

"Not yet. We've done everything. Nothing much from around the van. If there had been another unknown car parked on the drive no-one saw it. No sign of any forced entry to the house, so the killer didn't stay there. DI Greatorix thinks..." Noble flashed another apologetic look at Brook. "Sorry."

"Don't be. What does he think?"

"Not a lot."

"You don't have to bad mouth him to please me, John." Brook was pleased anyway.

"I know. It's just..."

Brook's breakfast arrived and he took up his knife and fork. "What?"

"Have you seen him eat? It's disgusting. And the way he sweats..." Noble broke off when he realised Brook had stopped spearing a mushroom onto his fork. "Sorry. Bon appetit."

"Does he have *any* ideas, John?"

"He thinks it was a neighbour with a grudge against Bobby Wallis."

"I wish he were right. What have Forensics come up with?"

"Nothing yet."

"Have they examined Jason's clothes yet?"

"His clothes? No."

"They're a bit slow, aren't they?"

Noble seemed a little put out. "Maybe, but when we found no blood on his shoes, he was in the clear. He couldn't possibly have been in that room. So we put his clothes on low priority. And you weren't here to give them a hurry-up."

Brook nodded. "Fair enough."

Noble rose to leave. "Well, have a good holiday."

"Thanks. And good luck with B.O. Bob."

Noble laughed. Was this really DI Brook? Going on holiday, tucking into a hearty breakfast, cracking wise. Noble pinched his fingers over his nose and Brook returned the laugh.

216

As soon as Noble left, Brook pulled out a pen and wrote 'International Hotel' on his paper napkin. He didn't need to write down the man's name.

*

After breakfast, Brook returned to his flat, retrieved the keys to the Sprite and climbed into the old car. The Mondeo was next to it. Being suspended, he wasn't sure he should still have it, but nobody had asked for it back and he hadn't thought to offer. But The International was only half a mile away and it would be as well to keep the Sprite ticking over.

Five minutes later Brook parked on the forecourt of the hotel and clambered out.

He entered the double doors, running his eye over the excessive Christmas decorations, and rang the bell at a deserted reception. A young girl appeared, trying her best to look helpful and confident. She was petite and full-figured with plenty of make-up and bright orange streaks in her hair. The studs in her ears reminded him of Laura Maples.

"Can I help you sir?"

Brook pulled out his warrant card and flashed it at her. The girl's face betrayed a glimpse of alarm and Brook wondered what she'd been up to. Drugs probably. She was young and, no doubt, badly paid. What else was there?

"No need to be alarmed, miss. I need some information on one of your guests. Apparently a man stayed here from the 16th to the 18th of this month."

"Ye-es?"

"He registered under the name Sammy Elphick."

"Ye-es?"

"I wondered if there was anyone here who might be able to give me a description of the man."

"Mr Elphick?" She turned to the desk to flip through the visitor's book. "That's right. One of your constables rang to ask us about single men staying in the area. What's he done?"

"It's just routine. Sally," he added after a glance at her tag.

"Sammy Elphick? Yeah here he is. I remember *him* alright. A right weirdo." She flipped the book round at him. Next to the name column the words "Harlesden, London" glared out at Brook.

"Was he?"

"Yeah."

Brook waited, wondering if Sally were some kind of comedian.

217

When it became clear she wouldn't be elaborating without further stimulus, he said, "Could you tell me about him, Sally?"

"Well he wasn't very well."

Brook's heart quickened. "How so?"

"It was his hands."

"His hands?"

"That's right. Burnt they were. So he said. He had to wear gloves all the time."

"Did he? So that's not his handwriting," enquired Brook, nodding at the folder.

"No, it's mine. He couldn't write."

"And he paid his account with cash for the same reason."

"That's right."

"What did he look like?"

"Old, a bit sad-looking. He didn't speak much."

"I'll bet he didn't eat in the restaurant either."

"No, he didn't. He said it was too bright. He had bad eyes as well you see."

"'Course he did. He'd need special glasses for that wouldn't he?"

Sally was impressed. "That's right. Big thick frames with tinted lenses."

"So he didn't take breakfast?"

Sally was starting to get into the swing of things. "No. We all wondered about that because it's included in the price. We can't knock anything off, you know. Not round Christmas. Not that he asked. I mean Cook was a bit put out. He does a good breakfast. One of the best in Derby," she added, reverting to a professional voice. "But even if it was crap, people always make a point of having it, don't they? I mean, when they've paid for it..."

"Any other distinctive features?"

"He wore a wig. I noticed that, though he kept a hat on most of the time." Sally was very pleased with her deductive powers. "Does that help?"

Brook nodded. "It would help more if you could tell me if he was bald underneath." Sally screwed up her face in concentration then shook her head. "I don't know," she concluded, a little crestfallen. "Like I said, he had a wig on. And not a very good one."

"How tall was he?"

"Quite tall."

Brook looked up. "Tall? Sure?" He looked Sally up and down. "How tall are you?"

"I'm five feet three," she answered, a touch sensitive.

"You look taller."

"I'm wearing platforms."

"I see. So, if you're five-three, someone five-seven/five-eight would look quite tall."

"I suppose so. But I was wearing my platforms, so I guess not. He must have been taller."

"You're sure you were wearing platforms when you met him?"

"Certain."

"Why so certain?"

"Because I always wear platforms." Brook looked a little dubious. "I do."

"If you say so." With a sudden inspiration Brook said, "Could he have been wearing platforms?"

"Possibly. I didn't notice." Sally was a little defensive after being branded unreliable.

Brook whipped out the old photo of Sorenson and handed it to her. "Was that the man?"

She studied carefully then handed it back. "I don't know. I don't think so."

"Well, thanks for trying." He pocketed the photo. "What time of day did he arrive?"

"It was the evening. Seven o'clock."

"Why so precise?"

"Because I work nine in the morning to seven at night. I was just getting off when he walked in. Kept me here for a few more minutes. Missed my bus, didn't I?"

"That's a long shift."

Sally shrugged. She didn't need his sympathy. "It's a job."

"Do you know how he arrived?"

"No. You could ask Mac – that's Bert Mackintosh. He's on the door five 'til twelve."

"Where can I find him?"

"He lives in a flat down the road. Number 25. Flat 4. It's only a hundred yards but I dare say he'll be asleep now. He works late."

Brook made to leave. Before he did, he rummaged in his pocket and pulled out a ten-pound note. He handed it to the girl who was surprised and pleased. "You've been very helpful. Get yourself a drink for New Year."

"Thanks a lot. I will. Happy New Year to *you*."

*

"Didn't she tell you I'd be asleep?" The man yawned and covered his mouth. Not before Brook got an eyeful of false teeth shifting slightly as his jaw distended. Mac was past sixty with a thin white pencil moustache and short cropped white hair. He had a healthy sheen to his skin and his build and general demeanour added to the impression that he kept himself fit. A military man most likely.

"She did, Mr Mackintosh. But it's important. And I didn't think a military man would be lying in bed all morning."

Mac's eyes widened, unsure whether to be pleased that Brook had noticed his army demeanour. His expression betrayed an injury. He tightened the cord of his dressing gown and waited a moment, assessing Brook and the situation. The habit of an old soldier used to giving orders. "When you work the hours I work, it's the middle of the night." He waited for Brook's acknowledgement that he knew he wasn't a layabout before adding, "You'd better come in then, Inspector…"

"Brook." He followed Mac into his two rooms, noting how the essential squalor of the accommodation was kept at bay by the man's sense of pride in his meagre surroundings.

The place was tiny and down-at-heel but spotlessly clean. The first room was a kitchenette into which the old man would have led his guest had there been space for two – it was only possible for Brook to join him in the doorway, where he leaned against the frame.

There wasn't much in the way of amenities – a sink, a worktop over a noisy fridge, a small Baby Belling electric hob with two rings – the same model as Brook's.

The worktop it sat on was old and warped and had been stained by the rings of hot pans lain on it over the years. A half full pan of water sat atop one of the rings. Mac took the pan to the empty stainless steel sink and doubled the amount of water from the solitary tap, before setting it down and switching on the ring.

Next to the hob was a small steel teapot with a teabag in. Mac added another. Next to the teapot was a bean-stained plate with knife and fork, neatly placed together. Mac picked it up and laid it in the sink. "Sorry about the mess," he said. "When you're on your own…" he shrugged.

"Don't worry."

Mac nodded and busied himself with the tea. He added milk from a carton in the fridge that Brook saw was otherwise empty. The lone cupboard set back on the opposite wall had glass doors similar to the one in Brook's kitchen. The supplies Brook could see consisted of 'economy' baked beans, outnumbered by dozens of tins of cat food.

For a second, Brook worried that this proud, impecunious old man had descended to getting his meat from pet food, until he heard the plaintive yowl of a cat in the room next door. At the same time he spotted the newspaper-lined litter tray on the far side of the fridge.

Mac must have seen him looking. For no other reason, he said, "I get most of my meals at the hotel. Go through into the other room."

Brook stepped next door. Another small room, with a low ceiling. A bay window covered by lace curtains looked down and out over the centre of Derby, every roof slick and shiny under the brief illumination of rain and low sun.

Most of the room was filled by a metal framed bed on which the cat lay. It glared nervously as Brook entered. It was a little black kitten with wide wary eyes. Brook cautiously held out a hand to stroke it and it immediately careened itself towards the pressure of Brook's fingers.

From a flat nearby a dull thudding music sprang up. Brook continued to look around. There wasn't much to see. A small coffee table, a wooden framed armchair with a uniform draped over it, a gas fire and a straight-backed chair with a small TV resting on it.

Brook could only stand and stare. It wasn't possible to move around, as the other pitiful scraps of furniture were jammed against the far wall. A deep sadness filled him. He couldn't explain why. He took no great pains over his own living conditions and it wasn't as though he hadn't seen such poverty before. Perhaps it was the denial of the occupant. Like poor dead Laura in her pathetic squat, clinging to the pretence that she was in control of her own life, her own environment.

"My alarm call," beamed Mac, holding a mug of tea towards Brook and nodding vaguely in the direction of the music.

Brook took it and had an appreciative swig. "Thanks. Just what I need."

Mac set his own mug on the floor and lifted one end of the bed. "Off you get Blot," he soothed, as he raised the bed into a recess and closed two doors on it. Now there was a little space and Mac moved the table and chairs to the middle of the room and sat in the stiff-backed one, resting the TV on the floor, before taking a sip of tea.

"Mince pie?" Mac held a plate towards Brook who took a mince pie and bit into it. It was turning stale.

"Very nice."

"I get 'em from the hotel."

"Right. Nice view," nodded Brook.

"We like it. The moggy and me."

Brook smiled, glad of common ground. He didn't know how to talk about the weather. "I've got a cat. It's a pain in the neck."

"I know what you mean. Bloody nuisance, this little puss. Aren't you? I'm stuck with you now though, aren't I?" Mac smiled with pleasure. "Found him out in the alley a couple of months back. Wet through he was. No bigger than my hand. Mewling and shivering. Must've been chucked out. Some people. Who'd do that to such a defenceless little mite?"

"How long have you got?" replied Brook.

"Now what did you want to talk about, inspector? A Mr Elphick, you said."

"That's right. Do you remember him?"

"Should I?"

"He stayed a few nights the week before Christmas. Old, not very well."

"Oh, him with the gloves and glasses?"

"That's him."

"I remember. Only 'cos he was such an odd looking sort. I don't know what else I can tell you, 'cept he wore a wig."

"Sally told me. Was there anything else? His voice? His height? Anything he said."

"He didn't say a word to me, inspector, and that's a fact. Not even thank you, when I opened the door. Not that he weren't polite. Just that he preferred to nod than speak, that's one of the things that made him stick in the mind. That and his appearance."

"Did he tip you?"

"He did. He was a good tipper for these parts. I only saw him twice and each time he gave me a pound. Tips like that make all the difference. My army pension goes nowhere. Not now I've got two mouths to feed." He beamed at Blot who was caressing his ankle.

"And his height?"

"Tallish. About your height I'd say. Even with a bit of a stoop."

"You're sure he wasn't smaller? Nearer five eight."

"Certain. I've seen over a lot of men and you gets to know these things without really looking. You'd know what I mean about that, inspector."

"Yes I suppose so." Brook was unhappy. The waters were muddying. The Reaper had gone out of his way to get Brook's attention and now all his long nurtured certainty about the case, about Sorenson, was being undermined.

"Was there anything else? Did you get him cabs?"

"No. He walked the night I saw him."

"Did you see how he arrived?"

Mac's face widened. "That's right. That *was* odd."

"What?"

"Well when he arrived he was dropped off down the road."

"By a cab?"

"No. A cab wouldn't have gone past the front entrance."

"And that was odd?"

"There were no cars parked outside the hotel. Why not just drop him off there? And the car was on the hotel side of the road, so it must have driven past deliberately. It was almost as though…"

"As though the driver didn't want to be seen," concluded Brook. Sammy Elphick had been a dummy, a distraction. Sorenson had been driving not staying at the hotel. But why bring somebody else to Derby? To flag up a name so Brook would realise The Reaper had been to town? Why, when there were so many other pointers at the crime scene. It made no sense.

There had to be another reason. There had to be a purpose, a need for Sorenson to have company. Perhaps he was too ill for the "job" and needed stronger hands to do the deed while he supervised – Brook had a momentary flash of Sorenson ticking off chores on a clipboard, with his assistant.

1) Deliver pizzas

2) Bring down baby

3) Cut throats.

But all the evidence pointed to a single killer, someone of Sorenson's height and stature, entering the Wallis house that night. But then again, he'd only been seen delivering the pizzas – even a sick old man could do that. Nobody had seen who returned later to kill the victims.

Brook showed Mac the picture of Sorenson but without success.

"Well thanks Mac," said Brook standing. "You've been a big help."

"My pleasure. What's he done by the way?"

Brook walked to the door and glanced again at the door of the empty fridge.

"I can't discuss it."

"'Ere, he's not the one that did that family, is he?" Brook's silence confirmed it. "The bastard. That poor little girl. What had she done to deserve that?"

Interesting how everyone zeroed in on the only aspect of the killings that was truly tragic, thought Brook.

"We don't know for definite. Listen. If this man comes back, I'd like you to ring me on this number." Brook wrote his home number on a piece of scrap paper knowing it wouldn't be needed for anything other than the smokescreen he was about to throw up. He handed it to Mac with a twenty-pound note.

"You don't need to pay me for doing my duty, Inspector Brook. I'm glad to do it." The wound in the old man was stark.

"Oh I know, I just thought...I need a good man on the job..."

"You've no call to insult me like that. I don't do the right thing for profit..."

"Please take it. Treat it as a tip. Get some toys for the cat."

Mac eyed the money with a mixture of longing and deep bitterness. Brook was appalled at the effect of his actions.

The old man stood before him, bereft even of the dignity he so scrupulously nurtured, unable to lift his dampening eyes from the money, the life-giving money. Every instinct told him to refuse it. He'd invited another person, as a guest, into his home. He'd assisted the police with their enquiries. They'd had a nice cup of tea and a nice chat and the old man had felt useful again. What could be more normal than that?

Being treated as an equal by a police inspector, an important man who sought his opinion, his help. Suddenly he was a member of society again and could make a contribution to a community from which he'd felt ever more alienated. For a short, wonderful moment he was a human being not a shuffling relic, not a lonely, desperately sad old man who would have opened his arms to death every day, had not a tiny kitten given him the unquestioning love and companionship he needed to keep him going.

Mac closed his eyes and his hands around the money. £20 for self-respect. Bargain.

Brook turned to leave. He turned back at the sound of the old man's voice.

"We have a saying in the army." Mac stared at the floor, gazing at his own headstone. "Life's like a gunshot wound. When it stops hurting is the time to worry."

*

Brook hurried to his car. What was he doing? Out of nowhere he was taking an interest in other people's lives, other people's pain. Years of living behind the barricade of his thoughts had been replaced by pity for the plight of others. Why?

He was throwing cash around like Scrooge on Christmas Day. He could afford it but it was the kind of scattergun palliative of which he'd always disapproved and which, as he'd just witnessed, could do as much harm as good.

Then suddenly he knew and it hit him hard. An old man in a hovel, clinging to the illusion of life and companionship, only a cat to care whether he lived or died. Mac was The Ghost of Christmas Future. Brook had dropped in on his own barren existence, twenty years on.

*

The next morning, New Year's Eve, Brook staggered to his door under the weight of two heavy boxes. He fumbled with his keys, balancing both boxes on his left thigh and let himself in. He stepped into the kitchen and snapped on the harsh strip light. He placed the boxes on the kitchen table and trotted back out to the Sprite for his shopping bags.

When he returned he opened the fridge. It was empty save for a carton of milk. A moment later it was full of comestibles, most of which he wouldn't eat but that didn't matter. For the first time in a long time, appearances were important. Appearances mattered. Not to Brook maybe but to everyone else, and it was stupid pigheadedness to put himself at such a disadvantage where human relationships were concerned. If his life were to be retrieved, he had to start where other people started – first impressions.

God forbid that anyone should walk into his flat again and see it as defeated and empty as old Mac's. Small wonder he hadn't seen Wendy for dust after that first night. What must she have thought?

*

Later that evening, Brook had set up his brand new TV and VCR – not without difficulty – and was able to put in the first of the tapes from the station CCTV. He settled down with the remote control and a ready meal chilli, briefly amused to have stumbled upon the nation's twin pillars of obesity, after a lifetime of emaciation.

It was dull going, so after the first half hour, he put it on fast-forward but this made it too difficult to pick things out, so he abandoned the experiment and decided just to leave it running. If he missed something, so what? Unless Sorenson danced across the footbridge in a blood-stained boiler suit waving a scalpel around, Brook knew this was a waste of time. They still had nothing.

He decided to ring Amy again, see how she was getting on. He'd rung her the day after getting back to Derby on some pretext or other and it was obvious she'd been crying. After he'd pressed her to confide in him she'd told Brook of Tony's departure.

"*I haven't told Terri yet. She thinks he's away on business.*"

225

She'd seemed composed. But when she read Brook the note, the tears had begun to fall.

> *"Dear Amy*
> *I have to go away for a long time. Maybe forever. I can't tell you why because you wouldn't understand. Please realise that it's nothing to do with you and that I love you. I can't face telling you or Terri but please try not to think ill of me.*
> *All my love, your darling Tony"*

Brook had kept her talking until she cheered up. He didn't usually have that effect but then he rarely made the effort. They'd had a few laughs about the early years making sure to skirt difficult areas. Maybe she just needed someone, anyone, to talk to, but Brook was still pleased to detect a note of affection in her voice he'd not heard for many years.

This time Amy picked up on the first ring.

"It's me again, darling. How are you today?"

"I'm O.K."

"And Terri?"

"She's fine."

"Have you told her about Tony yet?" There was a long pause at the other end. "Anything wrong, Amy?"

Brook heard her take a deep breath. *"Damen. I don't want you to ring again."*

"What is it?"

"I don't want you to ring again. I want you to leave us alone."

"Tell me what's wrong..."

The line went dead. Brook replaced the receiver.

At that moment Vicky hopped from the bottom step of the footbridge. The same flash of blue denim that Brook had first seen standing across the road in the cold a couple of weeks before, the same quilted coat, the same flash of blond hair.

He checked the date on the display. It was the day before Brook had met her outside his flat.

He watched her progress across the concourse. It was difficult to make her out, the cameras in the main station were high in the vaulted roof, but she seemed to be waving at someone off-camera, someone waiting by the entrance. She quickened her step.

Then a hand reached out from beyond the fixed camera position and Vicky swung her carpet bag into it as she walked off-screen. Brook surmised that a girl wouldn't offer to carry another girl's luggage. Vicky must have been met by a man.

226

Chapter 24

Brook sauntered down the corridor, grinning inanely at the tide of revellers washing the other way. "Happy New Year," he mouthed for the thousandth time, doing his best impression of a *bon viveur*. He was tired and would have preferred to slink off to his room, but there was work to do. He'd left Derby after sifting through all the CCTV tapes, searching in vain for a better view of Vicky's rendezvous, and had set off for London later than was wise, catching all the traffic rushing round to New Year party venues.

"You're going the wrong way, darling." A plump woman – mid-forties – in a French maid's outfit barred his way with a generous show of bosom. "The party's this way," she slurred, fixing Brook with her swaying proposition. "Come with me." She locked a flabby arm onto his and gripped him with her profiterole fingers. "I won't see you all po-faced on the best night of the year. Molly'll show you a good time, handsome."

"Well thanks, Molly. But I'm not allowed to drink..."

"Nor me darling. But what's one little drinkie on New Year's Eve?"

Brook smiled. Belle Vue certainly wasn't severe on its patients. Their wishes, or rather their money, seemed to override any consideration of clinical need. The place was little more than an expensive hotel, dressed up as a clinic to justify the kind of charges that hoodwinked guests into believing they were being treated. And at this time of year, peak time for self-loathing, the sky was the limit for fools and their money.

Brook himself had been relieved of £3,000 for a three-night stay. This included the fancy dress costume of his choice and a seven-course New Year dinner, with copious champagne. Carrot juice was available for those with a "problem." Not that anyone was checking.

For £1,000 a night, medical rigour could be overlooked. It was a critical time of year for the ailments of those whose money couldn't fill every demand they placed upon it, and at such a time of low self-esteem they required – at premium rates naturally – an uncommon amount of attention to see them through.

Perhaps the place had changed in the years since Sonja Sorenson had been a "guest." Perhaps she'd been more than the pampered wife of a rich businessman. She'd been at the Retreat for four years, after all.

Assuming he could prise the flabby knuckles of the determined Molly from his arm, Brook was about to find out.

"You can't get away that easy, you naughty boy. I can see you need a good time."

Brook decided to take the initiative and planted a huge kiss on her sloppy lips. "You said it, gorgeous. I'll meet you in the bar in twenty minutes. I'm just going to get my Tarzan costume on."

Molly stared, open-mouthed then broke into a sly grin. "Me Jane. Me come. Help put costume on."

"No, wo-man. That spoil surprise. You go now. Tarzan change. Ungowa! Ungowa!" Molly giggled as he shooed her along, stampeding the tottering beast towards the watering hole, tacking from wall to wall as she went.

When she was out of sight, Brook pulled a hand drawn map from his pocket and studied it.

A few moments later he stood outside a solid panelled door in a deserted corridor. There was no light under the door and this part of the building was quiet. Only the faintest noise of celebration penetrated here.

Brook went to the far end of the corridor to see where it led. Whatever Thalassic Therapy was, it took place in the rooms leading off there. The rooms were in darkness so Brook returned to the first door and took out a small bunch of keys.

The attendant who'd drawn the map and given him his keys, for a large consideration, had told Brook that all patient records were secured in the computer and he couldn't get access. However, any records over ten years old would be on paper in this rarely-used office.

Brook tried the keys. The first key turned the lock and he pushed back the door, closing it quickly behind him before snapping on the light.

He locked the door behind him, moved to the filing cabinet and produced a different instrument from his pocket, a thin metal probe like the blade of a hacksaw that he'd removed from a housebreaker a few years back.

After a few seconds probing at the lock, Brook heard a loud click then pulled open a drawer. He looked around. Footsteps outside. He scurried to the door to extinguish the light. The footsteps paused outside the office. Brook could see the shadow of two legs craning under the door.

A few seconds later the footsteps receded. Brook waited a moment longer to be on the safe side. Finally he returned to the cabinet and flicked on a small desk lamp nearby. He pulled open the S-Z drawer and found what he was looking for. There wasn't much for four years of a life, just a few sheets.

He made a cursory inspection and slid the most relevant papers under his shirt, returning the folder to its drawer. He locked the cabinet, with more difficulty than he'd opened it, leaving heavy scratching around the lock. But it was unlikely to be noticed any time soon, if at all, given Belle Vue's general lack of stringency.

He paused at the door to listen for human traffic, then locked up quickly and returned to his room by a circuitous route, to avoid bumping into Molly or anyone else trying too hard to enjoy the evening.

*

Back in his room Brook opened a complimentary bottle of champagne and sipped at a glass while he read Mrs Sorenson's case notes.

> *12/11/88. The patient harbours deep feelings of worthlessness for herself. Her husband, Mr Stefan Sorenson, fears that she might harm herself or her children. These fears appear well-founded. She speaks in violent language to denounce her husband and children and has shown every indication of violent intent towards them.*
>
> *Given her depleted self-esteem, I feel it necessary to admit Mrs Sorenson for an initial examination period of six weeks. Minimal medication is required at this point, though it may be worthwhile prescribing anti-depressants. The patient herself is in full agreement with her husband and has agreed to attend on a full-time basis on the grounds that she is allowed a visit by her children on a weekly basis. This visit will be subject to full supervision.*

The entry was signed by Dr David Porcetti, as were the others.

15/12/88. Patient making excellent progress. Is able to talk extensively about her childhood without trauma. Her trouble appears to lie closer to home. She is calm, rational and more aware of her own value away from her own home. She is loving and attentive towards her children, who are always escorted by their uncle, Victor Sorenson. Mrs Sorenson's husband does visit but thinks it best not to see his wife and upset her treatment.

3/1/89. Mrs Sorenson's condition worsened on the day before her release. She flew into a rage at breakfast and smashed several plates and bowls and threw missiles at staff attempting to calm her. Patient had to be forcibly restrained and sedated to prevent threatened self-harm.

Mr Sorenson has asked Belle Vue to continue her treatment and has sent appropriate remuneration.

PS (Must reiterate my suggestion of last year that all kitchenware should be plastic.)

After the initial attempts at diagnosis, entries became more routine dealing with medication, dosage, occupational therapy and so on. It was as though the clinic had forgotten she was there for a purpose and just wrapped her into their inviolable daily routine. She became a paying guest, not a patient with needs.

Brook was puzzled. Surely someone as successful as Stefan Sorenson would know what kind of place Belle Vue was. Surely he'd have done his homework, found a place where his wife's mental problems could have been properly addressed. It didn't make sense, unless her problems were so bad they couldn't be resolved. Could it be that Sonja Sorenson was being confined, hidden away for a reason? What had she done? Why was she such a threat that she needed to be removed from decent society, from her family?

Brook continued to skim until he came to Stefan Sorenson's murder, what should have been a seismic event in Mrs Sorenson treatment.

The patient seems to be in shock. Minimal medication required, however. Shows no emotion at all. Her husband's death leaves her numb. Questionable whether she understands the fact. Has become almost catatonic and refuses, or is unable, to speak. Patient's brother-in-law, Victor Sorenson, has requested that she no longer be medicated with a view to her release but we have advised strongly against this.

3/6/89. Prof Sorenson has continued to insist on no medication for his sister- in-law and has retained his own psychiatrist, Dr Lilley, who has endorsed his view. Dr Lilley has also agreed with his client that Mrs Sorenson should be on selective home release to which we strongly object. He believes that regular exposure to home life and her children will have a beneficial effect. We feel that the patient still represents a small, but active threat to her family and should be confined.

Unfortunately Mrs Sorenson is effectively a voluntary patient and our hands are tied.

We have put on record our objections.

<u>*CONFIDENTIAL!*</u> *It is also our view that the reductions in charges, resulting from Mrs Sorenson becoming an intermittent resident, can only affect the quality of her care here.*

And that was that. Over the next three years, Sonja Sorenson was effectively an outpatient, having decreasing contact with Belle Vue and virtually no clinical assessment. It was no surprise to Brook that Mrs Sorenson recovered without the expert care of its doctors, becoming no threat to society, herself or her children. All contact ceased in 1992. Brook nodded. 1992 – The Reaper's gap year. Maybe Sorenson was too preoccupied with Sonja's recovery to scope out appropriate victims.

Brook drained his glass and refilled it, deep in thought. The place suddenly disgusted him and he resolved to leave the next day – New Year's Day.

Then another thought struck him. This time last year Brook and Wendy Jones…it was their anniversary. One year ago. 365 days – 365 nights.

If Brook closed his eyes he could almost smell the perfume of her hair as she chewed urgently at his chest. He could feel the smoothness of her pale skin and the violence of her passion, all her sinews girding themselves to the rhythms of his lust.

On an impulse he rang her. He regretted it at once. No reply. Even though it was a night when the whole world was out enjoying themselves, Brook burned inside. Where was she? Gone out to find some solace amongst the emptiness, with another, more eligible, man? Maybe. Who could blame her?

He drank some more and rang Amy.

"Happy New Year, Amy." It was the best he could come up with.

"*Damen? I told you never to ring again. Ever.*"

"Just want to wish you a Happy New Year."

"*What?*"

"I know you're upset darling..."

"*Don't call me that. How dare you after what you've done?*"

"What have I done?"

"*You know damn well. Leave my family alone...*"

"Family?"

"*What?*"

"You said *family*."

There was a pause at the other end of the line.

"*Yes. Terri and me.*"

"So Tony came back." No answer – confirmation in itself. "He came back and you let him in. Tell me Amy. Did he come back with his tail between *his* legs or Terri's?"

"*Leave us alone you sick bastard.*"

"What's happened to you?"

"*To me? That's fucking rich.*"

"Your husband is having sex with our daughter."

"*He said you'd say this. You're sick Damen. Do you know that? Do you know what he's going through at work after what you did? Have you any idea? I had to go in and assure the partners at the firm that I have a mentally unstable ex-husband. And as for Tony, he can barely speak to us. His own family.*"

"Good."

"*He's at the end of his rope.*"

"Best place for him."

"*I should have you arrested for what you've done to me and our daughter, you bastard. I hate you! It makes me sick to think I was ever married to you.*"

There was a stunned silence at Brook's end of the receiver. He suddenly felt physically ill. "My God! You've known all along. Haven't you? Amy. Tell me you didn't know. Did you think you'd never get another man...?"

There was a scream of pain from the other end of the line, then a click.

Brook replaced the receiver and sat motionless on the bed for several minutes. He poured himself another drink. He felt nothing beyond his usual vague confusion at the ways of the world – nothing. Life was like a gunshot wound but suddenly it had ceased to hurt. Perhaps now was the time to worry.

He jumped off the bed and packed for something to do. He couldn't stay. The sooner he left this place the better he'd feel. Like Sonja. Better. He spied the empty champagne bottle lying on the floor and was tempted to order another. Strains of Auld Lang Syne filtered up from below and he looked at his watch. Midnight.

Brook needed some air so he opened a window. The grounds below were large and inviting. He'd go for a walk. Or perhaps a drive. The roads would be empty. Now was a good time. He took his case to put in the car, all the better for a quick getaway in the morning.

*

Brook pulled his jacket tight against the cold as he stalked along the damp pavement of Electric Avenue. The detritus of the market was everywhere. Rotten fruit and vegetables had been squashed underfoot by the day's pedestrian traffic and the ground was slimy and treacherous and, as he walked along the crescent shaped street, Brook had to divide his attention between examining the shop fronts and picking his way along the pavement.

When he reached the junction with Brixton High Street, Brook turned back to walk on the other side of the avenue towards his car. He was deflated now. There was nothing to be seen and the adrenaline of the chase was spent. All he wanted to do now was sleep.

As he walked he heard a door bang around the bend of the avenue and slowed his step to listen for anyone approaching.

A few yards further on, he could see the end of the street. It was empty. Nothing stirred. The wind had dropped and the sky had cleared and the dim lights were now augmented by the moon's pale light.

As Brook passed a doorway, something caught his eye and his heart began to pound. He bent to examine it. It was the large rectangular box containing the CD player he'd seen in Sorenson's house. It was empty.

He spun to examine the doorway. He saw a crack of light from the other side and pushed the door. It swung away from him and Brook stepped over the threshold. He was at the foot of a small flight of stairs. No sound. No movement.

Brook's face followed the stairs to the dim light at the top. He took as silent a pull of oxygen as he could manage and placed his foot on the first step.

*

Brook woke the next day to the sound of champagne bottles,

233

empty ones clinking together at his feet. He opened his eyes and looked at his watch. It was nearly midday.

Brook lay for several minutes in the warm bed, luxuriating, looking at the ceiling. His head didn't feel too bad. Then he remembered his call to Amy and pulled a pillow over his head.

He picked up the phone. *"Room service."*

Brook ungummed his lips and did a good impression of someone speaking normally. "This is Room 215. I'd like a full English breakfast please, with a pot of coffee and two jugs of orange juice and any other healthy liquid you can think of."

"I'm afraid we've stopped serving breakfast sir. I can do you lunch."

"Stopped? When?"

"Nine thirty, sir."

Brook laughed. "On New Year's morning. Did anyone struggle down before then?"

"One or two, sir."

"Well at a grand a night old son, you'd better make that three or I'll be down to damage some eardrums. Got that?"

There was a brief muffled aside. *"Certainly sir. Right away."*

Brook gathered his clothes and began to dress.

*

After a hearty breakfast and copious re-hydration, Brook felt much better. He paid his bill, resisting the temptation to have a swipe at the establishment then located his car and set off south into the heart of London. It was a grey day, not too cold, so he opened the sunroof to blow away the alcoholic haze.

Despite the dull ache in his head he felt better physically than he had in years but he worried now, after that day on the pier with Terri, whether his mind was gone. He'd changed that day, for the better, he felt. But now he wasn't so sure. He didn't know if he had the mental strength to cope any more. Going back. It had been a long time. The past seemed a long way away. Amy. London. The Reaper.

He'd left it all behind to find some peace and now he'd squirreled away a thimble full, he doubted the wisdom of coming back to face Sorenson. Today was the day. Charlie Rowlands had arranged it. But what good would it do? Let The Reaper play his games. Let him destroy who he wished. Most of them deserved it. What did it matter? Even Kylie Wallis. Stick thin, skin of alabaster. She was better off now. Well out of it. The sexual abuse. The pain. The hopelessness. No life

234

sentence for her, no clinging to the weekly mirage of the six-numbered parole.

*

Charlie looked up from his drinks as Brook strode into the Prince of Wales. He smiled. It was a smile of love and friendship. It was a smile of goodbye. His eyes were bonfire-red. They burned with the life that was seeping from the shrinking frame, hunched over Guinness and rum chaser. Blue smoke drifted from hand to face and he inclined his head slightly, like a sniffer dog, to secure maximum inhalation. Brook could see he was in pain.

"Smoking again?" smiled Brook, offering his hand. Charlie placed his bony claw in Brook's as though about to receive a manicure, not shake hands. He had no grip left.

"Seems daft not to. What'll it be? Orange juice?"

"I'll get them."

"No you won't, old son." Rowlands stood uneasily but with great distinction. This was an article of faith, affirmation that Charlie was still a man. Men bought each other drinks. Brook remembered the humiliation he'd heaped on old Mac the doorman and relented.

"Thanks Charlie."

"What'll you have?"

"Same as you."

Charlie grinned, his face a dusty old accordion. "Welcome aboard son. You won't regret it."

Brook watched him totter to the bar, fumbling for a note. Now he could see how wasted Charlie's legs had become. He hadn't noticed a few days ago but then he'd been on home turf, able to conceal such things under blankets and shapeless dressing gowns.

He returned with a tray of glasses and, like most career drunks, regardless of condition, was able to plonk it down not having spilt a single drop of the precious liquid.

"Cheers. Happy New Year lad."

"Cheers." Brook declined the second sentiment on behalf of them both.

"Sorry it's not the Hilton."

Brook laughed. "Don't start."

They talked over old times for a while and behaved like men. Rowlands smoked and drank heavily, between bouts of guttural coughing, and Brook did him the courtesy of joining in. They were friends again. Equals. Not a sick man with a disapproving colleague.

235

Death with dignity sat in their corner, waiting, listening and appreciating.

"Tell me guv, why are you here? I could have met Sorenson on my own."

Rowlands' face clouded for a second. "Don't you know?"

Brook looked into his friend's hooded eyes. The fruit machine couldn't drown the noise of Rowlands breathing. "Perhaps I do."

Rowlands smiled. A silence fell between them – not awkward, but of perfect companionship with no compulsion on either side. Finally Rowlands broke the silence. "It's going to be so good being dead, Brooky. So fucking good."

Drinks consumed, they rose without prompting and left the pub for the short walk to Queensdale Road. It was already getting dark and a cold wind was stirring. Brook experienced a tremor of disquiet and was grateful to be able to walk slowly, next to his friend. He was in no hurry to meet Sorenson.

Chapter 25

Brook knelt beside the girl. She was small but, no matter her size, The Reaper had seen fit to lash her to a chair, now on its side from the death struggle.

She looked eight, maybe nine years of age in physical development though she could have been older. Some kids, abused kids in particular, were often years older than their appearance, their bodies thin, malnourished, unable to grow. Sometimes only a look at the face could reveal how long they'd lived, how much they'd endured. The eyes had it. They had dead eyes.

This girl's eyes were very dead, glaring at Brook without judgement. But the creases around her eyes suggested a smile and Brook was beset by an urge to untie her bonds and get the girl to her feet. It passed.

Instead he stepped back for a better view. He couldn't see the girl's mouth – it was covered by a large sticking plaster – but he knew her teeth would be clenched in the rictus of death. A grin of pain and determination as life convulsed to a close – risus sardonicus, it was called.

On her neck the terrible wound winked at Brook, a cross-section of windpipe visible, a mocking vowel amongst the twist of pink gristle.

Brook stared down at her, his eyes equally hollow and lifeless. This was his daughter now. He was acquiring quite a collection. Baby Theresa, Laura Maples and now The Reaper's latest offering. He wished he knew her name.

He stepped away. The toe of his shoe was covered in blood. He cursed. Take care. A DS should know better. Do the job. Be a copper not a punter. Keep it together. He snapped on a pair of latex gloves to avoid further tainting of the crime scene and moved to the sofa.

The man and woman were side by side. Rope lapped their waists but they required no gag – Brook wondered why. Their heads lolled together in a sick approximation of romance. A pose staged by The Reaper as a parting joke, Brook was sure.

He bent to examine the woman, close enough to smell the blood which clung to her clothes as though they'd been freshly dyed – the deep slash across her throat had left no sanctuary for body fluids. Her T-shirt had a deep apron of gleaming scarlet still eating across its midriff. Only the material at her hips retained original colour. White to contrast with her brown skin.

Brook picked his way round to the man. There was something odd about him. Apart from a few lines of blood splatter from the woman, his clothes were dry and clean. How had he died? Maybe his heart had given out at the sight of his daughter being torn open in front of him. Shock – it happened. But this man was young, thirty perhaps, and looked lean and gym-fit, like many young black males in the inner city.

Brook stepped closer, being careful this time to skirt the blood pool on the bare boards. As he neared, he saw the bloody scalpel glinting from the man's lap. No, it was a razor – it had a mother-of-pearl handle and looked old – a cut-throat, the kind scraped on leather belts in barber shops in Westerns.

Two bits for cologne mister – give the ladies a treat.

He examined the man's neck. Nothing. No sign of a wound.

Suddenly Brook was overcome by the impulse to find a quiet corner and sleep. He'd been awake for days and now it got to him. But he couldn't sleep yet. Not yet. He'd missed his prey by seconds. For once he was there when it mattered – a living crime scene. Living but not breathing. Gone was the routine numb of detection, the banality of post-mortem bureaucracy. In its stead came the thrill and chill of participation. Brook was in the eye of the needle.

Then a noise – a hiss and a gurgle – and the man's chest moved.

Brook snapped upright in terror, his heart punching its way out of his ribcage. Pinheads of sweat moistened his top lip, his hair follicles tingled and his mind span on its axis.

Was the man alive? Why would The Reaper spare the father yet tear open the daughter? Had he been disturbed? Was he still...?

Brook was engulfed by the urge to flee, every sinew screaming at him to run, to stumble out into the cold Brixton night and fill his lungs with oxygen. He was in bad shape, he knew that. The last year on Sorenson's trail had taken its toll. If he left now he could get away and never look back – never think of The Reaper again.

But he didn't run. Couldn't. He'd waited so long. So instead he stepped away from the sofa, like a daredevil, walking backwards along a tightrope slung between high buildings. Don't look down.

238

You'll fall. Don't think. You will fall.

Back he stepped, inching his way to the wall 'til he could go no further.

As his heels bumped against the wall, his arm brushed something. Suddenly there was music. Something beautiful, sensuous almost. Mozart. The Requiem. It shocked him, brought him back.

Only then did he blink and begin to register his breathing, harsh and rasping through the tar. Only then could he think.

It made no sense. Why the child and not the father? The Reaper was too thorough. The man was dead. The noise was the onset of decomposition. Body gasses. Had to be.

Brook took a few moments to compose himself, still staring at the man to be sure. No movement. No more noise. Only the music. He was glad of it. The silence would have scorched his ears.

Calm now, Brook turned to the CD system. It was brand new. A half-smile drifted across his face. He set about concluding his business and turned to the wall to examine the word smeared in blood over the fireplace. His eye caught a glimpse of something else and his features darkened – a photograph in a frame on the mantelpiece. He looked closer, staring hard for what seemed like hours. There was no mistake. His mouth fell open. He shrank back, his face frozen in wonder, his eyes unblinking, his mind in turmoil, trying to make sense.

Then he knew. It all fit together and he nodded, his face set, eyes like slits to block out the visions. Of course. Now he understood. He'd got The Reaper's message. A smile cracked his features. Another noise behind him. Brook took a deep breath as he turned to face his nemesis.

*

Brook stood outside Sorenson's house waiting for Rowlands to shuffle the last few yards. It was dark now, snowing lightly, and Brook recalled the last nerve-shredding night he'd been in Sorenson's house, the night he'd found the brand new, still boxed CD player.

He sensed Rowlands looking at him, probing his reaction, waiting for him to be ready. "Well lad?" he panted.

"Just a minute."

"What's wrong?"

Brook put a finger to his lips. "I thought there might be music," he explained. "He played me something a long time ago. *La Wally.*"

"What did you call me?"

Brook laughed nervously. "Sorry Charlie. You're cold." Brook grabbed the bell pull and gave it a tug.

A light footfall crossed the interior and the door was opened by a vision of loveliness, an angel framed against the warm light of the hall.

"Hello Damen. Mr Rowlands."

"Hello Vicky."

She smiled nervously. "You don't seem surprised," she said, looking sheepish. Rowlands looked from one to the other, trying to be included.

"I wouldn't go that far. You look nice. Different somehow. More like your mother."

She smiled again. Brook wasn't sure he'd said the right thing. But he wasn't thinking his straightest. He'd suspected Vicky might be close to the case but seeing her now, at The Reaper's house, was still a shock to the system. He hid it well.

"Come in."

Brook and Rowlands stepped into the warm. Vicky took their coats and hung them up. She was very beautiful in the pale light. Gone were the patchy jeans and multi-coloured cardigans. Instead she wore black figure-hugging cords which tapered down to an expensive pair of tan Chelsea boots. A superfluous belt held her flat stomach against a dark velvet V-necked top which caressed her sculpted torso. Her hair was scraped back into a clasp, showing off her swan's neck and her ears, embellished by a pair of silver earrings – delicately worked filigree – shimmered in the half-light.

She led them to the room that Brook had cowered in, all those years before, waiting to be discovered by Sorenson. Then it was a bare room with only oddments of furniture, now it was warmly furnished, with plump dark armchairs and soft lighting. A blazing log fire crackled in the hearth.

Brook helped Rowlands to the chair nearest the fire. He gestured an inquiry at a decanter, warming on a table nearby. Vicky nodded and Brook poured a large measure for Rowlands and a less ample one for himself. Rowlands took a deep draught of his drink and closed his eyes. Brook took a sip and recognised the taste. All was as it should be.

Vicky threw a look at the door and Brook followed her back out into the hall.

"Thank you." Her face was soft and full of invitation.

"For what?"

"For not saying how you know me. I don't know Mr Rowlands very well."

"I'm surprised you know him at all."

"Uncle Vic and Mr Rowlands have become..." suddenly Vicky's eyes filled with tears. She looked very young again, as vulnerable as Brook had seen her that first time, lying defenceless on the bottom bunk, snoring gently in the room upstairs. "They share a common bond." She gathered herself quickly and gave Brook a brave smile. Uncle Vic clearly provoked much love in some quarters. "So how did you know our meeting wasn't an accident?"

"I didn't. Not for sure. Those ridiculous lies you told about the university gave me a hint, but that wasn't the clincher."

"What was?"

"Me."

"You?"

"Me. This battered piece of mid-forties driftwood you see before you."

"I don't understand."

"Well, you may find this hard to believe, Vicky, but I'm very careful to keep my awesome sexual magnetism under wraps – and with great success. A beautiful young girl like you could never be interested in a burn-out like me. Not without ulterior motives."

When she laughed, Vicky's eyes twinkled like diamonds. She contemplated his sad smile then cocked her head and leant up to give him the sweetest, softest kiss on the mouth. The merest hint of Gallic penetration aroused Brook more than a dozen skin flicks could have managed.

He felt her hot breath as she pulled back. Her eyes bored into his.

"Don't underestimate yourself, Daddy."

"I'm not your Daddy," he whispered.

She stiffened as if he'd flung an obscenity at her. Brook could almost smell the blood flushing her face.

"No." She turned away from him.

"I'm sorry. That was thoughtless. You still remember your father?"

When she turned back her face was streaked with tears. "No, *I'm* sorry. I'm embarrassing you."

Brook put his hands on her shoulders. He could feel the tension in her frame. "Don't be sorry. It wasn't your fault."

"No. That's what mum says."

"She's right." She looked up into his eyes now, searching for comfort, for affection. "You must have loved him very much." Vicky blinked again and buried her head in Brook's chest. He put his arm round her and patted her back in the manner required.

Incredible. All those years hadn't healed the scars of Stefan

Sorenson's murder. And Brook thought *he* had baggage. Little wonder Sammy Elphick and family were despatched with such relish.

Suddenly Vicky drew back and fixed him with her grey eyes. "Why have you got a picture of Uncle Vic in your Reaper file?"

Brook stared back at her. "Don't you know?" he finally said, managing to keep bewilderment from his voice.

A door opened at the top of the house and Vicky shrank back. Suddenly she was a frightened rabbit.

"Please. Don't tell them."

"What?"

"Please don't say anything about us. Please! Promise you won't."

Brook was stunned. The closer he came to answers the more confusing things became. "I thought your uncle sent you…" From the beseeching look she now gave him, he was wrong.

"Promise?"

"I promise." With that, Vicky turned and scuttled away leaving Brook nonplussed. Why would Vicky Sorenson go all the way to Derby to seek him out, if not with her mother or uncle's knowledge and approval? And who had met her at Derby Station? Not Sorenson, that much was clear. The answer came to Brook before the question was formed – her brother. The young man he'd seen that night many years before, sharing a bunk bed with Vicky. The young man with the baseball cap and the fast car – Vicky's lift to Brook's flat. Knowing who didn't help. Brook wanted the why.

"Hello again Mr Brook." Vicky's mother held out her hand.

"Mrs Sorenson."

She stood on the bottom step, level with Brook. He could see the similarity with Vicky more clearly now – the same sad expression, the same fragility.

"Thank you so much for coming. You don't know what it means to Victor." She stepped aside to beckon Brook up the stairs. He walked past her towards the first floor then turned when he saw her declining to follow.

"You know the way," she said. "He's waiting for you."

Brook paused on the stair and searched her face for clues to her reticence. Feeling foolish, he turned and climbed again. Past the Bosch triptych he'd been invited to interpret many years before, past the room he'd first encountered the sleeping Vicky and her brother, and on up to the study.

Brook quickened his step, keen to be there now, his trepidation replaced by burning curiosity to see his old quarry.

He held out a hand to push open the door but before he could reach it, it swung back sharply. A young Asian woman beamed at him. She was dressed in fresh white nurse's clothes with plimsolls to match. Her hair was invisible under a net. She had an air of brisk efficiency.

"Come in sir." She ushered him into the room he knew so well then stepped outside, closing the door behind her. Brook swept his eyes around the study that was etched into his sub-conscious. He wasn't disappointed. It was exactly the same as the day he'd first entered, except today the room was illuminated by lamps, not bathed in piercing sunlight. The only addition was a CD player next to the old stereo and off in one corner a video camera on a tripod. The books were the same. The desk was the same. The rest of the house may have changed, become friendlier under the guidance of a woman but this was still a man's room. His room.

Sorenson sat by the coal fire, his legs covered with a blanket – Charlie's trick – his eyes closed, feeble hands gripping the arms of the chair loosely. He was completely bald as he had been that final, fateful night in 1991, the night the Wrigley household had been removed from the world. He was the same, perhaps the skin was a little more yellowed, but it was the only difference.

A chair waited across from Sorenson so Brook sat quietly, not wanting to break the moment. Sorenson opened his eyes. Those black pools. He smiled. It was a warm and welcoming smile. Like a friend's. Like Charlie's.

"Welcome, Sergeant Brook. But it's Inspector Brook now, isn't it?"

"Yes." Brook leant over to shake Sorenson's hand. He didn't want to shake hands. He only did it now out of suspicion. To be sure he really was wasting away.

It was only the second time Brook had ever touched the man. The first time had been in the derelict house near Ravenscourt Park. Laura's squat. Sorenson had helped him to his feet before hinting to Brook that he would kill again that very night.

And it was true. He had the cold hand of death. It was limp, though not withered as Charlie's talons were. There seemed little strength there. And the skin was almost translucent.

As they touched, Sorenson's hand suddenly fastened round Brook's with a strength that belied his appearance. Brook's nerves ends tingled as though a mild electric current had been fed into him.

Brook tried to draw away. Sorenson's smiling face pierced him. Brook tried again to remove his hand from Sorenson's but his withered host held on, running a calloused thumb over Brook's knuckles.

Brook pulled away. He flexed his hand to dispel the pins and needles then darted a look at Sorenson who held his gaze. Finally the old man broke away, waved a hand at the drinks cabinet. "May I offer you something?"

"No. Why did you want to see me, professor?"

Sorenson's injured expression appeared genuine. "Why?" He shook his head. "Don't you know?"

"If you're ready to confess to The Reaper murders, I'm listening."

Sorenson laughed, though without amusement. "I wanted to see you because you're my friend. I haven't got long…"

"Then tell me. Confess to me, professor. You'll feel better."

"You've tried it?"

"Trust me. Then I'll be your friend. Talk to me. Tell me why you killed the children. Make me understand at least that."

"My friend, still you resist. Even now, with all the knowledge you've acquired, you plead ignorance. You'll never understand unless you clear away the fog that surrounds you. Society puts it there to take your sight. I thought you'd lifted the fog. I thought you saw clearly."

"I'm happy to disappoint you."

"Happy? You?" Sorenson chuckled. "Let me tell you about happiness, Damen. Two weeks ago I was in the happiest place in the world. Do you know where that was? The Terminal Ward at Hammersmith Hospital.

"You think I'm joking. I'm not. All those dying people under the same roof, not for long, by definition the population are transients. But yes, they are the happiest people in the world. You want to know why, Damen?" Brook shrugged. "Because they're finished with this terrible world. They've been given their notice, they have no more cares, no reason to fear, no need to wear a mask for the outside world. Just human beings looking at themselves and saying, 'Here I am. Take me or leave me. I'm happy either way.' Do you understand? You see Damen, in that place, people on the edge of the abyss, realise something."

"And what's that?"

"That they can't be hurt any more. Nobody can touch them. No body. No thing. Can you imagine the peace that brings?"

Sorenson suddenly laughed at a joke he hadn't yet told. Brook, taken aback, smiled on a reflex. "There was a man, two beds down from me, Colin – we had no use for surnames. Lung cancer. He was dead two days later. That afternoon his wife was with him and I could hear her complaining that the car kept cutting out when she braked.

"I remember looking over at Colin and as I moved my head, I must have caught his eye because he looked over at me and then down at his wife, blithering away.

"And on his face – I'll never forget it – was the most comical expression I've ever seen. I remember at the end, he couldn't contain it any longer and when she'd finished prattling away, he just said, "Oh dear. Oh dear, oh dear, oh dear." Then he looked back at me and started giggling. Then I started giggling. Then he giggled some more.

"And do you know what happened next, Damen? The most amazing, terrifying, wonderful thing. Within half a minute, every other patient in the ward had joined in.

"Do you see? They all knew. They hadn't heard what Colin's wife had said, how could they? But they knew what had happened to him, it had happened to them, this absurd euphoria you'd get when a visitor sat by your bed and tried to drag you back into their mundane little world – their world of sorrow and care – and suddenly you realised you didn't have to go with them."

Sorenson closed his eyes and took a large breath to extinguish the laughter. But still he smiled and shook his head. "Amazing." His enthusiasm had tired him. Brook stared into the fire, not knowing what to say. He was learning nothing and wondered whether to go. This whole idea had been a mistake. Sorenson would never confess.

"Do you still dream, Damen?" Sorenson kept his eyes closed.

"Sometimes."

"About the rats?"

"Sometimes."

"About Laura Maples?"

Brook was disgusted. What was this? Surely Sorenson didn't need leverage now. He decided there was nothing to hide. Sorenson couldn't touch him anymore. They were both terminal.

"Sometimes."

Brook's host opened his eyes to look at him. He nodded, thinking. "Interesting. I thought you'd be able to achieve closure in her case."

"I can. But I still see her. It was never her killer that haunted me. It was her suffering."

"Of course. Families do engender great suffering don't they?" Sorenson stared into the fire. "My family…" Brook waited for an indiscretion but none came. "How is *your* family, by the way?"

"Never better," Brook replied. He wondered if Sorenson knew about the break-up. He didn't have to wait long for an answer.

"Your ex-wife remarried, didn't she?"

"How do you know that?"

Sorenson smiled innocently. "I've no idea."

"Yes she did. We're still on friendly terms though."

"That's good. What do you think of my niece, Victoria?"

"She's very beautiful – a credit to you. She's grown a lot since I first saw her," Brook added mischievously.

Sorenson looked puzzled for a brief moment then beamed back at Brook. "Of course, you looked in on Petr and Victoria on your last visit."

"Amongst other things."

Sorenson was grave all of a sudden. His sigh was suffused with tension. "Poor Victoria. She's a very disturbed young girl."

"Oh? She seems pretty level-headed to me."

Sorenson ignored Brook's comment. "Since the death of her father. It's not natural. Such a long time ago but she can't get over it. She's obsessed by Stefan's death. What's worse is that she seems to have got the idea that this Reaper you talk about had something to do with it."

"Really?" Brook was suddenly alert. "I wonder how she got that into her head."

Sorenson grunted his amusement. It was only temporary. "Not from me, I assure you – a very unsuitable fixation for one so young, so much life in front of her."

Again he stared into the hot coals, thinking the unimaginable thoughts of the killer. He closed his eyes again.

"I'm tired, Inspector Brook."

"Of course."

"Please would you give my best wishes to Charlie." *Charlie* was it. Brook had underestimated the bonding they'd done together in hospital. "And feel free to call again soon. We still have a lot to discuss."

"How did you know Floyd Wrigley raped and murdered Laura Maples?" Brook stood stone-faced, waiting for an answer to a question that had haunted him for years.

Sorenson smiled sadly at him. It wasn't a smile to taunt Brook with his superiority and Brook knew then, no matter what happened, Sorenson saw Brook as his friend – perhaps his only friend. And friends share things.

"You were at the house where she died. Couldn't you feel it?"

"What?"

"The atmosphere, Inspector Brook. Never discount the power of atmosphere." Barely had the last syllable cleared his dry lips before his head slackened onto the wing of the chair. A soft snoring followed.

Brook flexed the hand that Sorenson had grabbed. He could still feel a tingle running through it. He waited a few moments then rose and left the study. The nurse was outside the door.

"Is he sleeping?" Brook nodded. "He should be having his injection."

246

"Is he in pain, nurse?"

"Constant. He's on Morphine. I don't know how he manages to keep his mind clear. He should be babbling like a baby. He's very strong-willed."

Brook headed for the stairs. He turned on the top step. "How long?"

"A month. Two at the most."

Brook nodded. Two months to closure. Not a chance. Not unless he confessed. Brook had to know everything. He knew then he'd have to come back, speak to him one more time. And Sorenson knew it too. And even if it meant Brook pouring out everything to Sorenson to gain an admission, he knew he'd have to do it.

*

As he descended the stairs, Brook considered the withered old man slumped in his study and wondered how someone so ill could have played a part in the deaths of the Wallis family. Everything in Derby pointed to The Reaper but Brook's chief suspect sat shrivelled in a chair, pumped full of drugs, awaiting his own end.

Brook paused by the Bosch triptych and stared blankly at it. Then he nodded. Atmosphere. He could feel it alright. It clung to Sorenson even now. An atmosphere of unstoppable power. Brook had felt it the night the Wrigley family had died in Brixton, the night he'd sat outside his own house and waited for Sorenson to take the lives of Amy and Terri – unable to move, unable to intervene.

It was a power like no other, a power that allowed Sorenson to spend ten minutes in the place Laura Maples died and be able to identify her killer. He'd solved a case that couldn't be solved and that same night, Laura's killer – and every member of his family – was dead.

No, he couldn't take Sorenson out of the equation – no matter how strenuous the deed, no matter what his physical condition.

*

Rowlands was in good spirits when Brook returned to the living room. Or rather, good spirits were in him. Booze gave him what little energy he had and he'd certainly filled the tank while Brook had been upstairs.

Rowlands looked at his friend's sombre expression with the blank curiosity of the drunk.

"How do you suppose Sorenson knows about my family's marital history, Charlie?"

After taking so much energy on board, Rowlands failed to detect the insinuation in Brook's voice. "Beats me laddie," he replied.

Brook shrugged. He helped Rowlands to his feet and led him to the front door.

"Damen."

Brook turned to Vicky. She held out a carrier bag. Brook took it. There were two brightly wrapped packages inside. "Uncle Vic wanted you to have these for Christmas."

"Thanks very much, lass," Rowlands slurred. "It's much appreciated."

"Thanks Vicky." Brook's affectionate tone was more of a surprise to him than to Vicky. "Look after yourself. And say hello to your brother for me."

She smiled her goodbye but said nothing.

*

Two hours later, Brook sat in the warmth of Rowlands' Caterham home, leaded glass in hand. It was dark outside and in. Brook didn't want light. He wanted to be alone, cut off from everything and everybody. Time spent with Sorenson had a way of inducing sensory overload and Brook needed to let his mind drift for a while or he'd blow a fuse.

He sipped on his Navy rum and ran the mellow heat around his mouth as an antiseptic. He could hear Charlie snoring heavily upstairs. Alcohol-induced stupor was the only medicine for him now.

Brook kicked off his shoes and warmed his feet before the gas fire. It had been a difficult two days but now they were over. He'd done it, he'd faced Sorenson and come through. He knew he could win now. Sorenson would confess, he was certain. Then he'd know why. That would be his victory.

Brook dragged the carrier bag from "Uncle Vic" towards him on the sofa. He pulled out the parcels and examined the labels. The bottle-shaped parcel read, "To my old friend Charlie Rowlands. Sleep well."

Brook snorted. This terminal illness deal was something else. He looked at his package. It felt like a book. His label read, "To Inspector Brook. So near yet so far. Don't judge this book by its cover. Victor."

Brook slid off the paper and turned the book. He could make out the title on its white background by the glow of the fire. His mouth fell open. It was an A – Z of Leeds, published 1993.

Chapter 26

DS Brook trudged through the office aware that he looked wilder than usual. He hadn't shaved or changed his wet clothes, his eyes were red-rimmed and his hair was dank and matted against his skull. Even the DC's, and other assorted grunts, who generally avoided his passing, were moved to stop what they were doing and stare.

Brook, aware of inquisitive eyes, locked his attention onto the plastic cup of black coffee he carried, holding it like a bar of plutonium. He didn't go out of his way to indulge in that fiendishly difficult small talk that others found easy so he hurried to the sanctuary of his office.

Once there, he slumped into his chair, took a mouthful of the black unction and rummaged through a drawer for cigarettes. He pulled out a dented pack, cracked the cellophane and lit up, closing his eyes to the bite of the smoke. Then he reached for the phone and dialled.

"Hello."

"It's me darling."

"Where've you been?"

"Working."

"All night? In that terrible weather?"

"'Fraid so."

There was a pause from Amy. She'd been down this route before. Since Harlesden. Since Laura Maples. Her husband was unreachable, not of this earth. But she couldn't let him off lightly. He had responsibilities. *"And were there no phones where you were working?"* She was about to add his name but thought it might signal weakness.

"I...It was difficult, darling. There was another family killed last night. It's The Reaper. He's taken another family."

249

"Oh God. Where?"

"Brixton. Can you hear me? Do you understand? It was The Reaper again." Brook closed his eyes and recalled Amy peering out of the window of the house the night before, ignorant of his presence, unaware how her simple reaction to a car horn had released such a tide of relief and self-loathing in him. He remembered the cold hand of fear tightening its grip on his shoulders, holding him, pushing him down into his seat, numbing him.

"Does this mean another year like the last one, Damen?"

"No."

"Don't lie to me. I can't stand it any more. Never seeing you and all the time dreading seeing you. You come home, sit in a chair and stare...I can't stand any more..."

Brook took the silver chain from his pocket and draped it around his fingers, playing with it. For a moment, he forgot he was on the phone and just stared at the necklace with its little hearts glinting in the pale light. He spoke again, his voice a mere croak.

"You can rest easy now Laura. Don't worry any more. It's over Laura. It's over." He replaced the receiver and slumped forward onto his desk.

The door opened. "Brooky. Fucking hell! Are you all right, old son? You look like shit."

Brook opened one eye at Rowlands from the cradle of his trembling arms. He lifted his damp head and caught a waft of the brewery from his boss. He drained the last of his coffee. "Sorry guv. Didn't sleep last night."

"Was that at home or in your car outside Sorenson's?" Brook opened his mouth to speak but thought better of it. "I thought so," nodded Rowlands. "Well," he said, looking at a wad of papers in his fist. "That might be a blessing in disguise."

"Why?"

Rowlands smiled. "Because now you'll know Sorenson ain't The Reaper. There's been another."

Brook nodded. "I know."

"What do you mean, you know?"

"The Reaper killed another family. I followed him."

Rowlands was speechless, his face pained. He turned away from Brook and slumped into the nearest chair, pulling out his flask. After a longer pull than usual, he offered it to Brook, as was his custom. For once Brook kept the tip of his tongue from the neck and allowed the cheap whisky to burn his throat.

"You're right." Rowlands was sombre. "In Brixton. A black man, name of Floyd Wrigley and his girlfriend and daughter. What happened to you?"

Brook looked away. "I lost him. In Battersea."

"What?"

"He went to my house first to remind me what he could do."

"Jesus, Brooky! Then you don't know for sure it was Sorenson."

"It was him, guv."

"Fucking hell lad. When will this thing end? You can't go on like this. You've got to get on with your life." Rowlands seemed like he was about to burst into tears. "Look, I'm your friend. You have to drop this now. Another year like this will kill you..."

"Guv!" Brook held up a hand. "Stop worrying. Sorenson's finished with me now."

"I don't follow."

"He's beaten me, he'll move on."

"Talk sense man."

Brook smiled at his incomprehension and decided not to disturb it. "I've nothing left to give. He knows that. After last night. That's why he went to my house. To show me he can do what he wants and I won't...I can't stop him."

Rowlands took another pull on his flask and looked off into space. After several moments he began nodding and even managed a smile. "Good. We'll let someone else worry about it. And you don't want any details then?"

"No."

"You really mean it, don't you?"

"Yes."

"And you don't want to reccy the crime scene?"

Brook paused. "No need."

"I'd better ring the Brixton Boys then. They were expecting you on a consult. I'll tell 'em we've got complete confidence in 'em." He winked. "They'll lap that up. Go home, Brooky. You've got a beautiful wife and baby waiting for you."

"Thanks guv. I will." Brook stood with some difficulty. He seemed to be on the verge of complete collapse. He shuffled to the door.

"What's this?"

Brook turned to see Rowlands fingering Laura's silver necklace, which lay on the blotter. He held out his hand and his boss dropped it into his palm.

"It's a present for Theresa."

*

Brook pulled his collar up against the cold and headed for the sanctuary of the café. He bought a tea and hesitated, surveying the available food. He was hungry but not that hungry.

The Leeds-Derby service was delayed but Brook didn't care. He needed time to think. He knew now what he had to do, but he needed support from McMaster and had to work out how to get it. Suspended or not, he must have her backing to go to Glasgow, even if unofficial, just drop her name into the conversation to get the jocks to speak to him about Roddy Telfer's background and try to find a link with the other Reaper killings.

It would be difficult. His visit to Leeds had been a mistake. He'd been refused any co-operation without back-up from a senior officer. Now McMaster would be hearing about Brook treading on toes in the North, sniffing around on a case from which he'd been suspended.

Brook sipped his tea. He pulled out the Leeds A-Z given him by Sorenson. What had he missed? Despite all indications to the contrary, there had to be something to learn from Telfer's killing in '93. But what? What did Sorenson mean? *"Don't judge this book by its cover."*

Well Brook had judged it. He'd marked Leeds down as a copycat but now he was being forced to reassess. The murder of Roddy Telfer and his heavily pregnant girlfriend was connected to The Reaper. Sorenson had told him that much, told him to dig deeper.

Brook stared at the A-Z, at the page with Telfer's old street on it. He wondered if Sorenson knew Telfer's building had been flattened to make way for a new link road and that there was no longer a murder scene to visit. Did that matter? Sorenson was telling him Leeds was important. Brook had missed something. Despite the botched MO, there was a connection with Harlesden and Brixton. Especially Brixton.

Something bubbled away beneath his consciousness but wouldn't surface. His mind drifted back to the face of the Wrigley girl on that terrible night in Brixton. The night Sorenson had shown him he could take any family he wanted, even Brook's.

Families. Sammy Elphick had killed Sorenson's brother in a bungled burglary. Floyd Wrigley had raped and murdered Laura Maples. What had Telfer done to interest The Reaper? What had Bobby Wallis done?

*

"How you feelin' Brooky?"

"Okay guv."

"You don't look okay. That baby keeping you awake?"

Brook nodded.

"How is she?"

"Terri's fine."

"Fine." Rowlands contemplated Brook. "You must be the first parent in history who don't gush at any mention of their new-born baby. And what about you, lad? Are you fine?"

Brook nodded.

"I can do this on my own lad. There's still time for you to bail."

"I'm okay guv," replied Brook and they both returned to their reading matter. Brook finished his toast and drained the last of his syrupy tea. He looked back across at Rowlands reading the autopsy reports and nursing his whisky-laced coffee. His toast lay untouched. He wouldn't eat on an empty stomach.

"There were traces of chloroform around the Wrigley girl's face and nose and she was given an injection. A mixture of Nembutal and Seconal. A lot."

"Nembutal?" Brook looked up. "That's a barbiturate. Relatively harmless."

"So is Seconal and you're right. It says here if they're taken orally, they're absorbed slowly. Injected into a vein it causes damage. It would have killed her."

Brook received this information with a small measure of relief. "So she may have felt no pain."

"But why cut her throat as well?"

"For show, like the Elphick boy," answered Brook. "What about the parents?"

"Smack. They were both users so it was probably self-administered, which means he didn't have to work hard to control them."

"That explains why they weren't gagged."

"I guess."

"Would you like the good news, guv?" asked Brook, nodding at his own reading matter. "Floyd Wrigley. Petty theft, possession, affray, ABH, GBH. It goes on." There was no mention of rape and murder. Now there never could be.

"Some comfort then," nodded Rowlands.

"It gets worse, guv. Or better. DS Croft reckons Floyd was living off immoral earnings to fund his habit. They had nothing solid but..."

"He was pimping his girlfriend? Classy."

"Not the girlfriend, Tamara, the daughter."

"Fucking...scum. How old?"

"Eleven. There's a note at the end of the autopsy. They asked the pathologist to look for it. She wasn't a virgin, guv."

Both fathers of daughters, one living, the other dead, looked at a space that couldn't look back at them, that couldn't see through the eyes, into their hearts where all the private things were.

Rowlands lit a cigarette and took a huge pull. "I don't envy you,

Brooky. At least Elizabeth..." Rowlands looked down at his coffee. In a trice that a gunfighter would have been proud of, he'd whipped out his flask and was replenishing his cup. "Look after Amy and little Theresa, lad. You only get one go at it."

"Guv..."

"I know. Sorenson's finished with you. But you're here aren't you?"

Brook examined his boss. He didn't look well. Then again he never looked well.

Rowlands squinted up through the blue smoke drifting across his face. "Ready?" He finished his coffee at Brook's nod and they manoeuvred themselves off the Star Burger's unyielding bucket seats.

They walked together down Brixton High Street, not speaking, not looking at each other. Instead they looked at the second-hand Christmas illuminations, cast-offs purchased by the Council, on the cheap from Blackpool. They even studied the famous railway bridge, straddling the main road with its patronising "We're backing Brixton!" message, its cluster of business logos a knee-jerk, post-riots affirmation of capitalism. They looked but they didn't see.

As they turned onto Electric Avenue, Brook had to make a conscious effort to stay half a pace behind Rowlands who was scanning the street to get his bearings.

He stopped outside a door sandwiched between two moribund shop fronts, daubed with posters for bands, concerts, jumble sales and obscure political groups. A constable squinted at their ID and stood aside. A gaggle of ghouls still loitered outside the murder scene four days after the event. They talked in lowered tones about the killings. They were shocked and horrified in conversation, but glowed inside, satisfied to be a spit from the spotlight of public infamy.

Brook glanced warily around for the empty boxes that The Reaper had left outside the doorway. They were gone. Rowlands passed through the entrance but Brook hung back.

"You coming lad?" said Rowlands from the bottom of the stairs.

Brook smiled and followed his boss. He made to close the door but the constable put his hand out to keep it open. "They want fresh air up there, sir." Brook nodded.

The lounge was the last room at the top of the rickety stairs. Rowlands nodded to the two SOCO's on their knees still sifting and scraping and measuring and combing four days after the fact.

Brook took out glossy photographs from the dossier and started handing them to Rowlands who examined them against the layout of the room. It was bright now because the curtains had been drawn back. On the photographs the curtains were closed and the room

254

was poorly lit. Rowlands looked around, getting the measure of what had happened here, acclimatising to where he could and couldn't walk.

There was a tatty, if comfortable looking sofa at one end of the room. It had once been a faded blue but was now covered in black stains, particularly on the seat cushions where rivers of blood had dammed against the thighs of the man and woman, sat side by side. The rest of the sofa was a patchwork of blood splatter.

The bare floor had also been stained – dry-black pools, in contrast to the scuffed dirty brown of the boards. The bloodstains were edged in white chalk and tape to alert pedestrians. At the edge of one such stain the smooth circular regularity of the encroaching blood had been breached and part of a footprint was clearly visible.

"What size?" asked Rowlands.

"The file reckons 10," said Brook. "Thereabouts."

"And what's Sorenson?"

"Size eight."

"Told you so."

"We can't say for sure it's the murderer's shoe, guv."

"Well it ain't the milkman's."

To one side, under the window, lay a small mattress with a couple of thin blankets for cover – perhaps the place of work for one wretched human being.

In the middle of the room there was an old straight-backed dining chair, lying on its side, facing the sofa. Another apron of black spewed out from where it had toppled. Black-red sprays extended out from the mass of the pool like flares under the great initial force of the severed artery. These thin jets of blood had escaped at several different angles. The girl, Tamara, had contested her fate, despite the drugs. She'd been bound, gagged and doped up but still fought against the ebbing of her scarred life.

What had she thought of the world in those last few terrible moments, Brook wondered? Tied to a chair, cold in vest and knickers, throat sliced by a stranger, facing her parents, drug addicts, who sold her for sex and were only able to stare back, saucer-eyed, uncomprehending, as their daughter convulsed herself into oblivion.

"Why her? Why the Elphick boy? Why the children?" muttered Rowlands.

Brook approached the top-of-the-range CD player. He squirreled a look at Rowlands who nodded back at him.

"Alright, don't rub it in, Brooky."

"Has this been dusted for prints?" Brook could tell from the powder residues that it had, so he switched it on before the SOCO's could reply. He opened the CD tray. It was empty. Brook reached into his overcoat and pulled out a thin plastic case. He flipped out the disc and fed it into the machine. Mozart's Requiem crept out of the speakers positioned in opposite corners, barely audible. Brook turned it up so the music flowed over them. This would be the only beauty young Tamara would have known in her life.

The SOCO boys turned round at the noise.

"Atmosphere, lads."

Rowlands examined a crime scene photograph and moved closer to the gas fire. He could still see the glint of broken glass on the boards. "This is where the picture frame was smashed Brooky." He peered at the trickle of blood on the wall above the hearth.

"Maybe it was in the way of his message," offered Brook.

"Yeah but why not just move it? Why would he smash the glass and remove the actual picture? He didn't take souvenirs in Harlesden." Rowlands moved over to the sofa. "Floyd sat here, the woman, Natalie, this side." Rowlands' tone conveyed his raised eyebrow. "Interesting. Look." He pointed to the photograph of Floyd Wrigley's body. "There's more than one cut here. It was a struggle. Like the killer had trouble. Or maybe there was a smaller, weaker accomplice."

"Look at his neck though, guv. There are some weights in the bedroom. He worked out. A real vain bastard."

"So?"

"Well, in a condition of heightened adrenaline, combined with the effect of the heroin, there's no telling how his neck muscles would react. They could have seized, making them difficult to cut."

"Maybe. I'm not complaining, laddie. One less piece of shit on the streets." Rowlands pulled out a glossy print and handed it to Brook. "This is interesting."

"What am I looking at?"

"The back of his neck. See that mark." Rowlands indicated the long thin weal on Floyd Wrigley's skin.

"Yeah."

"What do you think caused that?"

"No idea, guv." Brook became self-conscious under his superior's gaze.

Rowlands wasn't used to his sergeant not having the answers. "Maybe the killer helped himself to a trophy. Maybe Floyd wore a chain and the killer yanked it off as a keepsake." Brook said nothing. Rowlands turned to the SOCO boys still groping around on their knees. "Are there any family photographs in the flat, fellas? There's no mention in the inventory."

They both looked blank and shrugged back at Rowlands. Then one said, "You'll have to ask DS Croft, sir."

"Do you mind if we look around for any?"

Another shrug. "Go ahead. We've finished in the other rooms, sir."

Brook and Rowlands set to work. It didn't take long. Wrigley had clearly sold everything that wasn't required for sleeping or sitting. No camera, no photographs.

"What are we looking for, guv?"

"Snaps of the flat, family portraits, anything that might give us a clue about what was in that picture frame or what was round Floyd's neck."

Brook shook his head and looked at his boss. "It must be a souvenir. Like you said."

"Exactly." Rowlands nodded. "Which gives us a different MO."

"Perhaps he had no choice, guv. Perhaps, when he moved the frame, he cut himself."

"On the picture and not the glass? There were no traces of anything on the glass. No prints, blood, nothing."

"It's a puzzle, guv."

Rowlands suddenly looked at Brook, his face animated. "Maybe it's not a different MO. Maybe he took something from Harlesden that we don't know about."

Brook laughed. "You're on top form today, guv."

"One of us has got to be," Rowlands snapped back. There was an awkward silence. "I'm sorry, lad. I didn't mean that. I know what you've put into this case. I'm glad you're not getting too involved."

The awkwardness returned. Rowlands turned away and laid a consoling arm on Brook's shoulder for a few seconds.

"Forget it, guv. If Wrigley's got any relatives that aren't in hell with him, Croft should find out what was in that frame."

Rowlands nodded. "Good thinking, lad."

Brook broke away and went behind the sofa to check the last view of the parents, as he had in Harlesden. As with the Elphicks, they would have watched as their daughter died, and afterwards, seen the word SAVED written on the chimney wall, in the blood of their child.

"Why SAVED and not SALVATION?" mused Brook to himself.

"There could be a pattern. Something Biblical."

Brook couldn't suppress a curt laugh. "You'd know, guv."

"Cheers."

"It's more likely lack of space or time, if not blood."

"One thing puzzles me. If the killer brings this CD player as some phoney prize, like you say, why let the killer in? With Floyd's habit, I would think he'd just take the box at the door and keep it to exchange for drugs. Why let him in to set the thing up?"

"Our guy wouldn't hand it over unless he was allowed in to set it up. Part of the prize. Or maybe the parents didn't let him in. If they were tripping the light fantastic, maybe they were bombed out on the sofa."

"The girl." Rowlands nodded, his eyes and lips clenched.

"Yeah. How easy could it be? He comes in, sees the parents in the state they're in. He puts the girl under with the chloroform then ties and gags her then binds mum and dad. Just in case. Then the injection..."

"Enough to kill her?"

"Sure, but not before he gets to cut her throat."

"Then why give her the injection, lad? He didn't do that with the Elphick boy."

"No, guv. But he didn't have to. He'd smothered the boy before he hung him. Maybe, Sammy and his missus weren't as upset as they should've been, as they would've been if they'd actually seen him die. He cut off the fingers to show the Elphicks he was dead. But it wasn't enough. So now The Reaper feels the need to slaughter the girl while her parents watch."

"So he gives her a lethal dose of barbiturates because he doesn't want her to suffer. What a prince." Rowlands looked away deep in thought. Both men considered the scene. Mozart's portentous choir flowed over them.

"What makes someone with a life that shit cling on to it with such force? In her shoes..." Rowlands stopped himself in time. He snaked a look at Brook who pretended to be absorbed in something else. "So then what, lad?"

Brook took a heavy sigh and found his bookmark in the drama. "My guess is that he's already set up the CD player. He's brought Mozart's Requiem. He wants to hear it as he works. Or he wants the Wrigleys to hear it.

"There was a wet towel in the bathroom sink. My guess is he's revived mum and dad to make them watch. Then he cuts the girl's throat and stands back to watch Floyd and Natalie's reaction.

"It should be a good show. The girl's struggling for all she's worth. She knocks over the chair, fighting with as much strength as she can muster.

"But maybe Floyd and Natalie are on Cloud Nine and don't know what's going on. It's worse for the child than it was in Harlesden, but it doesn't make the parents suffer. They're too far gone." Brook's voice began to soften and he looked away as though watching a re-enactment unfolding in the middle distance. "He wants them to see. He wants *him* to see. He hates Floyd Wrigley. He's scum – the lowest form of life on earth. What he's done with his life demands punishment. He's wasted it and ruined others. Even watching his daughter choke on her own blood won't settle the debt." The other officers exchanged a look and stopped to listen. "Because you don't care, do you? You don't care about anyone but yourself. You fear your own death, not your daughter's, not your wo-man's." Brook spat out the word in the loud Jamaican patois he'd heard so many times from bejewelled Yardies. There was silence for a moment. Nobody moved. Only Mozart.

"Why no art to look at while they die?" Rowlands asked.

"Maybe he brought something but they were in no state to appreciate it so he didn't put it up."

"Or maybe he's changing his MO every time to try and fool the profilers."

"'Could be."

Rowlands studied his friend. "I've seen enough. Let's go. Be quick if you want that serial number."

Brook stopped the music and pocketed the disc. He knelt down behind the CD player with a small pad and pencil.

Rowlands was already on his way back down the steps. Brook watched him go and jumped up to follow. He put the pad and pencil away then paused and turned to one of the officers still toiling away.

"Have you found anything useful?"

"It's not looking good apart from that footprint. No fingerprints, no weapon, no DNA, no fibres. This guy knows what he's doing."

"If you do find something, anything from the killer, I want you to get it DNA tested."

"Obviously."

"I mean anything. And if you don't think the sample is usable, make sure you still store it carefully. It may be usable in the future. Clear?" With that triumphant demonstration of his interpersonal skills, Brook followed his boss out into the crisp, winter afternoon.

"And you can blow it out your arse, you fucking nutter," mumbled the officer to his retreating back.

"Wanker," agreed his colleague with venom.

*

Brook took the cigarette thrown in his direction and placed it in his mouth. The lighter followed. Rowlands sat opposite refilling his flask from a half bottle of Johnny Walker Black Label. It was unavailable in Britain, but he had a friend in Customs and Excise who sent him seized contraband from time to time. When he'd finished he took a swig first from the bottle, then the flask. Finally he looked back over at Brook. "Well?"

"Guv?" Brook looked back at his boss.

"Does the serial number match?"

Brook fished for his notebook and flipped it open. He stared at the blank page. Then rummaged around his drawer and drew out the delivery note he'd taken from the boxed CD player in Sorenson's house. It still had the brown tape clinging to it. Brook located the serial number and held it next to the blank page away from his boss.

Brook smiled. It was a bittersweet smile. A smile of loss. A smile that wished things could have been different.

"Are they the same lad?"

Brook picked up the lighter from his lap and ignited his cigarette. Then he held the flame to the edge of the delivery note. The tape crinkled and smouldered before the paper took light. Brook held it up for a moment to ensure the conflagration then dropped it into the metal bin at his feet. "No."

Chapter 27

"Well?" McMaster sat with her back straight and her hands interwoven on the desk. Her stony gaze was supposed to penetrate him, her silence pierce him.

But Brook stood impassive, staring at a fixed point above her blonde bob. He understood Sorenson's story about the terminal ward now. Brook was the same. Finished with life. Nothing anyone did could affect him, nothing anyone said could bring him back.

But he had a job to finish and a lack of concern, a refusal to play out this scene along its scripted course, would lose him the support he needed for a little longer. So Brook fought his instincts and concentrated hard to remember the next line.

"I screwed up, ma'am. I'm sorry."

"Sorry? Sorry is the pause you should've taken between thought and deed. I've had the DCC of West Yorkshire barking down the phone at me for half an hour..."

"I can explain..."

"Can you? I wish you would." She broke her gaze and unclasped her hands. She picked up Brook's warrant card from the blotter and began to fiddle with it. Brook shot a look at her spider plant. It was brown and withered.

McMaster waited but Brook said nothing.

"For God's sake, stand easy and speak to me Damen. Don't give me this strong, silent number. I've seen it a million times from coppers who aren't fit to lick your shoes. I thought I knew you. But I don't, do I? It's always the same. Whenever you bloody men are in trouble you clam up and play the hard nut..."

Her volume subsided and she put her head in her hands, before looking back at him. "And no I'm not going to cry." Brook's face softened into a half smile.

"No ma'am," he said. "Not you." He relaxed his shoulders into the break of tension.

"Well thanks. I think." Her voice was soft and measured once more. "They could have your job for this, Damen. Do you care?"

"Not really."

"I didn't think so. Well, what now?"

"Now? I'm going to Glasgow, ma'am. I'm going to do what I should've done years ago. It's in the past. Something they've done that's got them killed. Bobby Wallis abusing Kylie, Floyd Wrigley selling his daughter for sex. It's The Reaper ma'am. I'm sure of it now. He's back and he wants me to know it. So I need to go to Glasgow and find out about Roddy Telfer's past. That's why I went to Leeds."

"Did he have a daughter too?"

"What?" Brook looked at her as though he hadn't understood.

"Did Roddy Telfer have a daughter? I assume that's the connection you're talking about."

Brook stood there like a fish in a bowl staring out at a world misshapen by glass. He was rooted for several seconds while his superior looked on. "Are you all right, inspector?"

Brook's mind was in turmoil at this sudden spark. It was difficult not to show it. "Yes. I mean no. He didn't have a daughter, at least, none that I know."

"Are you sure you're okay?"

"I'm fine. I've got to go, ma'am. I need your help."

"Oh, now you need my help. Well you..."

"Look ma'am. Evelyn." McMaster blinked in surprise. "They can have my job after I've been to London. But do you really think that will satisfy them?"

"I thought you were going to Glasgow..."

"No. Maybe. It may not be necessary. Look ma'am. You must see. They don't want my job. I'm a harmless washout. But you, you're a woman in a man's world. And they're waiting and watching, every second of every day. Waiting and hoping for you to screw up. It's you they want, you must know that..."

"Inspector Brook..."

"I'm close. I'm close to The Reaper. After all these years. What better thing to give them? What better way to make yourself fireproof than to give them The Reaper?"

"And for yourself, of course?"

"I don't care about that."

McMaster looked down at her desk in apology. "No."

"There's my warrant card. Take it now if you think it will help your career, but I'm following this up to the end. I'm going to finish this, with or without your help."

There was a long silence in which McMaster clasped and unclasped her hands. She stood and turned away from Brook, then stepped across to her spider plant and rustled the dead fronds. Her mind made up, she turned back to her desk and picked up Brook's warrant card and tossed it at him. "What do you need?"

"Speak to whoever you need to, and get them to co-operate. I need to look at Telfer's record…"

"You can get that from the PNC."

"True, but Floyd Wrigley pimping his daughter wasn't on record. It was a whisper. So I need to look at all the scraps that may not be on his record and if I go up to Glasgow, I'll need to talk to any coppers, ex-coppers who had any dealings with him."

"If?"

"There may not be time. But meanwhile, get everything you can on Telfer faxed down."

McMaster sighed. "I'll make the calls now."

"Thank you. I know what this is costing you."

"Don't worry about me, Damen. I can always go to the tribunal. There's big money in sex discrimination these days," she added, with a laugh.

"It's never been about money for either of us, ma'am."

"Thank you for that. Now get out. And good luck."

*

Brook unlocked his office and stepped through the door. He walked over to his desk, bent down then stopped dead. "Hello *Bob!*" he said, without turning round.

Greatorix stood in the doorway. He was taken aback for a second. "Hello Damen. Come to clear your desk?" Brook turned to catch a yellow grin of satisfaction, which Greatorix made no attempt to hide.

Brook sniffed the air without being too obvious. There was an unsanitary current wafting over from his dank colleague. Greatorix had clearly worked himself into a special lather of anticipation at Brook's impending unemployment. Noble stood behind him, but not too close.

"Something like that, *Bob.*"

"I can't say I blame them." He stepped into the office, sizing it up for his own use. "A maverick like you on a case this important…"

"Did you want something? I'm in a hurry."

"I don't want to hold you up but you have some video tapes which belong to the Wallis investigation. I'd like them."

Brook looked blandly at Noble who shrugged his apology. "From the station's CCTV? Yeah I took them home to watch. I forgot all about them."

"Did you? Well I want them."

"There's nothing on them for you."

"Are you refusing to hand them over, inspector?"

"Don't be crass. They're at home. I'll drop them off in the morning…"

"I want them now!"

"I don't work for you, *Bob*."

"You don't work for anyone, *Damen*."

Brook laughed. "Tell you what. Lend me DS Noble for an hour and I'll give them to him. That suit?"

"It'll have to."

"Oh and Bob, speaking of mavericks, don't you know it's an offence to search the office of a serving colleague without some kind of permission?" Brook exhumed a malicious grin of his own, to crank up Greatorix's temperature. Greatorix turned to Noble with a malevolent expression. "No, DS Noble didn't tell me, Bob, it was the smell."

"Smell?" Greatorix narrowed his eyes. Noble stifled a laugh. "What smell?"

Brook took a pause to give his portly colleague time to stew. "Ambition Bob. Unfettered ambition."

"Unfett…?"

"It's in the dictionary."

Greatorix was on the wrong foot for a second before retrieving his own spiteful grin. "But you're not a serving colleague. In the words of the great Norman Tebbit, you're semi-detached."

"Shouldn't you be out arresting Jason Wallis, Bob?" asked Brook.

"My, our enquiries," he added with a curt nod at Noble, "have put young Wallis in the clear."

"Really?"

"He's even going to help with an appeal."

"On TV?"

"Of course on TV. I don't know why you didn't think of it."

Brook nodded. "So Jason's going to be a big-shot after all. Much as I dislike you, Bob, can I tell you that would be a mistake."

"Really? Why?"

"Trust me."

Greatorix smirked in Brook's general direction. "Just get those tapes." He turned to walk past Noble. "You've got an hour, John," and walked out as haughtily as he could for a man of his girth.

"'Sir."

Brook watched Greatorix retreat before continuing. "John. I don't have much time. Have you got your mobile?"

"Yes sir."

"Give it to me."

"Sorry?"

"Don't argue. I don't have one. Now if I've already left, I need you to ring me on your mobile. I'm expecting a fax from Glasgow about a small time villain called Roddy Telfer. When it arrives, ring me and tell me if there's any mention of him outside of Glasgow and Leeds. Is that clear?"

"I don't know…"

"And while you're waiting for that, I want you to run a trace on a Petr Sorenson. P-E-T-R – it's a Swedish name – Sorenson. Find out where he lives, his job etc."

"Has he got a record?"

"Unlikely."

"Well it may take longer than Inspector…"

"Forget him. Here. Take my office key. Lock yourself in, put a chair under the handle if you have to. Just do it. Tell him you were following another lead."

"O-kay." Noble was hesitant and Brook, for the first time, wasn't sure he could trust him. Unlike Brook he had a career to think about.

"Good. Let's get those tapes."

*

Brook led Noble into his front room located the bag of video cassettes and held them out to him. Noble made no effort to take them and Brook saw he was distracted by the surroundings. He realised that Noble had never been inside his flat before and his DS was as stunned as every other visitor by its decrepitude. It was a familiar reaction and one that, until recently, wouldn't have concerned him.

"This is just temporary, John. 'Til I can find a place to put down roots."

Noble was embarrassed now and tried to cover his error. "It's not bad to tide you over, it's only been…"

"Three years. Since the transfer. Come with me." He took Noble back into the kitchen and opened the fridge with a flourish worthy of Barnum. "Can I get you anything, John? I've got beer, cider, alcopops."

"No thanks."

"Something to eat then? Chicken, pate, dips, quiche, cocktail sausages?"

"No really, sir."

"What about tea? Or I've got coffee or orange juice?"

"Maybe an orange juice then," agreed Noble.

Brook cracked a carton from the brick, removed the attached straw and inserted it through the foil hole, before giving it to Noble with an air of quiet satisfaction.

Noble, unsure what to do took it from him and waited. But Brook would only stare at his guest, looking first at the carton then up at Noble until he shoved the straw in his mouth and proceeded to suck. "Mmmm. Delicious." Noble finished his drink and handed the carton to Brook. "Sir? What's wrong with Jason doing an appeal?"

Brook paused and thought for a while, the merits of long life orange juice forgotten. "It will cause embarrassment to the Force and whoever organises it, John. I want you to promise me you'll speak to McMaster and get her to block it."

"I don't understand."

"Promise."

"Tell me why."

Brook paused. "I think Jason was involved in the murder of Annie Sewell."

Noble raised an eyebrow. "Annie Sewell?"

"The old woman in the sheltered housing."

"You're joking?"

"There were traces of cocaine in Jason's system. There was cocaine in Annie Sewell's flat. She was forced to take some before she was killed."

"How do you know that?"

"I sneaked a look at her autopsy."

"That's Inspector Greatorix's case."

"So what? He wasn't interested in it. Has he made an arrest?"

"It could be anyone. A burglary gone wrong..."

"It was a contract killing."

"What? Who'd put out a contract on an old woman like that?"

"Good question."

"Are you saying Jason was paid to kill Annie Sewell then stole drugs and money from her?"

"He stole nothing. The tablets and cash were his payment."

"Someone hired him?"

"Not Jason directly. I suspect his participation was a mistake. He was supposed to be at home, remember. One of his lowlife friends probably asked him along for the ride."

"Why for Christ's sake? Who'd put a price on a harmless old girl's head?"

Brook paused aware of the effect his words would have. "The Reaper."

"The Reaper? What would The Reaper want with Annie Sewell? It doesn't make sense."

"It only makes sense if it *is* The Reaper. Think about it, John. Two sets of murders in one night. In Derby! The first, Annie Sewell, takes Bob Greatorix away because he's on duty. I'm on call so the Wallis case falls into my lap. Coincidence? I don't think so. But there's one screw up. Whoever The Reaper hires to kill Annie takes Jason along to help, when he should be at home eating drugged pizza and getting his throat cut. You see?"

"So killing Annie Sewell saved his life."

"Ironic isn't it?"

Noble was silent for a moment, casting his eyes around, trying to find an objection. "Why not just kill the Wallis family on a night you *are* on duty?"

"You've got me there, John. But I think her death serves some other purpose. I think *she* was punished for something – some skeleton in her cupboard. Like the others."

"What exactly?"

"No idea."

"I don't buy it. And even if I did, you're saying whoever had Annie Sewell killed, had a thorough knowledge of our duty roster."

"Mmmm," nodded Brook. "Interesting eh? But not too hard. What, with all the leaks we had last year on the Plummer rape, and Brian Burton spilling the beans on the Wallis deaths."

"Can you prove any of this?"

"I could do, given time."

"That's why you asked about forensics on Jason's clothes?"

"Right. If he was involved there might be fibres or hair samples on them."

"And if not?"

"There's the cocaine. Have it analysed. If both samples are the same purity it might be enough to have him in and lean on him. But he's a cool customer. He wouldn't crack. We'd need more."

"You think he's a killer yet you don't sound too bothered he's still out there."

"It's essential, John. We can't arrest him. Greatorix thinks he's in the clear…"

"I don't believe it…"

"It's not professional jealousy, John. You should know me better than that. He could have the collar if I was sure he put Jason away for a lot of years. But he wouldn't."

"What do you mean?"

"Suppose Jason's clothes are clean and you tell Greatorix about the cocaine. He hauls Jason in but he toughs it out. What do you think Bob would do, given there were multiple assailants?"

Noble thought for a second, running his tongue over his bottom lip. He eyed Brook with a quizzical look. "Offer him a deal?"

"Exactly. Possible reduced sentence, maybe even immunity, for putting his friends in the frame. Which stinks, you'll agree. No, Jason deserves what's coming to him. So he's best left for the moment, John. Wait for Forensics. He's under virtual house arrest as it is, afraid to go out, afraid to sleep with the light off. The Reaper's out there, remember, waiting to finish the job."

❋

When Noble had left, Brook gathered a few things for his own journey. Finally he descended the cellar steps to retrieve the folder from where he'd taken the necklace belonging to Laura Maples. He debated whether to put it back in but decided to keep it handy. Then he emptied out all the papers to get at the remaining artefact, small and slim and tightly wrapped in clear plastic. Without disturbing the plastic shroud, Brook placed it in his breast pocket and returned to the flat upstairs.

❋

Brook finished dialling Noble's mobile and returned his eyes to the white lines of the M1 flashing past him in the dark.

"*Hello.*" The voice sounded weary and under huge strain.

"Charlie. It's me."

"*Brooky!*" There was a pause. "*I haven't much time…*"

"I know. I'm coming tonight."

There was a noise of muffled emotion from the other end.

"*Bless you, Damen. You've always been…I didn't want to be alone.*"

There was silence for a moment then Brook said. "Leeds was a washout. Telfer's flat's been bulldozed."

No reply from Rowlands so Brook rang off. He didn't want to miss the call from Noble. Not that he needed it. It all fit together now.

Not for a court of law perhaps, but that was never the final destination in Brook's mind – or The Reaper's.

He thought of Terri for the first time since he'd seen her on the pier. Fathers and daughters. The things they do to each other. And yet the things they do *for* each other. He thought of Tamara Wrigley and what she'd done for *her* father.

What had Laura Maples done for hers? And Kylie Wallis. Fathers and daughters – a love that burned at both ends. Until girls became women. If they lived that long.

*

Half an hour later Noble's mobile rendered its tinny version of Volare. It was the owner. Brook listened. "When did Telfer move to Leeds, John?" He nodded. "And what about Petr Sorenson? Well keep trying. Anything else? I'm sorry to hear that, John. Did you tell McMaster I was against it? I see. As a friend, my advice is to be elsewhere. You don't want to be sat next to Jason when they're filming it. Find a way, John. It'll be played again and again if the shit hits the fan."

*

It was nearly two in the morning when Brook edged the car onto the drive of Rowlands' Caterham home and stepped up to the front door. It was a mild night for January with plenty of cloud cover. All was dark except for a dim glow somewhere in the back of the house. On a hunch Brook jabbed at the door with a finger and it creaked open an inch. He pushed again and the entrance yawned at him.

He looked around the front of the house again before crossing the threshold, closing the door behind him. He dropped the latch and adjusted his eyes to the gloom.

He could see light coming from the patio round the back. He moved towards it, not expecting to see Rowlands through the French windows on a winter's night, but there he was, loosely wrapped in his blanket on the sun lounger, head slumped to one side. In the pale gleam of the patio light, Brook could make out the dull sheen of a gun, an automatic, resting on his lap.

He stepped through and bent over the old man. He listened and watched the emaciated chest swell into a shallow pull for oxygen. He was alive.

Brook put two fingers onto the barrel of the gun and eased it away

269

from Rowlands' papyrus hand. The safety was on. He checked the clip. It was full. His old boss stirred and opened his eyes as Brook pocketed the gun.

He smiled in recognition – a smile of love. He held out his hand. "Laddie," he croaked. "Thanks for coming."

Brook smiled back. He slid his hands under Rowlands' meagre frame and hoisted him into the air like a child. With a speed which belied his condition, Rowlands darted a hand back to the lounger to clutch the half bottle of whisky to his chest.

"This doesn't mean we're married does it?" said Rowlands, as Brook crossed the threshold out of the cold. They both laughed. Brook placed his old boss onto the sofa and arranged a thin blanket around his legs. He sat down in the chair opposite. "What was the gun for?"

"In case the cold don't finish me. I'm off tonight, Brooky. To see my Lizzie." His eyes moistened.

"I need to know everything, guv."

"I know. He said you would. It's all written down. It's in the kitchen."

"How did you manage that in your condition?"

Rowlands smiled. "I did most of it years ago. Confession is good for the soul, they say. Well it's bullshit." He lifted the bottle to his mouth and took a long pull.

"And Derby?"

"It's all there. You'll be a hero again."

"I've never been a hero." He pulled up a chair and sat down with a sigh. "The things we do for love, Charlie."

"Ay. How long have you known?"

"A few hours. I went to Leeds. There's nothing to see. My Chief mentioned daughters and then I knew. It all clicked. It's a place I've been. With Terri. With Laura Maples. The Wrigley girl. The anger, the pain. I remembered your pain, Charlie. And then I knew what to look for. It didn't take long to find out Roddy Telfer lived in Edinburgh, for a couple of years, the same time as Lizzie. He was dealing, wasn't he, though he never got tugged for it? It didn't take a great leap to connect him with Lizzie. But it was still a leap. But that's part of my problem, Charlie. Everything I know about Telfer requires a leap. There are no solid facts. So tell me. How could you possibly have known Telfer supplied Lizzie's heroin?"

Rowlands shook his head. "I've written everything…"

"*Tell* me, Charlie."

Rowlands nodded after a long silence. "Ay. I suppose I owe you that much." He sat up now and beckoned for Brook to help with his cushions. "I need a cigarette. In the bureau." Brook fetched them and they both lit up. Rowlands nearly retched after the first mouthful and didn't inhale again but let the smoke curl up into his face.

"It was about a year after Brixton, you were still on sick leave after your...thing..."

"Breakdown."

"Right. Sorenson contacted me, said he had some interesting information, that we should meet and that I wasn't to mention it to you. Not that I had any intention, in your state..."

"And you went along with it?"

"Not at first. But then he mentioned Lizzie."

"Go on."

"So I met him. And he told me he knew who'd sold Lizzie the heroin that killed her."

"And you believed him?"

"Course not, lad. Give me some credit. But he had dates, he had times, he knew her friends, her movements and he had Telfer. He knew all about him, told me who he was, what he was like, where he was on the day of Lizzie's death..."

"All circumstantial."

"I know. But then he showed me this." Rowlands fished out a thin gold ring with an inlay of tiny sapphires and showed it to Brook. "It was hers. I got it for her eighteenth. Said she'd paid for her gear with it. Then he showed me a pawn ticket with Telfer's name and a description of the ring on it. And a price. £20. A score for my daughter's life. It cost me £400."

"But Charlie, how did *he* know all this? Where does he get knowledge of things he can't possibly have witnessed and aren't a matter of record?"

"I don't know, lad. But I didn't need to know. I was hooked."

"Then what?"

Rowlands flicked ash onto the floor and had another slug of whisky.

"Then it was just a question of when I'd kill Telfer. Sorenson offered to do it for me but he wasn't serious. He knew it had to be me. He knew I had to face Telfer – to look into his eyes. So we started planning it.

"I needed a gun, so I redirected a sawn-off from some blagger's car into mine. When the time came, I'd let myself in and wait for Telfer to come home. Then I was supposed to handcuff him to the chair. If not there was the radiator. I was supposed to do the girlfriend too. Sorenson gave me a bottle of chloroform and a scalpel but I was never going to fuck around with that. I think he knew I wouldn't do it his way.

"It was already winter so it had to be done soon. Dark nights, bad weather, you know the routine. I had no problem with that. The sooner the better. I wasn't sure about writing the blood on the wall but if Telfer was already dead...well, why not? I figured I owed Sorenson that much."

"Why did he need you to be The Reaper?"

"I honestly don't know. I think to get your attention again. He has a great respect for you. For your abilities." Brook snorted and Rowlands looked down at the floor.

"Did he give you music or a picture?"

"Music – a CD and a cassette. Beethoven's ninth. Telfer had to hear it as he died. I didn't ask why and he didn't offer to tell me. Listen Brooky. There's one thing you've got to understand."

Brook looked at the floor. Finally he returned his eyes to Rowlands. "The girl?"

"Right. You know...you know I'd never...I didn't mean to...do the girl. Sorenson insisted. For the MO. I agreed but I was never going to."

"So what happened? From the beginning."

He took another large pull on the whisky. "I went to Leeds. I stayed in a seedy hotel in Armley. Near the prison. A right shit-hole. Full of hollow-eyed wives and kids on the social, visiting husbands, brothers, fathers in the nick. Two weeks I waited..."

"Two weeks?"

"Yeah, I had two weeks leave in '93. Compassionate, remember. I was having a bad time over Lizzie."

"But you went to Leeds..."

"Damen. My marriage was over. Lizzie had choked on her own vomit. Making sense of her death was all I lived for."

"And what did you do for two weeks?"

"Waited. And watched. Watched that bastard go about his tawdry business, making a living out of other people's misery. But mostly I watched his girlfriend, to see when she'd be out of the flat so I could be alone with Roddy, so I could tell him why I'd come, watch him squirm, watch him beg me for his pathetic life as I begged God for Elizabeth's." He stopped to compose himself. Brook borrowed the whisky bottle from him and took a slug before placing it back in his bony talon.

"And then I was ready. Wednesday nights the girl had ante natal classes and Roddy always walked her to the bus stop. That was the kind of guy he was. He had his own van you know, but he let his eight-month pregnant girlfriend get the fucking bus in winter.

"So that was my chance to do him, without killing the girl. And the child." He paused. "I took my bag of fresh clothes and my sawn-off and I let myself in. Nobody saw me. Nobody took any interest in anything but their own business." Rowlands began to cough and took another draught of whisky to recover his breath. Brook tucked the blanket tightly around his legs for something to do. He knew the rest but resolved to hear the confession. It was better for Charlie to get it off his chest. There'd still be plenty left in there to kill him.

"When he came back I sat him down – it wasn't difficult, he was a snivelling coward. I showed him a picture of Elizabeth." Rowlands emitted a strangled laugh. "You'll never guess."

Brook's face broke into a sad smile. "He didn't know who she was."

"Not a fucking clue. Had me stumped for a while, I can tell you. But then I showed him the ring. The £20 ring. And I had him. He remembered the ring. He couldn't hide that.

"That's when he got scared. He realised. And I was right. He begged me. Begged me, Damen. Prayed to me like I was God. You should have seen his face. I've never seen anything like it, the look I saw in his eyes that night. That piece of shit begging me, crying for his worthless life. I couldn't believe it could be so precious to somebody like him." Rowlands shook his head in wonder. "So precious. After Lizzie died I could have sucked on my gun a dozen times a day and smiled doing it. I don't need to tell you. But Telfer. He wanted to live so much. It threw me.

"And I knew then I couldn't do it. And suddenly he knew it. So he started talking. Talking me down. Trying to get to know me. Make me believe him that he'd finished with all the drugs and the fencing and the nicking. Then he made a fatal mistake. He swore it to me on the life of his unborn child." Charlie looked at the floor and tried to get his breath back. He took another pull on the whisky.

"And then?" asked Brook after a short silence.

"Then I blew his head apart."

Brook nodded. "And wrote on the walls?"

"I don't remember doing it but I did."

"Then his girlfriend came back."

"Yes."

"And you strangled her."

"Yes."

"Why did she come back?"

"She was having…pains."

273

Brook ground out his cigarette in an ashtray took the bottle from Rowlands and poured a capful of whisky and drank it down. He looked at Rowlands. It wasn't a look of judgement. Rowlands stared back, waiting.

"Go on."

"Go on where, laddie?"

"What happened then?"

"I changed clothes and I left." There was silence. Brook sensed there was something more. He waited for Rowlands to continue. When he did there were tears in his eyes. "There are some things you should never see, Brooky. I see that little face as much as Lizzie's now…"

"Whose face?"

Rowlands head fell to the side, his eyes shut. Brook half stood and listened for the rasp of shallow breathing. He sat down again when he heard it. There was time yet.

Brook took another swig of whisky. He grimaced at its harshness and spun the cap back on the bottle. He went to the kitchen to make coffee.

When he sat back down, Rowlands was conscious again. He'd lit another cigarette. His eyes, bleary from booze and smoke, were trained on the floor.

For an hour they sat like that, saying nothing, Rowlands taking the occasional chug from his bottle. From time to time he would close his eyes and doze fitfully, his head lolling from side to side like a puppet, devoid of the strength to control its movement.

Brook didn't know what to do next so he resolved just to be there. If Charlie Rowlands was to die tonight, he would be there for him, as a friend, to bring comfort, to help him on his final journey to his Lizzie. He couldn't pressure him, couldn't judge him.

And Brook knew whatever Rowlands told him tonight was not for public consumption. No matter his promise to McMaster to bring her The Reaper, if it meant besmirching his old boss, he couldn't bring himself to do it. Yes he'd killed two people, three if you counted the unborn child, but it was a long time ago. Roddy Telfer and his common law wife hadn't been missed. The child was the real tragedy. The same as the Wrigley girl. And Kylie Wallis. And maybe, given what happened to them, Charlie Rowlands had saved the child from a life of misery and abuse. Saved the child. Saved.

Brook realised he was cold and went into the kitchen. He paced up and down to get warm before picking up the sheaf of papers from the kitchen table.

The first few pages were hand written and faded. Brook leafed through until he came to a newer section that had been word-processed. At the back was a wad of clippings from the Derby Evening Telegraph. His eye was taken by the headline, "Derby Schoolboy Accused of Attacking Teacher." Most of the clippings were about Jason's brush with infamy though he wasn't named for obvious reasons. There was no mention of Annie Sewell.

Brook lit another cigarette and turned back to the printed pages. He sat down and began to read.

To Damen, my friend

I hadn't seen or spoken to Victor Sorenson since 1993, until that day last year when he walked up to my bed in the cancer ward. I don't know how he knew I was there, said he'd come for tests himself and had seen me sitting outside Radiology. I'm not sure I believe him. Nobody, you included Brooky, had a sniff of my illness.

I should have known he wanted something. The next day he walks in with a bottle of my favourite rum and starts talking about the old days. Like we were old friends who'd worked together for years or something, not murderers who've killed kiddies before their lives had even begun. I'm assuming a lot to say he's a killer. He never admitted he was The Reaper to either of us, but what he don't know about his MO, isn't worth knowing.

Anyway he says he's got another proposition for me and tells me about this old girl he's met, Annie Sewell, and what she's done. Ask him what she did, he'll tell you. I don't know how he knows but he does. He's got the hospital records and you can see how she did it, and how it was missed. It's all circumstantial but we both know him too well to doubt it. And I guess he's right. She deserves to die alright. But I reckon she deserves to live more. Live with what she's done. Suffer like I've suffered since Leeds. And since Lizzie.

And he's telling me all this, like I'm interested, and saying I don't have to do anything other than point her out to some scumbag who's going to take care of her. And I'm looking at him, wondering who the fuck does he think he is, telling me all this shit. Like I'm going to help him kill the old bird.

So I tell him. I don't care one way or the other about this Annie Sewell. As far as I'm concerned, topping her is letting her off easy and he can do what he likes but there's no way,

275

nothing he can say or do to make me help him.

And he looks at me with those fucking black eyes and he thinks what he's going to say next. And I'm waiting for the threats, the blackmail, how he's going to turn me in over Roddy Telfer if I don't play ball. But he says nothing. He seems to know I'm too far gone to care about my reputation. Just sits there smiling. Then he nods and says it's okay and that he knew it would be too much to ask, even if it helps you, Brooky.

So I asked him what this had to do with you and he starts on about The Reaper, like it's another person. About Brixton, how Wrigley and his family died for you, because Floyd Wrigley killed that girl you found. Laura something. And he says that's why you packed in looking for The Reaper, because you knew Wrigley deserved to die.

Well I don't buy any of that shit either but on he goes. And now he's talking about Amy and Terri and how you've lost them and lost yourself. He says this is The Reaper's final job and he has to do it in Derby, for your sake, because you need to get back on the old case and catch The Reaper so you can put it to rest and find some peace for yourself. That's his only reason for doing it again. For you to heal yourself. He says we both owe it to you. We're responsible.

I don't know, Brooky. Even when I was telling him it was bullshit, I was thinking about it and persuading myself it was a good idea. Maybe this old bird feels like I do after Leeds. Maybe I'll be doing her a favour. And I reckon I was right. But that's not why I agreed to it. It was knowing you the way I do. Knowing you back then, how it got to you.

And the family The Reaper's going to take out won't be missed. Sorenson gave me some clippings about what the son's been up to and the dad's got form. I don't know who else there is but I can't lie and say I care. I've seen enough of these people to know how they turn out. I only care about Lizzie and you now.

And myself? I have to come clean. It was selfish but I knew if The Reaper came back I'd see you again. I don't have long and you're the best friend I've got left Brooky. The best friend I've ever had. Honest. Anyway I don't need to tell you my decision. And I don't need to tell you Sorenson didn't even pretend to be surprised when I changed my mind. He's too fucking clever by half.

Now I'm not sure how much you've already worked out about what happened in Derby but here it is.

Two days before the killings, he picks me up at my house. He's driving. I don't know if the car's his or hired but I think it's hired. It's clean. He drives us to Derby. It takes ages. He drives like a funeral director, which I suppose he is in a way. Fifty-five all the way up the M1.

I'm staying at The International Hotel in Derby, he tells me. On the way he gives me a wig and some specs to wear. Just to make things a bit more challenging for you. I'm to wear them at all times and I can't take my gloves off, I have to find an excuse for that and the fact that I can't sign my name.

I worked out that Sorenson wants you to think I'm him if that makes sense. I asked him how my dressing up like a freak is going to grab your attention and he says I'm to register at the hotel as Sammy Elphick from Harlesden. Well I knew that would do the trick. Like either of us could forget that night.

When we arrived in Derby, he dropped me at the hotel. He's not staying there but in some B & B up in the Peaks I think – miles away so you don't trace him. He says to meet him at a pub the night after. The Blue Peter it was called. So I meet him there, only this time he's driving a white van. Hired locally I think.

He gives me a holdall. Inside there's a brand new mobile. There are two phone numbers on speed dial – one's a mobile number, the other's local. There's a plastic bag with fifty ecstasy tablets in, a small bag of coke and two grand in cash. There's also a gun, one of those instant cameras that cough out a picture straight away and a street map with Annie Sewell's sheltered accommodation marked in red. Her flat number's on it – 20a.

I'm to meet some thug called Banger in the pub in half an hour. Give him the map, the coke and £100. Show him the rest of the cash and the tabs, which are his, if he kills Annie Sewell the next night between 7pm and 8pm. No earlier. No later. I've got to make sure he sees the gun in case he gets any ideas, and give him the camera so he can take a picture of Annie Sewell's body to prove he's earned the rest of the cash and drugs.

I'm to watch the guy go in, then ring Sorenson after seven on the mobile number he's given me, to tell him it's under way.

277

When it's over, I meet Banger back at The Blue Peter, check the photograph and hand over the plastic bag. I get a minicab back to the hotel and phone the other number. It's for the warden at the sheltered accommodation. I report a disturbance anonymously to make sure she's found at the right time.

The next day, I checked out and got a cab to a place called Long Eaton a few miles away and pick up the train back to London. My idea – so you won't get me on camera at Derby Station. I take the mobile phone apart and throw the pieces out of the train.

Sorenson says if the timings are right you'll pick up The Reaper case. Not some bumpkin who doesn't know his arse from his elbow.

And that's more or less what happened, except Banger did the job with a couple of friends and one turned out to be young Jason Wallis. When they walked into the pub after the job, they looked really young and they were high as kites. I'm not sure it was just the drugs either.

Of course, none of that would be possible without knowing your duty roster. Fortunately – that's the wrong word – nothing's been left to chance. I think Sorenson has a contact that has a contact in Derby nick.

Brook smiled. "Brian Burton."

Sorenson knows who'll be on duty and get the Sewell case and he knows you're on call if anything else happens. I don't know who it is but my money would be on that Burton journo from the press conference. Remember how well informed he was – slimy little pencil neck. I wouldn't think he knows who's pulling his strings but when has that ever bothered those vultures?

That's about it really except for this kid Banger. I had no idea he was a mate of Jason Wallis and he'd rope him and another kid into the murder and I'm not sure Sorenson knew either. And who says crime doesn't pay? The little punk murders a stranger and it saves him from a date with The Reaper. Funny thing. Sorenson didn't seem put out by that. In fact, he seemed pleased even though this Jason character deserves to have his throat cut worse than most. I even wondered if somehow that was all part of the plan but I don't see how. What the fuck. I've wasted enough time thinking

about it. You figure it out.
I can only think of Lizzie now. I'm dying to see her. A
favour though, Brooky. See me under the ground next to her.
And tell my ex to go fuck herself. I love you for everything
you've done for me, no matter what the cost to yourself. Time
for a drink. Cheers. Charlie. 29th December.

Brook folded the papers and slipped them inside his coat. Now
there was nothing to do but wait. He knew everything Charlie knew.
Almost everything.

Brook sat opposite his old boss. The old man's chest still moved.
His breath still whistled faintly through his teeth but the noise was
diminishing. There wasn't long.

Brook sat forward and cupped Rowlands emaciated hands in his.
For a split second he fancied he could see something. Something
terrible – blood everywhere, covering everything...and deep in the
blood a tiny face, eyes closed. He removed his hand then rubbed his
eyes and shook his head. He stood up to walk around. "I'm going
mad," he muttered. "Again."

There was a grating sigh. Rowlands' chest stopped moving. Brook
checked his pulse. There wasn't one. He held a withered hand in his.
Charlie was gone.

Brook sat back and closed his eyes. He took a few moments to
remember his friend. Then he reached into his own pocket and pulled
out the silver necklace he had carried with him for so long. Laura's
necklace. He removed the sapphire ring from Rowlands' waistcoat
pocket and slid it onto the necklace before refastening the clasp and
putting it back in his own pocket. "Safe-keeping Charlie. I'll give it
back when it's time. Goodbye old friend. Give my love to Lizzie."
Brook made to leave but turned back at the door. "And Laura."

Chapter 28

It was the early hours before Brook pulled onto the forecourt of The Hilton and stepped from the car. He handed the keys to the doorman and carried his small overnight bag to reception and registered. If the girl swiping his credit card recognised him from his last visit she didn't show it. He ordered a 9.30 breakfast and headed for the lift.

Inside his room he flopped fully clothed onto the bed and slept soundly for a couple of hours, his mind untroubled and his dreams at bay.

*

Later he sat on the bed, wet towel round his waist, downing the last of his coffee. He turned the TV to mute and picked up Noble's mobile and dialled.

"Can you speak, John?"

"*Yes.*"

"Anything on Petr Sorenson yet?"

"*No form at all but he's local. A student. He lives in halls at Nottingham University.*"

"Really." Brook was thoughtful. Vicky's brother was not more than fifteen miles from Derby. He had a more than reasonable excuse to meet his sister's train. On the other hand if Sorenson's nephew had taken up the mantle from his uncle, what better place to revive The Reaper murders than Brook's new home?

"*Sir…*"

"What's he studying?"

"*Er…Chemistry? Inspector…*"

"Interesting but not surprising. That's how the family made their money."

"Inspector Brook, listen. We've found something. I put a rush on Jason's clothes."

"I knew it. Get a team to Annie Sewell's…"

"It's not fibres. They're still working on that. It's not what we expected. It's blood."

"Blood? Whose?"

"His father's…"

"What? That means…"

"No it doesn't. Let me finish. We found minute traces in a series of small cuts on his jacket."

"Did you say cuts?"

"Yes. Cuts. Very thin. With what looks like the murder weapon. Someone cut the letter R into the material – R for REAPER. That's how the blood got there. It was very small and under his arm so it wasn't spotted at the scene."

"Jesus." Brook's mind was flooded with images and scenarios. Noble kept silent at the other end of the line to let the implications sink in. "The Reaper was still there when Jason got home, John. That's why Jason didn't hear music."

"Right. The neighbour, Mr Singh, said it was turned down for a few minutes. The Reaper turned it down after he killed Bobby. He saw Jason coming and waited for him in the living room. When he didn't show he guessed what had happened and went to find him spark out in the kitchen."

"So he cuts his signature on Jason, turns the music back up and then leaves. God." Brook shook his head in dismay, not bringing himself to say what needed to be said. But Noble said it for him.

"But why didn't he kill him? He had him."

"I'm not sure John. The only thing I can think of is that Jason was in no condition to know he was about to die. And that's key for the man we're dealing with. That's what gets him off. It's the knowing…"

"With respect sir, that's fucking bullshit. If Jason's the reason he's chosen this family he should do him right there. I mean, he's never going to have him in his sights again. He's left him for a reason, something we don't know yet."

"Maybe he knows Jason's a killer, John. Maybe he's leaving him to us."

"What? So we can send him to prison – maybe. You don't believe that for a second."

Brook sighed. "All right, all right. It's a mystery. We'll figure it out. Anything else? What? Is he?" He looked up at the TV. Jason Wallis filled his screen. "I'm watching it now, John." Brook stayed on

281

the line but turned the sound on the TV back on.

"I just wanna say if anyone knows anything to come forward. Speak to the police. Whoever did this to my family is sick. Dangerous." Pause for slumping of head and wiping of tear. Jason's aunt tightened her grip on his arm to give him the strength to get through. *"Me mum and dad and me sister…"*

But Jason couldn't go on and the camera moved onto McMaster and Greatorix seated next to one another.

McMaster, as usual, was immaculate and the same could almost be said for Bob Greatorix, now basking in the limelight he so craved, a hint of a smirk submerged beneath his mask of fake sympathy.

Brook grimaced at the sight of McMaster. After all her support he should have warned her about young Wallis personally. Now she was between a rock and a hard place. With Charlie's confession, Brook had the evidence to charge Jason with at least conspiracy to commit murder. Sorenson too. But now, after this debacle, even bringing her The Reaper wouldn't wipe the tape of her sitting next to a teenage killer, comforting him in the regulation manner. The press would tear her to pieces.

He turned off the phone, forgetting Noble was still on the other end, turned off the TV and finished dressing. Then he packed his bag and prepared to leave.

There was a knock at the door. "Who is it?"

A pause. "Daddy's Special Girl."

Brook put his bag and coat on the bed and walked to the door. "Vicky?"

"Yes. Let me in."

Brook raised a hand to the door but hesitated. "How did you know I was here?"

"Can we talk inside?" Still Brook waited. "Please!"

Finally, curiosity got the better of him and he turned the handle. Before he could pull the door open it crashed against his right shoulder and he was sent spinning onto the bed, knocking his bag and coat to the floor. He tried to right himself, but a wiry figure was on him, forcing a cloth into his mouth. Brook could taste a pungent chemical aroma and had already taken an involuntary gulp before swinging back onto the mattress and bringing his knee up into his assailant's crotch.

Brook felt the gust of breath through the man's teeth as he doubled up. His grip eased so Brook was able to flex his left foot into the man's chest and heave him off the bed. He fell heavily into the doorframe of the bathroom.

Vicky shrank back, unsure what to do, but a second later she flung herself onto Brook's legs and clung on tight while the man staggered back to the bed with the cloth.

Brook was already feeling the effects of one lungful of the chemical and tried to wriggle free from Vicky's grip. But the man fell on Brook's chest and forced the cloth back over his face. Brook grabbed his right arm to hold him off but he was young and strong.

As the man edged his arm closer to his face, Brook's head was forced off the bed towards the floor. The more the man pushed, the further off the bed Brook slipped until the back of his head was touching the floor. Now there was no retreat from the fumes as the man pressed his weight against Brook's defensive arm.

Finally, Brook felt the cloth against his mouth and held his breath. His eyes darted at the bag by his head. His coat, which had lain on his bag, was on the floor next to it.

With his free hand, Brook dragged the coat to him and slid his fingers into the pocket. After a few seconds scrabbling to get the correct hold, Brook pulled out Charlie's gun and thrust the nozzle against his attacker's forehead.

"Get off!" he grunted through the cloth. "Now!" Brook fixed his eyes onto the man trying to look calm. He didn't feel calm. His heart was pounding against his ribs and his head spun from the chemical.

"He won't shoot, Pete. I know him," urged Vicky, still clamping Brook's legs.

Brook screwed his eyes in what he hoped would appear a display of quiet determination. "Now!" he gasped.

Brook felt the man's arms relax and the cloth retreat from his face as he stood back from the bed. Brook leapt up to open the window and gulp in fresh air all the while keeping the gun trained on his assailant.

Petr Sorenson was a young man of medium height, a little taller than Vicky, and with the same slant to his eyes, the same blonde hair. His face was flushed and he panted heavily, all the while looking at Brook with that sullen hatred Brook had seen in Jason.

"Shouldn't you be studying?" Brook managed to say through urgent draws of oxygen.

"Fack you!" Brook expected the abuse but not the broad cockney accent. But with a wealthy background to live down in the college bar, perhaps it shouldn't have been a surprise.

"Face the wall. You too Vicky."

She looked at him, eyes pleading. "This wasn't my idea."

"Turn round."

"Please," she began to sob. "Please you have to tell us. Uncle Vic won't say, even though he's dying."

"Tell you what?"

"About The Reaper," she implored.

"I don't know what you mean." Brook threw the cloth at Vicky. "Put it over your brother's mouth and nose."

"What? No. I won't do it."

"Do it Vicky." Petr half-turned to his sister, nodding. His face was grim now. The flash of hatred was gone. Understanding and acceptance had replaced it. "Don't blame her mate. You don't know what he did to her."

"Why do you want me to hurt him?" she sobbed at Brook.

"I'm going to see your uncle now. He's expecting me. Put your brother under. Now."

"I don't understand." She was barely able to speak.

"He's right Vicky. Do it," said Petr again.

"I can't have any distractions, Vicky. Your uncle and I have been planning this day for a very long time. When he's...when we're finished I'll answer all your questions."

"I won't do it."

"It's better than a crack on the head or a bullet in the leg, sis. Do as he says." Expecting no argument, Petr dropped to his knees.

"He wouldn't do that. I know him."

"You don't know me at all Vicky. I'm a man. Capable of anything. Like your uncle – like your father."

Vicky eyes widened. Brook saw fear there. She picked up the cloth and pressed it over her kneeling brother's face. "I'm sorry Pete," she muttered. Brook watched Petr inflating and deflating his chest. It took longer than expected but eventually his eyes rolled skywards and he fell on his side.

Brook prodded a finger into his ribs. He stood to face Vicky and nodded at the bed.

She kicked off her shoes, moved to the bed and lay down like a corpse. Legs together, toes pointed away from her, arms folded, eyes staring at the ceiling.

Brook knelt beside her then a thought crossed his mind. "Is your mother home?"

"I don't know. I've not been home for a while. We were waiting for you outside Charlie's house. We followed you from there."

"How did you know I'd be...? Uncle Vic told you," he realised before he'd even finished the question.

"Is Mr Rowlands dead?" asked Vicky.

"Yes."

"I'm sorry."

"Don't be. He's not."

Brook raised the cloth. Vicky held his arm.

"Won't you tell me? I've got to know."

"Tell you what?"

She gulped now and her eyes widened. "My father. Is he still alive? Is he The Reaper?"

Chapter 29

Brook sat quietly in his chair and watched Sorenson sleep. He was content to wait. He'd waited a lot of years; a few more moments wouldn't hurt.

The house was empty. Sonja was nowhere to be seen. The nurse had let Brook in then left at once, according to her instructions. Everything was ready.

As Brook waited for his host to wake he took out Laura's necklace, slid Lizzie's ring from the chain and put it in his pocket. He held the chain up to the light and examined it draped around his fingers.

He imagined he was there, in that hellish place where Laura died. Everything was dark but his senses were keen. He fancied he could almost smell the stench of decay in his nostrils. Human waste, old food, damp walls. Something else. Sweat, bad breath.

There was an empty can on its side, a small stove on the floor. And then he heard the tears, the muffled squeals of pain. He could see Wrigley's face, teeth grinding, grimacing, moving towards the girl. Then away. Then back. And still the smell. The beer breath. The sweat. Another thing. Sickly sweet. The fear. Laura's fear.

Wrigley smiles. It's not a smile of pleasure, of happiness. It's a smile of triumph. Conquest. The fight has gone. He can do as he pleases. He tears at the girl's neck and the pain is fierce but quick. The necklace is taken. A keepsake dangled to taunt, to remind him of his greatest day. He's already invaded the present. Now he seizes the past, receding glimpses of childhood tarnished. He puts it round his own neck. Yeah. Now he's somebody. Now he exists. Laura knows. Brook knows. They won't forget Floyd Wrigley in a hurry.

But the moment fades and his power is gone. Wrigley takes a neck at a bottle. He's hungry. He wants back what he had. That power. To be a God and squash this ant. To take the future and complete the set.

There is a way.

Brook let the necklace drop to his lap. Poor Laura. Poor Vicky. He thought of her lying unconscious in his hotel room. As Brook had sat beside her on the bed, Vicky had revealed every appalling detail of her torment.

Sorenson groaned and Brook glanced across at the sleeping old man. Even unconscious the pain came, though you wouldn't have guessed from his countenance. Despite his years, despite the cancer, despite his every terrible deed, his expression was that of a dozing new born.

Brook got up from his chair and tiptoed to the desk. After a moment rummaging in the shelves, he emerged with a disc and dropped it on to the turntable in the corner.

As he returned to his chair the first strains of the lament from La Wally rent the air. Brook waited for Sorenson to wake, pleased with his little conceit.

Sorenson filled his chest and sighed though he kept his eyes closed. "Is that you, inspector?"

"Yes."

Sorenson's lids lifted and his black eyes blinked up at Brook then creased into a smile of warmth and welcome. "I'm glad you came."

"I'm here for your confession."

Sorenson grinned. "Why, what are you going to do with it?"

Brook was startled by the simplicity of the question, realising he didn't know the answer.

Sorenson smiled an apology for putting his guest on the back foot. "Thank you for coming. I'm tired."

"Charlie's dead."

Sorenson looked down at the floor in genuine sadness. "He was a good man."

"Tell me about the Dentist Game." Brook saw Sorenson flinch. He recalled, years before, bringing up the subject of his brother Stefan's death and seeing a similar reaction. Sorenson's eyes closed for a moment and when they opened there was the ghost of a tear.

"Ever since Vicky crossed my path, I've assumed you sent her to check on my progress. I was wrong. You didn't know she came to Derby. And she has no idea what you are or what you've done. That's why, when she stole a look at my Reaper file, she was stunned to see a picture of you there. *Uncle Vic.*"

"She would be." Sorenson paused. This hesitancy was new. It pleased Brook. He'd finally got to Sorenson and would soon know it all. But a small corner of his mind told him to beware. He was in the presence of a heartless killer and manipulator.

Brook continued to wait but his normally garrulous host didn't seem to know how to continue. Vicky was the key to Sorenson. She was the person he cared about most. Brook knew every sickening detail. Getting Sorenson to talk about it would be difficult. But when he did, if he did, the dam would burst.

"Tell me about the Dentist Game."

"You've seen what Stefan did to Vicky?"

"She told me."

Sorenson nodded. "But you've seen other things, haven't you? You've had episodes before."

"Episodes?"

"Visions, a sixth sense which allows you to picture things that have happened, that are going to happen."

"We all have empathy. We can all imagine another's plight."

"As you imagined young Laura's."

"I'm a policeman. It's my job. When I put a sequence of events together it's almost like writing a script or shooting a film."

"And the future?"

"Everyone gets a sense of something about to happen from time to time. Is that why you came to Derby for me? Because you think I have a talent."

Sorenson smiled. "No. If put to good use it will be a useful tool, no more."

"Good use?"

"Something to guide your future work."

Brook laughed. "You mean arrest people because I've had a vision of them committing a crime. Is that how you choose? You're crazier than I thought."

"The Reaper's victims choose themselves."

"But you're prepared to execute a family on the strength of a feeling or a vision you think you've had. You're a madman."

"Your contempt would be deserved if so. Those feelings, as you call them, merely point the way. The Reaper has great resources of time and money. Only when he's sure does he take his prey."

"So you *see* your victims before you kill them? Some kind of sixth sense. Do you touch them? Is that how it works?" asked Brook, remembering the handshake on his last visit.

Sorenson was silent. "You continue to personalise these acts, Damen. Is it deliberate? I can only help you understand The Reaper's work if you see it in its proper context."

"Which is what?"

"The Reaper is an entity, Damen, not a person. He's an idea that cannot die. He is not motivated by ego. He doesn't act for personal gain and takes no pleasure from his work."

"Semantic nonsense…" Brook took a breath. He had his own agenda and realised he was being drawn from it. After a moment he nodded at Sorenson to signal acceptance of the rules. "So The Reaper meets his victims and discovers the crimes they've committed." Sorenson nodded. "And these meetings are social?" Sorenson nodded again. "And accidental?"

Now he smiled. "Usually."

Brook nodded. "Unless The Reaper needs a…project in a specific city like Derby. Then you, sorry, The Reaper has to find somebody suitable."

"Exactly." Sorenson nodded, suddenly animated. "But it depends who The Reaper is helping. Roddy Telfer was difficult to find because he'd moved away from Edinburgh by the time…"

"By the time The Reaper wanted to help Charlie Rowlands." Sorenson smiled at Brook, taking no offence at his tone. "What about Floyd Wrigley? How could The Reaper prove he killed Laura Maples, even with all *his* time and money? There was no evidence to connect him once the rats had done their work."

"On the contrary, there was the best evidence of all. A witness."

"Second sight isn't evidence, professor." Sorenson said nothing but his eyes continued to bore into his opponent. Brook's eyes narrowed. "You mean a proper witness – someone actually saw him? You?"

"On the night of her death. I was in a cab, coming from Heathrow. I'd been in Stockholm for a few days. The cab stopped at lights, I looked out of the window and there they were, walking along Goldhawk Road together. It was very late. Three in the morning. But they held me, interested me. They were an odd couple. Ill matched. I knew something was wrong. She was nervous but he gave off an aura of tremendous self assurance. But I could sense it was a sham. His inadequacy filled him with a rage I could almost touch. They turned into Ravenscourt Gardens and were gone."

"What happened then?"

"I went home to bed."

"You did nothing?"

"What was I going to do? I didn't know he was going to kill her. It was only later. You said it yourself many years ago, on one of your first visits here. You can only act retrospectively. Your "after sales service" you called it," Sorenson chuckled.

"But afterwards you tracked him down."

"Not at first. It was of no interest until you told me how her death haunted you. And then…"

"Then The Reaper wanted to help me."

Sorenson beamed. He seemed pleased with himself suddenly. "Yes. Help you. Show you what was possible. It was the perfect opportunity."

"Why won't you tell me about the Dentist Game?"

"Vicky darling. Where are you? Where's Daddy's Special Girl?"

Sorenson looked away. "My brother's dead."

"Yes. The year before Sammy Elphick and his family were butchered. Cancer wasn't it?" Brook's face was hard. He'd trained for this moment, rehearsed every sentence and polished every nuance until the script gleamed like Greatorix's forehead.

"Vicky, where are you? Where are you hiding? It's daddy. I've got something for you."

Sorenson held his gaze for a long time. Brook didn't look away. The old man nodded at him, forcing his cracked features into a pained smile – Charlie's smile – communicating warmth and impending death.

"There you are, Vicky. What are you doing under there?"

"You're everything I could have wished for, Damen. Everything."

"It's okay daddy. My teeth are nice. See."

"You can't protect him any more, professor."

"I'm protecting her."

"But I know what he did."

"Then it needs no further discussion."

"Open wide. That's good. Oh dear. I think you need some of daddy's special toothpaste. Keep still. You'll wake your mother."

"My teeth are okay, daddy. They're new ones. Please daddy! I don't like it."

"It won't take long. Open wider. Only the best for Daddy's Special Girl."

Sorenson's faraway look as he stared into space reminded him of

Charlie at the end. Charlie on the way to his Lizzie. The pair did have a lot in common. Brook too. They had Vicky, Lizzie, Laura. And now Terri. Fathers and daughters and the unspoken sexual bond that tugged at both. Daddy's umbilical. Even death couldn't sever such a tie. Especially death. Death strengthened it, magnified it. Only life could break the bond – when a blossoming young woman tired of vicarious sex with her father in the beds of men who weren't him, yet were so like him. If she only wanted to sully herself, surely daddy had earned first refusal. A reward for everything he'd done for her. And all the things he didn't do because he was civilised.

"Only the best. That's it. That's it Vicky. It'll come. Good girl. Good girl, good girl, good girl, good girl...
Now swallow and rinse Vicky, swallow and rinse."

"How long had it been going on?"

"I don't know," answered Sorenson. "He died before..."

The music stopped which broke their concentration. There was silence for a while as each considered their next utterance. Especially Brook. This wasn't working out as planned. The spectre of death should have been a spur to confession but instead Sorenson had never been so reluctant to talk. The subject matter was delicate and perhaps too close to home. He decided to change tack.

"So, in a way, Sammy Elphick deserved a medal..."

"A medal?" Now Sorenson became animated. He pushed back his blanket and hauled himself to his feet. For a second Brook wondered if he was about to be attacked and fingered the gun in his pocket. Instead Sorenson moved over to the cabinet – Brook was surprised how steady he was – and pulled out a pair of leaded tumblers. He didn't ask Brook if he wanted a drink but came back with two generous measures all the same. Brook took his glass. "A medal for what? Bringing that brat into the world."

"Come on, professor. Sammy Elphick was a petty criminal, and maybe his kid wouldn't have amounted to much but neither deserved what you did to them..."

"Didn't they?" Sorenson smiled at Brook's anger. Control had changed hands with frightening rapidity and Brook was annoyed for letting it slip.

"No they didn't. I knew Sammy. He was small time. He wasn't violent. Killing your brother was accidental, I'm sure. He was backed into a corner and probably struck out..." Sorenson's smile widened. Brook was on the verge of pulling out the gun just to wipe the expression off his face and had to control himself with a few deep breaths and a large slug of whisky.

When he spoke again his voice was deliberate, restrained. He'd waited too long to spoil it now. "What Sammy did to your brother, saved Vicky. No matter how much you loved Stefan you must see that."

Now Sorenson laughed but it wasn't an articulation of pleasure. "Loved? Stefan?" Suddenly his gaze was far away. He spoke almost to himself and Brook had to strain to hear. "I hated him. From the moment he was born I hated him. Stefan was a monster. And you're right. He deserved to die."

Brook held the drink from his lips, his face impassive but his mind in turmoil. All his carefully constructed assumptions lay in tatters before him. Then he knew. "*You* killed him."

"Of course."

"And Vicky?"

"After what he did to her, she hated him then. She hates him still. Everyone hated him."

"And Sonja?"

"Especially Sonja."

"She knew about Vicky."

"Of course she knew, Damen. How can a mother not know these things?" He shot Brook a penetrating glance and he looked away, remembering Amy and Terri. "That's why Stefan put her in an institution."

Sorenson took a drink and considered how to begin. "When we were born, Steffi and I, in Stockholm, our paths were mapped out as soon we left our mother's womb. Steffi was first. The elder. The heir. Thirteen minutes. I took that as an omen. And so it proved for our mother. At the end of the thirteen minutes, she died. I left her body at the same time as her final breath.

"*If you hadn't been there,*" Steffi told me when we were old enough to understand these things, "*our mother wouldn't have died. You killed her.*" Sorenson shook his head. "What sort of mind can conjure up that much cruelty? Steffi must have thought I was a complete fool. I knew I hadn't killed her. He had."

"What are you talking about? You were babies."

"Identical twins, Damen. There's a difference. You see even in the womb I could feel him, his presence, his evil, attacking me, suppressing me. I was supposed to be first, you see."

"What?"

"I was supposed to be born first." He smiled and looked at Brook.

"I know what you're thinking and I know how it sounds. You can't understand." Sorenson's expression darkened. "Before we were born I could feel him. At first, just the occasional kick or fist, nothing important, but gradually, as we grew, I could feel him manoeuvring himself, pushing me behind him, thrusting himself to the fore. Even then he had to be first. He wouldn't accept second place even if it meant doing down his own brother. And so he was first and mother died of *complications.*

"First in all things. Bigger than me, stronger, faster, healthier. I was the sickly one, prone to colds and headaches, minor things. I was smaller, thinner, not as confident, and Steffi lost no opportunity to keep me that way. Generally I was less than him and our father, who was a good man, strict but loving, he tried his best to hide his preference for Steffi, but being such a weakling, I was cursed with great sensitivity and not just in my health. I knew. I could read it in everything father did, everything he said.

"It didn't matter too much when we were young. Boys will be boys. They can be very cruel, worse than girls sometimes. But they grow out of it. Steffi didn't. And, as we grew up together, things became worse. This knowledge lay between us, what had happened to our mother. I knew what he'd done to hurt her and he knew I knew and never stopped punishing me for it. I hated him for that. But that would have been all right if he hadn't made father hate me with his tricks and insinuations and lies. Father always took his side. He couldn't see what Steffi was."

Sorenson took a sip of whisky. "When our 21st birthday arrived our lives changed forever. Until that point, I was able to keep a rough parity with my brother. We both went to university to study Chemical Science. My father wanted us to take an interest in the business. And so, to please him, I got a first class degree. But Steffi? Steffi could only scrape a pass, and even then I'd had to give him my notes. It was more important for Steffi to get drunk and sleep with as many women as he could, which was a lot. He could be very charming when he wanted something from you.

"After university we were supposed to work at the plant and learn the ropes from the bottom up, like dad had done. But I'd performed so well that dad wanted me to go as far as my brains would take me. And I was happy to oblige, to shut myself away in academe. By this time I was having trouble coping with life. I was different. I'd discovered that I was more than sensitive. I was seeing things, visions, when I came into physical contact with people. Terrible things. Never anything beautiful. So I was happy to hide with my books while my brother went to work in the business.

293

"And to be fair to him, he did well. He became a good manager, a good entrepreneur. Like father. And when I finally went to work, we had the ideal partnership. I could supply all the expertise for the new processes for product development and Steffi could wheel and deal – under father's watchful eye of course. But it wasn't enough. He didn't have control over his own destiny. That's when he killed father."

Brook took a sip of his whisky, and rolled the burning liquid around his mouth. What he was learning was interesting and told him a lot about the psychology of his opponent but took him no nearer The Reaper.

"You don't seem surprised, Damen?"

"This kind of rivalry is well known, particularly in twins. It produces all sorts of imaginary hatreds and jealousies. Each believing the other is their enemy, each trying to promote themselves at the expense of the other…"

"I see."

"I mean he didn't really kill your father, did he?"

"Oh yes."

"You have evidence?"

"No."

"But you saw it – *in a vision.*"

"No. Steffi knew. After they found father with his neck broken at the foot of his office stairs, he never came near me. Never let me touch him. He was my twin. He could sense my abilities."

"I see."

"Do *you* have proof that I'm The Reaper?"

The directness of the question threw Brook for a second. "I did have. I destroyed it." Brook shifted a little in his chair and took another drink. "I searched your house that night, while you were asleep. The serial number on a CD system stored in your house matched the number on the system in Wrigley's flat. I removed the delivery note."

"But you destroyed it?"

Brook shrugged. "An illegal search. It was inadmissible."

Sorenson's knowing grin was close to an outright laugh. "Inadmissible. Of course." Now he did laugh. "You couldn't condone such corrupt practice. Another drink officer? Or would that constitute a bribe?"

"I'll risk it."

"Brave man." Sorenson went to put on some music and returned with another tumbler of whisky. Brook took an immediate sip. The heat felt good on his tongue, he swirled it around like mouthwash. He felt relaxed, at ease with his host. This was where he was meant to be, where he'd been so often in his dreams.

"So you can't prove I'm this killer?"

"I've proved it to myself." Brook decided against mentioning Charlie's confession. That was an ace he'd only use if he needed it.

The music drifted over from the speakers. Beethoven this time. Brook wasn't sure which.

"The Ninth – von Karajan conducting," said Sorenson, as though answering an audible question. "You'll enjoy it more than you can imagine," he said with a cryptic smile and set off round the room switching on lamps to dispel the gathering shadows.

Brook looked at his watch. Nearly four in the afternoon. This could be a long night.

"If you'll excuse me, Damen, I've got some medication to take. I won't be a moment," and he stepped through a door at the back of the room, behind one of the floor-to-ceiling bookshelves.

Brook picked up his glass and ambled around the room, wondering what Sorenson had meant by his remark about the music. He sniffed his glass and examined the bottom of the whisky bottle. If Sorenson had doctored his drink he couldn't tell. He took another hearty swig and positioned himself to admire the "fake" Van Gogh he'd seen on his first visit to the room. Everything about it was right – the bold brushwork, the light, the signature. It was an impressive mimic of Van Gogh's style.

He picked up an instruction booklet from the desk. It was for the video camera on a tripod in the corner of the room. He flicked through it then tossed it back on the desk.

He continued to wander round, stopping at his overcoat to pick out Noble's mobile. He turned it on. There were no messages so he returned it to the coat. The music played on.

Brook arrived at one of the bookshelves and examined its contents. A book caught his eye – *Empathic Depths of the Mind.* He browsed through it.

"Keep it," said Sorenson over Brook's shoulder. "A gift. You're going to need it." He returned to his armchair and arranged the blankets around his legs.

Brook made a show of replacing the book but Sorenson had closed his eyes. Brook stepped back to his chair and sat down.

"One thing Vicky didn't explain was why she latched onto me." Sorenson didn't respond so Brook pressed on. "She said she saw me on the News, at the Wallis Murders press conference, but if she had no idea you were involved why would she even be interested in The Reaper?"

"Vicky thinks he's still alive."

"Who?"

"Her father. She's terrified of him, of the memory of him. She thinks he's The Reaper."

"But she knew her father was dead."

"Not at first. She was very young. I couldn't tell her. Not after killing him. I said he went away."

"But she's not young any more."

"I know. When she was old enough to understand we told her, Sonja and I. Said he was killed by a burglar. But it was too late. It had taken root. Her father was a monster – a beast, preying on his family. Do you see? Families. That's how she connected to The Reaper. She fears the monster coming in the night, killing without mercy, destroying families then melting into the darkness. And to confront those fears she has to seek him out, to find him. It's not rational, I know. But our nightmares rarely are."

Brook nodded. "And your brother?"

No response. Finally Sorenson's eyelids parted slightly. Already he looked like a corpse. He opened his eyes and contemplated Brook.

"Sonja was home for the weekend. She'd been in care for a year, driven out of her mind by Steffi's cruelty. But he wouldn't allow her proper treatment. I'm sure he wanted her to go mad in that glorified country club he put her in, just to save himself the bother of dealing with her. He never visited. I did – without his knowledge. And that's when she told me about Vicky. That's when I first heard of the Dentist Game. She couldn't be absolutely sure. We're talking about a little girl. Her own father. But I was sure. I knew what he was like.

"One day, I waited for Steffi to go out and called round to see Vicky and Petr. I hadn't seen much of them that year. Steffi had hired a house-keeper to keep people away. Especially me. He knew better than to let me near them. He must have known I'd sense the truth at once. But Sonja warned me about her so I pretended to be Steffi. We were so alike. How could she have known? I'd forgotten my key, I said. It was easy.

"Poor Vicky. I didn't need to hold her tiny hand to know. It was so strong. Just seeing her, imagining her and Petr alone with that monster. And Sonja, going mad with guilt, powerless to protect her own children. I decided then to kill him.

"I left the house but before I went, I fired the housekeeper. I told her I'd made a mistake hiring her. I offered her £1000 in cash if she left immediately. Steffi never knew.

"Sonja was coming home for a visit the next day so I called round unexpectedly to see them. I took flowers.

"She opened the door. She was crying, her blouse was torn. Steffi" was in the living room. Drunk. He had an old cutthroat razor, a coming-of-age gift from my father, and he was waving it about in front of the children. They were terrified. Howling the place down. Sonja had finally got up the courage to tell Steffi she was leaving him and taking the children and he'd gone berserk.

"Strange. He couldn't have cared less about them. But his ego was bruised. The thought that his power was no longer taken seriously, no longer feared, mortified him. So he'd decided. Told them he was going to tie them up and cut their throats one at a time."

Brook looked up – another reason for Vicky to connect with The Reaper. "What happened?"

"I managed to distract him long enough to get the children out. Sonja brought them back here. When I came home the children were asleep. I made Sonja take a taxi back to the hospital, her alibi you see. Then I went straight back to Steffi's.

"He was even drunker by now. The violence in his eyes was savage. He attacked me, verbally, then physically. It all came out. All his poison. And then I saw. He'd wasted his life. He didn't deserve to live. It was easy. He was too drunk to stand. I tied him to a chair. I needed to make it look like a frenzied attack by a burglar so I beat his brains out with a poker. Afterwards I put a few antiques in a bin bag to suggest a burglary and left.

"Just like that?"

Sorenson smiled. "Not quite. Something happened. Something terrible, something amazing, something few people can understand. Even murderers don't get to see it. Most of them."

"What was that?"

"I think you know. You've seen it in Harlesden, in Brixton, in Derby. Those last few moments of life when people realise what's happening and beg for a little longer – a few minutes, a few seconds more. Everything changes in those moments.

"I saw that in Steffi. Those final seconds of his life he lived more than he'd ever lived before. Because suddenly he knew. He knew it was right. He knew he was about to die and every breath, every sight, became urgent, precious. He looked around the room at all the beautiful things and saw them as if for the first time. They were different, wonderful. He asked me to put on some music so I played him our song. La Wally. He cried. We both did.

"And to die, to give up your wasted life surrounded by the apex of human achievement, to end your time seeing such beauty and listening to the breath of Heaven, instead of gaping at a hospital ceiling or the bonnet of a car or a back street puddle…

297

"By the time I'd crashed the poker into his skull the first time, I'd changed him. *I* had changed him. He was different to the Steffi I'd always known. Better. At ease with himself, with his fate. I envied him for once. No more worry. No more having to hide the pain, the guilt. He was in the terminal ward. In rapture. If it were possible, I would have untied him so he could do the same for me. But I couldn't let him down. He was depending on me."

Sorenson had to take a pause now. His head slumped.

"There's something I don't understand."

"What don't you understand Damen? The urge to kill those who don't deserve to live. To destroy those who can't appreciate the beauty there is in the world – a painting, a piece of music, a glass of wine. To end the lives of those who, in deadening their own pain, spray their vile scent over others. To show them how precious life is by removing it. What don't you understand? Tell me."

"I understand the picture – Fleur de Lis – I understand the music, the wine. I even understand the arrogance which demands that only people who can't appreciate the things you take for granted should be slaughtered, people without your advantages, people that the wealthy, the well educated like you should be trying to help."

Sorenson turned to Brook with a look of such scorn and disgust that Brook worried that he may have gone too far and be disqualified from the endgame. But then Sorenson laughed as if realising he was being teased. "You don't believe that liberal nonsense for a second, any more than Charlie did. It's tried and failed. We live in a jungle, Damen. In the jungle, if you hold out a hand to help a suffering animal, it will be ripped to pieces. You understand that much."

"I understand the power, the mania. I understand the insanity of other people's lives and the desire to be God. But God *is* God, professor. Only the Devil ever *wants* to be God."

Sorenson laughed again. "You think I'm the devil? I'm flattered."

"No, any fool can have a God complex. You're no fool." Sorenson accepted the compliment with a nod of the head. "So tell me."

"Tell you what Damen?"

"Make me understand. If *you* murdered your brother why kill Sammy Elphick and his family? What had they done to deserve that?"

"Everything. Their entire lives were a monument to ugliness, to causing pain with their petty theft and casual violence. There was nothing to be achieved by extending their existence. Not when I could show them something better. Not when I could teach them how to appreciate life in those final minutes. I could show them beauty. They lived more in half an hour with me than they could in two lifetimes of drudgery and struggle."

"But how did you choose Sammy Elphick and his family?"

"A detail, Damen. Suffice to say they were chosen..."

"How?"

Sorenson's expression was blank. Finally he nodded. "Very well. I was in Shepherd's Bush one afternoon, trying to flag down a cab. A group of boys ran towards me. They were only young but they were very loud, very aggressive. I had no fear of what they might do to me but I was interested so I stopped to look. Fifty yards behind them I could see an old woman being helped to her feet and people shouting at these boys. One of them had the old woman's purse."

"What did you do?"

"I examined their faces as they ran past me. I watched them trying to look tough to discourage interference but I could see each of them was affected by what they'd done. They had that big-shot excitement on their faces but I could detect worry, some brief flicker that they knew what they'd done was wrong. Except one."

"The Elphick boy."

Sorenson nodded. "He charged towards me with such hate on his face and in his eyes. He had dead eyes. His parents were to blame. They'd trained him properly, to deaden every emotion, to care about no-one but himself and his own gratification."

"What happened?"

"He slowed in front of me thinking he had another opportunity to inflict himself into the nightmares of some meek soul. He screamed at me and clenched his fists. "Do you want some?" he shouted in my face.

"What did you do?"

Sorenson chuckled. "What his kind fear above all things. I laughed at him."

"And then he assaulted you?"

"No. I'd assaulted him. He was in shock at the idea that this lightly built, middle-aged man considered him so inconsequential, so hilarious. For a second he didn't know what to do."

"Then what happened?"

"He knew."

"Knew?"

"That one day I was going to kill him."

"And did *you* know you were going to kill him?"

"Yes. But not before he did. He realised that if someone like me could turn him into a figure of such ridicule, could strip him of all the power he'd invested in himself, he might as well not exist. In a sense, he died at that moment."

"What happened next?"

"He ran away. I watched him go. Then he stopped and turned to face me to try and get his power back. He gave me a V-sign."

Brook darted a look at Sorenson. "You cut off his fingers. You killed an entire family because of a V-sign?"

"Damen. When will you look at the big picture? The boy was a killer. How do you think that poor old woman coped with his act of thoughtless violence?"

"She died?"

"I've no idea. Does it matter? You must have met the teacher Jason Wallis assaulted?"

"So?"

"Is she dead?"

"You know she isn't."

"Think harder. Is she *dead?*"

Brook cast his mind back to the panic in Denise Ottoman's face when she couldn't find her cigarettes, remembered the hands wringing the damp handkerchief into a knot, her husband by her side, ashen-faced, staring into the distance. He didn't want to answer Sorenson but knew he must.

"Is she dead, Damen?"

"Yes. She's dead. Her husband too."

Sorenson exhaled deeply and stood to gather their glasses. When he returned, he fixed Brook as he handed him his drink. "And you say you don't understand. You've always known, Damen. Always. It's time. Someone's got to choose. Someone's got to decide…"

"Who lives and who dies?"

"Yes. Things can't go on the way they are. On every estate, law-abiding residents are thinking it. In every school, teachers are thinking it. On every street corner, policemen are thinking it. If we could just remove this family, this pupil, this yob from the face of the earth, the world would truly be a better place. Nobody would miss them. Nobody would mourn for them. If they could just cease to exist and the misery they cause die with them. No fuss, no mess. What a thing.

"But too many hands are tied, Damen. So while the meek cower behind their bolted front doors, the dregs of humanity are taking over. The weak can't choose. The politicians, the judges sitting on their hands – they won't choose. It's up to us."

"To play God. You're insane."

"Perhaps I am. But that makes God insane. And the billions who bend their knee in worship. A start had to be made. Do you question

300

that after what you've seen? Did you question God's right to act when you found Laura Maples?"

Brook didn't answer. He could see where this was leading.

"I remember you telling me about her death. You described the power Floyd Wrigley had over her perfectly. *'Suddenly he's a God. He is God.'* you said. *'He can choose.'* Maybe I am insane, Damen. But I know I'm not God. Yet thousands of apparently sane people, every year, become God. They assume the power. Power over life and death. The power of God.

"Take a Christian country like America." The sarcasm in Sorenson's voice was a little overdone. "I lived in Los Angeles from 1995 for three years. You didn't know that."

"Doing what?"

"Continuing my work in my small way. Not that anyone would notice in such a place. Los Angeles – the city of the angels. America – the home of the Brave. For such a humourless people, their sense of the absurd is delicious. Do you know how many people are murdered in America every year, Damen?"

No reply. Brook could see how long Sorenson had been preparing this and decided to offer no interruptions. He shook his head.

"24,000 people. Every year. On average, every week in the Land of the Free, nearly 500 people are murdered. They don't die in road accidents or of heart disease or cancer. They have their lives deliberately ended by another human being. So how many killers is that, assuming more than one person is murdered by the same killer?

"Let's be generous and say there are 18,000 killers in America. In any one year." Sorenson looked hard at his pupil, raising a bony digit for emphasis. "What do you suppose gave all those people – 18,000 of them – the right to assume the power of God and end the lives of their victims?"

"They don't see it that way."

"Exactly!" shouted Sorenson, slamming a fist down on his chair. "There's no guiding hand behind them. They see no power other than their own. If there is such a power, where is it? Why isn't it being used for good? Why won't this power stop them killing? And if this power is not to be used for good then *"Why shouldn't I use it?"* they ask. Each of these 18,000 murderers has realised that anybody can wield this power. What need have we of metaphysical God, when, with a squeeze of the trigger or a stroke of the blade, we can *be* God? We are God. What a power, Damen. What an awesome power.

"And who wants that power? Not those who have power, other power, power to affect things. No. It's those without the power to change anything that thirst after the ultimate expression of existence – the God-given power to take life. Our society has become infected by that power, Damen. The millions with no power and no influence have realised they can turn themselves into a celestial being with a single act.

"And then there are people like you and I. We look on in horror. We wonder what's happening to the world. Did God really die at Auschwitz? Where is the order, the rightness of things? We see God devolving His powers to decide who lives and who dies, without reference to any logical system.

"I'm not religious..."

"Neither am I, Damen. Neither are the 18,000 people who committed murder in America last year. *"God doesn't exist!"* they say. *"If He did exist He'd do something. If God does exist He doesn't give a damn so why should we?*

"And so we ask ourselves. A million questions. You know them as well as I do. It's the interrogation at the Theatre of the Absurd. Why can Hitler live to kill six million Jews, when an innocent baby can be snuffed out at birth? How can Josef Stalin die in his sleep when a bus full of schoolchildren can career into a swollen river and be washed away? Why do arms dealers get to sip martinis in the sun while the weapons they sell are used to slaughter women and children in the name of ethnic purity?

"Why? What is the point of it all, Damen? It's complete chaos. Does this God want us to hate him? Does he want us to despair of His creation?" Sorenson took a strained sigh and dabbed his brow with a hand towel produced from behind a cushion. "Excuse me. As you can see I feel strongly about this."

"And where do you fit into all this?"

"Me?" Sorenson laughed. "As you said, Damen, I am now God. I have assumed that power. *I am become Death, the destroyer of worlds.* If God refuses to bind a guiding philosophy to His power then I must do that for Him. I must show the world that power over life and death can be justly managed, so others can take up the mantle. The Reaper leads the way. He makes us see that the guilty can be judged and the innocent saved. The Reaper can decide. The Reaper does decide. It's the only way.

"The Elphick boy was young. I felt sorry but it was right. But his parents? They created him. They made him what he was. I was satisfied with their tears, their suffering. They learned a hard lesson and, by the end, they knew it was right. They saw I'd brought them beauty. They saw I'd brought them together as a family, for one last exquisite moment, and were grateful."

"And Wrigley?"

"Floyd Wrigley was chosen for you Damen, to prove to you the justness of The Reaper's work. But still you refused to see and I had to look elsewhere."

"Charlie."

Sorenson nodded. "His pain was so deep. The Reaper was happy to help him."

"By making him kill Roddy Telfer?"

"By showing him that he had the power to make the world a better place."

"And Tamara Wrigley? Kylie Wallis? Roddy Telfer's unborn child? Did their deaths make the world a better place?"

"Nature versus nurture, Damen."

"What?"

"Genetics or Environment? You look but you don't see. Is the way we're raised responsible for what we are and what we do or is it laid down in our genetic make-up, as unchangeable as the sunrise? I suspect you're an Environment man, Damen. It's the liberal choice."

"But you believe in Science, in Genetics."

"Believe? No. Like you I believe in nothing but my own ability to act. That's how the choice is made. Nature versus nurture. When you're the child of a habitual criminal your future is written. If the genes don't get you, the environment will. It's what the Americans call a slam-dunk.

"You saw the poor Wallis girl, her virginity torn from her at such an age." Brook looked sharply up at Sorenson. "Of course I knew, Damen, every sickening detail – more even than you. And how long before this poor child delivered the seed of some habitual criminal like her father? Three years? Two years? Six months? And the cycle of abuse begins again.

"She didn't suffer if that's what you want to know. She'd suffered enough before The Reaper took her. The parents cried. Finally they'd seen real pain and were forced to confront it, fear it. And they understood. I wish I could be certain they cried for their daughter and not for themselves. It was the same with the Wrigley girl…"

"She was called Tamara. She'd have been twenty-six now."

"Yes." Sorenson was unfazed by Brook's attempt to humanise his victims. "And how many young Floyds do you think she'd have squeezed out by now, strutting their stuff around the 'Hood?"

"So the Wallis baby was saved because there was still time to change its future by changing its environment."

Sorenson smiled warmly at Brook. "Exactly. Another drink."

303

"Is that why you write it on the wall?"

"Don't feign ignorance, Damen. Nobody in the Wallis family was saved. You know who benefits from The Reaper's work."

"Benefits?" From the depths, Brook hatched a bitter laugh. "From cutting the throats of little boys and girls."

Sorenson's grin forced Brook to look away. "Don't bore me with the response you think society requires of you. Who benefits?"

Brook remembered Kylie, skin like white porcelain, her top sliced open, her back scored like a joint of pork. He remembered her mother, he remembered Bobby Wallis. He remembered the aggression of Jason in the hospital. He remembered Floyd Wrigley and Sammy Elphick and his boy hanging from the light fitting, shorn of his V-sign.

"Tell me Damen." Sorenson's eyes bored into Brook and he couldn't hold the look. He'd tapped into the mother lode of his deepest, darkest instincts and he knew. He saw it all. Everybody said it. Charlie Rowlands, Noble, Hendrickson, Greatorix, even Wendy. Good riddance to bad rubbish. He said it himself in unguarded moments. Nobody cared. Nobody was affected by The Reaper's slaughter.

"Is it a bad one, guv?"
"I don't know. I need you to tell me!"

"Who benefits, Damen?" Sorenson was insistent, sensing breakthrough.

Brook's voice was barely more than a croak as he wrenched the words out. "We all do. The rest of us. We're saved from them."

Sorenson sat back with an appreciative sigh and continued to gaze at Brook a thin cruel smirk hovering around his mouth. "Welcome aboard, my boy."

Welcome aboard. Charlie's phrase. Brook's head spun. He was defeated. Not that Sorenson was the winner. But that made it worse. He saw how like Sorenson he was. Sorenson saw it too. They were of a kind. That's why he'd come back for Brook.

And in the midst of all the madness, The Reaper came to help. He brought salvation with him, not for the souls of his victims but for society, if there was still such a thing. Saving the world from the pain these families inflicted and from the certainty of future pain.

Brook's breathing was laboured now. He tried to return to the case to calm his mind. "There's something else. Annie Sewell."

"Ah. Charlie finally rid himself of the burden."

"No. Charlie said nothing. I worked it out but what I couldn't figure was why you'd take the trouble to arrange some anonymous old

304

woman's death just to get Bob Greatorix out of the way? Why not kill the Wallis family on a night, when I was sure to be first on the scene?"

"That was the idea before I met her."

"When?"

"More than a year ago. In Derby. I was in a hotel the Christmas before last…"

"The International."

"That's right. On a scouting mission," Sorenson added with a wink. "They were having a dinner, a Christmas treat. For the old folks," he added in a cockney accent. "Funny how, when you become old and senile, people automatically assume you're harmless…"

"And she wasn't?"

"Oh she'd become harmless, I dare say. But in her youth she carried a terrible anger. She couldn't have children, you see. An ironic circumstance for someone who's a midwife, don't you think? All those happy couples, all those babies. And sometimes, poor Annie's rage at the injustice of it all got the better of her. Sometimes the babies were weak and the slightest setback could take them away from their parents. It wasn't hard to cover her tracks.

"Eventually the anger subsides. Too late though for a dozen newborns and their broken parents. Of all the people who've come to my notice, she had the most blood on her hands. But worse, it was innocent blood. Killing a baby is unforgivable."

"But The Reaper kills children. What's the difference?"

"The Reaper removes those who are doomed to perpetuate the abuses of their parents. But a baby is the only true innocent, a blank canvas if you will. The Wallis baby now has her chance, a glimpse of a useful life where before there was only one road to travel."

Brook was barely breathing. Sorenson too sank back into his chair, exhausted. The music had finished but Brook hadn't noticed. He sat motionless, staring at Sorenson whose eyes had closed again. He looked at his glass. Empty. He wanted another belt of whisky but didn't dare move in case the spell was broken. Sorenson was in his element now and Brook was loath to disturb the ether.

But DS Noble's mobile phone hadn't read the script and the tinniest rendition of Volare seeped out of Brook's coat pocket. Sorenson opened his eyes immediately and Brook leapt from his chair to answer it.

He was a little unsteady on his feet at first, unaccustomed to so much alcohol so early in the day. He retrieved the phone and swayed gently towards the porthole window, opening it to a gust of chill air, which didn't make him feel any better.

"John?"

"Sir. We've been looking for you."

"What is it?"

"The thing is...are you alone?"

"What is it, John?" Brook rubbed his hand over his face.

"Is anyone with you?"

"Why? What is it?" Then Brook realised. Noble was ringing about Charlie. "John. It's okay. I know about Charlie. I was with him when he died."

There was a short pause during which Brook could hear mumbling and other noises. Someone was speaking to him but Brook couldn't take it in.

He felt dizzy and unable to focus. He dropped the phone to the floor, unable to grip it, and heard it break apart but couldn't look down for fear of losing his balance or blacking out. Instead he turned to Sorenson who was suddenly at his shoulder. He took Brook's elbow and helped him back to his seat.

Brook slumped down and Sorenson sat opposite him but in the same movement pulled his chair close to Brook's so he could see his face. He stared into Brook's eyes, changing the angle of his head to take in as much information as possible.

Brook tried to speak but his mouth felt numb and thick. As though a dentist...

"Worve u dun?"

Sorenson smiled. "I've given you something to help you relax. You didn't think you could get this close without a forfeit, did you? I can't let you act on Charlie's confession. There's still so much to do.

"Don't struggle. It'll do no good. This is for the best. Life's of no use to you now. Charlie told me what your daughter and her stepfather have been up to. Your poor ex-wife – Amy. Think how she suffers. She knew – a mother always knows. But she couldn't know, could she? She had to blind herself to it. The only way to get through. But you, Damen, you saw what was happening, yet you did nothing."

Suddenly Sorenson was back in Brook's face. "Don't you see, Damen?" said Sorenson, removing the gun from Brook's pocket and placing it on his desk. "What an opportunity wasted. It was your duty as a father to act, to do something but you let him live and, instead of him suffering it's you who are in pain. He's fucking your daughter, Damen, and he's not even her real father." Brook felt the words slapping his face and screwed his eyes shut. He opened them again and Sorenson had retreated from what little vision he had left. When he returned it was to the sound of The Ninth again. The Adagio began.

Slow. Melodic. Mocking the frenzy that was to follow.

Brook tried to breathe, to focus. His hearing, all his senses were supercharged. His sight was blurred yet enhanced. He could see colours he'd never seen, colours he didn't know existed, changing with every bleary blink, dancing around the winking lamps, like multicoloured angels gathering against the dark. No light without darkness.

And the music was wonderful. It seemed to be swooping and diving around in his head, each note erupting from a thousand orchestras. The choir rose up as one voice, to lift themselves for Brook's last hurrah.

Sorenson pulled his chair closer, so Brook could see his face framed against the gloom.

"You've failed me, Damen. You've failed yourself. I had such high hopes." He reached into Brook's pocket and pulled out Laura's necklace and smiled at Brook. "Still no closure? Don't worry. It's near." Then he took out and tore open the plastic bag and removed an old razor, a cutthroat with a mother-of-pearl handle. Sorenson examined it, opening it and closing it. "Perfect. Thank you Damen. I appreciate you bringing it. It was my father's before he gave it to Steffi. It was a terrible wrench leaving it in Brixton, but I knew you'd look after it. Is there anything you want to say before the end?"

Brook tried to fix his eyes on Sorenson's face. It wasn't easy. His head felt like it was on a stick. "Let... me... hear... you say it. Just once."

"Say what Damen?"

Brook gulped with the effort of speech. His mouth was arid, his tongue cracked as he spoke. "Say the words...tell me you're The Reaper."

Sorenson permitted himself a little chuckle. "But I'm not The Reaper, Damen. You are." Brook squinted back at Sorenson. "You saw. You had the power. Remember how good it felt in Brixton. Remember how sweet it was to find Laura's killer. Did you put the music back on? Did you cry afterwards? Tell me." Brook let his eyes fall to the floor.

Sorenson slapped him on the cheek. He grabbed his hair and lifted his head. "Look around. Don't waste it. Look at the beauty. Feel the wonder. It doesn't get better than this. Then you can let go. Cry now. It helped the others. Think of Amy and your daughter. Think of Laura. She's waiting for you."

Brook swallowed and for a second was able to keep his head still as he stared back at Sorenson's wizened pate. His mind and vision cleared and Brook found some control over his speech had returned.

"I'm not like you. I made a mistake."

"You are me Damen. You're ready. I came to Derby for you. Charlie did his best but you were always the one. Cry now, Damen. Like the others did. It's good for you."

"Don't cry," Brook began to giggle, "for me – Argentina." Sorenson looked on in disbelief. "D'you think…I care? I'm terminal. There's nothing left…you can all… go fuck yourselves." Brook's body shook with laughter.

Sorenson smiled. "You never cease to amaze me, Damen. Never! I'm proud to have known you."

"Magnificent peaks, Uncle Vic. Peaks and troughs." Brook's vision cleared though his head continued to roll. Tears of laughter rolled down his face. He could see Sorenson smiling down at him. "Help me…help me soar…Mozart, Beethoven, Van Gogh." Sorenson nodded. "If you can't…love beauty, you are dead," Brook gulped as the Finale picked up.

Sorenson sat down and opened the razor. "I've waited years for you. Now you're ready." He looked down at the glint of the razor. "Tell me you want to live and I'll spare you."

Brook fought to keep his eyes open. He wanted every second to count. This was how it should be. What a feast. What a way to die. Overwhelming. Humbling. To be so blessed. Make it last. The choir rising and falling. Calling him. The clashing of cymbals, the urgency of the orchestra, the climax erupting in his head. Make it last.

He tried to breathe but could feel nothing from the neck down. It was how he imagined death coming. Shutting up shop, organ by organ. Finally the mind. He gave up on his eyes and closed them and through the starburst he watched the rats scuttling towards him, watched Laura's leg fall open for him, watched Sorenson through the rain, watched Vicky brush her hair, watched Jason sleep in the hospital, watched Amy support her womb with an arm, watched Charlie beckon him into the flat above the launderette, watched Mac the doorman put down a saucer of milk for his kitten, watched Wendy Jones vomit behind a bush, watched Harry Hendrickson laughing and pointing at him, watched Terri gurgling in her cot.

"Kill me."

Chapter 30

Brook took a few moments to compose himself, still staring at the man to be sure. No movement. No more noise. Only the music. He was glad of it. The silence would have scorched his ears.

Calm now, Brook turned to the CD system. It was brand new. A half-smile drifted across his face. He set about concluding his business and turned to the wall to examine the word smeared in blood over the fireplace. His eye caught a glimpse of something else and his features darkened – a photograph in a frame on the mantelpiece. He looked closer, staring hard for what seemed like hours. There was no mistake. His mouth fell open. He shrank back, his face frozen in wonder, his eyes unblinking, his mind in turmoil, trying to make sense.

Then he knew. It all fit together and he nodded, his face set, eyes like slits to block out the visions. Of course. Now he understood. He'd got The Reaper's message. A smile cracked his features. Another noise behind him. Brook took a deep breath as he turned to face his nemesis.

"You killed her!" Brook stared at the man on the sofa.

"Wassup?" groaned the man.

As Brook watched, he tried to lift his head and open his eyes but the effort was too much and his head fell back against the corpse of the woman.

Brook turned back to the chimney breast and picked the picture frame from the mantelpiece. He squinted at the image again but reflection from the lights hindered his inspection so he hurled the frame face down onto the floor and stooped to recover the photograph from the shattered glass.

Brook fixed his gaze on the picture of the man who sat incapacitated amongst the wreckage of his family not ten feet away. He grinned for the camera, proud of his naked torso, smooth and toned.

There was no mistake. Brook saw the necklace clearly. Silver hearts. It once belonged to Laura Maples and now it strained against the man's thick neck.

Brook let his hand fall to his side, his head dropped and he stood, dazed. He listened to the music – the only way to be sure time was passing. With his eyes closed he could almost imagine he was at a concert at the South Bank with Amy, looking forward to his half time gin and tonic and then perhaps a meal. Finally the music stopped and Brook opened his eyes, refreshed by the beauty in his mind. Then he saw the savagery around him.

As if by remote control he turned to the CD player and started the Mozart again. The Requiem. Then he pushed the photograph deep into his overcoat pocket. He returned to the man on the sofa and pulled down the neck of his T-shirt. The necklace glared back at him, each tiny heart a Cyclops from his dreams. Brook twisted his hand between the man's neck and the delicate chain and pulled hard. It came away first time and Brook buried it in his pocket as well.

Then he buttoned his coat up to the neck and pulled the collar around his ears to be completely weather proof.

In the bathroom he soaked a towel in cold water and padded back towards the sofa. He slapped the towel onto the man's face. He revived at once though he was still groggy.

"Can you hear me?" enquired Brook.

The man was trying to open his eyes and was blinking in a manner, which suggested they'd never been opened before. "Wass happen?" he muttered, his head still lolling from side to side. "Wer you?"

"Who am I?" asked Brook in genuine alarm. Good question. He didn't know, couldn't remember who he was. He tried to think, tried to piece together his past, his identity, but it wouldn't reveal itself. He knew he wasn't a new-born, he knew that much. But who was he and why was he here?

As he moved behind the sofa, he gave it serious thought. A moment later he smiled with sudden child-like pleasure. He'd remembered something, something about who he was. It sounded strange when he spoke. "I'm The Reaper," he said. "And this is for Laura." Brook plunged the blade of the razor into the soft tissue below the man's left ear and dragged it as hard as he could across his throat.

Although the blade was sharp, Brook lost his grip before he could reach the windpipe but the blood still began to hiss from the artery. The handle was stuck deep in the man's neck and Brook had to struggle to yank it out, his hand slipping on the now crimson stock several times.

310

At first the man didn't react, such was his stupor, but after a few seconds the pain, and the sight of warm blood steaming down his chest alerted him to his fate and he began to struggle.

"Easy," whispered Brook. "Easy." He had to hold the man's forehead with his left arm to pacify the shuddering. He dropped the razor and put the wet towel across the man's nose and mouth to stop any noise, pulling the man down against the sofa with his left arm to minimise the spasms. "Easy. Listen to the music. It's Mozart. It's greater than us. It was written for you. Don't fight. It's over. You're better now. That's it. That's it."

Brook held on for longer than he needed. If he was going to kill a part of himself tonight he had to be sure. There was no turning back.

Some time later Brook relaxed his grip. He blinked rapidly as though waking from a coma. He stood and looked at the razor on the floor as though he'd never seen it before. Then he gave a nod of recognition, picked it up and closed it into his pocket. Slowly, deliberately, he unbuttoned his blood-soaked overcoat, turned it inside out then rolled it up under his arm, like a child on the way to the swimming pool. Then he returned to the CD player and turned up the volume before walking down the stairs and stepping back out into the night, humming the Requiem all the way to his car.

*

Brook stirred and opened his eyes. His lids were too heavy and it was an effort to force them open. All was black and still. Nothing, no sense got through. He couldn't hear, couldn't part his welded lips. He tried to move but was paralysed.

Knowledge surfaced. So this was Death. Falling through space. Blackness. No sights, no sounds. No tunnels. No hopes. No bright lights. No dead relations to show him the ropes.

Then it dawned. He was on his way to Hell. There'd be no flames. No barbecued flesh. The Devil knew. Man was a gregarious animal. Perpetual loneliness was the refined torture. On your own to the end of time.

Well the Devil was a wimp. Solitude was bliss. God was spot on. He knew how to inflict pain. Hell was other people. The Devil should have done his research. Then he'd know about the rats. Could give Brook a hard time. But maybe it wasn't set yet. Perhaps there'd be an interview…

*

Brook came round with a start. There was light now. Blurred, but

311

definite. He tried to focus but it was too hard. He couldn't distinguish shapes but there were colours, indistinct, shimmering, but definite colours. And he could hear. A dull rushing. Constant. Punctuated by sharp notes. Traffic. Traffic and the sound of horns.

He shifted his position, aware now of his limbs. He could move his hands from under his legs. He was in a chair. The one in Sorenson's study. He was alive. Sorenson had miscalculated. No. That didn't sound right. Must be a mistake.

Brook tried to stand but a black hole engulfed his head and he slumped back into the pit.

*

"Inspector! Inspector Brook!" A voice he knew. "He's alive!" It was Wendy. She'd come for him.

Brook awoke to her face. He could see it clearly but the rest was a haze. She smiled at him. An angel. Perhaps he was dead. But then where was Charlie? Wouldn't he be on hand for the welcome drink?

As if in reply Wendy said, "Sir, can you hear me? You're alive. Do you understand me?"

Brook lifted his weary eyes. He puzzled over the information as though it meant nothing then blinked his eyes at her. He gulped and tried to speak. Wendy Jones craned to listen. Brook could smell her perfume. "Sor…"

He passed out again.

*

Moments later Brook felt a jolt. He was lying down. There were people around him, carrying him. They had knocked into Sorenson's desk. He opened his eyes. Sorenson sat at the desk. He was white. His desktop was red. Brook saw a clenched fist smudged with blood. Laura's necklace was wrapped around the marble knuckles. Brook closed his eyes.

Chapter 31

He knew at once he was in a hospital. The smell told him: the pungent aroma of heavy duty cleaning fluids couldn't quite overpower the aroma of sweet dried blood and stale body wastes that permeated these places. And the low hum of misery was unmistakable. Hushed despair. As if to speak at greater volume might remind a delinquent God to attend to His roster of death.

Brook blinked and looked around and, trying to sit up, winced at the pain in his stomach. He rubbed it through the heavy cotton of his NHS pyjamas. It felt as though he'd been kicked by a mule.

He sat back and stared upwards. The ceiling was high and he had an impression of space on the other side of the screen that ran alongside his bed. He guessed he was in a large ward rather than a private room.

Beside the bed on a hard-backed wooden chair sat a large leather bag. Brook tried to reach it but was hampered by a sharp nip in his left arm. He was hooked up to a drip and had given it a nasty yank so, with his right arm, he pushed himself and his pillows right back so he could sit up properly. He rubbed the tape on his left arm then reached over again but the bag was still out of reach.

He gave up and turned his attention to a selection of Get Well cards arranged on his bedside cabinet. Four of them. He couldn't make out any of the inscriptions except one. The smallest card, complete with 49p price sticker and black thumbprint on the back was the work of Greatorix. Brook couldn't decipher any of the handwriting but recognised the large childlike B for Bob and the even larger G and X. The rest was just wavy lines.

Brook remembered something. It came to him now. He hadn't been hallucinating. Sorenson was dead and his career was over...

Wendy Jones walked into view carrying a cup of coffee. She looked wonderful in figure hugging white polo and tight jeans and the

313

look of delight and affection in her expression gladdened Brook's heart.

"You're back, sir," she exclaimed and hastily put down her coffee to grab his hand. "How are you feeling?" She withdrew it after giving Brook's hand a squeeze but there seemed to be none of the awkwardness that had characterised their encounters since their trip to London. Instead her eyes shone brightly, burning into him, eager to talk.

"Tired." Brook smiled back at her. "Hungry."

"I'm not surprised." She moved her bag onto the bed and sat down to rummage through it. "You've been out cold for days. It's lunchtime in half an hour but I got some things in case you came round. I've got a cold bacon sandwich or an apple or a banana." Brook raised an eyebrow and she cracked into a grin. "Bacon sandwich it is."

One bacon sandwich, banana, apple and packet of crisps scrounged from the duty nurse later, Brook lay back and took a sip of coffee. "I'm ready."

"What do you want to know?"

Brook was hesitant now, doubting his memory. "When you found me…"

"You didn't imagine it. Sorenson's dead."

"I see. Does Amy know anything about what's happened?"

"She's knows you're in here…"

"But she's not been to visit?"

Jones looked at the floor. "That doesn't mean…"

"Don't humour me, Wendy. I tried to wreck her marriage."

"You confronted her husband about your daughter. That's all you did. Any father would have done the same. You can't blame yourself for that."

Brook smiled at her. "I don't. And Sorenson?"

"He cut his wrists with an old razor."

Brook found it hard to accept. A part of him was dead. He'd lived with the thought of Sorenson for so many years. Now he was gone.

"And is there a reason why you're out of uniform and I'm not handcuffed?"

Jones was taken aback. "Handcuffed? Why?"

"A prominent citizen commits suicide in the presence of a suspended police officer. Not enough? How about possession of an illegal weapon? It's not hard to figure out a sequence of events…"

"What weapon?"

"I had a gun. It was Charlie's…"

"There was no gun."

"There wasn't?"

"Sir. Damen. Don't you know? You're a hero, or you will be when

314

this all comes out. You've found a killer that nobody else could. From what McMaster has been saying you're a guaranteed DCI. And your success is our success. We're all…"

"Stop, stop. What are you talking about?"

"He confessed. Sorenson. He made a videotape."

"What?" Brook remembered the camcorder on the tripod in Sorenson's study.

"It's true."

"Confessed to what?"

"To being a killer."

"The Reaper?" Brook saw the hesitation in her manner.

"Well, no. He said he killed his brother…"

Brook closed his eyes and nodded. Of course. Closure for Vicky – the dying act of a loving uncle. But not The Reaper. He would never admit to that. Sorenson can die but The Reaper must live.

"…there was also a girl."

Brook sat bolt upright despite the tubes restraining him. "Girl?"

"Yes. One of your old cases, from your time at Hammersmith. He had her bracelet in his hands…"

"Laura."

"That's right. Laura Maples. He confessed everything. He knew all about it." Brook was sombre. "And that poor old woman in Derby, Annie Sewell. He said he arranged it."

Brook was deep in thought. "Did he say why?"

"He claimed she killed several babies when she was younger. She was a midwife…well? Who knows? It was a long time ago. They're looking into it."

"Did he say who he got to kill her for him?"

"No. When we get back to Derby…"

"Derby? Where the hell am I?"

"Still in London. Hammersmith Hospital. You were too ill to move."

"Terminal ward?"

"That's not funny, sir."

He stroked her hand. "No it's not. And please call me Damen."

"I *can* tell you something funny, Damen."

"I'm listening."

"Sorenson thinks he killed you. On the tape he said he poisoned you. Said he was sorry because you were such a brilliant detective and nobody else could have caught up with him."

Jones smiled with pleasure but Brook was sombre. "Then why am I alive?"

"He must have got the dosage wrong."

"I don't think so. If I'm alive it's because Sorenson wanted it that way. He staged it."

"Staged it?"

"To convince me he was going to kill me. Otherwise it would have been phoney. I wouldn't have believed it, wouldn't have gone through what the others went through. It had to be authentic."

Jones was baffled. "Authentic?"

"The same as the other victims. He needed to show me things, the despair and the hope and the beauty of dying. The joy of letting go. Of being saved." Brook could see he was losing her. "He wouldn't kill me. I was his friend." Brook took a sip of water. "He said I was a brilliant detective?"

"Words to that effect – what's wrong with that?"

"He's trying to manipulate me, Wendy."

"He's dead. How can he manipulate you?"

"You didn't know him. He never said or did anything without an ulterior motive. And now, being a hero, I get to stay in the Force. That's what he wants."

"Sorenson. Why?"

Brook pondered how to say it. "Access."

Jones was mystified but Brook showed little sign of enlightening her. "Access to what?"

Brook had closed his eyes and was drifting off to sleep. "Deserving cases." In a barely audible voice he added, "He came to Derby for me, Wendy. And dead or alive, he's not going to give up until he gets me."

Chapter 32

The next day Brook demanded his clothes and insisted on leaving his sick bed despite the protests of Wendy Jones and the doctor. The toxin pumped from his stomach had yet to be identified.

"What's the worst that could happen, doc?"

"You could collapse and die, Inspector Brook," she replied.

"Then you better get me an organ donor card."

"If you died we couldn't use them."

"You could if I stepped under a bus."

"Then take a cab."

Having discharged himself, his first task was to recover his car from the Hilton. His bag, containing Charlie's confession, was in the boot and Brook couldn't risk leaving it. Jones refused to let him go alone in case he became unwell.

After picking up the car, their first call was the local police station for Brook to make a statement about the events at Sorenson's house. Jones assured him it would be routine as McMaster had already liaised with the Met over Brook's presence in London. The fact that Sorenson had confessed to a murder in Derby was a plus, but Brook knew how sensitive locals were about jurisdiction and suspected the Hammersmith crew would be gearing up to give him a hard time.

Sonja Sorenson, Vicky, Petr and the nurse had already been questioned about Victor Sorenson's state of mind. All were able to suppose that Sorenson was a potential suicide because of the nature of his illness. But nobody could shed any light on his videotaped confessions or his relationship with DI Brook.

Sonja had been questioned closely about her husband's death but could offer up no useful leads and because of her history of mental fragility she wasn't pushed too hard. After all, the murder was an old one and they had a confession. Case closed.

Brook believed the Laura Maples murder would be the fly in the ointment, and for that the local CID would need to speak to him. It was his case. It was unsolved. Unsolved murders spawned obsessive behaviour. And if by chance the obsessed detective found his killer but was unable to prove it...

*

Jones was directed to the canteen when they arrived and Brook was ushered towards an interview room once his refreshment order had been taken.

He sat down in a bare, windowless room. It was illuminated by cheerless strip lighting, had a battered table and three chairs – two on one side, one on the other. A clean ashtray sat in the middle of the table. Bad sign – the room wasn't left over from a previous interrogation, it had been chosen for a purpose and set up with forethought. Now he was alone with a chance to stew and coffee was being brought to maintain the pretence of routine friendliness. Brook knew what would come up – his breakdown.

The two detectives entered the room together and sat opposite Brook. One of them smiled a welcome. The senior man. "I'm Detective Chief Inspector Fulbright. This is Detective Sergeant Ross."

"Detective Inspector Damen Brook, Derbyshire CID."

"Feel free to smoke, inspector," said Fulbright.

"No thank you." Brook wanted a cigarette but still felt queasy in his stomach. He decided against it. In Brook's experience, the guilty smoked like chimneys during an interview.

"Given up?" Brook turned to look at Fulbright more closely. "You don't remember me, do you inspector?"

"Should I?" Brook knew he'd made a mistake as the words left his mouth.

"No reason at all. I was just a lowly PC back then, on crowd control at the first Reaper killing. Harlesden. A family was butchered. Do you remember that case?"

"It rings a bell. And no..."

"No what?"

"...I haven't given up." Better. He smoked but didn't need a cigarette because he had nothing to hide. Brook hoped that would cancel out the disrespect he'd shown.

"Now..." began Fulbright.

"Before we start I think I need to see the video."

"So you can get your story straight?" DS Ross had a thin wiry body and complementary mean features. He was quite small, close to minimum regulation and Brook had never yet met a male officer of similar height who hadn't overcompensated with an aggressive manner.

DCI Fulbright raised a lazy hand to intervene. "I think we'd like to hear your side of things first *DI* Brook."

Brook noted the emphasis on rank and studied Fulbright's face. Yes. He remembered him. He'd transferred from uniform and had been an untalented DC ten years ago. He could recall Charlie once tearing a strip off him for some bumbling evidence gathering. Now it was payback time.

"Is this the bit where I cross my legs so you can see I'm not wearing underpants?" Ross half stood and was halted by a more urgent hand from Fulbright. Brook beamed to annoy them.

"Funny." Fulbright held out a hand and Ross passed him a piece of paper. Brook knew what it was but continued to beam across the table at his two interrogators. "I've got a report here about your psychological condition. This report was compiled in 1992..." – Fulbright shot Brook a glance which aped a concern he didn't feel – "...and refers to a, and I quote, 'period of obsessive stalking' by yourself, DS Brook as you then were."

"Can you tell us anything about this period, Inspector Brook?"

"Is the report not clear?"

"I'd like to hear about it in your own words."

"Can you remember who you were stalking, inspector?" put in Ross.

Brook continued to smile but it was wafer thin. He took a pause to think then decided he had nothing to hide. "It was a long time ago. Sorenson was a killer. Only I knew it."

"You admit you went off the deep end on this guy..."

"It happens in this job. I did nothing illegal."

"As far as we're aware."

"If you've got something to say, get it said."

"Okay. You're a fucking fruitcake, mate," sneered Ross.

"I'm not your mate."

Ross stood over Brook, bearing his teeth. A blue vein on his shaved scalp stood out and distracted Brook. As yet, his personal space hadn't been violated but he felt it was a matter of time. "You're finished as a copper by all accounts."

"So you decide to right a few wrongs from the past," chipped in Fulbright.

"You went to Sorenson's house, forced a confession out of him, cut his wrists and took just enough dope to make it look like you'd been poisoned." Ross stood with a leer and went to stand behind Brook. "And you thought we'd swallow it. What do you take us for?"

"Let me guess," Brook said, pointing at Fulbright, "you're the good cop and," slinging a thumb over his shoulder at Ross, "he's the really bad cop."

"We're just honest coppers like you used to be. Asking questions that have to be asked. And answered."

"Harassing an officer who's clearing up your old cases?"

"By killing the prime suspect," sneered Ross from the back wall.

"He wasn't a suspect in either of those killings," Brook observed.

"No. But you had him down for The Reaper." Fulbright looked down as if to check the details. He looked back at Brook with an expression of great sympathy. "I mean, we've all been there inspector. We're just the same as you. Flesh and blood. I saw what he did at Harlesden. And Brixton was pretty grim by all accounts. All these years the bastard's been free to go about his business. It rankles, doesn't it?"

"Pisses you off big time," Ross interjected, as though his superior's vocabulary was too obscure.

"And it all gets too much for you. So you decide to do something about it."

"Just like that," said Brook.

"It can happen in this job."

"But with your *history* it looks iffy, you making him cough for The Reaper. So you tag him for something else."

Brook laughed and turned to Ross. "You still watching Sweeney re-runs, sarge?"

Ross leapt over to Brook's chair and put his mouth next to Brook's ear. "You think you're the dog's bollocks, don't you, you toffee-nosed, university cunt?"

Brook felt hot breath on his neck. "I'm bored with this. We all know I didn't kill him. He was terminal, for Christ's sake."

"How would you know that?" enquired Fulbright.

"Mrs Sorenson told me and she will testify to that. In fact, she probably has already. I didn't kill Sorenson and if you could prove I did, you would have charged me by now. You're just blowing smoke. Let me see the video. I'm willing to bet Sorenson mentioned things about Laura Maples and his brother's death that only the killer could have known."

Ross and Fulbright exchanged a look. "You were the investigating officer on the Maples murder," rejoined Ross, "you could have clued him up, given him a script."

"And Stefan Sorenson? I was nowhere near that investigation and you know it." Brook stood. "Unless you have any intention of charging me, I'll be on my way."

There was a pause before Fulbright shrugged his shoulders. He stood too and motioned Ross to the door. "You're free to leave, inspector. This was just a friendly chat. It's been good to see you again after all these years. No hard feelings I hope?"

"'Course not."

"When are you going back to Derby?" asked Fulbright.

"Now."

Ross opened the door for Brook. "I like your bird. Just my type," he added with a leer. "Nice arse, big tits."

"Bit tall for you though," Brook observed, passing him. The leer evaporated and Ross took a half step towards Brook's retreating frame.

"Sergeant!" snapped Fulbright. "I'll see the inspector out."

Ross managed to wrench a "Yessir!" through his gritted teeth and stalked away, his fists clenched.

"I see you haven't lost your ability to piss people off, Brook."

"It's a gift. Sir."

Fulbright gave him a smile of grudging respect. He studied him for a second. "You've changed."

Brook fixed his eyes on Wendy Jones walking towards them. "Oh?" he said.

"I watched you in Harlesden, moving round the Elphick family like you were measuring them up for a new suit. You didn't give a shit about what happened to them, did you? I saw it in your face. But now you're worse. Then you didn't really understand what had been to done them. Now you know and still you don't care. You've become hard." Brook turned to face him and their eyes locked. "Like a killer."

Brook stared at Fulbright for a moment then smiled.

Fulbright held out his hand and Brook shook it. "Stay out of Dodge, Brook."

*

"How was it, sir?" asked Jones on the way to the car.

"Like you said. Just routine."

Chapter 33

Brook buttoned his shirt and knotted his black tie. Immediately he loosened it. No sense being choked before getting to the church. He hated wearing a suit, he hated going to churches, but it *was* a funeral and McMaster had been very specific. The press would be there and the TV cameras. Nothing less than sartorial elegance would suffice – Greatorix was minding the shop while the division turned out to pay their respects to the Wallis family.

He checked his watch. Half an hour before Noble and Jones picked him up. He looked again at the Van Gogh propped on his sofa and shook his head. What on earth would he do with it? He knew he shouldn't keep it. But getting rid of it could be trickier than hanging on to it.

He read again the accompanying letter from Sonja Sorenson which said that it was always her brother-in-law's wish that it be given to Brook. "For being my friend and understanding the importance of my work," was how he'd expressed it to her. And she echoed her brother-in-law's claims from his first encounter with Brook. The painting was unknown to the art world but was a genuine Van Gogh.

Brook stared at the picture. It *was* magnificent. And if the Sorensons were to be believed, an undiscovered treasure worth millions nestled on the plastic sofa in his grubby flat. He found it hard to take in – harder even than the two handlers from Fine Art Conveyors who had marched the bubble-wrapped masterpiece through Brook's hovel to its nicotine stained dungeon. Their jaws had hit the floor when they saw the living room and they departed in stunned silence, eyeing each other all the while, unaware even of Brook's attempt to give them a tip.

Brook removed his jacket, hung it on a chair to avoid the cat hairs and sat down. Something else had arrived that morning through the regular post. Unlike the painting, Brook had been expecting it since reading the transcript of Sorenson's taped confession several days before. DCI Fulbright had refused Derby CID's request for a copy of the videotape, so Brook had been forced to rely on the written word.

He'd examined the transcript thoroughly, but had found nothing that he hadn't expected – a thorough account of Stefan Sorenson's murder and less detailed confessions to the killings of Laura Maples and Annie Sewell.

What surprised Brook was the absence of a hidden message, something personal from Sorenson to Brook, something for his eyes only, that he alone could decipher. He didn't know what he expected to find – a last goodbye maybe or a final plea for understanding. But there was nothing.

It was possible Sorenson had included a visual message on the tape but Brook thought it unlikely. Given their knowledge of each other's thinking, it shouldn't have been difficult for someone with Sorenson's intellect to speak to Brook with a few well chosen buzzwords, a few coded references. But he hadn't. The confession left in Sorenson's study was for public consumption only. There had to be something more – something for Brook alone. It had bothered him for days until the morning post arrived.

Brook examined the padded envelope for the umpteenth time since it dropped onto his mat. It was postmarked London and had a return address. 12 Queensdale Road, addressee, Peter Hera. He squeezed the package trying to guess its contents. Finally he tore it open and pulled out a video cassette.

Brook checked his watch. He lit his first cigarette since leaving hospital and let the nausea wash through him. He fed the cassette into his shiny new VCR, pressed the play button and turned on the TV. All was white noise.

Sorenson's face appeared and Brook exhaled nicotine relief. A grisly voice inside his head had warned him he might have to endure a filmed account of the Wallis family being torn open.

Instead Sorenson sat in a chair, at his desk in his study. The room was lit by lamps and Sorenson held his father's cutthroat in his hand. He raised a glass to the camera.

"Hello my old friend. I'm dead. And you're alive. I'm sorry to have let you down like that. I know how much you wanted to go.

It's strange addressing you through the camera when you're actually slumped in a chair on the other side of the room. I hope you understand my motives for making you

323

think I was going to kill you. I had to make it real for you then you'd know how good the others felt when they went. I'd given them a gift. Life as it should be – every second precious. Don't forget that.

"I know you can forgive me for Laura. Floyd Wrigley has paid in full – we saw to that. I saw how she died in that terrible place. It was easy to convince the police I was her killer. Case closed.

"And I'd have gotten away with it too," Sorenson smiled, *"but you tracked me down, Damen, at great risk to yourself. Now you're a hero. And so you should be. It doesn't sit well, does it? But don't fight it. It's the credit you should have had for finding The Reaper. And it'll make your work easier. There'll be plenty of opportunities. You'll see.*

"Look for father and daughters. Daughters are your speciality."

Brook grunted. Even death didn't stop Sorenson's probing.

"Remember, this is your time, Damen. Your time to be who you've always been. The person many would like to be but only you have the power and the knowledge. Use it wisely. I know you will. And if you still have doubts speak to your forensic people and then go to it. I hope you enjoy the painting. You always admired it. And yes it is genuine. It's a long story and time, for me, has run out. So another occasion for that. Goodbye old friend."

He stood and raised his glass. *"The Reaper is dead. Long live The Reaper."* Then Sorenson walked out of shot. A couple of seconds later the screen was white again.

Brook rewound the tape and listened to the toast again. He froze the image with Sorenson facing the camera, arm raised. Then he paced around the room for a couple of minutes before disappearing into the cellar. "Something's not right." He emerged with the sheaf of papers taken from Charlie's kitchen, leafed through for a moment to find the section he needed, then read aloud.

"And who says crime doesn't pay? The little punk murders a stranger and it saves him from a date with The Reaper. Funny thing. Sorenson didn't seem put out by that. In fact, he seemed pleased even though this Jason character deserves to have his

throat cut worse than most. I even wondered if somehow that was all part of the plan but I don't see how. What the fuck. I've wasted enough time thinking about it. You figure it out."

"Funny thing," Brook whispered. "Noble was right," he said to the screen. "Jason was at your mercy. Why didn't you kill him? Why?" He stubbed out his cigarette then re-read the transcript of Sorenson's confession.

"You always have a reason. Every action serves a purpose. One – you confess to killing your brother so Vicky can get on with her life. Two – you confess to killing Laura Maples so you can give me credit for tracking you down.

"Three – you admit to arranging Annie Sewell's murder. Reason:" – Brook hesitated then shrugged. "So you can put Jason and his low-life friends in the frame for her murder. So why haven't you done that? Funny thing."

"What's funny?"

Brook spun round. "Wendy!"

"I knocked but there was no reply. I hope you don't mind."

"Not at all." Brook turned off the TV and moved Charlie's confession under the Sorenson transcript on the table.

"What's funny?"

"Nothing's funny."

"You do realise that talking to yourself is the first sign of madness?"

"Yeah but it's the only decent conversation I can get since the cat stopped confiding in me."

"You've got a TV," she breezed. "It's almost like a home."

"Keep pushing."

Now she giggled. "Sorry."

"No need. I've given notice. I'm looking for another place."

Jones tried to hide her blushes at the possible reason for the move. "Oh? Nice painting," she added quickly.

"Yeah it's an original Van Gogh."

"Lovely. Shall we go?"

*

Brook sat on the hard wooden bench with his head lowered in the traditional manner. It was good manners to hide the boredom. The priest was droning on somewhere in the back of Brook's head but no words got through his blanket of taciturn solitude.

325

He hated churches. To Brook they were monuments to futility. Weddings were the worst. And christenings. All that misplaced hope of future happiness. At least funerals offered release – a way out. And now Brook was looking for his way out. He was suffering from mourning sickness. He smiled at his joke then covered his mouth with his hand to hide it. No funerals for years then – like busses – three happen along at once and each one a keepsake of his former life. Funny thing.

Charlie's funeral had been first, a happy occasion for Brook, knowing the release his old boss felt at the end. No more pain. No more guilt. No more tiny faces to haunt him.

And it was a pleasant surprise to be reminded what a legend Charlie was in the capital's law enforcement annals. Anybody who was anybody in West London policing was there. They'd even managed to dig up a junior minister for the occasion.

DCI Fulbright and DS Ross were there and a few other faces from the past. No relations though. Charlie had outlived all the ones he'd ever bothered with. His ex-wife wasn't there and Brook wondered if she was still in London but couldn't think of anyone to ask.

Fulbright exchanged a polite nod with Brook but Ross wouldn't even look at him, which was a disappointment as Brook had prepared a couple of visual taunts about his height.

After the service, in which he did a reading from John Donne, Charlie's favourite poet, Brook swapped a few pleasantries with barely remembered colleagues and made his excuses. His main excuse being that he had another funeral to attend – Sorenson's. Before he left, Brook lingered by Charlie's newly dug grave, next to his Lizzie.

"Goodbye Charlie and God bless." Then he bent over Lizzie's unkempt grave and burrowed six inches into the soil. He pressed in the ring from which she'd been separated before her death, and filled in the hole.

*

Sorenson's funeral was a much more sombre affair. The piercing winter light had given way to gun metal skies and the whole process was suddenly oppressive to Brook as only he and the family were attending.

Petr looked more strapping than Brook remembered. He was flanked on each arm by Vicky and Sonja, sobbing throughout. He was the man of the family now.

Again nods – the chief currency of funeral communication – were exchanged. Nothing was said. No readings were given. No stories were told. Sorenson left this life without ceremony and without sentiment and Brook felt it appropriate to the way he'd conducted himself in life. Few words were needed for someone who had so much to say for himself.

As the priest rattled through the service, Brook left the tiny chapel. He didn't look back. If he had, he'd have seen Vicky turn to watch him go. He would never see her again.

Outside stood Laura Maples' father. Brook didn't know him at first. He was a defeated old man. He stared at Brook leaving and walked towards him. Brook halted in sudden recognition and held out his hand. Maples ignored it.

"Did you know it was him, inspector?" Brook let his hand fall.

"Why are you here Mr Maples?"

"I don't know. Why are you here? To pay your *respects?*" The venom from the old man wasn't a surprise to Brook. He'd seen such bitterness fester in many victim's families. It had no outlet over time and to store it was to nurture it, until the roots grew out of your soul.

"Go home to your wife, Mr Maples."

"She's dead." His eyes burned into Brook's with a defiance borne of suffering. But suddenly a curtain fell over them and he lowered his head and cried. Brook took his elbow and guided him down the crisp drive towards the main road. Maples surrendered to his prompting and trudged in formation with Brook.

As they neared the gates, Maples pulled a hand from his pocket and offered it to Brook. "This is all we have left, inspector. The only thing for all that love, all that work. The sleepless nights…"

Brook, long the custodian of the keepsake, gazed at Laura's necklace wrapped around the withered claw, its little hearts reflecting the occasional peep of winter sun.

"The man who killed your daughter is dead. Go home, sir. Keep Laura alive in your heart, as I do."

Maples turned sharply to look at Brook's face and saw the depth of feeling there. He was taken aback. For a moment he seemed nonplussed and Brook wondered if he'd said the wrong thing.

But suddenly Maples broke into a watery smile, tears trickling down his hollow cheeks. He wasn't alone in his grief and it gave succour. "Thank you Inspector."

*

Now Brook stood with the rest of the congregation. All heads bowed so he let his eye wander around the crowd. He caught Brian

327

Burton's eye. Brook's glare was greeted by a frosty smile and both looked away.

After the prayer, Brook – positioned at the end of a row for a quick getaway – excused himself and tip-toed out of the church. He grimaced as he went, holding his recently-pumped stomach in case anyone took exception to the speed of his escape. Once outside he pounced on a cigarette and inhaled deeply.

"Inspector."

Brook turned to see Habib smiling at him. "Doctor. You've slipped out for a quick one too?"

"I'm sure I haven't. Religious differences, so it is." Brook nodded. "And how are you, inspector?"

"Same as ever."

"Ah, still no improvement, eh?" Habib chuckled.

"None." Brook eyed the good doctor, thinking how to avoid causing offence. It wasn't his strong suit. "Any developments in the Wallis case you haven't told me about, doc?"

Habib looked at him shifting from one foot to the other. "Developments?"

Brook glared at him, wondering what nerve he'd struck.

"This is hardly the place…"

"Doctor." Brook continued his stare but Habib failed to meet it.

"Inspector. I don't think it's right. It's no longer your case."

"It *was* my case. And there's something you didn't tell me, isn't there?"

"Not exactly." Habib was embarrassed and continued to avoid Brook's eyes.

"Tell me."

Again Habib cast around for suitable words. Brook let him sweat. It was coming. "We were short-staffed, inspector. I wasn't looking for it."

"Looking for what?"

"Inspector. It's not your case any…"

"And Annie Sewell wasn't my case. It didn't stop you giving me a copy of the report."

Now Habib looked into Brook's eyes, clearly injured by the threat. "You wouldn't?"

"I won't have to because you're going to tell me."

Habib was tight-lipped. Brook pressed him with his silence. Finally Habib said, "I begin to think you're not a very nice person."

"Get used to it, doc."

Habib sighed. "I should have spotted it sooner."

"What?"

"There were four deaths in the Wallis family."

Brook's brow creased. "What are you talking about?" Now it was Habib's turn to be still and watch Brook thinking.

"How do you kill two people and have one body, inspector?"

Brook stared hard at Habib. "Mrs Wallis was pregnant?" Habib shook his head. Light dawned and with no more than a croak Brook managed to wrench out one more word. "Kylie."

Habib nodded.

"God!" said Brook. "How long?"

"A month, five weeks. No more."

"At her age?"

Habib shrugged. "Girls these days…" He let it hang.

"And what's being done about it?"

"Done? Nothing. Kylie Wallis is dead. Inspector Greatorix and Chief Superintendent McMaster agreed that no purpose is served…"

"No purpose. A young girl's been raped. There must be tests…"

"The victim is dead, inspector. And most likely the culprit too."

"Most likely? You mean you're not even sure it was Bobby Wallis?"

"We know he didn't kill her. No-one in her family did. And now I think I'll bid you good day, inspector."

Habib walked away stony-faced. Brook felt the heat of the cigarette on his fingers and let it fall to the ground.

At that moment the doors opened and the coffins were carried out by the pallbearers. Brook stood aside to let them pass. As the coffin of Bobby Wallis passed him, Brook turned his back. One of the pallbearers noticed and narrowed his eyes at him.

Mrs Wallis followed and Brook turned to face the coffin. Kylie hadn't yet cleared the doors so not one of the following cortege noticed Brook's indictment.

A second later he was joined by Noble and Jones. McMaster was sticking close to Jason and his aunt to be sure she offered maximum comfort.

"You didn't miss much," said Noble, trying to keep levity out of his tone. "Feeling better?"

"No." Brook was far away, thinking of Sorenson.

"*…the poor Wallis girl, her virginity torn from her at such an age. Of course I knew, Damen. Every sickening detail. More even than you.*"

"Every sickening detail." Brook stared without blinking.

"Are you all right?" asked Jones, concerned to see the expression he wore on Brighton pier reappear. "Sir?"

Now Noble was curious and Brook became aware he was causing concern. He roused himself. "I'm fine, Wendy." He clenched his lips in an approximation of a smile to confirm his wellbeing. Jones and Noble mollified, Brook disappeared again into the comfort of the trance. Nothing much registered. Time passed without notice. When he needed to walk, he stumbled along with the herd. When he needed to stand still, he was kept upright by the proximity of others.

Senses returned. Brook knew he was still breathing because he saw the condensation leaving his mouth. He could feel the bite of the cold nipping his ears, hear the far-off cacophony of crows, the click of the cameras and the low hum of the generators feeding the news teams at a discreet distance.

He was okay. He wasn't beaten yet. Sorenson couldn't get him that way. He fumbled for another cigarette and somehow worked out a way to light it. McMaster glanced over with a tic of disapproval but soon regained her mask of professional sympathy.

And then it was over and Brook was able to walk where he chose. He broke away from the pack of stern-faced mourners hugging and clucking and kissing, and headed for a bench away from the tumult.

The next second Brian Burton was in front of him. Brook looked beyond him, searching for a way past. Freedom was only a yard either side.

"Inspector," he said.

Brook tried to plot a way round him but Burton moved across to block him.

"Inspector. Or should I call you Chief Inspector after your heroics in London?"

"Whatever you call me, Brian, I suggest you do it from a safe distance."

"Come on, inspector. No hard feelings." He held out his hand.

Brook ignored it. "Get out of my way, you parasite."

Now Burton lowered his voice. "Listen Brook, I can be a useful ally. Why don't you do us both some good and start playing ball?"

Chief Superintendent McMaster had spotted the two old enemies locking horns and made her way across to them. Others followed.

"Get out of my way," Brook insisted.

Burton saw McMaster coming and adopted a much friendlier expression. "How about a shot of the hero of the hour for the local taxpayers, inspector?" he shouted.

Burton's increased volume alerted Brook to the presence of others. He looked round and saw McMaster marching purposefully towards them. He turned to walk to his superior but Burton grabbed his arm. Brook stiffened and clenched his fist.

"Just one shot."

"Don't tempt me," mumbled Brook.

Burton scanned the oncoming faces. "How about one of you with Jason, Inspector Brook? To show your support for his loss."

Brook was aware of a warning glance emanating from McMaster and uncurled his fist. "Great idea, Brian," he muttered under his breath. "You could call it *The Hero and the Zero*."

Burton stared at Brook for a second then broke into a grin. "Oh I will, inspector. I will. Jason, I want a shot of you with the inspector."

"Fuck that! The way he treated me after me family were killed," snarled Jason. A volley of abusive muttering from his posse of friends followed.

Brook smiled his apology. "Sorry Brian. Looks like we'll have to give it a miss." He saw McMaster nod her approval at his manner. She stepped towards Brook to escort him away.

But Burton wouldn't be denied. "Come on Jason. It'll be on the front page."

Jason affected reluctance but finally was able to give in. "Yeah alright. But make it quick."

"That's it gents. Move a bit closer. Great. One more. Jason. Shake the inspector's hand."

Before Brook knew what had happened his hand was being shaken by Jason. He blinked at the flash of the camera and stared at Jason who was posing for the cameras, affecting a brave smile. Jason caught Brook's eye and felt the weight of his hand. His face clouded slightly and Brook could feel him attempting to pull his hand away – ever so gently at first but then more insistently. But Brook held on, narrowing his eyes as though to examine something close at hand, yet gazing, unblinking into the distance.

Now Jason struggled to remove his hand but Brook's grip tightened.

"Geroff yer fucking headcase."

Brook held on, eyes now fixed on Jason who tried to extricate himself with greater vigour. Then people began to huddle round, pawing at Brook's arm. All the while Brook was vaguely aware of the urgent flash of the camera. Still he held on.

"Geroff yer twat!" screamed Jason.

Suddenly a voice in Brook's ear. It was Jones, insistent but calming. "Control is what they pay us for."

Brook blinked and opened his hand. Jason pulled his own hand away, rubbing and flexing it and showing it to his aunt. "That's assault that is. You saw it. That's assault. I'll have you in court yer fucking nutter." He marched away with his aunt ministering to his hand and his posse egging him on to greater heights of rhetoric.

Brook stood his ground, a strange grin contorting his features. It was an expression of resignation, of regret.

McMaster gripped his elbow and with Jones and Noble gathered around Brook, they marched him away from the cemetery as nonchalantly as they could.

"Have you completely lost it?" McMaster muttered.

Without changing his expression or even looking in her direction, Brook nodded. "Lost? Yes ma'am. I've lost."

Chapter 34

The man brought the car to a halt. He killed the engine and lights and sat back, waiting for the rain to ease. He closed his eyes to let the music flow over him. It was difficult to hear over the beating of the rain on the bonnet and roof of the car. He turned it up.

He squinted through the rear window, trying to distinguish shapes through the distorting effect of the water. Nothing stirred. No cars. No pedestrians. No animals.

Every living creature had taken shelter tonight. It was a night to seal oneself off from the outside world and curl up to hibernate. Curtains were closed against the cold, fires were roaring, hot winter food was being consumed and the hypnotic pulse of the TV nurtured life in a flickering cocoon. Every home had returned to the womb. Comfortable. Safe. Warm.

The man located the wiper button and held it while the windscreen cleared. Mist rolled up Station Road from the Trent and for a moment he was sightless. A pocket of clearer air revealed a door opening across the road. A figure stepped through and out into the inhospitable gloom.

A moment later the figure stood next to a small red car, hesitating, rummaging. Keys found, the figure hopped into the car. Headlights snapped on. A cat skittered from beneath as the engine coughed into life. It ran to the next vehicle then turned to glare at its former shelter. Eyes unblinking. Head still.

The red car swung out into the road and away.

The man watched it recede then turned the music off. The rain had slowed to a steady rhythm. He stepped from the vehicle and retrieved a bag from the back seat. He closed the door, but didn't lock it, then walked briskly across the road to the house the other driver had left.

He rang the bell, and stepped back from the mottled glass of the front door to look around. No reply.

He rang the bell again and looked around, humming the music to himself. He could see the cat beneath the parked car, flattened against the ground, inching forward, restrained power, eyes rigid, ready to pounce on unsuspecting prey.

*

Jason heard the front door bell and lowered his mobile, the text message forgotten for a moment. He stood up from the bed and picked his way carefully round the baby's cot, to avoid waking her. The light was already off so he felt able to peer out of the window. He could make out a figure but couldn't tell who it was in the dark.

It didn't look like any of the officers assigned to protect him, since the slaughter of his family, so he decided to ignore it. Whoever it was carried a bag – probably someone flogging stuff. He tiptoed back to the edge of his bed and sat down.

Jason waited a few minutes in the dark, listening for the figure to go. He heard nothing except the wind and the gentle breathing of his baby sister.

After a few moments listening, Jason returned to the glowing display of his phone. As he started keying a message, the bell sounded again.

This time he growled in annoyance and made his way softly to the top of the stairs and squinted down at the door to the frame standing motionless on the other side of the mottled glass.

Again he hesitated, watching, waiting. When the bell sounded again he lost his patience and stomped down the stairs.

"Who is it?"

"It's DI Brook."

"'Fuck do you want?"

"To talk."

"What about?"

"Police business. And I want to apologise…"

"It won't do any good. We're not dropping the complaint so fuck off!"

"It's important." He paused then dangled the carrot. "I've brought your money."

Silence. "What money?"

"The money we confiscated when we arrested you."

Another pause. "All of it?"

"All of it."

Jason moved to unfasten the many new locks on the door. It

opened and Jason peered out at Brook through a crack. "Give us it."

"I can't just hand it over. You have to sign for it. Can I come in? It's cold."

Jason looked Brook up and down, a superior scowl on his face. The door opened and Brook stepped inside. Jason nodded him towards the kitchen.

"Was that your aunt I saw leaving?"

"Yeah, she's on nights."

"You're not going out?"

"I'm babysitting which is gay." He looked peeved, weighed down by the excessive responsibility.

Brook shook the rain from his coat but kept it on. He put the bag on the table, unzipped a side pocket and pulled out a bottle of whisky.

"What's that?" asked Jason.

"Peace offering."

Jason's face cracked into a slow smile of triumph. His aunt and that solicitor were right. They *were* holding all the aces. This was gonna be wicked. Watching this pig grovel. Like he was going to pass up a shot at compensation for a bottle of whisky after the way he'd suffered. Still. Keep it coming. It wouldn't hurt to string him along. "Cheers," he said trying not to gloat.

Jason pulled a single glass from the drainer and plonked it on the kitchen table. Brook spun the top from the bottle and poured Jason a generous measure.

Jason picked up the glass and hesitated, savouring his moment of victory. Wait till his crew heard about this. Maybe they had the pig on bribery, as well as supplying booze to an under-18. The bastard was finished.

Jason drank his whisky straight down and pursed his lips against the fire. "Where's my money?"

Brook turned to the bag and pulled out an envelope. Jason snatched it from him with a grin and began to count it. Brook replenished Jason's glass like an attentive barman. Jason put the envelope on the table and smiled. Fucking result.

"What do you think of the whisky?"

"It's shit," he replied with relish. "But as long as it gets the job done, who gives a fuck?"

Brook smiled. "No-one does."

Jason emptied his glass again and filled it himself.

"Steady on. Don't forget you're babysitting," said Brook, without conviction.

Jason leered in his direction then bent down to a cupboard and

335

took out a bottle of cola. He topped up his whisky to the brim and this time took just a sip. "I can handle it. I've been drinking since I was eleven."

Brook allowed himself a thin smile as the boy sniffed his pride at such an achievement. He really was a special young man.

He eyed the money and grinned at Brook, "Thanks for the dosh. Was there owt else?" He took another draught of his whisky and cola.

Brook smiled and pulled up a chair. "You need to sign for it." Brook placed a piece of A4 and a pen on the kitchen table. Jason sat down and squinted at the paper. He picked up the pen. He turned to Brook. "Where do I sign?"

"At the bottom."

Jason looked again. "This paper's blank. I'm not signing it. You could put anything on it."

Brook moved his face close to Jason's and spoke slowly and clearly. "I'm not going to write anything. You're going to give me a list of names, the friends who killed Annie Sewell with you. *Then* you're going to sign it."

It took a moment for Jason to register what Brook had said. He thought for a second then laughed. "You never give up, do you? Get the fuck out of here. I can have your fucking job, coming round here and interviewing me without an adult. You're abusing my rights, pig. Plus I'm under age and you've made me drink whisky..."

Jason decided to stand to show Brook the full force of his indignation but stumbled and fell back in the chair. He giggled and tried again but was still unable to get to his feet. The humour faded from Jason's expression. He was puzzled. He couldn't feel his legs. He tried again but gave up. Instead he stared off into the distance, alternately opening and screwing up his eyes to gauge the level of his intoxication.

Brook stood and sauntered around the kitchen, hands behind his back, not looking at Jason. Jason just watched him, head swaying slightly.

Brook stopped to admire a large framed picture of a lighthouse being ravaged by the sea. He then lifted the frame from its nail and placed it on the floor.

"Fuck you doing?" snarled Jason. "I've told you. Get out yer twat. You're trespassing. I can have you done..." Jason began to sway in his chair now. He looked at the glass on the table and squinted at Brook, then at his hands. He flexed his eyelids and mouth like a fish. Again he tried to stand, placing his hands on his chair's wooden arms to lever himself, but this time he couldn't even lift his body. Still he tried, face straining, sweating with the effort, but it was no use. He looked in

336

Brook's general direction but couldn't focus so he just stared, muttering as best he could. "Get'n me drunk. Bastard!"

Brook said nothing but continued to move around the kitchen. He moved to his sports bag and took out a portable CD player. He plugged it in, put on a disc and finally turned to contemplate his immobile host. He was out cold.

*

Jason felt the shock of the icy water on his face and jerked his head back. He batted his eyelids and sucked in oxygen. He opened his eyes to look at Brook, who sat to one side of him. Brook was looking at something on the wall, then back at him.

He could hear music. Classical shit. As if to answer, Brook smiled across at him. He seemed sad. "You can hear?" Jason nodded. As he did so he felt the rope lapped around his forearms and waist.

"This is Tchaikovsky's sixth symphony. One of the pinnacles of human achievement." Brook listened, his eyes far away. Jason watched him. He could see clearly now, though every image was edged with bright colours. He could make out something on the far wall where his aunt's favourite lighthouse picture used to be. There was a man dressed in black, with grey hair, standing on a rock, looking out over a raging sea or maybe he was on top of a mountain looking down.

"You can see?"

Jason gulped. "Yes." His voice was tiny, far away and his throat hurt from the effort of squeezing out even that whisper.

"That is a poster of The Wanderer over the Sea of Clouds by Caspar-David Friedrich. It caught my eye the other day." Brook smiled his appreciation at Jason. "Stunning isn't it?"

Jason made to speak but had to abandon the attempt. He looked at the picture and back at Brook. Not having the physical control to shrug, he did nothing.

Brook studied Jason while removing his leather gloves. "You're taking this better than I expected son."

Jason was unsure what he meant. Brook stood up. He looked different. Jason could see his coat was off and he wore some kind of black overalls. Then he saw the latex gloves underneath Brook's leather gloves and his brain began to register. His eyes widened.

"I envy you Jason. The last image you'll see on Earth is that painting. The last sound you'll hear is Tchaikovsky. This will be your finest hour. And you'll have what you've always wanted – a place in history."

337

Jason was panting now and tried to stand again but he couldn't move. Instead he looked down at the table and tried to speak. "You're police." His speech was a little stronger but still no more than a croak. "Please! Don't."

"Don't? Is that what Annie said to you? Don't kill me. It hurts. Take my purse but don't hurt me any more."

Jason's eyes widened. He looked away.

"How do I know you killed Annie Sewell? Don't waste time on that now."

"I never killed her. I never killed no-one."

"Did you laugh when you made her snort cocaine?"

"Not me." Jason found his eyes stinging from the sweat and the tears. No blood yet.

Brook stepped up close and showed Jason the brand new cut-throat, before putting it on the table in front of him. Jason's eyes began to close so Brook gently slapped his face to concentrate his mind. "You're not fit for this world Jason but, hopefully, if you can die right, you might be fit for the next one."

"No. Please. I didn't kill her. It weren't me." He struggled again but it was useless. The ropes immobilised him from the shoulders down. Talk. That's all he could do to stop this. Think what to say.

Brook's face was close and Jason could see the glint of the old fashioned razor. He felt a hand on his jaw, pulling his head round.

"Look at the picture, Jason. Listen to the music. Let go and feel the beauty. Look for some in yourself. There must have been some once."

"There's coppers...watching."

"We pulled them away two days ago, Jason. According to our budget, you're no longer at risk."

"You're supposed...to protect...to help..."

Brook smiled and nodded. "Protect the innocent, Jason. That's what I'm doing. Obeying the law sometimes makes that harder. I've seen too much thoughtless destruction, too many victims. I've seen Mrs Ottoman cowering in her living room after what you did to her, I've seen young girls raped, torn apart by lowlifes. Jason, I've seen Kylie. I can see her now."

"Don't."

"It's true."

Jason's eyes squinted through the tears. "What?" What was the copper saying to him? "Where?"

Brook placed a hand on Jason's head. "Here in your thoughts. I can see her struggling, fighting to be free. Her hair's trapped under your elbows. She can't move. Her pyjama bottoms are in a heap on the floor.

You're hurting her. It burns! She doesn't like it, does she? She wants you to stop…"

"What you saying? Give it a rest. You're creeping me out."

"…but you didn't stop, did you, Jason? Even though she begged you. She promised not to tell her mam if you stopped. But you weren't worried about that. Did your mother already know? Did she care? Your dad didn't. He told you what women were for, didn't he? Only good for one thing, son – even your own sister."

"How do you know all this?"

"The Reaper showed me when he let you live. It's the only explanation. I thought it was your father but I was blinded by The Reaper's other victims. Fathers and daughters you see."

Brook stepped away from Jason. The music played on. When he looked down the razor was in his hand. He stared at it as though he'd never seen it before.

Jason's eyes bulged. "*You* killed my family."

Brook shook his head. "No Jason. You killed them."

"Well yer can't kill me. It ain't right."

"Listen to the music Jason."

"Don't do it. I'll do owt you ask."

"Look at the picture Jason."

"I'll sign the paper. I'll tell you everything. You can have the names."

"You'll die with angels kissing your face."

"Please don't. Kill Bianca. Not me. I haven't lived yet."

"You shouldn't have been so anxious to start…" Jason tried in vain to get to his feet. The chair fell onto its side. Brook was reminded of Tamara Wrigley. He hoisted it upright again and burned his eyes into Jason. "Fantastic isn't it, Jason? The last minute, the last second. Have you ever felt so alive?"

"Don't. Please."

"Savour every second." Brook stepped behind him and pulled Jason's head back by his hair and touched the cold steel of the blade against the bulging, contorted neck.

"Feel the air going in. Feel your lungs filling. Feel the blood coursing, your heart pounding away under the hammer of adrenaline. Life. Amazing isn't it?"

"Please…" Jason was sobbing now. Brook remembered the exhilaration this moment brought. The music surged through Brook's consciousness, echoing around his mind like a shout in an underground cavern.

"The Reaper had you at his mercy. He could have killed you. But he knew you were special. That's why you're still alive, Jason. He left you for me. He came to Derby for me. Not you. The Reaper can't die you see. He must go on. His work must continue."

Jason howled, "Please. I don't wanna die. Let me go. I won't tell. Nobody would believe me. Please! I'm sorry, inspector. I'm sorry. You're right about Kylie and me. And the old woman. We killed her and we enjoyed it. It was a laugh at first. But I wish I never. I see her at night when I go to sleep." Jason sobbed violently, his shoulders shuddering. He tried to bury his head in hands that couldn't obey. Then more quietly, "I'm sorry. I'm real sorry for what I've done, mister. Swear down. I can't change it. But if you let me off, I'll change. I will. I'll turn myself in. And the others. Just give me a chance."

For a moment there was only the music and the quiet sobbing. Brook didn't move as he stood over Jason. His face was set in stone. The music played on, climbing and descending but the sobbing stopped and finally Jason looked up at Brook.

Brook took a pace forward and lifted the razor. He slashed the blade at the rope.

The boy was unable to speak. His face crumpled and he broke into a flood of tears and as he began to free himself, Brook pulled on his leather gloves and gathered the rest of his things into the bag including the whisky bottle. After rinsing the whisky glass, he folded the severed rope under his arm.

"You've got seven days to give yourself up. I'll leave the picture to remind you," said Brook, moving to the door.

Jason stopped rubbing his wrists and turned his tear-streaked face to Brook. "Remind me of what?" His eyes were fearful again.

"That The Reaper's watching."

Chapter 35

Brook stood as upright as he could manage given the weight of his rucksack and the steepness of the slope. In a few metres he'd be at the top, but the fire in his lungs and calves demanded immediate rest.

He turned to look back down the sharp incline of Thorpe Cloud and watched Wendy panting after him some thirty metres below.

"Hurry up. It'll be dark in eight hours," he shouted.

An indecipherable grunt emanated from below accompanied by a vigorous V-sign to guarantee clarity. Brook grinned and struck out for the summit.

Once there he flung the rucksack to the ground and, when his lungs had recovered, did a full turn to take in the sun-dappled panorama – the sleepy houses of Ilam, dozing in spring warmth to the north-west, Bunster Hill to the north and the deep scar of Dovedale, gouged out by the river, further east.

By the time Jones joined him ten minutes later, he had the flask and the sandwiches ready and was comparing the map to the view of their route along the River Dove to Milldale and Hartington beyond.

Jones flung herself onto the ground next to Brook and sucked in air until her breathing slowed. "Thanks for waiting," she gasped.

"Have some coffee."

Wendy took the plastic cup, drained it, then laid her head next to Brook's and closed her eyes to the morning sun. "It's beautiful up here."

Brook sat up and looked down into her face. "Yes."

"So what did you want to talk to me about?" She opened her eyes briefly to check his face then closed them again.

Brook paused, sweeping his gaze around the horizon. "I'm resigning…"

She sat up now and searched his expression. "You're giving in?"

"No Wendy. I'm getting out while there's still a chance for me. Carrying on is what Charlie did so he wouldn't have to live with himself, wouldn't have to face up to a life without hope." He looked back at her. "I've found something to live for. And a way to live with myself."

"Is this anything to do with Sorenson?"

"Yes. He had plans for me."

"What plans?"

"A way for me to cope with despair." Brook gave a half-laugh and looked into the distance. "But he needed me in the Force. He didn't envisage my finding happiness and making peace with the world."

"And have you?"

"Not yet. But I think I can."

"But you have to resign."

"Yes."

"Even though that's what some people want."

"Part of being happy involves not caring what other people want…"

"Even if Harry Hendrickson and Greatorix think you're a loser."

"They'd think that either way."

She looked away. "I suppose," she muttered some while later. "You mustn't blame yourself, for not catching him…"

Brook halted her with a brush of his hand against her cheek. "Don't worry, Wendy. I don't. The Reaper won't be stopped. Not by me."

Jones nodded and fondled his face in return. It had been a long time since she'd last touched him and Brook felt a thrill of electricity at the prospect of further contact. They didn't talk after that but sat there drinking coffee and munching on their sandwiches, looking at the view, spring-cleaning their minds.

After nearly an hour of peace, they heard the panting of other ramblers so they packed their rucksacks and headed down towards the River Dove.

At ground level, they moved off at a steady pace along the path to the east of the river and followed its course up the steep, wooded gorge cut from the limestone rock over millions of years.

As they walked, from time to time, Brook would produce a small guide book and give a name to various natural features along the way – Lover's Leap, The Twelve Apostles, Jacob's Ladder, Tissington Spires – almost everything bigger than a boulder seemed to have a name.

After the hamlet of Milldale, the terrain eased and the river's course became more sinuous. The path was no longer overhung by rock but wide and man-made. Occasionally it would take them away from the river as it cut across an alluvial plain.

On they walked, saying little, comfortable in each other's silence. In Wolfscote Dale herons watched them briefly before taking to the skies, Jones unable to get her camera out in time.

When they passed into Beresford Dale the river became slow and wide for a time and they trudged wearily across the flat landscape until they rejoined the water at a small footbridge. They crossed the river and plodded on, damp and sweaty in the afternoon sun.

"You look like Greatorix," laughed Jones, as Brook mopped his brow.

Around the next bend the water swirled gently into a large, deep pool, shaded by trees and guarded by a huge boulder. Large trout glided gently in the depths.

There was a "NO SWIMMING" sign on the boulder so Brook and Jones stripped down to their underwear and dived in.

As they lay, drying on the bank, they held hands while they sunbathed. Refreshed, they dressed and marched the last mile into Hartington with increased vigour.

After a late, leisurely lunch in the Devonshire Arms, their eyes began to droop.

"It's been a lovely day, Damen. Thank you."

"My pleasure. Pity you have to work in the morning."

"I know."

"What time are you on?"

"Early turn." Brook nodded. Jones smiled. "Are you thinking what I'm thinking?"

"It's unlikely." Brook laughed at her stern face. "What are you thinking, Wendy?"

"That we should get a room."

Brook frowned and looked into the log fire. Finally, he said, "No. Let's go." He rose and headed for the exit carrying his rucksack. Jones followed, trying not to appear insulted.

"What's the hurry?" she shouted at his retreating back. She struggled to throw her rucksack over her shoulder and trotted after Brook, who turned a corner and started striking up a steep street, not bothering to look round.

"Where are you going?"

Brook didn't answer and didn't slow down, so Jones ploughed on, trying to catch him, wondering what she'd done to cause offence. A minute later, Brook stopped and turned to face Jones still puffing along in his slipstream.

As she approached, he propped himself against an estate agent's board and waited.

"What the hell's the matter?" gasped Jones. She was ready to blow her top.

Brook could keep up the pretence no longer. He smiled at the aggression on her face.

"Well?"

Instead of an answer, Brook leant over the old dry stone wall he'd been sitting on, and wrestled with the pole.

"What are you doing?"

Brook finally extricated the pole from the ground and flung it into the tiny, lavender-scented front garden.

"Damen!" Jones looked at the pale limestone edifice of the house, expecting the front door to open and the owner to appear. "I'll have to arrest you if the owner complains."

"Don't worry, officer." Brook cracked into a wide grin. "I am the owner."

"You're what?" Jones laughed and pummelled Brook's shoulders with her fists. "You shit. I thought I'd done something. When did you...?"

"A couple of days ago."

"You never said."

"I wanted it to be a surprise."

"It is that. When did you decide to do it?"

"When someone very important to me asked me why I didn't live properly."

Jones looked at him and walked slowly into his arms, not moving her eyes from his. She put her hand behind his head and pulled him onto her mouth, kissing him long and hard. When she broke for air, she pulled his head onto her shoulder and whispered into his ear. "Take me inside."

＊

Two minutes later they were making love as though it were their last night on Earth. Every touch, every stroke, every thrust was urgent. They burrowed into each other, as if determined to emerge from the other side and when it was over they held each other, molten in their physical union, for a long time.

When they de-coupled they lay on the bed talking and touching, feeling the breeze billowing through the curtains, cool their hot skin. They made love again, this time taking pleasure in the exploration of the other's face and neck and torso.

Later they showered together, dressed and returned to the pub for urgent supplies of liquid and solid food, as Brook had not yet been able to transfer his copious supplies of party food from the fridge in his flat.

Brook slept better than he had for many years that night and, when he woke, spent many minutes gazing at Wendy's sleeping frame.

Then he dressed and went down into the kitchen. He made coffee and sat on a bench outside the back door, on a small flagged patio which overlooked the rest of his steep, walled garden as it fell away from the house.

He drained his cup and went back inside for a refill and a cigarette. On his way back to the patio, he picked up his resignation letter for a final perusal.

There wasn't much to check. Four lines got the job done. Three of them were used to thank McMaster for all her support and wishing her well for the future. He signed the letter and folded it into an envelope.

As he lit up, Jones stuck her head round the door. Her hair was tousled and she seemed groggy. "What time is it?" she asked, pulling Brook's towel robe tighter.

Brook examined her. She was even more beautiful in the early morning light. "Gone seven."

"Is that all? I should have slept longer."

"You'll miss this lovely morning. Why don't you have a shower? I'll go get something for breakfast."

"Sounds good."

An hour later, full of hot buttered muffins, Brook ignited the Sprite, and he and Jones set off for Derby.

*

Brook looked around the Chief Super's office as she read his letter of resignation. It seemed more spartan than usual. The spider plant had long since perished and several objects which usually adorned the desk had disappeared. He craned his neck over the desk and caught sight of a cardboard box full of the detritus of a career.

She looked up at him, nodding sadly. "So you're giving in."

"If that's the way you want to look at it, ma'am."

"It's how your enemies will look at it."

"They can think what they want. What about your enemies, ma'am?"

McMaster screwed her eyes and stared beyond Brook to the window. "I found out last night. I'm being transferred out."

Brook nodded. He had no need to ask whether it was voluntary or not. "I see. But you fight on?"

345

"Of course I fight on, Damen. I believe in what I do, and how I do it. I'll be back. Mark my words." There was anger in her eyes.

Brook smiled to comfort her. "I envy you, Evelyn. And pity you. How can you keep going?"

"What should I do? Take the easy way out, like you." Brook laughed. "I'm sorry, Damen. I didn't mean that."

"Yes you did. And yes, you should take the easy way out. Caring can damage your health."

"I can't. I won't let them beat me."

"I didn't for a minute expect you would."

McMaster stood and gathered her dignity and held out her hand. Brook shook it warmly. "Good luck, Damen. The Force needs people like you. I'll hold onto this letter for forty-eight hours…"

"Why?"

"It's standard practice – unofficially. In case you change your mind."

"I won't."

*

Brook gunned through the lights and roared up the Uttoxeter Road. As he approached the flat, he saw Old Mrs Saunders standing on the pavement, arms folded, looking up and down the road. She was just a tiny thing, barely five feet in height. She raised an arm when she saw him and watched as he slowed to a halt and jumped from the car.

"Anything wrong, Mrs Saunders?"

"I've already called the police, dear. Some lads kicked your door in. I rang straight away but they weren't in there long. They only left a few minutes ago. I'm sorry, dear, but I didn't dare come outside until they'd gone."

"You did the right thing, Mrs Saunders. Wait there."

"Oh, inspector." Brook turned. "One thing. I know it's a weird name but I definitely heard one of the young men call another one Jay or Jace. Is that a help?"

Brook nodded. "Maybe."

He ran to the flat's wrecked kitchen entrance and stopped in the doorway. The door hung from its hinges now and Brook had to lift it to go inside.

He looked down at his feet and stepped back. The floor was flooded with the water still spurting from where the sink had once been. It had been hammered into three large pieces and water was sluicing around the floor.

Various plastic food packets bobbed on the water. The fridge, which had had its door wrenched off, had then been pushed over. Brook could see a selection of cocktail dips and cooked chicken being showered by the fountain from the decapitated cold water pipe. The fridge door itself had been thrown at the kitchen window and lay half in, half out, of the shattered frame.

Brook lifted up his trousers and tiptoed across the sopping floor to the hall. From the living room, an acrid stench assaulted his throat forcing him to clench a handkerchief over his mouth.

He kicked open the door through which he'd watched Vicky brush her hair those many months ago. The smoke hit Brook in the eyes, so he bent low and forced his way through the room to the front door, satisfying himself that there was no heat from a blaze. He flung open the front door and stepped through to let his lungs pull in the fresh air. The acrid smouldering of Brook's sofa began to dissipate and Brook was able to see into the room.

He looked at the devastation. The brand new TV and video recorder lay pulverised on the floor. His chair and table were blackened by the smoke but were otherwise intact. The telephone and answering machine had also been placed on the sofa, to share its fate. They had begun to melt but were still recognisable. Fortunately the Van Gogh was in his new house.

The smoke cleared somewhat and Brook headed for his bedroom. He opened the door to the words "OINK, OINK. YOUR GOING TO PAY PIG" daubed on the wall in red.

"Oh no." Brook stepped to the bed and sat besides the remains of Cat. He placed a hand on its still warm body and stroked what was left. For once the cat didn't careen itself around Brook's hand. Its head was pulp though he could still identify the stub of pink tongue poking through broken teeth. Two grapefruit-sized splashes of dark red on the back of the door told its tale.

He closed his eyes to remember his only friend.

Sirens in the distance grew louder. He roused himself to look around. He reached to pick a towel from a hook and wrapped Cat reverently into a bundle.

He went outside to his car and placed the body gently in the boot. He hesitated. "I'm sorry Cat. I should have named you." He closed the boot and turned to face the squad car screeching to a theatrical halt behind him.

*

It was after midnight when Brook returned to his new house in

347

Hartington. He was on his own. Except for Cat.

He pulled up to the kerb and silenced the ear-splitting cacophony from the Sprite's exhaust, oblivious to the disturbance it must have caused in this sleepy village. He opened the boot and removed a carrier bag and newly-purchased spade. He took both in the house and returned to the car. He picked up the bundle containing Cat and took it to the back garden.

In darkness, he dug a small hole in a corner of the garden and placed Cat down. He replaced the soil on top and patted it down before putting a large stone on top to discourage scavenging foxes. "Rest in Peace, little friend."

Brook climbed the path to the house and sat down on the patio bench. He pulled the bottle of whisky and two packets of cigarettes from the carrier bag, poured himself a large measure and lit up.

"Cheers Cat." He took a swig and flinched as the fiery liquid burned its way to his stomach. "Cheers Charlie." He took another, smaller swig. "Professor." This time he merely held the glass aloft, declining to drink.

*

The next morning Brook was woken by birdsong. He was on the bench with a thin blanket for cover and a cushion for a pillow. He sat up and looked at his watch. Then he stepped into the kitchen and picked up the phone. He dialled, asked for an extension number and lit a cigarette in the pause to be connected. "Chief Superintendent McMaster. DI Brook, ma'am. About my resignation – I've been thinking it over…"